A Wizard Awakened

A Wizard in Las Vegas
Book 1

Brittany Fichter

A Pandora Effect Book

To Gretta,

You're the kind of fun that inspired this book. I wish I could drag you out to Las Vegas to look for vampires with me. I miss your beautiful voice and your equally gorgeous face.

Chapter One

Everleigh

I PAUSED at a metal bench to put my backpack down and fix my ponytail, doing my best not to look alarmed. As I'd just left the gym, my hair wasn't really messy enough to need fixing, but the pause allowed me a second to peek over my right shoulder at the wide concrete path behind me without looking too suspicious. To my relief and unease, however, I saw no one.

Well, no one out of the ordinary. Dozens of college students were walking to their next classes, most wearing hoodies and jeans, as March was in the middle of another cold snap. No one stood out. No one even looked my way. Most were either looking down at their phones or staring blankly ahead, lost in thought. But just like last Thursday, I couldn't shake the feeling that I was being watched. Or rather, followed.

Unable to find anything out of the ordinary, I huffed and briefly closed my eyes. Then I reached out with my senses, searching the air around me for any magic that might be floating nearby. But again, I felt nothing. Nothing except the cold, dry air of an early Las Vegas spring. Of course, that didn't necessarily mean there weren't any supernaturals in the vicinity.

Still, what else could he... or she be? Whoever had been

following me around the campus seemed to disappear and reappear too quickly not to be supernatural. Creating the illusion of invisibility would be a simple parlor trick for an experienced fae. And anyone with the money to do so could purchase a fae glamour. Elves couldn't disappear entirely, but they could often alter their bodies to somewhat blend in with the world around them. Heck, it could even be a shifter or vampire. They were fast enough to often appear invisible to the human eye.

That thought made me shiver.

I was no coward. But I *really* hoped it wasn't a vampire.

Once my ponytail was fixed, I grabbed my bag and resumed my walk as I decided to try something else. A glamour maybe, to make me look like another person? Or would a simple invisibility spell work?

Even before the ideas were fully formed, however, I knew they wouldn't work. If I'd been a full-blooded fae or elf, either would have been feasible. But if I attempted either one, especially in broad daylight, I would just end up looking *more* conspicuous than I apparently already did.

A snack shack stood at the corner of the path I was walking, right across from the education building. I hurried to its entrance and ducked inside, fighting my way through the crowd toward the back, where I could keep an eye on the front door.

Unfortunately, that didn't do me any good either. There were too many people for me to identify any suspicious individuals in the mass of college students trying to buy chips, soda, slices of mass-produced pizza, and pre-made, pre-wrapped sandwiches before their next classes. Besides, I wasn't tall enough to see over the towering group of guys who had just walked in. They had to be on athletic scholarships because not a single one of them was under six foot three. So finally, I gave up, dug my pepper spray out of my backpack, and pushed my way back outside.

Maybe, if nothing else, I'd lost whoever had been following me.

And if not? Along with several forms of martial arts, my parents had made sure I excelled in the art of pepper spray.

But just as I stepped out the door, I heard my name called, and my entire body sagged with relief as Julia and Georgie hurried toward me, Julia's thick blond ponytail blowing like a flag in the wind, while Georgie stuffed his hands in his hoodie pockets.

"Why aren't you answering your texts?" Julia demanded. But Georgie adjusted his glasses as he frowned down at the small black can in my hand.

"I think a better question is why she's walking around with pepper spray," he said, nudging Julia. Julia followed his gaze and gasped.

"Everleigh!" she began.

"Let's get some tea," I said quietly, forcing a big smile. "I'll tell you about it there."

Julia started to protest, but Georgie shook his head at her. It was subtle, but enough that she got the idea.

"Sounds good," he said with a grin. As he spoke, he casually draped an arm around my shoulder and walked on my left side as Julia hurried to walk on my right. And while Georgie seemed just a *tad* too comfortable putting his arm around my shoulder, I was glad for my friends' company. They weren't supernatural, which meant they wouldn't be any more use in a fight than I would be, should anything go down. But they were with me—clearly marking me as theirs. And though they were completely unaware of it, their possessive behavior ensured that any supernatural who attacked me at that moment would be in heavy violation of some of the supernatural world's strictest laws.

As we walked, I wondered if my stalker would risk continuing to follow me now. Did he really want to pursue me badly enough that he would risk exposing us to the humans?

To my relief, however, the next time I glanced over my shoulder, the feeling of being followed was finally gone.

We made our way across the street from the university campus to a small tea shop, the place we went when we didn't have anywhere else to go, which happened at least once, often twice a week. The sign above the door said *Ji-a's Pearls*. Underneath the name was a picture of a cat wearing a pearl necklace, drinking purple bubble milk tea. The bell jingled as we walked in, but none of the eight seated customers so much as looked up from their books, laptops, or tablets as we entered. Only the girl behind the counter nodded our way.

"The usual?" she asked as all three of us sat at the bar in front of the counter. There were at least half a dozen stools that lined the bamboo countertop, but after two and a half years of college, we were, to my knowledge, the only ones to ever use them.

"I don't know," Julia said, looking up at the backlit menu screen on the wall behind the bar. "We always get the same thing." She wrinkled her pretty nose thoughtfully.

The girl behind the counter played with her ponytail, its single pinkish purple streak standing out against the rest, which was silky and black. She grinned a little too widely, and her large brown eyes gleamed. "I have a new flavor–" she began to say, but I gave her a look.

"Soo Min, the last time you gave her a new flavor, she barfed all the way home."

Okay, so Julia's barfing was actually my fault, as I'd been the one to give her one of the precious magic emergency tablets my father kept me well supplied with. But it *had* been an emergency. Soo Min had apparently been under the impression that day that Julia was being a bit too clingy, so she'd infused my best friend's tea with some weird essence of fae magic that had given her a danger-ously high dose of independence. As in, she'd decided she didn't need crosswalks or streetlight WALK signals because she could cross the four-lane road all by herself without any signs telling her what to do. I'd been forced to crush the tablet up and blow it in her face when Georgie wasn't looking. The tablet had done its job, purging poor Julia's body of the influencing magic by the time we'd returned her to her apartment, but I wasn't about to risk having to do it again.

For reasons not shared with me, Soo Min was *not* a Julia fan. How or where this resentment started, I didn't know. The supernatural community is small enough that I'd known Soo Min a long time, and she didn't seem to mind me. Not that we'd ever been what Anne Shirley would call bosom friends–not the way Julia and I were, at least. But we were friendly enough. What made it worse, however, was that Julia wasn't even aware of Soo Min's resentment. She was under the impression that Soo Min liked her because she always tipped. (And Julia tipped pretty well for a nearly broke college kid.)

Really, it wasn't much of a surprise, though. Soo Min was a fae, and fae are known for being... nosy. For example, despite it being illegal, Soo Min liked to add essences of fae magic to the teas she made for people–supernatural and regular human alike.

"I see what they need, and I make their days better," she sniffed once when I called her on it after catching her trying to charm Julia's tea yet again. "Or," her eyes brightened, "I give them what they *deserve*."

Today, however, Soo Min just rolled her eyes as she wiped off the counter. "*Yes,* it's a good tea," she snapped. "Now, are you going to order or not?"

I held her gaze a moment longer to remind her that I *was* watching before ordering my usual–a rose green tea, twenty-five percent sweet with double tapioca pearls. Julia tried the new flavor, matcha mint, and Georgie just ordered fried fish balls.

"I've got to watch my weight." He grinned, patting his very flat stomach.

"Forget all that." Julia scowled as we seated ourselves at the barstools, and Soo Min moved away to make the tea. "Everleigh, what is going on?"

I paused as I toyed with my napkin, trying to think of what I ought to say. My friends' concern for me was sweet. And I had known Julia long enough to know she'd die for me in an instant. But they were... human. Just human. Which meant telling them about a possible supernatural stalker was out of the question.

Humans weren't allowed to know about us. Even if we *were* hiding in plain sight, and had been for the last few hundred years–ever since human technology had gotten too advanced to live safely out in the open. When that had happened, our ancestors had been forced to put away the storybook lives they'd once lived where elves, fae, shifters, dragons, and oracles lived openly in the country-sides together. Heck, back then, humans had even known vampires existed.

And basically useless half-breeds, like me.

"I... I thought someone might have been following me," I finally said. That was truthful enough. I just didn't need to go into detail. "But," I hurried to go on when their mouths dropped open in horror, "I didn't see anyone after all. Just being cautious. That's all."

"You should tell your parents," Julia said quietly, her eyes wide.

I rolled my own eyes. "Who do you think taught me to be cautious?"

"No, I think Julia's right," Georgie said, frowning as he scratched at the red stubble that was starting to cover his chin.

"Look, I'll tell my parents," I said hurriedly as Soo Min's father walked up with our order. Fae hearing wasn't any better than that of an average human, unlike that of elves and shifters, but there was no need to let him in on this particular conversation. Vegas might be big, but it's really a *very* small town. And the supernatural community within it is even smaller. If he caught wind of this, there was no way my parents wouldn't find out before they made it home from work.

"But they're on duty tonight," I said quickly. "I've already tried texting my mom, and they're not answering. Which means they're busy on a case. And if I text something like, 'Hey, I think I might have a stalker,' they would totally blow the case they're on. I'll tell them tomorrow, when we've all had sleep and caffeine. Besides, my house is like... super safe." I gave them a forced grin. "Can you imagine *my* parents living in anything that didn't have state-of-the-art security?"

My friends, who knew my parents were protective to the point of being obsessive, reluctantly agreed, and I sighed with relief as the conversation turned to classes and papers that were soon due. And I hadn't been lying. My house *was* super safe. As in... it was spelled to a ridiculous level. Fae wards. Elven wards. Even a dragon ward—and those were *really* hard to get.

Even if I didn't have a supernatural stalker, I knew better than to flaunt my parents' installed safety measures. My parents were too well-known in the supernatural community to be casual about security. So after my friends kindly walked me to my car, and I finally arrived home in my very spelled—albeit beater—of a car, I pulled straight into the garage. And as the garage door closed behind me, I could feel the layers of magic descending with it like an embrace.

A part of me wished I could have helped create the spells with them. Once a month, my parents rewove their respective elf and fae magic into the protective wards that surrounded the house. Other supernatural kids started helping their parents with magic around the time they turned twelve or thirteen. I, on the other hand, had learned early on that it was best if I stayed far away from the wards whenever they were being raised.

But there was no sense in crying over what couldn't be. I sucked at magic, and everyone knew it. That didn't negate the fact that I had great parents, good friends, and was only two and a half semesters from graduating with my bachelor's degree in criminal justice.

I had a good life, dang it.

And I wasn't about to let some stalker ruin everything I loved.

Chapter Two

Everleigh

I awoke the next morning to a text from my mom saying they would be home late, but that I could use her credit card to get groceries from the store if I was hungry.

As I read the text, my stomach soured slightly. It wasn't an unusual message. I'd awakened to similar messages countless times since my parents had been promoted to detectives at the local police department. They'd been on this missing persons case for the last week, stopping at home only to eat and sleep before racing out again.

Besides, I scolded myself, it wasn't like I was too young to be left on my own. I was twenty-one and a junior in college. I had a friend from high school who was already married and had a baby on the way, and she was six months younger than me. But after yesterday, I suddenly missed my parents a lot more than usual.

A stroke of genius hit me, however, as I threw my backpack into my car. And when I backed the car out of the garage again, my trunk held my bike.

Lots of people biked around campus, I told myself. Some skateboarded or even scootered, often in an attempt to cut the time it took to cross the campus between classes. I wouldn't stick out any more than usual, and I would spend a lot less time out in the open where I was vulnerable.

The morning had warmed considerably by the time I found a parking space, and I sucked in a deep breath of spring air as I climbed on my bike. *You may be fast,* I thought as I made my way through the parking lot toward my first building, *but today I'm faster.*

Unfortunately, despite my newly improved speed, the sense of foreboding returned before I'd made it out of the parking lot, and it grew stronger as I neared my Crime Prevention class. And though I still couldn't catch a glimpse of whomever—or whatever—was following me, the sense of magic that floated just beyond the edges of my senses tickled my mind again.

Just as I caught sight of the bike rack in front of the building where I would have my first class, I felt a sticky sensation on my hand. Lifting my hand off the bar, I found a golden goo, similar to honey, glittering on my knuckle in the sun, a long, thin string stretching from my hand back behind me like a spider's web.

A *Seira* tracker.

Any doubts I still harbored about the possibility of a stalker disappeared in that instant as I started to pedal as though my life depended on it.

In a way, it did.

For the first time in years, I *purposefully* searched my hands for the magic I knew lay dormant there, the magic I worked so hard to suppress. On the best of days, my magic could make a royal mess, which was why I hated to use it. But now I needed something—anything to destroy the sticky golden string that was growing longer by the second.

I gritted my teeth, calling my temperamental magic to the surface as I continued to pedal. And to my surprise, my fingers fizzled for the briefest of moments, and I nearly cried out for joy. A *Seira* tracker charm could be as strong or as weak as the elf who had made it. If I was fortunate, I might be able to set fire to this one and burn it up. If it had been crafted by an elf with experience, that wouldn't work, but in the off-chance it was made by a novice, perhaps that would set me free. College students weren't known for being loaded with cash. Hopefully, this one had purchased the tracking charm on the cheap.

Unfortunately, whether or not it was bought on the cheap, I never found out. Because instead of summoning fire the way I meant to, I accidentally zapped my own bike with a small but sharp jolt of electricity. Nothing strong enough to injure me, but just enough to send an uncomfortable shock through my body.

But not strong enough, I realized with a huff, to break the *Seira* charm. If anything, the sticky golden string looked thicker.

This was why I didn't use magic.

My building was approaching fast. I didn't stop at the bike rack, however. Instead, I leaped off the bike as I hurtled toward the building's automatic doors, slowing just in time to avoid crashing into them. The moment I was inside, I let the bike fall to the ground and yanked off my backpack. My fingers fumbled the zipper in my anxiety, and only on the third try did I get the bag open.

I was further slowed by the fact that I couldn't use my left hand. Instead, I had to hold it away from my body to keep the sticky substance as far from my belongings as possible. Then I wasted several more seconds attempting to find the little mint tin that had fallen to the bottom of my backpack.

To any human, this strange coincidence would most likely be interpreted as having touched some sticky surface earlier without realizing it. And had a human tried to wash the *Seira* tracker charm off, he would have succeeded just as easily as if he had put his hand in a drop of honey. But this wasn't honey, and I wasn't a human. Washing it off would only have succeeded in getting the sticky goo on my other hand as well.

Finally, the tin popped open, and I searched desperately for the single lavender tablet that should be inside. *Don't let anyone see me,* I prayed fervently as I searched. Not a human. Not a supernatural. And not the jerk who had set this trap.

Finally, I found the purple tablet. Throwing up a prayer of thanks, I pressed the tablet against the sticky golden goo, which was now growing and spreading toward my fingers. I clenched my teeth as the tablet and then the goo began to fizzle. It burned as it worked. Like... really, really burned. But I felt like I could breathe again when the golden goo dried until it turned into dust and floated harmlessly to the tile beneath me.

I sighed in relief as I watched the charm die. *Seira* tracker charms were elven-made spells that stuck themselves to their victims and left a magical string that stretched indefinitely behind them, so the one searching for the victim could always find them. The goo itself latched onto the supernatural victim's magic, meaning it couldn't be washed or wiped away. It would also grow, as it had tried to do on my hand, and spread until it was impossible for the victim to go any farther. Only my parents' forethought in sending me the magical tablets had allowed me to escape.

And not a second too soon. At that moment, three students walked in and stopped, staring at me where I crouched with what looked like a tin of mints in front of me, my bike sideways on the floor, and the contents of my backpack surrounding me.

"Are... you okay?" one of the girls asked with hesitation.

I did my best to smile, but it was harder than usual. "Just needed my medicine," I said, holding up the tin, the contents of which cost more than my car.

"I get that." One of the shorter of the girls gave me a sympathetic smile. "My sister gets migraines, too, and she has to take medicine real fast."

"Yeah, not much time," I added lamely as they walked by, the short girl telling me to feel better.

Now that my suspicions had been confirmed, leaving my bike unattended was out of the question. The last thing I needed was for someone to charm it so it took me somewhere against my will.

So instead of leaving it, I glanced around and then wheeled it toward the ADA elevator. Bikes technically weren't supposed to be taken upstairs, but I doubted anyone would care if I left it in the back of the classroom. Besides, I was early. It was unlikely anyone else would be in the classroom for several minutes.

Unfortunately for me, someone else was.

"Good morning, Everleigh."

I jumped at the low, smooth voice coming from the front of the room.

"Oh." I gave him the same sad excuse for a smile I'd given the girls downstairs. "Hi, Professor."

"I see you brought your–" His smile faded as he sniffed twice, and then his eyes opened wide, and his voice dropped to a whisper. "Do I smell... is that a *Seira* charm?"

I stared at him, unsure of how to respond. Only supernaturals knew about *Seira* traps.

Before I could answer, two other students walked into the classroom, and my professor closed his mouth and gave me a grim nod. With humans present, there was no way we could talk openly about the charm. But the suddenly fierce look in his usually gentle eyes promised me that this wasn't the end of our conversation.

Still, I had escaped whoever was chasing me, and I'd made it to class. That was reason enough to sit and thank the Lord. And now I had a whopping hour and twenty minutes to process what had just happened before having to venture back out again.

I didn't particularly love Crime Prevention as a class, but I did like Dr. Petras. I'd taken several of his other classes as well, and he was a good enough professor that I'd maneuvered my schedule so I could take this class from him as well. He was young for a professor–like, ridiculously young. My friends and I had a bet that he was twenty-five, tops. Word on campus had it that he was some sort of genius and had earned his doctorate by the time he was twenty-two.

Julia had taken one of his classes last semester, and she was also convinced that he wore sweater vests and glasses just to appear older so his female students wouldn't flirt with him. (Not that it worked. Several always vied for teacher's pet before the end of the semester no matter what the man wore.)

I had no desire to bark up *that* tree in any way, but I did genuinely like and respect him. I'd gotten the feeling before that he was some kind of supernatural, though I couldn't tell what. Today only confirmed that. My first guess had been that he was an elf or something similar, but now my money was leaning toward a merman shifter. Whatever he was, he'd smelled the trap, which meant there was magic in him of some kind.

That might work for or against me. I hadn't yet figured out which.

He started the lecture soon after that, and I did my best to get my mind on the lesson, taking notes and answering questions as he gave them. But I must not have done a very good job because he asked to speak with me after he released everyone else.

"Miss Clarkson, do you want to tell me what's going on?" he asked after the last student had gone. His light brown brows furrowed behind his glasses. "Let's start with the *Seira* charm."

I blinked at him. "I...um. Yes," I finally said.

His eyes narrowed slightly. "So where do you think you acquired it?"

"This morning on my way to class," I mumbled.

He opened his tablet and began scribbling furiously with his stylus. "And is this the first brush with danger you've had recently?"

I thought about trying to lie to him. But being half-fae, I was really terrible at lying. Also, for some reason, I realized I *wanted* to tell him the truth. "No," I blurted out. "I mean, not directly. But I've had this weird feeling since last week that... that someone might be following me. Around campus, I mean. Not home or anywhere else."

Yet.

"Have you talked to campus police?" he asked with a frown.

I shook my head. "There's nothing to tell. I haven't seen anyone. I couldn't even give them a description if I tried." I smiled wryly. "And I obviously can't tell them about the charm."

He crossed his arms, which I now noticed were thicker than I had previously thought. Had he started working out?

"I don't mean to pry," he said slowly, his voice suddenly low and cautious, "and I didn't want to say so in front of the class but... I know your parents and a bit about what they do. I've actually acted as a consultant for them before. And if you haven't told them yet, I think you ought to."

I nodded at the floor. "I know. But they've been on a case since last week. And I didn't want to distract them."

"You're their daughter." His frown deepened. "I hardly think your safety would be a distraction."

"Everleigh?"

We looked up to see Georgie standing at the door of my classroom. His eyes widened as he took in my professor. "Oh, sorry. I don't want to interrupt, but Julia sent me to find you so I can walk you to the smoothie shop in the student union. They're selling half-price shakes today!"

I gave him a grateful smile, but Professor Petras only pursed his lips before turning back to me.

"I'm fully aware that I'm just your professor, so take this advice as you will," he said slowly. "But I do think all the same you shouldn't wait to tell your parents." His voice grew so quiet I could barely hear him. "Your safety affects more than just you, Everleigh."

I stared up at him. Was he trying to say something else without saying it? It almost seemed that way, as his eyes bored into mine. But then he fixed me with a sad smile and blinked. "It's always that way when you have people who love you the way your family and friends do." He looked back over at Georgie. "You say Julia will be there as well?"

Georgie nodded, unperturbed, it seemed, that my professor didn't seem to trust him enough to release me into his presence without Julia expecting us as well. It was sweet and... strange. But then again, everyone on campus who knew us seemed to now see the three of us as a single unit.

My phone buzzed, and I pulled it out and glanced at the screen. "She texted me just now." I smiled up at him, true gratitude filling my chest. His kindness, particularly in light of my mixed lineage, was unusual in the supernatural world.

Still... the way he spoke hinted at something beyond simply knowing who and what I was. Sure, my parents were minor royalty in the supernatural world, but to most supernaturals, children born of two different bloodlines were generally considered to be of less worth than the average human, no matter what their parentage. Why was this brilliant professor worried about me? I mean, he was a nice guy. It was one of the reasons I'd signed up for his classes. But his concern was nearly as confusing as someone choosing to stalk me in the first place.

***

"So he's back, is he?" Georgie said as soon as we were back outside.

I sighed. "It would seem he is."

Georgie looked around, not even bothering to hide his search. But then again, he was two heads taller than me. Maybe he would see something I'd missed. "I'd like to find him so we can confront him and figure out what he wants, once and for all," he said.

I gave him a look. "You think *talking* to my stalker is going to help?"

He frowned and shook his head. "Stupid," he muttered.

"Excuse me?"

"Oh, I didn't mean you!" He shook his head. "Sorry, I just meant all the hiding. It's stupid. Because hiding is *cowardly!*" He snapped the word loudly, as if he was hoping the stalker heard him.

As he did, he stepped closer, as though he might shield me with his six-foot-two frame that looked as though he might blow away in a strong wind.

Still, I couldn't help but smile. I had good friends.

Julia spotted us outside the student union, and she did not look happy.

"Let me guess. You already told her." I let out a gusty sigh.

He blinked down at me in surprise. "Of course I did."

"Georgie, what you guys are doing for me is so sweet, but—"

Sure enough, before I could finish my sentence, Julia was marching toward us. "So that sicko is still following you, is he?"

"Hi, Julia," I said with a wry grin. "How are you?"

"They ran out of smoothies, but that's okay because we're going to the police station *now*." She linked her arm through mine and put her pretty nose in the air. "Georgie, you can walk us to the car."

I opened my mouth to remind them that I could ride my bike easily enough. It was annoying to walk with the thing anyway. But when I saw the determination on Julia's face, I just sighed and nodded. Maybe it was for the best. Whoever was following me was *still* close by. I could feel him, even now with my friends walking on each side of me, making us an Everleigh sandwich. He hadn't even been *that* bold yesterday.

"I'm going with her to the station, too," Georgie announced.

But Julia shook her head. "No, you can't. You have that makeup test today, and your professor said she'll flunk you if you miss it again."

Georgie scowled. "I don't really need that stupid class anyway."

"You might not, but your GPA does," I said dryly. "Look, Georgie, just walk us to my car and know you've done a gallant deed. It's not like you're going to save us from anything while we make our way through the traffic." I gave him my best smile. "Really, that's the best way you can help."

"What about you?" Georgie pouted at Julia as we turned onto another path. "Don't you have class this afternoon?"

"Yes, but I can attend online." Julia smirked. "That's not important, though. What *is* important is that from now on, until we get this figured out, you, Miss Everleigh, are not going to spend a moment alone. Either Georgie or I will walk you to and from class and to your car until your parents track down this weirdo and wring his neck." She sniffed.

"She's right!" Georgie gave a sharp nod. "We'll make sure you're always with one of us." He paused. "Though I'll try to be with you both as much as I can."

"That's really sweet of you guys," I said, giving them a sad excuse for a smile. "Only, you forget. One word of this, and I'm going to lose every ounce of privacy I ever had. And I mean, there's a *really* good chance my parents aren't going to even let me come back to campus. You *know* what they're like."

As we spoke, we made our way west, toward the parking lot I usually chose. The air smelled like smog and pollen, and it made me sneeze.

"Well," Julia said, her voice less bright than before, "as much as I would hate that, if it's safer for you, then I would accept it."

"Yeah," Georgie said. "Though it really... really would suck." Then his eyes brightened. "We could hang out with you more when you're home or out and about, though. Your parents are always working. It would be another level of protection."

"You do realize that you're both putting yourselves in harm's way as well," I said as we started across the crumbling parking lot, the asphalt crunching beneath our feet.

"I'm thinking of it as an excuse to get one of those collapsible sticks you can use to smack bad guys with." Julia grinned. "They probably have a pink one on sale somewhere."

"Is it even legal to carry those on campus?" I asked. But as soon as I thought about it, I loved the idea. Julia might be a mere human, but she was a born athlete–tall for a woman, strong, and fast as a race horse. We'd taken two different kinds of martial arts together as kids and teens, and she'd lettered in multiple sports in high school. The only reason she wasn't playing on one of the college teams now was because she was planning on applying for a kinesiology internship soon that would take a ton of her time. If she was determined to be around me, she'd be far safer walking around with a big stick.

"Maybe this is my sign to get to the gym more often," Georgie laughed nervously, running a hand through his fiery red hair.

"If you're weak, it's your fault for not letting me train you," Julia shot back. "I told you I'd train you for free after I got my license last year. I should charge you now, though. Just on principle for being lazy."

"For the last time, I have an online job! Testing strategy games on my PC is not being lazy if I'm making money!"

They were still arguing by the time we reached my car, and I smiled as they vowed to continue their "discussion" later. But my smile didn't last as I put my ancient sedan in reverse and pulled out of my spot. As much as I liked leaving school, I wondered when I would be on campus next.

If it was left solely up to my parents, I might never set foot on the campus again.

Chapter Three

Everleigh

I DID my best to appear relaxed as we walked through the front doors of my parents' police station. My smile became more genuine, however, when we were greeted by the lady behind the U-shaped desk.

Technically, the *elf* behind the U-shaped desk.

"Well, look who's here," Miss Lillian gushed as she hurried to stand. Her Irish accent wasn't as strong as my parents said it once had been, but it softened her words so they were even sweeter. Almost as though she were always speaking a song.

"Hi, Miss Lillian," Julia and I said as she hugged us both.

"Now, Everleigh I recognize because she's been in here just enough to remind me how much she's gone." Miss Lillian gave me a false glare from behind her cat-eye glasses. "But Julia! You've grown six inches since I saw you last!"

"I was here last week!" I protested as Julia gave me a smirk.

"Dropping off your parents' lunches in such a hurry that you couldn't say more than hello and goodbye." Miss Lillian sniffed and adjusted her graying hair, which was pulled back into a neat ponytail.

"If it isn't Everleigh and Julia!" a booming voice called from the hall behind Miss Lillian's desk.

I grinned. "Hey, Chief." And then the scoldings and teasing started all over again.

My parents never told me much about why they left the lavish lifestyles of their families behind, other than to say they hadn't wanted to raise me in the supernatural courts. *That* I understood. What little I'd seen of the courts was more than I ever needed or wanted to know.

It also made me grateful that—despite being raised as supernatural royalty—they had immediately focused on getting our little family settled in the human world. They'd both joined the local human police force and worked their way up the ranks, each reaching detective the year I started high school. This police station was a home away from home, and I had countless memories of playing beneath Miss Lillian's desk, attending work picnics, and Chief sneaking me lollipops when he thought my parents weren't looking. (Although, he hadn't been chief back then.) And eventually, Julia had come with me so often that the station had come to treat her as an extension of my family as well.

"Are my parents here?" I asked Chief as he prepared to launch into a rant about last night's hockey game. Both Chief and Julia *loved* hockey. "I need to tell them something."

"Sure thing, kiddo. They should be at your dad's desk."

I thanked him and headed past him down the hall, my footsteps muffled by the sound of the cheap carpet beneath. As I did, my heart began to race. And by the time I reached their work area, full of cubicles and desks, I was starting to wonder if I might pass out.

Which was stupid. It wasn't like this was *my* fault. So why was *I* nervous?

As soon as I turned the corner, however, I breathed a slight sigh of relief. My mom was sitting in my dad's rolling chair, and my dad was leaning against the desk, their heads together as they studied something on his laptop. And it wasn't until I neared them that I realized just how anxious I had been.

"Everleigh!" My dad stood and strode toward me, his arms outstretched. I threw myself into his hug and squeezed my eyes shut, reveling in the slightly earthy smell all elves had—one, however, that I had come to associate exclusively with him.

He was wearing his usual work attire, khaki slacks with a button-up shirt and black boots. Also hidden on his person, though no one could see it, was the glamour stone.

Nearly all supernaturals carried glamour stones. For those of us with features that differed from humans on an everyday basis, such as pointed ears, unusually brilliant eyes, or attention-drawing height differences, the fae-spelled stones softened our features, giving us the illusions of rounded ears or human eyes, allowing us to blend into the crowd just a little better. For shifters, who can change forms in seconds, the stones could make them nearly invisible until they were able to get into hiding. Just as with anything else in life such as food, clothing, and weapons, you got what you paid for. The quality stones cost more.

"It's nice to—Hey, Everleigh. Look up at me."

I swallowed and peered up at him, trying to give him my best smile.

But he wasn't fooled. "Everleigh." His voice dropped so low it was tinged with magic. "What's wrong?"

"Nikos." My mom's voice was suddenly near. "What is it?"

"I..." I looked around. There were several officers looking at us, waving and giving me smiles. I gave them a weak smile in return and waved back.

"Come on." My dad gently tugged me toward the break room. "We'll talk in here."

It was empty, to my relief. Once we were all inside, he locked the door and pulled the inner blinds down.

My phone buzzed with an incoming text. I glanced at it and smiled when I saw Georgie's name.

Did you make it safely to your parents?

I shot off a quick reply so he wouldn't worry while my parents worked on isolating the room. Just as I put my phone away again, my dad finished adding a silencing ward. Then he turned back to me and crossed his arms. "All right. Now we can talk."

I nodded but swallowed. This was already turning out to be way more dramatic than I'd wanted it to be. But really, what had I expected? *Hey, Mom and Dad. I think I've got a supernatural stalker at school. It's just your worst nightmare come true for your daughter who can't do magic. No biggie. Anyway, I'm going to take Julia home now. Bye.*

Yeah, that wasn't going to happen.

That was the frustrating thing about being the daughter of two of the most talented detectives on the force. Not only were they excellent at their jobs (which I'm pretty sure broke regulation—spouses working together and all), but that was *before* factoring in my parents'... natural abilities. Between the two of them, they could sense just about anything. Any attempt at a lie or hint of untruth. Heck, they could sense my *anxiety*. No use in beating about the bush now.

So I told them. And the more I talked, the more my fears about never being allowed out of the house again seemed to materialize in front of me. My mom's gentle brown eyes had hardened into something more akin to copper, and my dad's face looked as if it had been chiseled from granite. I could almost see his ears growing sharper by the second, despite knowing he was wearing his glamour stone. But then again, my dad's power was stronger than most elves', as he was from a royal line—which meant that when he felt *very* strongly about something, the glamour stone sometimes struggled to keep up.

Like now, it seemed.

"Everleigh." My mom put her fingers to her temples when I

was done. "*Why* did you not tell us about this as soon as it happened?"

"Because." I rolled my eyes. "I wasn't even sure about it until yesterday. I thought maybe it was a fluke last week, the first time it had happened. That I was just imagining things. And you seemed so busy last night I didn't want to–"

"Everleigh," my dad snapped so sharply I jumped. "When in the world have we ever told you *not* to come to us for help?"

Mom whipped her phone out as he spoke and began texting furiously. A moment later, there was a familiar knock on the door, and I resisted the urge to put my face in my hands and groan.

"This," I muttered, "is exactly why I was hesitant to come."

But no one heard me. Or if they did, they pretended not to. Because my dad was already ushering in Mr. and Mrs. Nomos, two of the other detectives who worked at the station.

They also happened to be my parents' closest friends–friends who had escaped the royal supernatural world as well. They weren't family, but I was closer to them than I was to any blood relatives other than my parents.

"What happened?" Mrs. Nomos asked in a low voice as soon as my dad's ward was resealed. Then her green eyes fell on me, and despite the anxiety in her voice, she smiled, and her voice was velvety and warm. "Hi, Everleigh."

"Hey, kiddo," her husband said, nodding to me as well before turning to my parents.

"Everleigh," my mother said in a strained voice, "thinks she has a stalker on campus." Her eyes met theirs. "A supernatural one."

I had known Mr. and Mrs. Nomos my whole life. They were technically my godparents, and I was pretty sure Mrs. Nomos had changed as many of my diapers as my own parents had. Never before that moment, however, had I seen both of them go completely still, as though frozen in time.

My father gave them a single meaningful nod.

"Wait," I said. "Is there something going on that you're not telling me?"

But they ignored me, all four now deep in whispered tones I couldn't hear. They didn't have to answer, though. The longer I watched them, the more I was convinced that they acted as though...

As though they had been expecting something like this.

First the stalker.

Then Professor Petras.

Now this.

As if summoned, Professor Petras's words came back to me from earlier that morning. *Your safety affects more than just you, Everleigh.*

Had he been speaking in code, too?

My mind worked quickly as they continued to whisper. Something was definitely going on. And whatever it was had started way before last Thursday.

"I need to take Julia home," I said loudly.

I thought they would continue to ignore me or tell me no, but my dad turned and reached into his pocket. After pulling out his keys, he tossed them to me. "Take my car and leave me yours. I've just had it respelled. You can take Julia home, but don't go in or linger. Then drive straight home." His green eyes narrowed. "*Straight* home. We'll meet you there."

I thought about reminding them that I was twenty-one, not fifteen, but another look at the anxiety on all four faces kept my mouth shut. They were truly worried. There was no need to make it worse.

Chapter Four

Aithan

My phone buzzed as I surveyed the empty hotel suite yet again for any sign of mischief. When nothing appeared to be out of the ordinary, I pulled the phone out just long enough to glance at my boss's text.

Everything's clear in the lobby and halls. Done with the rooms yet?

I'd already been through the hotel suite's multiple rooms three times. That was the company's policy. Whenever we were providing security for a client as famous as the Hollywood heart-throb we'd booked that day, my boss insisted on going over every inch of the hotel multiple times. Any corner we were legally allowed to touch, we did—something most hotels had no problem with. After all, no resort wanted to trend online because a celebrity was ambushed in his or her bedroom by a crazed fan.

Unbeknownst to my boss, however, I did more than look through every closet, under the bed, or in the bathroom cabinets. I did what my human boss could never dream of doing.

Closing my eyes, I reached out with my magic to give the suite one final test, searching for any active or lingering remnants of magic in the air. Nine times out of ten, there was nothing to find. After all, this was one of the nicer resorts on the Las Vegas Strip–elf-owned–and they had their own security. It was unlikely that anyone had...

My senses sharpened as I tasted a hint... just the barest whisper of magic. So I reached out further, focusing my mind on following the source of magic that had momentarily flashed across my senses. Like a candle being lit and then extinguished, it had been there one second and gone the next.

Of course, there was always the chance that there was a super-natural member on the cleaning crew, and he or she had left a remnant of magic behind, but I doubted that this time, as I'd performed this same magic sweep when I'd first entered the room. If that had been the case, I should have picked it up the first time. But this...

If I was making a bet, I would say there was someone here now. And that someone had just made a mistake.

There. I opened my eyes and went back to the closet I'd checked multiple times. And as expected, when I opened the door, I saw nothing. The sensation of magic, however, grew stronger. This time, I felt it enough to look up.

"Well, look at that," I said, peering at the ceiling of the closet. Sure enough, a nymph had squeezed herself between the top closet shelf and the ceiling, and she was clutching a small bottle of wine to her chest.

I held my hand out. "Come on. I see you. Might as well climb down."

The woman–who was dressed seductively–huffed and rolled her eyes before climbing down. When she was finally standing in front of me, I took the bottle.

"Made this yourself, did you?" I asked, noting that the wine's seal was gone. "Going to snare yourself an expensive whirlwind marriage and divorce?" I uncorked the bottle and inhaled just enough to give it a sniff. The potency of the drink made me cough several times before I put the cork back in and stuck the small bottle in my sports jacket pocket. "Good grief. He would have died of asphyxiation before you ever got him to drink it. What possessed you to make the seduction spell so strong?"

"It would have been *fine* if you could have minded your own business," she pouted, her green wings giving an annoyed twitch. "I know what I'm doing." Then her eyes lit up, and I wanted to curse as recognition flooded her face. "Wait, you look familiar—"

Before she could finish, however, I sensed a second presence in the room. And not a moment too soon. My spelled knife was in my hand milliseconds before a cheetah pounced on me from behind.

If I had been a rookie at security or magic, the shifter might have succeeded in knocking me to the ground the way I knew she'd planned. But I was experienced at both, and by the time she landed on all four paws, I spun around and landed a sharp jab to the back of her head.

She hissed, and without pausing, sprang at me again.

I rolled, landing on my back and kicking up with one leg, sending her sprawling on the floor behind me.

The nymph lunged at me, grabbing my utility belt and yanking a leather handle from its loop. She squealed with delight until she held up it up, frowning when she realized there was nothing attached to the other side.

I only grinned, holding up my hand and conjuring a magical whip that crackled with lightning.

"I'm not sure why you think this is an easier way to leave the hotel," I said. With a snap of my wrist, I wrapped the lightning whip around the cheetah shifter. She screamed in rage as I yanked her toward me, her claws extended as she tried to scratch my eyes out.

"Now, that's just rude." I grabbed the nymph's arm as she tried to flee. "I'd prefer you wait here." I flicked my wrist again, this time loosing the whip and then wrapping it around them both, pinning their backs together where I could hold them both in place.

The cheetah shifted back into her human form, but she continued to struggle. So I tightened my magical whip around her before taking the decoy whip handle from her partner.

But the nymph woman seemed determined not to go quite as easily as her partner had. Her smile turned alluring, and she blinked up at me through wide, brown eyes, her red hair framing her face in adorable ringlets. "You know, if *you're* not busy after work—"

I just sighed and shook my head before waving my hand. The nymph gasped as her seduction spell floated away and disappeared, leaving a beautiful but average fae woman gawking up at me.

"How did you—" she began, but then paused and stared. I was already unbuttoning the top of my dress shirt. After undoing the top three buttons, I leaned over to show her the tattoo just below my collarbone.

She sucked in a sharp breath and stumbled sideways as hard as if I'd shoved her, dragging the other woman with her. The doe-eyed look was gone, replaced now by a nearly violent shiver. Her partner shivered as well.

"Nomos," she whispered. "But you..." She looked around wildly as if searching for somewhere to go. The shifter woman behind her had gone stone still.

"I gave you the chance to leave," I said, buttoning my shirt up once more. "But you chose to try to seduce me instead. Which was a really terrible idea, if you think about it. And that terrible idea means I have no choice but to hand you over to resort security."

"Please. Oh, please, no!" The nymph, who had managed to slip out of her bonds, threw herself back against the closet wall. "Just let me go! I promise you'll never see me again!"

"You'll never see *us* again!" the shifter whimpered.

"I'm sure I won't, as I have nothing to do with the resort itself," I said, flicking my wrist and closing my hand. A second cord of magic appeared in my grasp and wrapped itself around her arm. I gave the cord a tug, yanking her toward me so I could firmly grasp her arms and press her down onto the ground. "I only work as hired security for rich men like the one you tried to snag tonight. My uncle, however, owns this hotel. And I have no doubt that his security will be *very* glad to see you."

The nymph wailed so loudly at this that I was forced to create a silencing ward around her as I dragged her and her friend back out to the suite's front room and tied them up again. For a moment, I wondered if either of them would try to run. But the sight of my family crest seemed to have destroyed their confidence in their own abilities. The shifter began to plead, but the nymph only slumped, still wailing, to the ground. If they hadn't been attempting to ruin not only my client's life, but my own as well tonight, I might have felt sorry for them. My uncle *didn't* deal kindly with people like them. But this wasn't my hotel, and that wasn't my decision to make. So once I was sure they weren't going to run, I called my boss. It didn't even have a chance to ring.

"What's taking so long?" my boss barked.

"I found two very avid fans here," I said, giving the fae woman a warning look as she gazed longingly at the door. "I'm sure the manager would prefer us to be discrete. Can you get him up here?"

"On it." The line went dead, and I shoved the phone back into my pocket with a grimace. Talking to hotel management was *not* what I had planned to do that morning when I'd been assigned to scope out the movie star's rented rooms. But this particular celebrity was an A-lister, and management would be very put out that these... *ladies* had somehow managed to get past them and into the hotel room at all.

Unfortunately, of course, that meant I would have to deal with–

The suite door clicked with the sound of the electronic key, then it opened. Four very large, suited men entered the room, and behind them, a fifth, younger man. I did my best to look professional and detached as the man in the front did a double take upon entering. But it was hard not to groan as the young man's face transformed into a wide smile.

"Aithan! I didn't know you were working for my father these days!"

"I'm not," I said calmly as the shifter began to struggle again at the sight of the men. "I'm on your esteemed guest's security detail for the next few days. We were doing a sweep of the room, and I found this lovely lady hiding in his closet with..." I pulled the bottle of wine from my pocket. "Whatever concoction this is of her own making."

The young man hardly spared the women or the wine a glance. "You know the offer still stands. My father would love to hire you any time. Just because your parents chose a life with humans doesn't mean you have to." As he spoke, he motioned at his men, who took charge of the two women and the fae's illegal elixir.

"Tell my uncle thank you," I said with a slight bow. "But I'm quite happy where I am."

But rather than taking the hint, my cousin's smile faded, and he drew near, his expression serious. "Grandfather would be pleased–"

"You mean the grandfather who cursed me and my brother as children because my father displeased him? No." I let out a harsh laugh. "I think I'm much better off where I am, thank you."

"You never know." The young man looked down. "If you came back, he might be able to... to mitigate it somehow."

"He *cursed* me, Angelo," I spat. "Unless he's been searching for a way to to alter curses, then I'm not interested."

Angelo scoffed. "No one tries to break his own curse. Isn't that asking a little much–"

"Well then, there's your answer." I clapped my cousin on the shoulder as I headed toward the door. "Keep an eye on that one. She tried to seduce me as well."

Once I was free of the room, I made my way down to the security office, where my team was waiting for me.

"I'm going to say it again. I'm impressed!" The movie star's manager was telling my boss as I walked in, shaking his hand almost violently. "Our people brought up his luggage hours ago and looked that room up one side and down the other. We would have had no idea he was locked in there with whatever lunatic she was!"

"Here he is." My boss, a human who was nearly as large as a modern giant, jerked his head in my direction. "He's the one who found her."

The movie star's manager beamed at me and offered his hand, which I shook. It was a weak shake, cold and clammy, and hardly one from someone I would have ever entrusted with my own well-being. Still, when the man handed me a wad of cash for my troubles, I thanked him yet again. Private security may not have been my parents' dream for me after graduating with honors from the local human university. But it paid really well.

And yet, after getting my schedule set with my boss to relieve some of my coworkers later, I couldn't help feeling somewhat hollow as I walked back to my car in the resort's cold, windy parking garage. I suddenly wished I could call my brother and talk to him. Alexander was always good at putting things in perspective. But these days, Alexander was very rarely available to talk, as he *was* working for our grandfather—work of a nature he couldn't share.

Well, then maybe I would get something to eat and go back to my apartment. Then, after loading up on carbs, I could do the workout of the century. I'd been craving Thai lately. Just as I was putting the car in reverse, however, my phone buzzed again.

"Aithan?" my dad's voice came in loud over the car speaker.

"Hey, Dad. What's up?"

"Are you alone?" came my dad's reply.

I hit the brakes and frowned down at my phone where it sat in the cupholder. "Yeah," I said slowly. "Why?"

"We need you to come home as soon as you can." My dad paused. "It's about Everleigh."

Chapter Five

Everleigh

By the time I got home from dropping Julia off at her apartment, my parents had already arrived, and I could tell as soon as I saw them that they were much more their usual calm and collected selves.

Which meant they'd reached a solution I probably wouldn't like.

If only, the thought flashed through my mind, *I was a normal elf or fae who could properly defend myself without a sidearm or pepper spray.* Not some half-and-half who had to rely on my parents and friends to keep me safe.

Of course, this would also be easier if I could carry a firearm on campus. Even elves, with their ability to manipulate matter in the world around them, had to be decently powerful to stop a bullet. My dad had not only put me through his own (very extensive) firearms training when I was a teenager, he had then hired experts from all over the country to come and personally train me in self-defense. Who needed magic when you had a gun?

But guns weren't allowed on campus, so that put me back to square one.

"Hey, sweetie!" my mom said as I walked in. "Come sit down."

Trying to keep my heart at a somewhat healthy rhythm, I tried to look nonchalant as I dropped my keys by the door and plopped down on the love seat across from their couch.

"So," I said. But that was all I could think of to say.

My mom and dad shared a long look, the kind that said all kinds of things they weren't going to say out loud in front of me. And it made me want to beat my head against a brick wall.

Instead, I sighed. "I'm twenty-one. You don't have to hide things from me like I'm ten."

"We're aware of that," my mom said in a voice so patient it nearly drove me berserk. "And... we're grateful that you've been so willing to live within the parameters we've given you for so long, seeing as most human children are usually less... compliant by your age."

"Well," I chuckled wryly, "having extended family members who will kill you if you step out of line will do that to a girl."

My parents didn't laugh.

"What we mean to say," my dad continued, "is that we understand your degree is nearly done. And as such, it's important that you're able to attend class."

I sat straighter. "You do?"

He nodded. "We're also glad you spoke with us this afternoon because we got an interesting email from Dr. Benedict Petras just after you left, saying he was worried about you."

"Interfering merman," I mumbled under my breath.

Mom smiled wryly. "He's... not a merman. But he *is* a powerful ally, and we're glad he was *thoughtful* enough to consider *your* safety by telling us."

I sighed. "I know."

"That said," she continued, "we talked it over with the Nomoses, and we've decided that Aithan will be attending school with you for a while as your bodyguard."

I jumped out of my seat. "He *what?*" I could feel the blood drain from my face. "Aithan... Aithan doesn't even *like* me! We're not friends anymore, remember? He went off and did his own thing after graduating, and I'm absolutely certain he has no desire *whatsoever* to babysit me."

That, and I had no desire to be babysat *by* him.

"Well," my mom shrugged, "it's either that, or you'll be attending school online for the rest of the year. According to Dr. Petras, that is a perfectly acceptable option if we submit the right paperwork."

I put my hands on my head and began to pace the living room. Of all the ways to finish my junior year! With *Aithan Nomos*. As my *bodyguard*.

I wanted to throw up and throw rocks at the same time.

"I know this isn't what you wanted." My mom's patience was quickly draining from her voice, and the hard, no-nonsense tone I was all too familiar with was taking its place. "But whether you like it or not—whether you reject your magic or not—you *are* royalty in supernatural society, Everleigh. And while your father may not be the son of the high king like Mr. Nomos is, his family—and mine—are not of little consequence in our world."

Dad was frowning down at his ring, the one he never took off. I knew its shape and image by heart. It was the family crest that no member of a royal elf family ever took off—*ever*. It was a seal of the connection an elf had to his family line—a ward of protection in its own right provided by the family magic. Its dark green stone glimmered even in the low light of the living room against the gold band it was set in, and from across the room, I could see glimmers of magic seeping out from it even as we spoke.

"Sweetheart," he said slowly, "have you ever really stopped to consider *why* you're being followed?"

Only every other moment since last Thursday. But I wasn't going to admit that out loud. So I huffed instead. "I don't know.

Probably because I have two X chromosomes." It obviously wasn't for my magic.

My parents exchanged another one of *those* looks, then my dad let out a gusty sigh and ran his fingers through his blond hair.

"Have you…" then he stopped and made an annoyed sound in his throat. "I can't," he said after a moment, looking at my mom. "I've thought of every way to try, and I just *can't*."

"What your father is trying to say," my mom said slowly, "is that…" But when she opened her mouth again, nothing came out. She closed her eyes and swallowed before trying again. "If you read the histories we gave you of royal courts and the esteemed…' Then, once again, as though someone had hit the mute button, she put her face in her hands and let out a huff. After a second, she looked at my dad and frowned. "We need the *sanguis colorum*. Now."

"Did he say when it would be done?" my dad asked.

My mom shook her head, her face still in her hands. "No. He's still working on it."

I shook my head. "The… what?" My annoyance was quickly turning to utter confusion the longer this strange conversation went on. Why couldn't my parents say whatever it was that they obviously wanted to say? Were they being… magically prohibited? It was the only explanation I could come up with for their strange behavior and unfinished thoughts.

My dad rubbed his eyes. When he looked at me again, he looked much older, and much more tired than he had ten minutes before. "I wish we could say it aloud, sweetheart. I really do. We've tried so many times."

"But that doesn't mean," my mom said firmly, almost fiercely, "that you can't find out for yourself! We need you to try, Everleigh! To really *try!*" Then she stood and looked down at her clothes. "I need to change and make dinner. In the meantime," she met my eyes again, "*read* the histories. I know the supernatural is not the world you love–"

"It's not my lack of love," I reminded her. "The supernatural world never wanted *me*."

"Be that as it may," my dad said, standing as well, "you're a princess. On both sides. Which means even if the human world doesn't recognize such things, it's your duty to find out what you can for our people." He frowned slightly. "For all of us." Then he turned and followed my mom upstairs. But I could only stare at his back as he walked away.

Find out? Find out *what?*

I slowly followed them up the stairs, then turned toward my room. There I changed mechanically, only half aware of what I was doing. But after putting on my comfy old pajama pants and one of my dad's softest t-shirts, I couldn't bring myself to go back down to the kitchen to eat with them. After all the weirdness that had just taken place in the living room, I needed some time alone to think.

To *find*, apparently. So I headed instead to my parents' study, where my dad's library boasted nearly every dry supernatural history book ever written.

I'd heard this command for years, of course, the constant reminder to learn more about the fae and the elves, and about supernaturals in general. It was all part of being a royal. Blah, blah, blah, all my royal duties. All as royal as my royal homework, royal bathrobe, and royal slippers with pictures of those naked sphynx cats all over them.

And yet, despite my annoyance, I had—to a point—actually searched. And that research was part of the reason I was so compliant when it came to my parents'... *unusual* restrictions, despite being twenty-one. For in my reading of the supernatural histories, I had learned just enough to know that all those Las Vegas crime bosses from the nineteen-forties on—the supposedly Chicago-based mobs that had run the Las Vegas Strip for decades— had just been a front.

The real money and influence behind the rich and affluent on the Las Vegas Strip came from the most powerful supernatural leaders in the world. The high elven king had chosen to make his seat there on the Strip, as had many of the lower elven courts. Likewise, though not as powerful in magic or numbers, were the lower elven courts and likewise, the fae kings and queens. Even the vampires had their headquarters in town, as did a growing number of shifter groups. And the betting and entertainment they provided the humans via the facades of the hotels, resorts, and casinos not only hid their activity, but kept the monarchs' bank accounts fat as well.

I was *also* aware that the supernaturals who rebelled too openly were quickly brought to heel by those same rich and powerful monarchs. They kept eyes not only on the Strip itself, but all over town. They had even stopped a number of plots by the less-than-moral supernaturals who wanted to take advantage of humans. And as the granddaughter of not one but *two* supernatural monarchs, it would have been very... *very* stupid of me to draw attention to the magic I barely possessed and used even more poorly. Lying low and living like a human was the safest bet.

And really, that was all I wanted, I mused as I browsed my father's shelves. I loved my life, and I had no desire to interact with the supernatural world at large. It was they who had rejected me, as they did all half-breeds. "Weakening the blood pool," as it was called, wasting reproduction on supernaturals who, by birth, possessed magic but could not generally use it well. I'd had enough supernatural friends as a kid to learn how many turned tail when they found out that my parents were of different races. Heck, the one serious boyfriend I'd ever had had ghosted me after his parents objected to mine.

Aithan Nomos hadn't, of course, rejected me because of my parentage. He and his older brother, Alexander, had been raised right alongside me, as our fathers were best friends. But Aithan wasn't much better than the average supernatural in that aspect either. Years had passed since he'd done more than occasionally acknowledge my existence between his continual revolving door of girlfriends and arm candy. In fact, I decided as I yanked a book off a shelf, he was worse. And I had no desire to see his stupid, expensive car pull up next to my beater at school the next day so I could tote him around like some hot, smug security guard.

But I would stew about him later. Right now, I apparently had mysteries to solve.

This in mind, I continued to wander around my parents' study. Unlike the rest of the house, which would appear very normal to the human eye, this room was full of proof that my parents weren't, in fact, run-of-the-mill police detectives. Sure, it had a large wooden desk, the kind executives kept in expensive corporate offices. And the very full floor-to-ceiling bookshelves on every wall looked like any well-designed library. But little crystals and other magical artifacts were hidden all about the room if you knew how to spot or sense them. And if you read some of the book titles, you'd find that they weren't written in English.

Or in any human language at all.

I wasn't looking for the old books, though, I decided. I didn't have time for those. Instead, I put my chosen book back and logged onto my dad's computer instead. Then I pulled up a blog post I'd stumbled upon years before when he'd accidentally left it up on the screen.

Disquiet for Daniil? read the title.

It might come as a surprise to many humans, but yes, supernaturals had our own blogs and websites and social media apps. Heck, we even had our own hashtags that trended every now and then, something so innocuous the humans never guessed the actual meaning or origins. If one knew what to look for, they weren't that hard to spot.

Generally, these sites contain a type of formatting that looks like it hasn't been updated in about twenty years. And this site was one of those. The font was all tiny and off-center, and the images were blurry. Annoying to a human, but perfectly readable for those with magic. It had taken the fae brownies (many of whom specialized in information technology) a few years to figure out how, but they'd eventually worked out how to bespell the code so it looked different to those without magic. And that was quite a feat. I think a few of them were even knighted for it by King Kostas.

This particular article was dated the year before I was born. And even though I knew the article by heart, I scrolled through it again.

Prince Nikos of the Elven House Ethelia, close friend of the heir to the high elven King Kostas of the House Nomos, has fallen out of favor with his father after marrying Princess Erin, daughter of King Daniil of the Fae House Gallagher against the crown's will.

Along with the article was a picture of my father, who looked to be in his early to mid-twenties, frowning as he held my mother's hand. They were both wearing sunglasses and hats, much in the way movie stars might at a grocery store. But then again, they were celebrities in their own right. It only made sense that they would try to escape the photographers like the one who had taken that picture.

There wasn't much else in the post, just a few vain speculations about how the other family members were reacting to the split, most of them as mean and petty as anything I might expect from jealous cousins.

The second post was about how the one of the fae princesss from the House Gallagher had also married against her father's wishes. But this article went further to mention that rumors were swirling that she was pregnant, and that the High Elven King's personal oracle had foreseen that they would give birth to an *Anikos*.

A magical dud, essentially, and a disappointing way to end the hopes and dreams of two prominent supernatural royal families.

The third post was about how King Kostas of the Nomos line was angry with his own son for staying loyal to his best friend, cursing him and his children after the crown prince had made an oath to follow his closest friend out of the courts and into the human world.

I shook my head with disgust as I closed the browser window. All of this anger and angst and cursing had happened because of me.

I was under no delusions about Aithan's avoidance of me when he graduated from high school. Given, we hadn't been close since I'd been in middle school. But still, it didn't take a genius to figure out that he wasn't super fond of the kid whose appearance in the world had brought his grandfather to *curse* him when he was a *preschooler*.

Was it any wonder I wanted nothing to do with the supernatural world?

And now it was all happening again. My family and friends were completely rearranging their lives to protect me. But what for ultimately? To what purpose? And how long could my parents really expect this ridiculous level of security to last? I happened to know that Aithan had a job that paid very well. I highly doubted he wanted to follow me around all day when he could be making that kind of paycheck.

As anger flashed through me, a bright light shot from my hand into the desk's polished wood where my hands were resting. It then traveled all over the desk, until each little branch fizzled out. The sound of breaking glass followed.

I closed my eyes and leaned my head back so I could count to twenty. Only when I was breathing normally again did I slowly open my eyes to see my dad's empty water glass in shards all over the desk and the hardwood floor.

This was why I didn't use magic. All it ever did was make a mess. Slowly, I pushed the chair back, got up, and went to find the mop.

Chapter Six

Everleigh

THE HOUSE WAS quiet when I woke up the next morning. Usually when that happened, it meant my parents were already at work. Sure enough, my mom had already texted to let me know that they'd left early that morning, but that her car (which was also extra spelled, in case their suspects got any ideas) was still in the garage for my personal use. My dad was determined to get me a newer, safer one next Saturday.

Apparently, my goal to buy my own car with my own money was out now, too. I tried not to sigh too much at this. But, I supposed, such was the life of a princess.

Even if she didn't want it to be.

Usually, when I woke up to find my parents gone, I got up to get ready, too. But as my first class had been canceled that morning, I didn't have to be at the school until ten. So I reveled in the warmth of the spring sun streaming through my window and stretched lazily before snuggling back under my covers. The blankets were perfect comfy, and I was in no hurry to race back into the world that seemed determined to complicate my junior year of college.

That was... until I heard a door open and shut downstairs.

All thoughts of sleep dissipated as I leaped silently out of bed, threw open my desk drawer, and yanked out my 9mm pistol and a loaded magazine. I shoved the magazine in until I felt the telltale click, chambered a round, then peeked out from behind my door.

No one was in the hall, so I hunched low and cautiously made my way toward the stairs. The thick padded carpet gave me the advantage of silence. Once I was close to the top of the stairs, I moved close enough to peer down into the living room.

But it was empty.

Only then did it occur to me that I should have paused long enough to text my parents. Better yet, I should have locked my door and hidden in my closet with my gun. But the desire to end this torture had driven me forward, and now I waffled, unsure of what to do. If nothing else, I should have at least told them someone was in the house. But then again, I needed the advantage of speed. The time it would take to fire off a text could be the difference between life and death, *and* it would have meant less control over my gun.

And I, for one, was not going to have it said at my funeral that I died because I was texting.

Another clunk sounded from below, and I swiveled to the left. The intruder was in the kitchen.

After creeping down a few more steps, I could just make out a black shirt and jeans. Whoever it was was almost in my sights...

"If you don't want me here, you can just say so," the man called lazily.

Aithan's voice made me jump, and I was extra glad that my dad had taught me not to walk with my finger right on the trigger. If I had, I might have accidentally shot my bodyguard. Of course, with Aithan being a Nomos, he would have deflected it easily.

Still, he never would have let me live it down.

"You're kidding," I said as my heart threatened to beat out of my chest. I'd expected to meet him at school. Not for him to show up *in my house* before I woke up!

"Put the gun away," he said patiently, as though he were talking to a five-year-old wielding scissors. "And come get some caffeine. If I remember right, you don't function properly without it." As he spoke, he finally turned to look up at me with a smug smile.

A smug, *breathtaking* smile.

I hadn't seen Aithan Nomos since last Thanksgiving, when his parents had hosted our two families and several work friends for the big dinner, but even that had been a drive-by viewing. He had work, he said, which meant he'd appeared when the house was the most crowded, greeted his parents, loaded a to-go box with food, and then had disappeared again. I think I might have gotten a nod of acknowledgment while his mouth was stuffed with food.

And yet, somehow, he'd managed to change even in the months since. His shoulders had widened a bit, and the angles of his face seemed sharper. His hair was darker now, too, not the same light blond the rest of the Nomos family had. Instead, it had slowly turned to a rich brown with hints of red and gold. But that might also have been because it was shorter now than I remembered. And while he had never gotten quite as tall as his older brother, Alexander, he was now a head and a half taller than I was.

Okay, so that wasn't difficult for most people—human or supernatural. But still...

And now, as if to accentuate his new height and strength, the black button-up he was wearing open over a white undershirt made him seem...

I don't know.

Extra.

Just... extra.

Okay, so Aithan Nomos was hot. And everyone knew it. He *definitely* knew it. Which made everything about him that much more annoying.

I glared at him for a moment longer before releasing my magazine and then pulling the action back so the round fell out of the gun and into my hand. Shoving the loose round back into the magazine, I stomped the rest of the way down the stairs and into the kitchen to sit on the barstool across the island from him, where I could glower at him with all my might, trying not to think about my messy braid or the fact that I was in my fuzzy pajamas and hairless cat socks, with no makeup and dark circles beneath my eyes.

"This is a good look for you." He waved his coffee mug in my direction, his green eyes laughing as he took a sip of the coffee he had apparently made in *our* machine. "You should keep it. Hey, you just got here. Where are you going?"

Before the words were all out of his mouth, I was pushing off my barstool and heading back toward the stairs, pretending I wasn't abandoning the cup of coffee he'd placed in front of me.

"What?" he called as I went. "I'm serious. It gives off that 'I don't care' vibe."

"I was going for the 'Go away, Aithan' vibe," I shot back. 'Now, if you'll excuse me, I'm going to get dressed."

"Confidence is very attractive in a woman," he called after me. "Don't change on my account."

I could hear the smirk in his words, but I didn't bother to look back. He thought he was so funny. He'd thought that back when he was twelve, too, and he treated me like the annoying little sister I basically was. But he wasn't the one who had awakened thinking the bogeyman was coming after him. No coffee was worth this humiliation. Even if it did have my favorite lavender creamer stirred in.

He'd better *not* have finished off my lavender creamer.

I hurried up the stairs.

As I soaked in the hot shower, trying to wash away the shock and mortification of the morning, I fumed about how it... How he... How what *should* have been a good morning was now ruined.

Okay, if I was completely honest with myself, I was most upset about how Aithan Nomos apparently still made me feel. For as many dry insults as I could sling his way as though nothing about him bothered me, Aithan Nomos did very much bother me. And though I had tried very hard over the years to forget the way it felt to be around him, I suddenly felt as though I was a doe-eyed seventh grader once again.

He hadn't always made me feel weird and uncertain of myself. Heck, we'd been raised almost like siblings when we were kids. Our parents had done—and still did—nearly everything together. And we'd all just been dragged along.

And all of that had been fine until I'd turned thirteen. I remember distinctly looking at him as a brother-sort-of-friend one day, and being very aware of him as a young man the next. Not that I would have ever admitted to such. Still, I had, for some stupid girlish reason, wondered for a long time if he would ever notice me the way he seemed to notice every pretty girl on the face of the planet.

On the contrary, he'd started acting as though I didn't exist. Years went by while he pretended I wasn't there, except to some-times tease and prank me at the high school we attended together, often in front of the ridiculous string of girls he serially dated. And then, just when I'd begun to give up on him ever actually acknowl-edging me again, he'd told me we could be friends, and that he would be there for me...

Before going back to being cool and distant again the next day.

And now he was my nanny until further notice, in *my* house, drinking *my* coffee, and stealing *my* creamer. He'd even had the audacity to remain calm as a nun when I had just nearly shot him.

Really, I growled to myself as I scrubbed my scalp, *What gives?*

Still, maybe I didn't need to be so put out. After all, it had been years since we'd had a real conversation. I knew next to nothing about him now. What did he even do to make all that money? How many girlfriends had he dated since I saw him last November? Or had the impossible happened, and he'd actually dated one longer than three weeks at a time? A stranger. That's what he was. And that was the way I was going to treat him.

Still, I might have taken more time than usual to get ready after my shower. Partly to annoy him. Partly to spend as much time away from him as I could.

But really, to prove him wrong. He may still see me as a little kid, but I was an adult, darn it. A practical adult who didn't need the supernatural world to succeed. I would make it on my own, misbehaving magic or none.

My phone buzzed, and I found a text from Georgie.

> Will you be coming to class today? Or should I get notes from your professor?

My wrath subsided slightly as I texted my friend back.

> I'll be there, but I appreciate the offer!

I'd barely hit Send when another message appeared.

> Everything go down okay with your parents last night?

> Yes and no. You'll see when I get there today.

And just like that, my annoyance surfaced again.

"Well, look at you," Aithan remarked casually as I walked back into the kitchen. This time, I was dressed in a white camiscle with a thin green sweater over it and my "fancy" dark blue jeans. My hair was coiled into a neat braid, and I had taken the time to put my makeup on—something I forgot to do at least half of every week. "All cleaned up, you look at least old enough to have your driver's license."

I drew in a long breath through my nose before pouring myself a new cup of coffee in a travel thermos and giving him a plastic smile. "Good morning, Aithan." A stranger. That's all he was. A stranger my parents were paying to keep me safe.

"What, and no gun to aim at my head this time?"

"Can't waste all my fun before school starts." I took out my creamer and carefully shook it to see how much was left. Once I was satisfied, I poured and mixed to my desired sweetness. Then I grabbed a granola bar, my backpack, and my mom's keys, and I headed for the garage door. Aithan followed, still carrying the mug he'd pilfered from our mug tree.

"Um, Everleigh, where are you going?"

"To the car. Because I'm not walking."

"I can see how that wouldn't be preferable. What I meant to imply was that we're taking *my* car."

I turned and stared at him. "Why? Can't we just meet there? Like... park next to one another or something?"

He flashed me another smug smile. "Princess–"

"Don't call me that."

"You are what you are. And it is precisely because you *are* a princess..." He stepped closer as he spoke, until he was close enough I could feel his breath on my face.

Dang, he smelled good.

"...That it's appropriate," he continued, "for you to have a bodyguard. Hence," he bowed, "yours truly."

I hadn't been expecting him to come so close, or my pulse might have remained at a healthy speed. Unfortunately, he took me by surprise, and I suddenly found myself looking up at the man my ridiculous thirteen-year-old self had stupidly dreamed about for a very short but formative part of my life.

"You're..." I fought my voice to stay even, "of a higher rank of royalty than I am, if we're going to be technical. Which means, *Your Highness*," I dropped into a curtsy, "that you have no obligation to chauffeur me around." But when I stood up, I realized the keys were no longer in my hand. "Hey!" I protested.

"Come on, Everleigh." He dropped my mom's keys back into the bowl by the door then whirled me around and gently but firmly pushed me toward the door. "Your royal carriage awaits."

"I really can drive myself," I grumbled as we went outside. "This is ridiculous. I only have trouble with this weirdo at school, and my mom's car–" But I came to a halt when I stepped out onto the driveway. Whatever I was going to say, the car–if it could be called that–made me forget.

I wasn't well–versed in car speak, but I did know a fast car when I saw one. And this car made the term "sports car" sound like someone's grandpa. It was silver and yellow, and had obviously been modified. The engine, which started without any audible signal, was a smooth purr, and I could *feel* its vibrations within my chest, even from several paces away. But it could have been Aithan's magic making it do that too.

"Your mother's car is very nice," he said patiently. "But with all due respect, your mother isn't a Nomos." He smiled smugly as the doors slowly rose up instead of swinging out. "Which means her car is *not* bespelled like this. Nor," he continued, ushering me toward the passenger door, "does it go this fast."

As much as I wanted to argue with him, I was a little too in awe of the machine in which I was now sitting. My parents did well enough, as they were both detectives, and I had the sneaking suspicion that they had money reserves from their days in the courts, but when they'd left their families behind, they'd abandoned the continued streams of income that came with positions in the royal family. This car probably cost more than they made in a year.

"What do you do again?" I asked as he climbed into the driver's seat and hit a button that made the doors lower themselves into place.

"Personal security." He handed me a blue rectangular velvet box. "And that's for you."

With growing trepidation, I opened the box, my heart hammering within me again. This was very clearly a jewelry box, and the name on the front belonged to one of the stores I'd never dared to do more than peek inside. Had he gotten me...

I gasped slightly when I found a necklace with a glittering white gem the size of my pinky fingernail, a heart sparkling in the sunlight where it hung from a thin golden chain.

"Um... thank you?" I looked at him with wide eyes. "But did you—"

"It's from my parents," he said, looking behind him as he backed out. "My mom knows the store's owner, and she got this on short notice. Both they and your parents charmed it with a number of spells to help us keep an eye on you throughout the day."

For some reason, this answer was both a relief and...

A disappointment. The thirteen-year-old inside me wilted slightly before I had the chance to mentally chastise her for her hopeful stupidity.

This was Aithan Nomos, after all. Serial dater of the supernatural world. Definitely a look-but-don't-touch kind of guy.

"What's wrong..." He paused, and I could feel his eyes on me. "Are you blushing?"

"That's a stupid question." I bent my very hot face down as I focused on opening the necklace's clasp.

"Everleigh Clarkson," I could hear the laughter in his voice, "why in the world would you be blushing?"

Tell him, a voice in my head hissed at me. *He's just given you the in. Remind him how he told you he would be there for you, and then went back to being a total and complete—*

No, I interrupted myself. He might still be acting like a spoiled teen boy, showing off his pretty toys and making sure the world was watching him, but *I* had grown up since the last time we'd spent any time together, and *I* was more mature than that. What good was bringing up broken hearts after the fact, anyway?

"So," I said in a firm voice as I fastened the necklace behind my neck, "security, huh? Security bought you *this?*" I gestured at the car.

"*Some* people value their security," he said with a smirk. "Very prominent people who will pay lots of money to make sure no one gets too close unless they're invited."

That made sense. Not only was Aithan an elf, which meant he was stronger than the average human, but he was a *Nomos*—the most powerful elven line in the whole world. For the last several thousand years, only dragons had been known to rival Nomos power and magic. I glanced at his ring, which had a green stone similar to my father's.

"Speaking of security," he said, his smirk melting into a hard glare as he kept his eyes on the highway ahead of us, "tell me exactly what you've seen of this creep."

The way his face went from its familiar teasing expression to apex predator made me shiver. But I did my best not to let him see as I told him what I had told my parents, from the sensation of foreign magic to the *Seira* tracker charm, watching his face carefully as I did.

Like all supernaturals who were interacting with the human world, Aithan was wearing a glamour stone hidden on his person. The expression on his face as he listened, however, was so ferocious it made me think of the stories of the ancient elf warriors my father used to tell me at bedtime.

"I really think my parents are overreacting," I finished with a shrug, trying to sound casual as I did. We'd come to a stoplight and were only a few blocks from the university now.

He turned, his green eyes searching my face. "Do you?"

Unable to read his gaze, I held it until the car behind us honked, and he looked ahead and began driving again.

"So," I said, trying to think of something to erase the awkward quiet that had just taken place, "what's our cover going to be?"

"Cover?"

"Yeah. I mean, it's not really normal for college students to drag bodyguards around campus."

He pulled the car into a parking space and then added the

parking sticker my mom had apparently given him so the car wouldn't be towed. "The truth," he said simply, the predator demeanor from just moments ago gone once again, and the casual flippancy was back on his handsome face.

"The *truth?*"

He shrugged. "There's been someone bothering you, and as professional security, my job is to make sure they leave you alone. Simple enough."

"And *that* will get you into all my classes?" I asked as I got out of the car. "I'm pretty sure there's a rule–"

He sighed dramatically. "See, half-fae princess, if you were willing to hone your magic, you'd be able to do this all on your own. But as you're *not* willing, one of the charms your mother put on that necklace is that we should be able to convince anyone who objects to let me stay. Besides," he came to walk beside me, giving me a snarky smile, "I may not be Alexander, but I'm not grotesque. Does it offend your sensibilities to have me at your side, milady?"

I drew in a deep breath and blew it out slowly. It was going to be a long day.

The day with Aithan wasn't as bad as I thought it might be.

It was worse.

On the upside, the charmed necklace did seem to work, as none of my professors argued when we explained Aithan's sudden appearance. Professor Petras actually seemed pleased, although I'm pretty sure it was because he–being a supernatural–knew who Aithan was and approved of my parents' choice.

My female classmates, of course, did all but drool on my protector, and he flirted shamelessly back with them. The guys avoided him at all costs. Except, of course, for poor, sweet Georgie, who spent most of our time together sending Aithan lots of annoyed, nervous glances as he tried to talk to me in complete sentences.

"Is *that* who I think it is?" Julia blurted when I greeted her in the student union a few hours later. As if to be yet more conspicuous, she pulled her sunglasses down to look over them at Aithan, who was studying the line of food court options.

I rolled my eyes. "Yes, it is."

"No wonder you weren't answering my texts."

I elbowed her slightly. "Julia! He can *hear* you!"

"No, he can't. Look at that redhead, chattering up at him and giggling as if he's responded to a word she's said. He can't hear himself think over her."

"And thank goodness for that!" I pursed my lips, then lowered my voice again. "Julia, I was right about my parents' reaction to all this. They had him at my house *before* I woke up! I almost shot him because I thought someone had broken in!"

"And you're... sure nothing could happen between you? Because, Everleigh, I'm not going to lie. He is *so* nice to look at."

"Julia, did you miss the part where I nearly *shot* him?" I shook my head and let out a huff. "Besides, you were there in high school! You saw all the ways he pretended I *wasn't* around!"

"Except for the pranks." She smiled. "You have to admit that those were some pretty good pranks."

"Well, you're no help," I scowled. "Whose side are you on, anyway?"

"The one that gets you a boyfriend, so you'll put the books down and go out on a date now and then."

"Believe me," I hissed, despite the noise of the busy food court. Elves had excellent hearing. "Even if I wanted to date him, he's not into girls like me."

"And how would you know that? You were like... fourteen."

"Do you remember Athena Bakas?" I hissed.

In spite of herself, Julia grimaced and looked back over at Aithan. "Yeah, it's probably best you're not his type after all."

Well, that didn't make me feel any better either.

"Look," she said, "I have economics next. After that, could we meet at Soo Min's place? I have a project I want you to look over."

I nodded. "Sure. Meet you there at three-fifteen."

I expected Aithan to object when I told him about the planned rendezvous. He wasn't really a milk tea guy. But to my surprise, he seemed pleased when I told him.

"I have something I need to ask Mr. Song," he said when we arrived at the little shop a few hours later. "Will you be okay out here with your friends?"

"I'll be fine," I promised him. "The weirdo hasn't ever followed me in here."

Mr. Song, Soo Min's dad, didn't seem nearly as eager to see Aithan as Aithan was to see him, but he grudgingly gestured to the back of the store upon request. Julia arrived just as they stepped out.

"Julia," Soo Min called sweetly from the other side of the counter. "I have a new flavor I want you to try." She held up a green and pink milk tea.

"I'd *love* to taste it," I interrupted loudly as Georgie came through the door.

Soo Min scowled at me, and I smiled sweetly back at her.

"I didn't make enough for everyone," she pouted quietly before putting the cup of milk tea back behind the counter and prepping our usual orders.

"You two have the weirdest friendship," Julia murmured as Georgie came to sit on my other side.

I snorted. "You have no idea. Now what was it you wanted me to look at?"

"After you're done," Georgie said quickly as he leaned forward, his eyes darting around the shop, "I had something I wanted to ask you, too."

"Okay." I nodded and smiled, my mind already on the graphs Julia was placing in front of me. This occupied the next ten minutes as I asked questions, and Julia gave me answers. I'd taken the same class the semester before, and I remembered this chapter being particularly complicated.

"Um, Everleigh," Georgie said, his words even more hurried this time. "Before we go, I was wondering what you were doing next... next Friday evening." He pushed his glasses up his thin nose for the fourth time that minute.

I looked up at him. "My dad and I are going car shopping. Why?"

Julia rolled her eyes. "Georgie, if you're considering a group outing, Everleigh is *not* allowed to pick this time." She glared at me.

I gave her a guilty smile. "I really did think you'd like ziplining. You're all buckled in and everything."

"Oh, just like I *loved* bungee jumping!" Julia scoffed. "In case I never told you, Friend-of-Over-a-Decade, I have a thing against courting death!" Then she straightened and sniffed. "Besides, I'm busy on Friday."

Georgie rubbed his neck and gave a self-conscious laugh. "Yeah, I remember. You've got that date. Actually, um... I was going to ask Everleigh." He took a big breath and spoke in a rush. "If everything settles down by Friday night, or Saturday even– '

"Ready to go, Everleigh?" Aithan asked loudly as he emerged from the back of the store. "Your parents don't want you out longer than you have to be."

"How does he know Mr. Song?" Julia asked, realizing for the first time where Aithan had been.

"Oh," I waved casually in Aithan's direction. "Our parents know a lot of people in this area. Having a large network helps with detective work and all."

Of course, Aithan also just happened to be the son of the abdicated crown prince of the most powerful elven line in the world. He knew a *lot* of people. But I wasn't about to say that out loud.

"Oh." She tilted her head thoughtfully. "I guess that makes sense."

"Sorry, what were you saying?" I turned back to Georgie. But before Georgie could stammer anything else out, I was plucked off my seat and pushed toward the door by my bodyguard, barely having time to grab my drink.

"Walk now, text later," Aithan said. "Your parents have a schedule, and I plan to stick to it."

"That was really rude," I said when we were finally outside again and on our way back to the campus parking lot. "You couldn't wait thirty seconds?"

Aithan lifted his hand to muss my hair, but I darted out of the way. "You should be thanking me, Princess. I just saved you from a really embarrassing situation and the unpleasant, awkward experience of turning that toad down flat."

"Georgie is not a toad." I bristled. "And I have no idea what you mean."

The sideways look Aithan gave me was unimpressed. "You're seriously telling me he doesn't hang on your every word?"

I scoffed. "Georgie's just a friend. We've been friends for two and a half years, and he's never once asked me out or made me uncomfortable." Even as I said the words, though, the memory of him draping his arm over my shoulder made my conviction seem less sure. Even more telling was the text that popped up on my screen from said subject:

Are you okay? Is he bullying you?

No, this is my parents' fault. Not his.

"If that's not what he was about to ask you," Aithan smirked, "what do you *think* he meant by asking about your plans for Saturday night?"

"I..." I shook my head as we moved from the crosswalk onto one of the campus sidewalks. "He was probably asking me and Julia if we wanted to meet him at the Pinball Hall of Fame. We do that sometimes."

"Was he asking Julia?" Aithan raised one dark brow. "Or just you?"

I tried several times to answer—to come up with a good reason that Aithan must be wrong. But the more I thought about it, the more I realized he was right. He *had* just saved me from an embarrassing situation. Because as much as I loved Georgie, I had absolutely zero desire to date him. He was cute and lovable and sweet. But so were corgis. And I wasn't about to date one of them either.

Of course, that didn't mean I was going to admit any of that to Aithan. I did have *some* pride, after all.

"What if I wanted to go out with him?" I asked, lifting my chin rebelliously. "Besides, I've never interfered with any of your dates, even if they were shallow and rude."

Aithan opened his car doors, but when he looked at me again, there was a dangerous glitter in his green eyes. "Never?"

"Well... Athena didn't count. I didn't specifically *try* to meddle with your date. She was rude to Julia, and... my magic reacted. That was all on her."

That was also the night Aithan had promised to be a better friend to me—to always be there—a promise he had never, it seemed, intended to keep. But I wasn't about to embarrass myself by sounding desperate and lonely enough to bring that up.

"Which makes me wonder," I said in a lighter tone as he pulled back out into traffic, "who your number of the week is now. Do I know her?" Aithan had dated both human and supernatural girls throughout our time in high school, and from what I understood, college. He might have run out of one or the other if he hadn't. I sent him a sideways smirk. "Is she obsessed with her feet like the last one?"

He gave me a look of scorn. "I haven't dated her in months. And she was a *foot* model. Of course she was obsessed with her feet. They paid the rent."

"Fine. She was a foot model." I sniffed daintily. "And she smelled like feet."

"I have never dated a girl who smelled like feet, and you know it."

"I don't write the news. I just report it." I pretended to study my fingernails, but secretly watched him out of the corner of my eye. "You have to admit. She had an unusual... aroma."

"It was her moisturizer."

"Aha!" I pointed at him. "You admit she smelled weird!"

"If anyone is weird here, it's you, Clarkson."

I grinned as I settled back into the leather seat. "At least I don't smell like feet."

He gave me a furtive glance. "So I take it *your* social calendar is teeming with offers from eligible young men?"

I pursed my lips. "I go on dates, yes."

"Perhaps," he nodded. "But no more than two in a row, I suppose?"

I gaped at him. "Wh–Why would you say that? Do you think I can't get someone to go on three?" He was drawing me into a trap. I knew that as soon as the words left my mouth. But the insult was too strong to go unchecked.

Aithan let out a strange chuckle. "Oh, I have no doubt you *could* get someone to go on as many dates with you as you pleased. But I say three because three," he held up three fingers, "would indicate the possibility of a future. And it's hard to find a future when you refuse to even consider supernaturals, so by default, you choose to date humans you can't share your world with. Yes? Or no?"

Ouch. That stung more than I would have thought it could. What had begun as playful banter had suddenly entered dangerous territory.

"Come on, Clarkson," he said, coming to a stoplight and using the pause to poke my shoulder. "Admit it. You never go on more than two dates because–"

"Because it's not like supernaturals are lining up at this half-breed's door," I grumbled.

"Whoa, whoa, whoa, Everleigh." He hit the brakes so hard that my seatbelt locked. Then he pulled into a parking lot where he put the car in park and turned to look at me, but I refused to meet his gaze. "I told you years ago. I don't want you calling yourself that," he continued, all playfulness draining from his voice. "It's a terrible term, and I wish society would let it die."

"Yes, Aithan," I said, hurt making my voice heavy with sarcasm. "Because you've been the pinnacle of a friendly, encouraging presence since you said that seven years ago. Right before you quit talking to me *again*."

I hadn't meant to let it slip, and I was immediately annoyed with myself that it had.

To his credit, he had the decency to look somewhat disconcerted for the rest of the drive home.

When we finally pulled into my driveway, he turned off the engine and turned to look at me again. In a softer voice than I'd heard him use all day, he spoke again.

"Your parents will probably be home late tonight. What do you want to do while we wait for them? We could order Chinese and watch that sissy man, Mr. Darcy, fail to–"

"I'm good, thanks," I said, grabbing my backpack and getting out. "I'll pop a frozen dish in the oven, then get started on my homework."

He looked as though he wanted to argue, but after a moment of waffling, he didn't. Instead, he simply got out and unlocked the front door. Then he said he was going to check the security wards before my parents got home.

He hadn't meant to hurt me. I knew he hadn't. He never *meant* to hurt me. Sure, he liked to tease, but with me, Aithan was generally all bark and no bite. Still, I thought to myself as I closed the door and sagged against it, if only he could understand how lonely my life really was.

Because of the magical problems that mixed-race supernaturals usually faced, supernaturals with functioning magic generally dated solely within their own race pools. Marriage and reproduction between the races just didn't happen. And my parents were the obvious object lesson for those whose hearts might be tempted to overrule their heads.

And usually, I didn't mind. I loved my parents, and I was, for the most part, very comfortable being me. I didn't even mind not being able to use magic properly. I was perfectly capable, I'd assured my parents countless times, of living as any magic-less human did. I had a strong body and two strong hands and (in my opinion) a rather capable brain. What did I need magic for, anyway?

Nothing.

Except finding love, it seemed...

The moment supernatural men found out I was half-elf and half-fae, they lost all interest. And the only serious boyfriend I'd ever had in high school had eventually followed suit.

But dating humans wasn't really an option either. Because Aithan was right, I fumed silently to myself as I dumped my backpack by the door. As much as I might like fitting into the human world, I couldn't tell a human man about who and what I really was, nor could he ever really be brought fully into my family.

No, I was alone. And as if to rub salt in the wound, the constant friendship I'd had with Aithan and Alexander when we were small was gone too. They had moved on with their lives, and I with mine. And that was all there was to it.

I sighed as I went to the fridge and opened it to stare inside. But there weren't any answers in there. Just dinner. So I did the best I could do. I pulled out a partially thawed chicken parmesan and set it on the counter with a *thunk*.

Chapter Seven

Aithan

I SHOOK my head in disgust at my own stupidity as I stalked around the outside of the house, checking the security wards and looking for potential tampering.

Mr. and Mrs. Clarkson—Prince Nikos and Princess Erin, to be precise—were both highly skilled when it came to creating and maintaining wards. As they were both from royal lines, they'd both been gifted with more magic-wielding abilities than most supernaturals, so it only made sense that their magic would be of a higher caliber than the average elf or fae. Their families had also spent small fortunes on their magical training and education, starting when they were both quite young. Still, neither Mr. nor Mrs. Clarkson were from the highest lines of their races the way I was. So while I was here, it was up to me to strengthen the wards the same way my parents had been doing for them as of late.

But my confidence in my ability to secure the Clarksons' wards had no effect on my mood. I might be keeping her safe from the stalker, but I'd hurt her feelings. That was the ugly truth.

"It wasn't as though I meant to hurt her," I grumbled to myself as I peered behind the large bush beneath the living room window. I was just teasing her—the way I always had since we were little kids. But I'd gone too far this time, and I knew it the moment her shoulders hunched in, and she refused to look at me again in the car.

This was why I kept as much distance as my vow would allow. Well, this and the curse my grandfather had placed on me when I was a little kid. Things had been simpler when we were little. Everleigh was an annoying, endearing little kid who could dish insults like she could take them—really well. But now we were adults, and Everleigh wasn't a little kid anymore. And that... complicated things.

Things were complicated enough as it was. It was the reason I spent so much time away from my family and Everleigh's. The moment I was old enough, I'd hightailed it out of our weird friend-family dynamic. Not to abandon them. I loved them all too much for that. But to chase the freedom I knew would one day end.

That was possibly ending now.

I walked back into the house to find it seemingly empty.

"Everleigh?" I called.

"Yes?" she replied from upstairs.

I nodded. "Just checking. Carry on."

"M'kay," she called back, sounding distracted.

I paused at the foot of the stairs, wondering if I ought to apologize, to say something to explain my stupidity. But in the end, I just shook my head and made my way to the guest room downstairs where I'd already stashed my suitcase that morning. Then I changed into my workout clothes and headed to the Clarksons' basement gym.

From the outside, the Clarksons' house looked very much like any upper-middle-class home. It was a four-bedroom, two and a half bath, two-story house with nice, plushy carpet and a stone countertop in the kitchen. But what passersby couldn't see was the massive gym they'd built into the customized basement beneath the home. Everleigh thought it was there because her parents were obsessed with fitness. They were police officers, after all, so it made sense that they would want to stay in shape.

What she *didn't* know was that they'd really built it in order to prepare her for the inevitable war that would one day erupt in the supernatural community when someone discovered who–and what–she was.

I hopped on the treadmill to warm up, but even as I ran mile after mile, I couldn't outrun the guilt that made my chest ache.

I'd done my best to temporarily escape the fate that would one day swallow me. But Everleigh had never had that choice. She was younger than both Alexander and me, and after we'd flown from home, she'd been left alone. Her human friend, Julia, had been a fixed part of her life from fourth grade on, and from what I gathered, they still spent nearly every waking moment together. But Everleigh had brought Julia only as close as her life could allow without exposing the supernatural community. In fact, she'd probably brought her too close. But if that was anyone's fault, it was mine. To her, I'd been nothing more than an unfaithful friend.

I groaned as I stopped the treadmill and leaned against the handrail. Why had I let my parents talk me into this? But then again, I didn't really have a choice either. They might have asked me this time, but I'd been the one who took the Keeper's Oath. I'd agreed to be a part of their society. Given, I'd been twelve when I took the oath. And faced with the choice of promising to protect Everleigh at all costs, or leave her all on her own should something happen to her parents...

What was I supposed to say? No?

I had just finished working out and was in the kitchen to get a glass of water when the oven timer went off. I stared stupidly at the thing, realizing for the first time that I didn't actually know how a stove worked. When you can use your fingers to heat a frozen dish, why bother with electronics? Now that I thought about it, I'd never even taken the plastic off the brand new oven that had been installed in my apartment before I moved in.

"Out of the way, Martha Stewart." Everleigh hip checked me with the ferocity of a hockey player, ignoring my protest as she grabbed an oven mitt out of the drawer I'd apparently been standing in front of. Then she opened the oven door and pulled out a steaming, bubbling casserole dish full of something that smelled like perfection.

If the dish's smell caught my attention, however, it was Everleigh who held it. And for the first time that day, it really... *really* dawned on me.

Everleigh Clarkson had become a *woman*.

She was wearing loose athletic sweatpants that had been cut off at the knees and an old t-shirt, hardly an outfit that begged for attention. And yet, it still drew my eyes to the soft but undeniable curves that I had somehow missed over the last few years. Her legs were athletic, covered in lean muscle from all the kickboxing I knew she was currently into, and her arms, now pushing the steaming casserole dish to the back burners, were equally defined.

It was a domestic scene, really, and one that appealed against my better judgment to my male sensibilities. And the way my heart slightly sped as she studied her creation–

"Did you make that?" I asked, forcing my mind away from the curves of her calves as she moved across the kitchen.

"I did." She sounded pleased with herself. "I like to surprise Mom on nights when they work late."

"I'm impressed," I said. When she turned and gave me a suspicious look, I held up my hands. "I'm serious. That looks really good."

She shook her head and pointed at the fridge. "We have some TV dinners–"

Apparently, I'd teased her so much she didn't know how to take a compliment. "Let me rephrase that," I said, following her. "Behold, I am a helpless, clueless male. Please, *please* feed me, for I cannot feed myself."

She gave me another skeptical look, but then rolled her eyes and grabbed two plates out of a cabinet.

"Fine. You can have dinner. But behave yourself, or no seconds."

Soon we were seated in the living room with TV trays in front of our respective seats. She was curled up in the large armchair, and I was on the couch. We'd both agreed it would be weird to eat at the dining room table without our parents.

"So, I hear you're still kickboxing?" I asked, desperate for something not-awkward to talk about. She might have fed me. But that didn't mean I was forgiven.

"Yeah, but I've also been taking Kenpo for a while too, and I might move exclusively into that soon." She cut a piece of chicken, releasing a little column of steam as she did.

I took a bite of my food as well. It tasted as good as it smelled, but I was distracted by the thought of sparring against Everleigh. It nearly had me asking if she wanted to spar downstairs after our dinner settled. I didn't get to face-off against supernaturals nearly as much as I would have liked, and seeing that side of Everleigh— even if she didn't use magic—was surprisingly intriguing. I would love to see her throw a kick at my face. But, a voice inside warned me, facing off on the gym's sparring mat would be dangerous for more than one reason. So instead, I asked another question.

"How is your magic coming along? I know you don't use it on a regular basis, but do you ever practice it at all?"

She shrugged, her eyes on her phone. "Same as ever."

I hesitated, wondering just how far the magic would let me go. Not only had my grandfather placed curses on me and my brother when my father abandoned his place in the Nomos high court, but he had also been generous enough to place restrictions on Everleigh's family as well—a favor to her father's father, I always supposed. Consolation for his own son leaving him.

And his curse was that no one could talk to Everleigh about the specifics of her magic.

Of course, my grandfather had only doled out the curses and magical restrictions out of malice. In his mind, he was ensuring her parents' half-elven child would always struggle with her magic. But he'd had no idea the repercussions of his hasty words. He couldn't have. After all, Everleigh was the reason her parents had run in the first place.

"Everleigh," I started slowly, "have you ever wondered *why* your parents put you through every kind of self-defense training available in this city?"

Her blue eyes met mine, and her brows went up. "Because my parents are obsessed with safety? You know that. They're detectives. They've seen the worst of the worst." She looked back down at her phone as though it was the most obvious answer in the world.

"I know that," I said. "But... have you ever wondered if they wanted you to..." I tried to push more words out, but they wouldn't come. My grandfather's edict was just as strong as ever. No wonder she'd never figured out the truth.

Obviously ready to be done with the conversation, she held up a finger as she scrolled through her contacts and then dialed a number. A few rings later, a voice I recognized answered the phone.

"Everleigh! How can I help you?" It was our parents' police chief.

"Hey, Chief," she said, a sweet smile lighting her face as though she could see him. "I was wondering when you think my parents will be home tonight."

Oh.

Wow.

I was apparently so aggravating that she couldn't wait to get rid of me.

There was a brief silence before the chief answered. But this time, his words were slow and confused. "They didn't tell you?"

"Tell me what?" Everleigh sat up straight.

"They took vacation time today. Three weeks of it."

I was off the couch before she could respond and holding my hand out toward her. *Phone,* I mouthed.

For once, she didn't resist.

"Hey, Chief," I said. "If you don't mind me asking, how did they request the time off?" As I spoke, my mind was already spinning with questions. This was unusual. Generally, our parents would request time off beforehand. And they would never have done so without telling us.

"Oh, hello, Aithan." Chief sounded surprised. "Um, your parents requested time off, too. A last-minute thing, they said."

My heart dropped into my stomach.

"They said it was a family emergency of some kind," he continued. "I know you're not all technically family, but you might as well be. So it made sense they would want it at the same time..." His voice trailed off. "You're telling me neither of you knew?"

"Thanks for letting us know," I said firmly, knowing better than to answer him. "Have a good night." I hung up the phone and turned to face Everleigh, who was slightly pale. "Something isn't right."

Everleigh nodded but didn't say anything.

"I need to make some phone calls," I handed back her phone. "And I think you ought to finish eating and go to bed." As soon as the words left my mouth, I regretted them. Those were exactly the kinds of suggestions that were sure to get her riled up.

But to my surprise, she only nodded again before gathering up her plate and cup and heading slowly toward the kitchen. I shot off a few quick text messages before looking up to find her emerging from the kitchen, frowning at the ground.

"You need anything before I start making calls?" I asked.

"Aithan..." She swallowed, seeming not to have heard my question. "Do you think they're okay?"

For a moment, I considered lying to her. But whether it was my new realization that Everleigh was no longer a little girl, or the determination I saw in her eyes, I only shook my head. "I don't know." She deserved to hear that much. She was an adult now, after all. "But Everleigh?"

"Yes?" She looked at me through wide eyes the color of the ocean.

"Keep your gun handy tonight in case someone else shows up. What you did this morning? Do it again if something feels off. Whatever you need to make it to the study and take the emergency portal to Finn's bookshop. Yes?"

She stared at me for another long moment before nodding. Then she was gone.

Once I was certain she had locked her door, I looked down at my phone and drew in a deep breath. Then I dialed a number I hadn't called in two years.

He answered in two rings. "Hello?"

The sound of my brother's voice made my throat thick with emotion. But I knew better than to let my feelings get in the way. We had limited time before he would have to go again. So I cleared my throat and used the emergency code words we'd agreed upon just before he'd gone to work for my grandfather.

"That part you ordered? They're all out of it."

There was a slightly longer silence before he spoke again. "It's all good. I don't really need it that much." I heard the sound of a door closing on his end of the line. "What's up?"

"Have you heard from Mom or Dad today?" I asked.

Another pause. But when he spoke again, his voice was low and hard. "What happened?"

Chapter Eight

Everleigh

I BREATHED a heavy sigh of relief as we walked out of the stuffy university office and headed toward the stairs. The sounds of the student union's food court below echoed up to the second story where the offices were, filling the air with a low din.

"You did well," Aithan said, just loud enough for me to hear him above the noise.

"Thanks." I paused. "For a minute, I didn't think she'd let me switch to all online classes after all."

After neither of our parents had appeared last night, Aithan had decided that it was no longer safe for me to attend school. Having someone sporadically follow me was one thing. Both of our parents disappearing took things to the next level. There was no way this could be the work of one person. So, with a heavy heart, I had agreed.

Unfortunately, if I didn't want to flunk out of the semester and lose my scholarships, I still needed to attend online, which meant I'd had lots of paperwork to do.

Aithan glanced behind him in annoyance at the office from which we'd just come. "That woman is particularly obsessed with rules."

"It seemed for a minute like the convincing spell in my necklace wouldn't work." I reached up and clutched the little heart-shaped gem in my hand. It made my parents feel somewhat closer, their warm, familiar magic heating my hand like a hug.

"If anyone less skilled than your mother had made the enchantment," Aithan said in a low voice, "it wouldn't have." Then his eyes narrowed ahead of us. "Incoming."

I turned to find Julia hurtling toward me as we reached the bottom of the stairs.

"Everleigh!" she shrieked.

I wanted to groan. Of all the times for her to find me... But there was nothing I could do about that now. So I pasted a smile on my face and opened my arms just in time for her to fly into them. "Hey, Julia."

"Don't 'Hey, Julia,' me!" She pulled back and glared at me, pushing her blond braid out of the way. "Why haven't you been answering my calls or texts? Or Georgie's? I've been worried!"

"Let's take this outside," Aithan murmured in my ear, the heat of his breath on the side of my face making me jump. But he was right. We were going to attract attention standing inside the student union like this. Especially if Julia was about to give me one of her dramatic lectures. And they *were* dramatic.

"Has that creep come back?" Julia hissed as I grabbed her arm and started towing her with me toward the nearest door. Then she glanced up at Aithan. "Has *he* not been doing his job?"

"No, that's not it." I did my best to look casual as we walked, but I was really searching for one of the quieter paths that would lead back to the parking lot. No one needed to hear this conversation, even the edited version I was giving to Julia. "My parents... think it would be best if I went off the radar for a while."

As I spoke, I turned right, then left, down a thin concrete path that edged the business building. It was lined on both sides by thick shrubs and old trees that created a heavy ceiling of leaves stretching over the path, making the way darker and shielding it from view. If Julia threw a fit in here, it was less likely that we'd be seen.

"Everleigh Clarkson, I have known you for *twelve* years, and I know that something isn't right! What aren't you telling me?" She came to a stop in front of me, blocking my path, arms crossed, her large hazel eyes boring into mine.

Before I could answer, I felt a brush of magic against my arm. Aithan tensed up beside me, meaning he could feel it too. He drew both his daggers.

"Everleigh, if you don't answer me–"

"Julia, I have to go *now!*" I hissed. "I'll call you–"

"Not until you tell me what's going on!" she argued.

The stone statue of a former basketball coach behind her made a deafening crack before leaning heavily to one side of its base. Julia screamed as I grabbed her arm and yanked her behind me. But Aithan, moving in a blur, was between us and the statue before it could topple off.

"Get to the portal!" he ordered as he threw his hands out in front of him to create an invisible barrier. "The one at the fire–"

"I know!" I shouted back. As if my parents would let me attend college without memorizing the location of *every* single emergency portal on campus.

As I spoke, the statue continued to move. Rather than tilting and smashing against the concrete sidewalk, however, the statue landed on its feet and fell into what I recognized as a fighting stance.

"What is that–" Julia squeaked, but I had already hauled her around and was getting ready to run when a female figure appeared before us, walking out from where she must have been glamoured in the shadows.

She had translucent lilac-colored wings, and her eyes and hair–both unglamoured–were a similar shade of lilac, stark against her dark skin. At the same time, a third figure, though I couldn't see details, rolled in from the side. Whatever it was was glamoured as well to camouflage with the trees and shrubs it had been hiding behind, but from the way it rolled, I could only guess it was a troll.

I snatched my pepper spray out of my backpack's netted side, but even as I did, I knew that it wouldn't do much. Trolls are faster than they look, and if he rolled at me the way he had a moment before, the spray wouldn't do a thing against his stony exterior. The woman, whose wings identified her as a fae, would be more susceptible to the pepper spray. But fae were also fast.

My fingers itched for my gun or even my sword.

Julia let out a scream, nearly breaking my right ear drum, but I did my best to stay focused.

"Everleigh!" Aithan shouted from the wrestling match he and the statue were engaged in. "Get a move on!"

"I've hit a few roadblocks!" I shouted back, my mind working quickly. Stretching my fingers, I prayed for the elven lightning I so often zapped myself with by accident. Then I threw my can of pepper spray in the air over the fae and aimed my hands at it. To my delight, a short bolt of lightning did emanate from my fingers. Unfortunately, it did not hit the can that was now rolling uselessly on the ground. Instead, it shot out wildly in several directions all around me, making Julia scream again, and striking the troll by accident.

Whatever. It was an accidental win, but I would take it.

The troll's body slumped against the concrete, losing the tight ball shape trolls so often used to bowl others over.

Which left the fae.

She stalked up to me and grabbed my wrist. On instinct, I maneuvered out of the hold with a wrist escape I'd learned back in my first year of Taekwondo. Then I slammed my elbow into her side, while Julia, much to my surprise, had recovered enough to deliver a hard roundhouse kick to her head.

It shouldn't have been that surprising, though. Julia and I had met as sparring partners in Taekwondo when we were nine.

Unfortunately, the fae had other abilities as well. She leaped back out of our reach, rubbing the side of her head several yards back. Then she fixed a glare at my friend.

Oh no.

"You don't need to fight," she said in a singsong voice, directing her dazzling smile at Julia. "I've come to help your friend."

"Julia, don't listen to her!" I snapped as the fae continued to weave her convincing spell.

But Julia's eyes were already wide and doe-like as she tilted her head to the side in wonder. "But she's so pretty," she breathed. "And she wants to help!"

I rolled my own eyes and huffed. So many times I'd wished I could share my world with Julia. But this was not what I'd had in mind.

With no weapon other than my own body, I bolted forward, sprinting directly at the fae. Before I could reach her, however, the troll rolled directly into my path, knocking me over so hard I hit my head on the concrete. The world around me spun, but I had enough sense of direction left to scramble to the side as the troll rolled around, aiming for me again.

"No, idiot!" the fae called to the troll. "She's supposed to be alive and unharmed! Not with her brains bashed out!"

They were supposed to do *what* now?

The troll paused its rolling.

The hesitation wasn't long, but it was just long enough for me to jump to my feet and leap up onto the short concrete wall that separated the trees from the sidewalk. If I was fast enough, I could leap over the troll toward Julia again–

A wave of magic so strong that it made me breathless pushed me off the wall. Thankfully, my head had cleared by then, and I landed on my feet. The troll, however, who was still in his ball form, was now rolling down the sidewalk, far past its fae ally like a ping pong ball carried away in the breeze.

Everyone looked over to find Aithan stalking toward us, the statue broken and still against the concrete. A piece of his thick brown hair had fallen in his face, and he had blood dripping down from a cut on the side of his cheek. And he did not look happy.

"Everleigh," he said in a low, dangerous voice. "I want you to get to the portal. *Now*." His eyes were trained on the fae as he flicked his fingers, and a snaking whip made solely of raw magic fizzled and crackled to life in his hand.

Knowing I would only hinder him in this fight, I took off in the direction we'd been going before we were attacked, dragging a lolling Julia along with me.

Hopefully, the fae magic that had Julia dazed now would wear off *after* I reached the portal. I'd send Soo Min a text as soon as I was safely on the other side, and she would run across the street and wipe Julia's memory of the whole ordeal. Then Julia could go on to her next class as though nothing had happened. Fae magic could be awesome that way.

Unfortunately for me, however, she came to just as I reached my destination.

"Everleigh!" she cried, her voice shaking. "What... what was *that?* Were *they* the ones following you?" She swallowed loudly and looked back in the direction from which we'd come. But, of course, there was nothing to see. Aithan would have had the sense to activate a field glamour as soon as the fighting began. From here, the sidewalk looked empty.

The bigger problem, however, was that our fae attacker was apparently really bad at magic. Julia had just gotten a heavy dose of fae relaxing magic while seeming to remember *everything*.

"Look," I said quickly. "I need to get out of here. For your safety and mine." A sound erupted from the empty path behind us. Julia's eyes widened, but I only shook my head. "I need you to go *directly* to Soo Min and tell her what happened. She and her father will be able to help you."

And I had no doubt they would. Soo Min might not like Julia, but she would do a memory adjustment spell in this case without question. Any semi-conscious fae would do the same to keep the higher-up supernatural courts from sniffing around for breaking the law.

Because revealing ourselves to the humans was not dealt with kindly. For us or the humans involved.

"No!" Julia's sharp retort made me jump.

"No?" I echoed stupidly. I really, *really* needed to get into the portal.

"No." She glared at me. "I'm not leaving you alone like this. Not when *that*," she pointed at the path, "is what's after you!"

"Why do you think Aithan was sent here to stay with me?" I asked in exasperation. "Julia, I'll be safe if you just let me–"

"Everleigh!" This shout was from Aithan. I turned just in time to see the glamour flicker. This time, there were four figures facing off against him. "Portal! Now!"

As he shouted, the figures turned and looked at me. And all four began to charge.

If I hesitated any longer, I would be risking Aithan's life even more. So with a groan and a prayer that Julia would just do what I said, I pressed my hand to the top of the fire hydrant. The magic within me, broken as it was, immediately connected with the magical pathway, and I could feel myself being dragged inside. But before the portal could close behind me, a familiar hand closed around my wrist as Julia screamed my name.

***

The portal spit me out in a red overstuffed armchair beside a fireplace at the back of a cozy bookstore. Then, to my horror, it spit out Julia beside me, still clutching my hand with a look of terror on her face.

That would have been bad enough. I'd accidentally just broken the cardinal rule that all supernaturals were bound to follow.

Because of me, Julia had seen magic.

But our adventures, it seemed, weren't over yet. Standing right in front of us were two tall male fae who had been browsing the *History of Intoxicating Magic* section. And for a long moment, we only stared blankly at one another as I scrambled to my feet and did my best to push Julia behind me.

"Everleigh," Julia finally whispered. "What—"

"What's this?" one of the fae asked in a silky Eastern European accent. He took a step toward us, his purple eyes shining brilliantly, their distinctive ring of bright pink encircling the iris. "From the smell of it, a half-breed–and a human."

"I've never seen a human go through a portal before," said his friend, who wore a bemused smile. "Do you think she's a pet?"

My heart dropped into my stomach like a rock. "Uncle Finn?" I called, not moving my eyes from the fae.

These fae were not glamoured. There was no reason for them to hide. My uncle's bookstore was glamoured on the outside to look like a dumpy cigarette shop. Which meant the supernaturals on the inside could dress and act any way they chose, as long as they remained within supernatural law. It was meant to be a place of supernatural respite, my uncle had explained.

Unfortunately, that was not how it felt at the moment. These fae were obviously well-to-do, probably favorites of one of the lower fae kings or queens. The brightly colored silk pantaloons and flamboyantly frilled shirts that they wore attested to that, cut to emphasize their lean, powerful physiques while also making them look like something out of a cartoon. Their dark hair, shimmering with hints of purple and blue, had been curled and shaped with great care. Fae were nothing if not colorful.

"Girl," the one with purple hair addressed me, "is this your... pet?"

"What does he mean 'your *pet*?'" Julia whimpered.

"What my brother means to ask," said the second with a growing leer, "is to ask you, human, whether you are untethered."

"Uncle Finn?" I called again, this time louder.

This. This was why humans couldn't know about the world of

magic. It was too dangerous for them, too fraught with opportunities to lose oneself to the games played within the courts. They were fiercely protected by the supernatural courts... as long as they were ignorant of the world around them.

But once a human *chose* to dive headlong into the supernatural world–which Julia had just done, albeit unwittingly–all bets were off. My best friend was now fair game.

"If you are," said the first fae, his eyes moving up and down her person in a way that made me want to kick him, "I should very much like a pet of my own. And you will do quite nicely."

"Everleigh!" Julia rasped, yanking hard on my arm. "What are they talking about?"

"You've seen magic, which means you're compromised. And you came here... willingly." I swallowed, not moving my eyes from the two fae who were slowly but surely cornering us. "Which means by supernatural law that you're legally up for adoption as a pet to any fae who claims you." My voice didn't shake, but my insides did. Had I just ruined my friend's life forever?

"I'm *what?*" she shrieked.

"Uncle Finn!" I shouted. Where *was* he?

"Well," drawled the first fae, removing the glove from his right hand, "if she's not taken, in that case I–"

"She's mine!" I blurted out, grabbing Julia with my right. "I tether her! She's my pet, and our lives are entwined until natural magic itself can sever them!"

As I spoke, I could feel the vow already linking my life to hers. Like an invisible chain connecting the two of us, Julia's life was no longer her own. If I died, she died. Wherever I wanted her to go, she would go. If I ordered her to die, her heart would never beat again. Within seconds, a pink filigree band appeared like a tattoo around her left bicep. Julia rubbed it, but I watched in horror, knowing it would never rub off.

What had I done?

"Everleigh, what's all–" a familiar voice growled from around a tall bookshelf. A second later, an unusually burly fae appeared at the end of the aisle and looked around. When he saw the two fae facing us, he scowled. "Are either of you bothering my niece? There will be no trouble in my store!"

"We were just leaving," said the second fae brother, sneering at me once more before turning and walking down another aisle. "Come, Claude."

Claude gave me another dirty look before following his brother, his silken cape swishing indignantly behind him. No one spoke a word until the sound of another portal on the other side of the store quieted. They were gone.

As soon as they disappeared, Julia fainted. I moved to catch her, but my uncle was faster. Carefully, he laid her in another blue armchair across from the red one before turning to me with a troubled look.

"I assume... this is not good," he finally said. His eyes moved back to Julia's arm, and his brows bunched again. Then he shook his head and turned before walking in the opposite direction.

"Where are you going?" I asked.

"To close the store," he answered. "And then to get a drink. I'm going to need something stronger than Diet for this."

Chapter Nine

Aithan

I GLANCED at the makeshift portal—which had apparently been built into one of the sidewalk squares—to find it trying to open yet again. Fortunately, whoever had made this portal wasn't skilled. One of my now five opponents had gotten stuck twice before someone else had run to help him climb out, and it seemed another supernatural was stuck now as well.

Well, four opponents. There had been five, but the troll had been unusually stupid and easy to deal with. A single kick to his rolling ball form had allowed me to deliver a fossilization spell, keeping his stone form immobile for the near future.

Which meant I was left with the purple-winged fae, a vampire, a shifter of some kind, and something with the body of a male humanoid. But he had the hood of his sweatshirt drawn too tightly for me to see the face beneath.

They all faced me now. And as they sized me up, I did the same to them.

I had no doubt that they recognized me. I might not be at the center of Nomos court life, but I wore the Nomos ring, and I looked too much like my father to be anonymous. Which was probably why the original attackers had called for backup.

I would take the vampire last, I decided. He wouldn't be able to use his full powers in the direct sunlight. If I drew the other two out into the light, it would make this fight one against three rather than four. Then I could take him last. So the fae, the humanoid, and the shifter it was.

I backed up quickly so I was out of the shaded part of the path. As I did, I reached into my pocket and touched the glamour stone I always kept there, boosting the field glamour it currently provided. Unfortunately, keeping the field glamour boosted meant I couldn't use all of my magic against my opponents. But the repercussions of having a supernatural fight on a university campus in front of hundreds of students was an equally unpleasant thought.

The fae attacked first. She threw a persuasive charm at me—a small porcelain flower—with rather poor aim. When the charm hit the ground, it exploded and released a wave of apathy that hit me directly from the side. I felt the unpleasant experience of the left side of my body going numb before I snapped my energy whip at the charm's remains, breaking it and the spell.

As I destroyed the fae spell, however, the shifter was attacking from my other side, turning into a wolf mid-jump. Whirling around, I barely had the time to bring my energy whip up and wrap it around the werewolf's body, intending to slam it against the ground.

Unfortunately, I miscalculated. The size of the werewolf's human form is usually indicative of the size of its shifter form. A werewolf the size of an average human male will usually shift into a wolf of equally average size. But this werewolf, while on the slim side for a human male, somehow transformed into the largest werewolf I had ever seen outside the direct alpha lines. And the amount of strength I had to put into yanking him away from my body with the whip threw me off balance just enough for the humanoid to run in and kick my left side.

His kick wasn't hard or even well-aimed, but it was just enough to knock me over. I hit the ground, but the fall gave me the momentum to tuck into a shoulder roll, putting more space between myself and my attackers. The humanoid followed, throwing another punch as I jumped to my feet.

But this time, I was ready. Like Everleigh, my parents had put me through as much martial arts training as possible when I was a kid. I didn't even need magic to grab his arm and yank him closer, slamming my knee into his face.

He went down quickly, making way for the fae to jump over his body as she tossed a handful of smaller apathy charms at me. I conjured a wave of fire that emanated from my arm, making the charms—which she'd latched onto sticky flowers—sizzle before they ever hit my skin. Even these, however, were so strong they nearly made my arm go limp with exhaustion, and would have if I hadn't known precisely how to break them.

To my relief, whatever creature had been in the portal seemed to have given up on going through, as the portal had stopped lighting up. That it wasn't active was confirmed when I grabbed the hulking but dizzy werewolf by the scruff of the neck and threw him at it. He hit the ground with a whine, but the cement square itself did nothing. It was either broken or whoever had created it had shut it down.

The humanoid creature took one look at the portal as well before climbing unsteadily to his feet and sprinting away from me. Then, to my surprise, the fae did the same. I considered going after them, but froze when the vampire, who had been standing in the shadows, did the unthinkable.

He walked out into the sun.

I stared at him as he squared off against me, a smirk on his powdery white face, his red eyes glowing brilliantly even through his dark sunglasses.

"This is an unexpected twist," I said. As I spoke, I created an energy sword in my left hand and snapped the whip in my right. "You want to tell me why you're trying to abduct a half-elf, half-fae college student?"

Of course, *I* knew Everleigh was more than a typical college student, and that she wasn't simply half-elf or half-fae. But I wanted to know whether *he* knew that.

"I think you're confused, Your Highness," he said in a low, smooth voice, lowering his sunglasses slightly as he spoke. "We're not trying to abduct anyone. We only want to speak with her."

It was a novice mistake on his part. Experienced vampires knew not to try to use controlling magic with their eyes from a long distance, and he had just shown me his hand.

I shot toward him, whip and sword raised. Newer vampires, as this one seemed to be, hadn't had time for the blood they drank to fully touch all parts of their bodies. Which meant he would be much weaker than the vampires I'd trained against. All I needed to do was–

My plan to physically beat him into submission was thwarted when he rushed at me headlong as well. And using speed he shouldn't theoretically have had yet, he grabbed both my arms and squeezed them against my body.

In shock, I tried to shake him off, but somehow–impossibly–he was stronger. As I squirmed and did my best to free my arms, he opened his mouth, his slightly extended canines glistening in the reflection of the sun.

If he bit me, I was going to be in a world of hurt. Not because I'd become a vampire. Vampires couldn't turn other supernaturals into vampires–only humans. But his bite would deliver a serious dose of toxins to my blood that would leave me vulnerable to anything else he desired to do to me.

Inexplicably, I couldn't beat him in strength. But there was a reason elves were higher than vampires on the supernatural food chain. I let my energy whip and sword disappear and transferred my power so that flames covered the entire surface of my body instead.

The vampire let go with a shout.

I took advantage of his momentary pain and broke his

sunglasses with a single punch. Then I pinned his arms behind him and whipped him around to face the sun.

The vampire screamed so loudly I wondered if his shriek would penetrate the edges of the field glamour that my glamour stone projected. Not only did it shield us from human view, but it also insulated sound. Well, most sound. I'd never tested it to know whether it was stronger than a vampire scream.

The vampire fought back, but each tug and pull was weaker than the last until he went limp in my arms. I then took his unconscious body and none-too-gently tossed it back into the shadows. If I killed him, I would have no one to question later. But that didn't mean I was going to be gentle.

Breathing hard, I looked around me at the mess the attack had caused. Trees were scorched, and the bushes had holes in them. There were also burn marks on the sidewalk and enchanted flowers had sprouted where they shouldn't have. Usually, in this instance, any average supernatural would call the number that connected them to my grandfather's court to come and clean up and investigate the situation.

Whatever this situation was, however, it was undeniably linked to Everleigh. Which meant I couldn't have my grandfather's court or any others sniffing around. So I called another number in my phone instead.

"Your Highness?" the low, languid voice answered in a British accent.

I rolled my eyes. Vampires—even the one I had just fought— were nothing if not impeccably polite. But I supposed that came from living far longer than most other supernaturals.

"I need an emergency cleanup at the university." I looked up and squinted in the sunlight. "On and around the shaded path beside the old business building. I'll send you the location." Unfortunately, as I spoke, the unconscious bodies I'd immobilized disappeared before my eyes. An elven transporting spell, no doubt. I let out a curse.

Dorian paused at my exclamation. "And Miss Everleigh?"

"She's safe. I sent her through a portal to Finn's shop. But someone was after her." I looked at the disorder and destruction surrounding me. "*People* are after her. They're a lot stronger than they should be... and they're reckless. It was like they didn't even care if anyone saw us."

"Which means her parents were right," Dorian said with a sigh.

"First she has a stalker, then our parents disappear. Now this. Something's definitely up," I said. "But I don't know what."

There was another pause. "Understood. My lunch break is soon. I'll be there in two minutes."

<hr>

True to his word, two minutes later the vampire stepped out of at same the portal Everleigh had used to go. He was still wearing his long white lab coat, though I could smell that he'd changed into clean gloves.

"Will anyone at the lab notice you're gone?" I asked. "This might take longer than usual."

Dorian smirked at me, the single streak of gray hair running through his otherwise black locks gleaming in the sunlight. "That's the fun of being a forensic pathologist. You generally work alone."

I knew for a fact that Dorian had actually chosen his line of work specifically so he could work with my and Everleigh's parents on a regular basis. But I didn't have time to banter, and I was grateful he had shown up to fix what had become my mess.

"Have you heard anything about your parents?" he asked again, the smirk disappearing from his face. "Word has it at the station that there's something strange going on with their requested vacation time."

I shook my head. "No, but I'll let you know when I do. In the meantime, I need to follow Everleigh."

He nodded. "Of course. Find the princess. I'll fix this."

"Thanks, Dorian.

A moment later, I was stalking toward the same portal Everleigh had used just a few minutes before, hoping very much that she'd really gone to her uncle's store. Just as I neared it, however, something black and shiny caught my attention. A cell phone lay in the exact place the fae had tried to take Everleigh. As I picked it up, its screen flickered, letting off a distinct puff of magic. Then it went blank.

Chapter Ten

Everleigh

I watched Julia nervously as I sipped the mug of hot cider my uncle had given me. Julia was conscious now, but after waking with a scream, she'd done nothing but stare blankly at the little table that sat between the four armchairs on the rug in front of the glamoured fireplace.

"Julia?" I asked tentatively. "Would you like a drink?" My uncle had poured her a mug as well, though I suspected he'd infused calming magic into the cider. But she barely lifted her eyes to meet mine before staring, unseeing, back down at the table.

I sighed.

"So," my uncle said, leaning back in the green armchair across from mine, his long legs crossed elegantly beneath his blue robes. "You're sure you've told me everything?"

I nodded and stirred my cider with the little silver spoon that had been charmed to keep the liquid hot. "I... I don't know what's happening, Uncle Finn." When I met his vivid blue eyes–the color of my mother's... and mine–they tightened. Uncle Finn was the one relative who had been allowed to watch me grow up. Probably because he was also a fish out of water within my mother's family.

"Where is that boy?" he growled, glancing at the clock.

But just as he started to stand, the false flames within the fire sputtered, and Aithan popped through. His hair was matted with sweat, and he had smears of blood on his arms and neck. Hopefully, the blood wasn't his.

"Aithan!" I exclaimed, jumping out of my chair and spilling my cider on my jeans. "What–"

"It wasn't just a kidnapping," he growled at my uncle. "It was an ambush. Three more showed up after she left, and if their portal hadn't been so badly made, there would have been more."

"Who was behind it?" My uncle gestured to the yellow armchair and began to pour Aithan a drink.

"That's the weird part," Aithan said, flopping into the chair. "I have no idea. Every attacker was of a different race. They wore no crest, no colors. And..." He glared down at his mug as though it were the cause of our troubles.

"And what?" my uncle asked, his vivid blue eyes seeming to burn.

"They were strong," Aithan finally said, meeting his gaze. "Much stronger than they should have been, considering their lack of skill."

I stared at him, trying to process this. But it just wouldn't compute. A group of supernaturals had set an ambush–to take *me*?

Just as Aithan had been dragged to his fair share of my performances, competitions, and tournaments when we were kids, my family had attended his and his older brother's activities as well. And I could say without a doubt that Aithan and his brother were physically the strongest elves I'd ever seen, with the exception of their father. Aithan beat my dad in arm wrestling the month he turned thirteen. And my dad–an elf prince himself–was one of the strongest among his own kin.

"How did you beat them, then?" my uncle asked.

"I had to use skill," Aithan said, taking a sip of his cider. "They weren't particularly well-trained. They didn't even seem to have any attack plan. That's what makes it even weirder." He pulled something out of his pocket. "But I did find this." He tossed me a shiny black phone.

I hit the button on the side. The screen lit up, but rather than displaying the usual date and time, it was perfectly blank.

"A wiping charm?" I guessed.

Aithan nodded. "From what I can guess. I'm hoping we might be able to get something off of it, but I won't know until I can get it to an IT person."

I turned the phone around in my hands, studying each scratch and line. "There's something here," I said, squinting at the corner of the phone. "It's inscribed. It says... no, it's not words. It's a symbol. A key." I frowned at the phone. "I don't know of any company or organization that uses that emblem."

My uncle reached for the phone, so I handed it to him.

"Everleigh."

We turned to see Julia blinking rapidly as she sat up, her eyes suddenly widening in terror. Though her eyes had been open for several minutes, only now did she seem to truly wake up. "Everleigh!" she cried. "The woman! With the purple winged costume and wig! And the two men who... who wanted to make me a pet!" She looked wildly around. "What's going on?" she whispered.

I bit my lip as I considered what to say. If I told her the truth, she might faint again. If I didn't tell her the truth...

Well, she was going to be very confused when she wondered why in the world she was thinking about me nearly every waking moment for the rest of her life.

"She's *your* pet," my uncle told me with a shrug. "It's not going to help anything if you keep her in the dark now."

Aithan's brows rose. "She's *what* now?" He looked at my uncle. "Just how much did I miss?"

"I want to know *everything*!" Julia snapped, glaring at me

through red-rimmed eyes. "Because if you tell me I didn't see anything, I'm going to go—"

"Julia..." I began. I tried to smile at her, but I probably just looked like I was about to be sick. After the events of the morning, I very well might be.

"You know how you've always wondered why I... why I don't talk to certain people? Why I can't–leave Vegas? Even for a vacation?"

She stared blankly at me, sniffing pitifully but not arguing, so I forged ahead.

"Those fairy tales we used to read... The retellings with fae and elves and wizards and ogres and magic?" I lifted my shaking hands and let some of my useless elf magic dance over them, my unruly green and pink magic alternating between the tips of my fingers.

Julia gaped, then slapped her own two hands over her mouth. I expected her to scream, but instead, she began to cry and her whole body began to tremble.

This was going great.

"The two men you saw were fae," I continued in a rush. "Like my Uncle Finn."

She turned to give my uncle a look of terror, but he only gave her a polite smile in return.

"And my mother," I went. Then I paused. "And... me."

Julia looked wildly back and forth between my Uncle Finn and me before turning her eyes on Aithan. "And what's *he*?"

"I'm an elf," he said softly.

"The people who attacked us at school were... well, they were supernaturals. Like all of us here. You saw another fae woman–the one with the purple hair. And the rock one was a troll."

"So... so there are *magic* people everywhere." She drew in a shaking breath. "I get it. But where does the magic come from? How does it work? Because this..." She let out a strangled laugh that turned into a sob. "This is insane, Everleigh. I wouldn't believe it if–"

"Just... assume most of the old fairy tales we read as kids are true," I said slowly. "As for the magic–Do you remember when we studied string theory in high school?"

She blinked at me a few times before giving me a slow nod. Given how much she had detested that class, I took her nod as a *no*.

"Well, essentially the idea is that all subatomic particles– protons, neutrons, and electrons–are made of even smaller one-dimensional particles called quarks. And inside those quarks are strings of some kind of energy. And the behavior of those strings determines the attributes of the subatomic particles' substance–"

"English, please, Everleigh. Besides, I don't see what *this* has to do with these supposed fae who are out to kill us." Julia sniffed.

I held up a finger. "I'm getting to that. Basically, humans have the idea of string theory... *mostly* right. But what they don't realize is that supernatural beings already knew this from ages past. I mean, we had different names for everything, but basically, the behavior of the strings in one's body determines the supernatural's ability to interact with and change the world around him. What you call magic is really just science."

"I don't..." Julia began to shake her head.

"Elves," Aithan held up one of his hands, "have the distinct ability to warp and change the physical world around us. When we're children or untrained, this can only be done through physical touch. We have to be in direct contact with whatever we want to change in order to alter or enact change upon it." He dipped his finger in his cider, and the golden-brown liquid turned a distinct shade of green.

For a moment, I wondered if Julia's eyes might fall out of her head.

"But for those of us who've been trained," he continued, "we don't need the direct contact. We can create our own avenues of change." He held up his other arm, and a sword made of pure energy appeared in his hand.

Julia squeaked and leaned back into her chair as far as she could go, nearly tipping it over as she did.

"Fae, meanwhile," my uncle hurried to explain, probably worried she would pass out again, "have the ability to influence the *perceptions* of others. Our magic is more of a... convincing kind." As he spoke, the room transformed from a cozy book corner to a gleaming city in the clouds, and his face changed to look much more like a human's with rounded ears and eyes of a duller blue. His shiny blue robes became cargo shorts and a Hawaiian shirt. Julia began to breathe as though she was going to hyperventilate, so my uncle let the room melt back into what it had been before.

"Many supernaturals," I said, "are what we call shifters. Their ability to bring about change is limited to their own bodies. Were-wolves, for example."

"Werewolves are *real?*" Julia clutched her hands to her chest.

"They are. But they're not quite like the movies make them look." I smiled. "They live in packs, yes, but they're generally quite productive members of society. Lots of discipline and order and such. *Major* gym rats. Lots of them join the military and police force."

"Werecats, on the other hand..." Aithan murmured and made a face.

"But... but they can still bite people and change them. Right?" Julia asked.

"They can," I said slowly. "But the supernatural world has pretty strict laws about transforming humans. The same goes for vampires."

"Although vampires are different in their *own* way," my uncle added.

Julia leaned back into the armchair and closed her eyes, and began to breathe slowly in and out through her nose. I glanced at

Aithan, but he was staring blankly into the glamoured fire, seeming lost in his own thoughts.

"So," Julia said, opening her eyes again. "Magic is basically physics. And there are magical beings walking all over the world."

I nodded slowly, not sure what she was getting at.

"So what was all that nonsense about pets and claiming me?" she asked, her eyes narrowing at me.

I winced, then looked at my uncle. But he just shrugged and leaned over to hand her her mug of cider. She took it without breaking her glare.

"So..." I scratched my head, searching for the right words. "A lot of our supernatural law is rather... antiquated. Supernaturals are forbidden from telling humans about magic." I gave her an embarrassed shrug. "It's why I couldn't always tell you why I did certain things. I wasn't allowed."

She frowned slightly but didn't interrupt.

"If the supernatural courts–largely the elven Nomos court–find out that humans were made aware of magic, and the problem wasn't addressed with a fae memory charm or something like that, there can be dire consequences."

"Like what?" she asked. "Paying crazy fines or something?"

"Like punishment by death." Aithan turned to look directly at her. He'd allowed his glamour stone to rest, which meant he looked fully elven–something I knew she had never seen. And I didn't miss her shudder. "Or," he continued, "having fangs or wings or something else important removed."

Julia stared at him, her mouth falling slightly open.

"That's why I told you to go to Soo Min," I said with an apologetic smile. "She and her father would have used a memory charm to make you forget what happened when we were attacked. You would have gone home none the wiser. But when you grabbed my arm and came with me..." I sighed and rubbed my eyes with the palms of my hands. "You purposefully entered the world of magic.

Which meant that when we got here, you were legally up for grabs by any supernatural who happened to see you."

"That's... but that's unfair!" Julia protested, her voice growing louder with each word. "I didn't know that! I grabbed your arm because I was worried about *you!*" She was shouting now, and sounded on the verge of tears again.

"And that was very kind of you," my uncle said gently, putting a hand on her arm—no doubt also giving her a rather heavy dose of relaxing magic, as she hadn't yet sipped her cider.

"I know," I said, suddenly on the verge of tears myself. "And... I don't deserve you as a friend, Julia. I really don't. But when those two fae saw you, they could see that you were untethered. And I–"

"Untethered?" she interrupted.

I grimaced. "That you weren't *connected* to any supernatural."

"Basically," Aithan said in a bored voice, "you were a bagel floating in a harbor of seagulls."

"*You* weren't there," Julia said with a sniff. "How do you know what happened?"

Aithan gave her a hard smile, accentuating the sharp angles of his face. "Fae are rather predictable. And if Everleigh had to tether you to herself, you should be thanking her."

Julia lifted her chin defiantly. "And why is that?"

"Because if she hadn't, you would now be some strange fae's plaything. And he could have done with you or made you do whatever he wanted."

Julia paled.

"*Whatever* he wanted," Aithan repeated. "Your best friend just saved you from a life of very colorful servitude."

"So..." Julia turned to me and said in a small voice. "I'm. . your slave now?"

"No!" I cried. "Well, I mean, you're... tied to me. I could *technically* make you do what you didn't want to do. But I'm not going to! I don't want to! I just... wanted to keep you safe!"

"And... and there's no way to undo it?" she asked in an even smaller voice.

"There are ways to break the tether," I said slowly. "But they're... not easy." Not that I knew what they were. Only that it was so difficult a lot of people didn't even bother trying.

"And neither is our next topic of conversation," my uncle said firmly. "And I'm sorry, but it's one that *can't* wait."

I blinked up at him as he stood. "What's that?"

He gave me a wry smile. "My dear, I'm afraid it's *your* turn for a surprise."

I stared after my uncle as he stood and walked gracefully to the back of the store. When he returned, he was holding a contraption that looked like one of Leonardo da Vinci's sketches.

The only parts of the small machine that didn't appear to be made of copper were the stone base into which it was secured, and the single red gem suspended at the center of three large fixed copper rings, which had been fitted to whirl about one another in different directions without colliding. Beside the copper rings stood a long point that looked a lot like the spindle from Sleeping Beauty. And the sharpened point was facing straight up.

The entire machine was no bigger than a basketball, but I could feel its ancient magic before he'd even crossed the room with it.

"What is that?" Julia asked, sitting up slightly to see it better.

My uncle placed it on the table before us and stared at it with a slight frown. "We're going to try something tonight," he said, ignoring Julia's question. "It took me nearly a decade to track this down. Very few exist in the world today. And the only reason the owner sold it to me was because it was broken." He met Aithan's eyes. "But I think I've tinkered with it all that I can. It's time to try."

"What is it?" I asked.

"It has a few names, but most know it as a *sanguis colorum*. It means 'blood colors.'"

"I thought you couldn't get it to work," Aithan said.

"I couldn't at first. Why do you think I spent so much time in Italy these last few years?" Uncle Finn snorted. "Apparently, they were invented there. But even then, it was still hard to track working parts down. And it certainly wasn't good for business. That said," he turned back to the contraption, "I think it might actually work. It's done so the last few times I've tried it."

"We'll find out, I guess," Aithan said.

My uncle glanced at me. "You can tell different magics apart by looking at them, yes?"

I nodded. "I know most of the colors. The main ones, at least." My ability to see and sense magic wasn't as good as Aithan's, but it wasn't nearly as stunted as my ability to use it.

"Good. Then this will be that much less complicated. Aithan, prick your finger, please."

Aithan reached out and pressed his finger against the spindle-looking thing. A drop of bright red blood appeared at the top of the point. But it didn't stay there when he removed his hand. Instead, it was... absorbed?

I stared at the place where his blood had been. There wasn't even a red stain left behind on the shiny copper surface.

A moment later, the rings began to whirl, and I heard every-one—myself included—gasp.

Arcs of green power began appearing and disappearing inside the rings, fizzling and snapping the way Aithan's magic did when-ever he conjured it in his hands.

"Elven power," I told Julia as the green arcs began to sputter out.

"Which means it's my turn next," my uncle said, pricking his own finger on the sharp point. A moment later, we were all watching pink arcs of power float between the rings.

"Fae magic," I told my friend. But she pretended not to hear me.

"And now," Uncle Finn said, pushing the contraption toward me, "it's your turn."

I stared blankly at him. "Um... we know what I am."

"Do we?" Aithan asked.

I turned to scoff at him, but he just gave me a wry smile.

"Of... of course we know." I looked back and forth between my uncle and Aithan. "My mom is fae, and my dad's an elf. What else is there to know?"

"If that's the case," my uncle said, a dangerous glitter in his eyes, "what is there to lose if you just try?"

My heart sped as I looked back down at the contraption. He had a point. What did I have to lose?

Only your entire world, a voice inside me whispered. Whatever this contraption revealed, I instinctively knew there would be no going back.

"After all," my uncle added, "this was created to show supernaturals like you the truth."

"The truth?" I echoed. "Can't you just tell me the truth?"

Aithan snorted. "Do you really think after cursing both his grandsons, my grandfather would have left you untouched as well?"

"He didn't." I frowned. "He created boundaries so we couldn't leave Las V–"

"That was to keep an eye on *all* of us." Aithan shook his head. "Just try."

I licked my suddenly dry lips, wondering if I ought to change my mind. But it was no use. While I was certain... mostly certain that I was just another half-breed, memories of all the odd things that had happened recently began to fill my head. And once the questions were spinning in my head, I knew I needed answers.

Desperately.

So without pausing to think again, I put my hand out and pricked my finger.

Just as it had done for the others, the blood beaded for a moment on the copper point before being absorbed. I leaned forward, fully expecting to see pink and green magic arcs crossing weakly from one side of the rings to the other. Heck, my magic being what it was, I wouldn't be shocked if the machine just blew up.

Before any light appeared within the rings, however, the little machine began to shake... and then stopped working completely.

"What happened?" Aithan leaned forward.

My uncle peered down into it. "I could only suppose..." He glanced at Aithan. "Do you think you could boost it? Add more power, I mean?"

Aithan nodded but frowned. "Why do you think it needs more? It has the stone–"

My uncle let out a humorless laugh. "Consider the source." He glanced at me, then back at the contraption. "Give me a moment. I think I can..." He stood and retrieved a screwdriver from the back of the shop. Then he returned and used the screwdriver to snap something back into place. "That should do it! Now, if you wouldn't mind, Aithan."

Aithan put his hand on the base and sent a low level of power into the machine. After a few sputters and false starts, the machine began to whirl and twirl once again, continuing to absorb the blood I'd already left on the spindle.

I expected it to begin the same slow spinning it had done for Aithan and my uncle. But to my surprise, it spun faster and faster until I was worried it might break again. And then a small–*very* small–green arc appeared within the rings.

That made sense, of course, as I was half-elf. This was followed by a pink arc, which I had also expected, being half-fae.

But then a yellow arc appeared, and my heart seemed to stop in my chest.

Then turquoise.

Blue.

Orange.

Red.

Dark blue-green, gray, and white. Lime green. Peach.

The more colors appeared, the more frozen in place I felt as I stared at the contraption, which continued to whirl and shake like it might actually explode.

Only after more than a dozen different colors appeared as arcs in the center of the spinning rings did the contraption finally begin to slow.

"But that... that can't be right," I finally managed to sputter when the rings were still. "Where did all those colors come from?"

"Your magic," my uncle said with a shrug. "You used your own blood, did you not?"

"Yes, I know." I ran my fingers through my hair. "But there must be some mistake. I already saw my colors. Where did all the other ones come from? Who has that many kinds of magic in their blood?"

The question hung in the air like a crystal chandelier that was hanging by a thread, ready to crash to the ground.

"Who," my uncle said slowly, "or rather, *what?*"

Lessons from all my parents' dry history books suddenly echoed in my head, and the word was on my lips before I could stop to consider what I was saying.

"Wizard," I whispered.

As though on cue, both my uncle and Aithan gave a sigh of relief before sharing a look of long suffering.

"Finally!" Aithan said, cracking his knuckles.

I stared at him stupidly. "What... what do you mean *finally?*" I turned and looked at my uncle. "How long have you been trying to tell me?"

"My grandfather's official edict was that no one was allowed to discuss your magic with you in detail," Aithan said. "He meant it as a punishment, of course. A way to confuse you, since he assumed you were a typical child of two races. It was his way of getting back at your father for leading my father away from the courts. In his mind, you wouldn't only be bad at magic, your parents would never be able to directly tell you why."

"So your grandfather knows I'm a…" I couldn't finish the question.

But Aithan was already shaking his head. "No. He was just being malicious. Unfortunately, his pettiness complicated things for our parents." He frowned at the machine. "A lot."

"But it seems we can talk with you about it now," my uncle said, leaning back and sipping his cider with a satisfied smile. "Seeing as you know what you are. We just couldn't be the ones to reveal it to you."

"But why is it bad to be from two races?" Julia asked. She'd been sipping her cider in silence, and my uncle's added calming magic seemed to have taken effect.

"Most supernatural children born of two races have nearly useless magic," my uncle explained. "But while Everleigh's mother was still pregnant, a court oracle revealed in private to her parents that the child would be a wizard. It was then that her parents and their close allies began to plan their exit from the courts."

"The courts," Julia said with a frown. "You keep talking about courts. Like… royalty or something?"

"Everleigh," Aithan said, "is technically a princess."

"As are you," I retorted.

My uncle let out a snort and Aithan scowled, but Julia closed her eyes and inhaled deeply again. "Of course you are," she muttered. "Because what else could make this day seem less real?"

"But why would they leave when they found out what I was?" I asked, fingering the stitching on the armrest.

"You should know this," my uncle said disapprovingly. "Wizards are rare, yes?"

I nodded. Wizards, unlike the other supernaturals, were not

really their own race. Three or four generations would often pass before an old one died and a new one was born.

"A wizard is basically a harbinger," my uncle said, "a sign that difficult times are coming."

"Translated," Aithan said, "it means wizards are only born when something big and bad is about to happen in the supernatural world."

Julia and I stared at one another. And for once, I felt just as shocked as she looked.

My phone buzzed just then. In a daze, I pulled it out and glanced at the text. It was from Georgie.

> Where are you guys? I can't find you or Julia, and
> she won't answer her phone. Just let me know
> you guys are okay.

"We tried to tell you," Aithan said calmly. "Over and over again. Why do you think your dad had you memorize so many random facts about the supernatural world? And I know for a fact that your mom told you every story in the supernatural history books. Including stories that had wizards."

I opened my mouth, but no words came out.

"Unfortunately," my uncle said, "you grew so angry with the world for your 'broken magic,' as you called it, that you refused to touch your magic at all. You turned your back on everything supernatural as much as you possibly could."

As he spoke, I shifted uncomfortably in my chair. As much as I wanted to deny it, he was right. I *was* comfortable in the human world. In fact, I'd made it my goal to live as though I were a human. I'd focused so much on getting along without magic that I did everything in my power to ignore it.

Had I really spent my entire life being that blind? That jaded?

Apparently, I had.

But why?

"Once they knew what you were," your parents immediately

began gathering a small circle of trusted friends," Uncle Finn said, staring at his purplish-pink family ring thoughtfully. It was the same one my mother wore. "Their plan was to escape to a small town in the Midwest. Somewhere off the map while you grew up. They wanted the monarchs and courts to be totally unaware of you so they couldn't try to use you for their own purposes while you were still young."

"What happened?" I asked, my breath suddenly tight.

"Someone ratted on them," Aithan said bitterly. "It's why my grandfather had time to summon them and think up so many *helpful* curses. He let them go, but only within the confines of the city."

As he spoke, a thought occurred to me, and I sat up straight. "Is that why no one ever talks about *your* curse?"

"Unfortunately, my grandfather put similar bindings on my curse the way he did yours," Aithan said in a sour voice. 'Those who heard it know of it. *I* know about it because it's the earliest memory I have. But we're not allowed to speak directly of it.'

"Still," my uncle said in a softer voice, "your parents' friends were loyal. And those who escaped the king's notice set up a network around them to support them and protect you as you grew." He fixed his vivid blue eyes on me in a way that reminded me entirely too much of my mother. "More people than you're aware of love you, Everleigh. They've arranged their lives around keeping you safe. It's why your parents were comfortable leaving you with Aithan. They knew that he and the others in their organization would take care of you, should something happen to them. They've been planning for this moment your whole life."

And I, I thought miserably, *just sat by and let it happen.*

"I just got a text from Dorian," Aithan said, standing and shoving his phone in his pocket. "Your house has been searched and cleared. It's safe, so we need to go."

For the briefest of moments, I thought about refusing. What if I didn't want to be a wizard? I hadn't the slightest idea what being a wizard entailed. I wasn't a hero. I couldn't even use magic without blowing things up or electrocuting myself.

But if what they said was true, people were risking their lives to keep me safe. My parents were missing, as were Aithan's. What good would it do to refuse? It wouldn't change any of the unpleasant truths that seemed to continue popping up around me.

"Dorian had my car brought here," Aithan said as I pulled Julia to her feet. "We'll go to Julia's apartment on the way so she can get whatever she needs. Then we're heading home."

Neither Julia nor I responded. We simply followed him out.

Chapter Eleven

Aithan

JULIA GAVE me her apartment address in a monotone voice before turning and staring out the window as I pulled out onto the street. It was dark now, and a good deal colder than it had been the last time any of us had been outside. Neither Everleigh nor Julia spoke or even looked at one another as a heaviness settled in the car like a fleece blanket on an August night.

A part of me wanted to say something–anything to lighten the weight of the moment. Not that I had to. These girls weren't really girls anymore. They were both twenty-one–old enough to suck it up and handle this situation like adults. And yet...

When I looked in my rearview mirror, I didn't see two grown college students. I saw the two little girls who had tagged along and annoyed me for the better part of our lives. They might as well be wearing braids and swinging their sparkly plastic-clad princess shoes over the floor. Everleigh's parents had worked hard to protect her, and due to forced proximity, Julia with her. Was it possible, I wondered, if maybe...

Had she been protected for too long? We'd all known her blissful ignorance would one day end.

But that didn't mean I wanted to be there to watch.

Now wasn't the time to coddle, though. I steeled myself for what would have to be done as I turned onto the freeway. I didn't know who was looking for Everleigh or what they wanted, and I had no idea where our parents were. Of course, it could be elves behind this whole thing. Crediting my grandfather for any unknown evil was often a wise guess. Still, judging by the poor fighting capabilities of Everleigh's attackers, I doubted this was his work. Neither my grandfather nor any of the lower courts employed people who left messes in their wake. And yet...

The enemy might not be skilled. But they were far too strong.

Julia's apartment wasn't far from the university. As we pulled into the apartment complex, however, my skin began to crawl. Half of the parking lot lights were broken, and a group of men loitered on one of the darkened porches, their cigarettes glowing orange in the shadows. Several windows had been broken and poorly patched up, and I could feel the presence of at least three vampires in the vicinity. And there wasn't a single sign of security anywhere to be seen.

"You live *here?*" I asked, wanting very much to immediately whip the car around and drive back out.

Julia glared at me in the mirror. "Not all of us are *royalty.*"

I let out a heavy sigh. I had no desire to judge Julia's budgeting choices. But if Julia lived here, it meant Everleigh had no doubt spent her fair share of time here as well. And that thought had my fingers itching to whip a U-turn even harder than before.

"Look," I said, pulling into the spot in front of her apartment. "We're all going in. Everleigh, you can help Julia pack. I don't want to be here more than eight minutes, tops, so take only what's necessary. We can come back for more later."

"No."

I turned around and stared at Julia. "*Excuse* me?"

"I said no." She folded her arms across her chest. "This is my home. And you can't just waltz in and ruin my life because you've got weird physics!"

"I'm sorry, but *I'm* not the one who ignored Everleigh's very explicit instructions and decided to be a hero," I snapped.

"Well, I'm not going."

"Julia," Everleigh began in a tired voice, but I was done arguing.

"You see those guys over there? You want to ask one of them to protect you when whoever is chasing Everleigh traces her to you?" I leaned a little farther into the backseat. "Want to know which one's a vampire?"

Julia's eyes widened, and her gaze shot over to where the men were now studying us with open interest. After a moment of seeming frozen in place, she dug her key out of her backpack and mumbled, "Fine."

I tried not to look too relieved as she climbed out of the car and Everleigh followed. After sending the men a discreet but very poignant wave of magic to warn them away from trying anything while we were inside, I followed the girls.

My relief was short-lived, though. As soon as Julia had unlocked her door and let it swing open, we all stopped short

"Oh no," Everleigh whispered.

Chapter Twelve

Everleigh

JULIA's neat little apartment looked like an earthquake had hit. Dozens of books lay on the floor where they had obviously been carelessly tossed. The couch cushions had been slashed, and white stuffing covered everything. Dishes lay smashed all over the floor, and open food boxes and their contents covered every inch that wasn't littered with glass or porcelain.

The apartment had been ransacked.

"Shut the door, but stay right in the entrance," Aithan murmured, gathering magic at the tips of his fingers. "Everleigh, I don't care what shape your magic takes. If someone attacks you, you use it against them. Yes?"

I swallowed and nodded, trying to focus on my hands but having a hard time as I took in the carnage surrounding us.

"I have a stun gun over by the window," Julia whispered. "Should I get it?"

"Yeah, get it," I whispered back. Then I paused. "You *do* know how to use it, though, right?"

Julia made a face at me. "I took a class," she muttered as she climbed over the couch and retrieved what looked like a black plastic handle from behind the curtain.

Aithan had moved silently into the back of the apartment, but after a few minutes of silence, I began to feel uneasy. The apartment only had one bedroom. Surely by now, he'd had the time to–

Julia screamed and raised her stun gun.

"Julia, no–" I began, but I was too late. Aithan let out a cry of surprise as the electrodes jumped from her weapon to his chest.

"Julia!" Aithan snapped as he swatted the stun gun's barbs away. "What the heck?"

I unsuccessfully tried to hide a smile, but Aithan saw and scowled at me.

"Oh, come on," I told him. "It's not like it really hurt you "

"That doesn't mean it was fun," he retorted. "Now, go help Julia pack before I throw her dirty dishes into a suitcase and call it a day. Whoever is looking for you has discovered that you're often with Julia."

This thought sobered me enough to stop my teasing, and I followed Julia into her apartment's only bedroom.

"You should know," Julia snapped as she ran around her room snatching up articles of clothing, "that I don't care if you're two inches shorter than me. I'll be borrowing all your best clothes as payment for all of this."

I gave her a wry smile, glad she was at least talking to me again. "Tell me what you're looking for." As I spoke, I got another text from Georgie. Julia's phone buzzed, too.

"For the love of my sanity, could you please answer him so he quits blowing up my phone? Then find my favorite jeans."

I shot off a quick text. Vague, but one that I hoped would quell his fears. "He's just making sure we're okay. Now, tell me where your jeans are."

"They should be in that drawer over there. And then..." Her words faded as she paused and frowned at the top of her dresser.

"What is it?" I asked.

"My picture. It's gone." She stood and went to her dresser. "I had a picture of us here. The one from our day at the chocolate museum." Her frown deepened. "And my friendship bracelet is gone, too. The one you made me in sixth grade."

I stared at the empty shape in the dust where something like a picture frame had obviously sat. "Well, that's not creepy at all."

Julia turned to look at me, all signs of anger draining away. "What is going on?" she asked in a brittle voice.

That question haunted me as we got back in the car and drove across town toward my house. A few blocks out, however, Aithan shut off the music that had been filling the silent space.

"Things are serious enough that I called in backup. So be ready to have a few extra bodies hanging around the house for the foreseeable future."

I sat up. "Like... people will be in my yard?"

"In your house is more like it. Though I'll have someone patrolling the yard, too."

"Aithan, I can't ask a bunch of people to put their lives on hold just for–"

"Everleigh, I'm going to say this once," Aithan said in a low, dangerous voice. "People have *already* dedicated their lives to keep you safe. They made that decision years ago." He turned and gave me a sharp look. "You were born here and now for a purpose. And it would be nice if you were alive long enough for us to find out what that is."

"But–"

"So you're going to shut up and say thank you like the nice girl your parents raised. Yes?"

I leaned over to Julia. "You should have stunned him twice."

"Too late," he said, pulling into my driveway. "Our muscle is already here."

Chapter Thirteen

Everleigh

Knowing I had no other choice, I grabbed one of Julia's bags and waved her out of the car behind me. She still looked annoyed, but I was grateful that she didn't try to stay in the car–which would have been a perfectly logical thing to do, all things considered. When we rounded the corner of the garage to the front door, however, she jumped and let out a small shriek as we came face to face with a man whose eyes appeared to be made of orange fire, lighting up the dark entryway with an eerie glow.

His eyes weren't the only threatening thing about him. Julia probably couldn't see them, but I knew he also wore two firearms on his belt, and I had no doubt there was a third hidden somewhere else as well. Because fire, apparently, wasn't scary enough.

It was also rather risky when one wore no less than three guns on one's person at all times.

"Hey, Christian," I said as I tried to slow my racing heart.

He nodded but didn't smile. "Everleigh." His fiery gaze moved to Julia, who had grabbed my arm, trembling so hard I wondered if she might knock me down.

"He's a phoenix," I said, as if that explained everything. 'And you've seen him before."

"I... I have?" she echoed, looking back and forth between me and the phoenix.

"Yeah. His name's Christian. He goes to my church." I sighed and met his fiery gaze. "You going to let us in sometime tonight?"

"I've been to your church many times," Julia hissed, "and I think I would remember if I'd met a man who was on *fire!*"

The man in question frowned back at Julia. "A human?" he asked Aithan, who had come up behind us.

"Long story." Aithan shook his head. "We'll talk inside. Anything unusual since you got here?"

Christian shook his head and then retreated to open my front door.

It had been deathly quiet outside, but as soon as we walked inside and stepped into the foyer light, we were heralded by a cry of joy from a voice I knew all too well.

"Aithan! You made it!" A young man with dark hair and even darker eyes walked out from the kitchen, one of my favorite protein bars half-eaten in his hand. He and Aithan did that guy thing where they grabbed hands and then pulled each other in before slapping each other on the back. Then he turned to beam at me. "Look who grew up today! Everleigh's a *big* girl now!"

"Hi, Jamie," I said wryly.

"What is he?" Julia whispered.

"He's a chupacabra shifter," I said as Jamie tried to engage Aithan in a mock fight.

"Wait... You mean, like, the Latin American monster?" she hissed.

"They're rare," I murmured back. "He's an orphan. To his knowledge, everyone else in his family died years ago. He was raised by a childless werewolf couple and has been Aithan's best friend since their first year of college."

Honestly, I'd never been able to see what it was that made them such good friends. Aithan was cool and collected, and Jamie was a goofball with confidence so inflated it could barely fit through the front door. But for whatever reason, their friendship was tight.

"You guys are back." A fourth man walked in. This guy was bigger than both Aithan and Jamie, his frame probably twice the size of mine, and he had unusually thick hair on his arms and legs. I wondered if Julia would guess that he was a werewolf. But his expression was as clear and kind as it ever was, which was probably why Julia almost started giggling like she was thirteen again when he stopped and smiled at us. "Is that Julia Mayburn I see?"

"H-hi, Aaron," Julia stuttered. "You... remember me?' Her voice squeaked at the end.

Aaron chuckled softly as Aithan greeted him as well. "Of course. Everyone at school knew where one of you was, the other was sure to show up eventually."

Julia giggled nervously again. I was about to drag her up to my room to cool off when an elf woman in her fifties appeared at the kitchen door with a wooden spoon and wearing my mother's apron. This time, it was my turn to shriek.

"Miss Lillian!" I ran and threw my arms around her neck, closing my eyes so I could drink in her motherly affection as she hugged me tightly. I'd only seen her two days before, but Miss Lillian's warm countenance suddenly made today's situation seem just a little less awful. Both with her presence and her fantastic hugs.

"I came as soon as I heard they were recalling members of the group," she whispered in my ear before pressing a kiss against my head. "Oh, hello, Julia, dear! It's so nice to see you again so soon."

"Hi, Miss Lillian," Julia said with a nervous smile. But I could tell she was glad to see the older woman, too.

"Oh, look," called a familiar monotone voice. "The whole gang's arrived." Soo Min appeared behind Miss Lillian, her shiny, dark hair with its signature streak of pink pulled up in a messy bun.

She pursed her lips at Julia before turning to me. "Why am I not surprised?"

"Soo Min?" Julia said, taking a hesitant step closer. Then she looked at me, her eyes wide. "So... just how many of your friends are actually human?" She looked around. "Because that number seems to be rapidly shrinking."

"We'll explain at supper, dear," Miss Lillian said kindly. I sent her a grateful look. Bringing my human best friend back home with me as a pet to meet all my parents' supernatural allies had *not* been on my agenda for the day. But Miss Lillian, to her credit, acted as though nothing was amiss, waving us off to get ready and promising that dinner would be done soon.

Aithan had already put Julia's bags in my room by the time we made it upstairs. I, for one, couldn't wait to get changed. Maybe if I put on clean clothes, the royal disaster this day had turned into would end up in the dirty laundry hamper with my socks. As soon as we were in my room, however, Julia locked the door and leaned back against it, arms crossed, to face me.

"So let me get this straight," Julia said, her expression not happy. "You're a wizard."

I winced. "I have my own doubts, but that's what I'm told."

"Aithan's an elf," she continued, counting on her fingers. "The church guy–"

"Christian?" I supplied.

"Yeah, him. He's a phoenix?"

"Yes. And he works as a private firearms instructor. Don't ever mishandle a gun in front of him, or you'll find yourself out on a shooting range for a three hour lecture." I grimaced. "Ask me how I know."

"Noted. And Jamie's a... a–"

"Chupacabra shifter," I finished for her.

She shivered before going on. "And Aaron..." Her annoyance flickered slightly. "What's Aaron?"

I smirked. Aaron had been in the same grade as Aithan, and Julia had been rather in awe of him since she'd met him our freshman year. But then again, *everyone* had been in awe of Aaron until he graduated. "Aaron is a werewolf."

She blinked at me. "Um... oh."

"But he's a good one!" I hurried to add. "Everything you liked in him is the same! Just... bigger. Because that's what werewolves really are. Just... more of their human selves." And furry. They had so. Much. Fur. But I wasn't about to add that now.

She nodded slowly, then shook her head as if to clear it. "Okay, moving on. Wait... What are Miss Lillian and Soo Min doing here?"

"Remember?" I said. "Soo Min is fae. That's why I wanted you to go to her. She and her father could have used a memory charm to wipe your memory of the fight." I sighed. "Then we would have been spared this entire mess. But... We can't change that now. So to answer your question, Miss Lillian is an elf. She's one of Aithan's cousins."

"And... will there be any vampires that pop out at me tonight?" She eyed me warily. "Because I'm not in the mood to be someone's dinner."

I paused to think. My parents probably had more contacts than I knew about. They'd spent years building them during their time as detectives. There were several names and faces I thought about that might show up. But only one vampire came to mind.

"Dorian from forensics?" I shrugged. "But you've known him a long time."

She gaped at me. "Wait. Dorian is a– No, wait." She wrinkled her nose. "Now that I think about it, that actually checks out."

"I know it's a lot," I said in a rush. "And I know they're.. a lot. But you're going to be way safer here than you ever were back in your apartment. And now that you're technically... technically under my protection, you don't have to worry about any more fae trying to take advantage of you. Dorian will watch your back—and your neck, and Aithan, Miss Lillian, Aaron, Christian, and even Jamie would die before letting anything touch you or me." I paused. "Does that help?" I wondered if I ought to add Soo Min's name, but as I wasn't entirely sure, I just let her be.

But Julia wasn't looking at me. Instead, she slowly wandered over to my bedroom window and stared out at the lights of the city in the distance. Trying to swallow my guilt, I followed her and put my arm around her shoulder.

"I just... I don't know how to take this, Everleigh," she said quietly.

I thought back to the dozens of magic colors in my uncle's ancient contraption and cleared my throat. "Me neither."

"Girls!" Miss Lillian called from downstairs. "Dinner's ready!"

Taking a deep breath, I stood and forced a smile as I held my hand out to my friend. "Everything will seem better on a full stomach. And believe me. Miss Lillian's cooking is *exactly* what you want in your stomach."

Julia pursed her lips for a long moment as she stared at my hand. Whether it was my promise of something better, or the cheesy aroma of whatever Miss Lillian was cooking wafting up from downstairs, I don't know. But after another moment of hesitation, she took my hand, and I gave her a hug as we made our way to the door. Just before I opened it, however, I stopped.

"Just promise me this. If Soo Min makes you something to eat or drink, don't taste it until I or someone else does first."

She stared at me. "But I thought Soo Min–"

"Not a sip or a bite," I repeated with a wry smile, "until I've had it first."

"All right, everyone, find a seat," Miss Lillian was saying as everyone crowded around the dining room table. "Jamie, don't you dare sneak a bite until Aithan has said the blessing. I'm watching you. And don't think I won't put an itching curse on your hand again if you disobey me!"

I smiled back at Julia as we took our seats, making sure we were all the way across the table from Soo Min. But Julia only looked lost and small again as she took the seat I offered her. As I sat, I sighed. This was going to be a long night. But maybe Julia's presence would be helpful after all. Worrying about her kept me from driving myself crazy with my own anxiety.

Anxiety over the truth I wasn't sure I was ready or able to handle.

Aithan, who was sitting at the head of the table, across from Miss Lillian, prayed for the food as she had asked him to. Then he looked around the table.

"I want to thank everyone for coming tonight on such short notice. And for remaining here for the time being. I don't know what you were told, but here's what we know. Everleigh began sensing a supernatural following her around the university campus last week."

Last decade felt more like it.

"After she told her parents two days ago, they contacted me to keep an eye on her while they were away from her. Then they apparently requested time off work." He looked at Miss Lillian. "Is that correct?"

Miss Lillian nodded. "They came to me first thing yesterday morning and requested immediate emergency time off work—as did your parents. Then they left after that." She frowned. "I wish I'd thought to ask what was wrong."

"You wouldn't have been able to," Aaron said kindly. "Not at the station in front of everyone else."

Miss Lillian nodded again, but she still looked troubled.

"I escorted Everleigh to school yesterday and today," Aithan continued. "While there this afternoon, we were attacked on campus in broad daylight by a group of reckless, misfit fighters. They were unskilled, but surprisingly—"

"Wait." Jamie held up a hand. "Were they, like... crazy strong?"

Aithan stared at him. "Yes, they were. Why?"

Jamie frowned. "Something about that reminds me of something else that happened last week. But I'll have to think on it. Keep going."

"Anyway," Aithan continued, "I was able to send Everleigh to Finn's bookshop before the fight heated up. Unfortunately, she had a well-intentioned human stowaway. Which, through a weird series of events, led to her best friend, Julia, becoming her pet."

All eyes were suddenly on me and Julia. Julia was nearly as white as a vampire's victim, and I wanted to melt into a puddle on the ground. But Soo Min only snorted. When everyone turned to look at her, she held her hands up.

"What? They've been joined at the hip for forever. It was bound to happen sooner or later. Might as well be joined for life."

"For... *life?*" Julia echoed, her lips trembling.

I sent Soo Min a dirty look before Aithan rolled his eyes and continued.

"Thanks to Finn's dedication and hard work, Everleigh was finally able to figure out what she is and why her parents have basically recruited a small army to protect her."

I felt my face burn as everyone looked at me again. Was it really so hard to think I might not know? I mean, good grief! The stinking high king of the elves made a royal edict to prevent me from learning about my magic. I stared down at the lasagna Miss Lillian had made, my appetite suddenly gone.

"And—hold that thought." Aithan pulled his phone from his pocket and frowned down at it before his furrowed brow cleared. "I've just received word from my brother that both my parents and Everleigh's are safe and sound." He met my gaze. "They're okay."

I closed my eyes and said a prayer of thanks as the entire table breathed an audible sigh of relief. Then everyone started talking at once, asking questions and suggesting theories, until Aithan held his hand up for silence.

"Unfortunately, they won't be available to help us prepare or train Everleigh for a while. It seems my grandfather was concerned about their safety. So he had them brought back to the courts and confined there for the time being."

I stared at him. "So... they took my parents," I said slowly. "But not me?"

The whole table grew silent. Miss Lillian's eyes were full of sympathy, as were Aaron's and Christian's. Even Jamie looked down at his hands.

"Are we shocked?" Soo Min asked in a bored voice.

"Soo Min!" Miss Lillian scolded her, but Soo Min just shrugged.

"Think about it. They wouldn't need to fetch Alexander. He's already working for the king. They don't really *need* Aithan. He's the spare, and they probably knew he wouldn't come anyway, so why bother?"

"But the Clarksons aren't related to the Nomoses," Jamie pointed out.

Soo Min rolled her eyes. "No, but everyone knows Prince Nikos's parents are out of the country. Their lines are allies, so King Kostas probably took them in for 'protection' as a political favor." She looked at me. "And no offense, Everleigh, but they have no idea you're a wizard. To them, you're just the useless mixed race offspring who can't benefit the Nomos throne."

"Soo Min, that's enough!" Miss Lillian snapped.

I had the sudden urge to throw up. But I only shook my head. "No... she's right." I gave my protectors a sour smile. "I've never so much as received a birthday gift from any of my grandparents. As far as they know, I'm as bad at magic as I've ever been. It's... better this way." I finished with a shrug and an attempt at a smile. "I'm here, and... and you can teach me whatever you want."

To my immense relief, the resounding silence that followed my lame speech was broken by Christian's thoughtful question.

"Do we have an idea whether or not Everleigh's attackers are in any way connected to any major courts?"

"We don't know anything for sure," Aithan said. "I wondered that myself, but the attackers they sent were definitely untrained, and they were all of different races, which would be out of character for my grandfather. None of the courts that I'm aware of would use a motley bunch like this."

"Wait." I pulled the broken phone out of my pocket and held it up. "You found this at the fight scene after they left. And it has a little shape engraved on it." I tried to turn the phone in the light so everyone could see. "It's a key...with an infinity symbol on the end."

"I've seen that!" Jamie pointed excitedly, spilling Soo Min's cup all over her lap. She muttered at him while Miss Lillian helped her clean it up with a charm, but Jamie was too excited to notice. "That's what I was trying to remember! I saw a guy hanging around the car shop a few weeks ago with that key tattooed on his arm! He said he was recruiting! He tried to get me to join, but I told him he sounded crazy."

"Did he say what the group was called or what they wanted?" Christian asked.

"No. He just kept saying it was something that would make everyone stronger. Whatever that means."

"Stronger," said a low British voice from behind me, "and rife with anarchy."

Everyone turned to see the speaker. When I did, I felt myself exhale slightly, glad he'd showed up after all.

"Hi, Dorian," I said.

Dorian pulled up a chair beside Miss Lillian. "Your Highness," he said, giving me a nod. His gaze seemed to catch on Julia and her mark for a moment before he turned back to Aithan. "Your parents didn't have time to tell you what they'd uncovered only recently, but they gave me permission to share, should something happen to them. Which, in a way, seems to be the case."

"So you know who attacked Everleigh?" Christian asked.

"Not exactly," Dorian said slowly. "But I am aware that in recent weeks, the courts have been getting nervous about something. Portal records show a higher number of travelers coming into the city than usual, and it seems most of those coming in are members of the lower courts and their nobles."

"But why?" Aaron asked. "And which courts?"

Dorian hesitated. "All of them," he finally said.

Everyone in the room except for Julia stared.

I was the one to break the silence this time. "*All* of the courts have been calling in their members?"

Dorian gave me a solemn nod. "Those who can. Which had led your parents to believe something was amiss. Some sort of threat that the higher courts aren't sure they can handle." He paused. "There's even talk that a dragon marshal has arrived."

The dining room went perfectly quiet again. I traced the underside of the wooden table with my fingertips again and again to ground myself in the moment. This couldn't be real. It had to be a dream. One big, bad dream. Any moment now, I would wake up as the pathetic magic-user I had always been. My parents would be downstairs drinking coffee, and I would waltz off to school with my friends.

"I'm... confused," Julia finally said in a small voice.

"About what, dear?" Miss Lillian said gently. "You've had a lot thrown at you in one night."

"Everleigh told me that there are a few elven courts and some fae courts. But when you say *all* of the courts, how many exactly do you mean?"

"There are dozens of elven courts all over the world," I said. "And just as many fae courts. Maybe even more. We only keep track of the Seelie courts, which are those of the light fae. The dark fae–Unseelie courts–tend to hide in mountains and forests the way they did hundreds of years ago."

"And we prefer to *keep* them that way," Soo Min muttered into her tea.

"But there are other kinds of courts, too," Christian said. "Not as official in scope as the elves or the fae. But each race has its own method of governance–or some kind of pecking order at the very least. The werewolves have alphas and betas in each pack, but some packs are stronger than others. The strongest packs' alphas represent the werewolves to the rest of the races as a whole. Likewise, the vampires, the phoenixes, even the brownies have individualized hierarchies. All the other races have similar structures." He politely cut a piece of his lasagna with his fork as he spoke. "The elves are the strongest of all races, challenged only possibly by the dragon shifters. But there are so few dragons that they keep their whereabouts mostly hidden."

"What's important right now, though," Soo Min interrupted, "is that while the courts might not have seen Everleigh as important enough to take today, there's a good chance they will come for her soon. She's still technically royalty. And they won't want any potential vulnerabilities out in the open."

A vulnerability. That was a good description for how I currently felt.

"The good news," Miss Lillian said firmly as she stood to collect the empty plates, "is that they haven't come yet. Which means we still have time to train Everleigh the best we can."

"Actually," Aithan said, "we have more than time. My parents have been in contact with another wizard for a while."

Everyone stared at him as though he'd spoken a new language.

"There's another wizard?" I breathed. "I mean, one that's still alive?"

"If he's not, that's an even bigger problem," Aithan said wryly. "Because I'm going to the airport tomorrow to pick him up and bring him back here. He charged a substantial amount to come train you, and I'm guessing he'll want even more when he's done." He fixed me with a hard stare. "Which means your job is to listen and learn as fast as you can before he out-prices us all."

"Yeah, got it." I licked my lips. "No pressure."

But Aithan wasn't done. "No, I'm serious, Everleigh. No more of this 'I'm human,' stuff. The whole point of our parents giving everything up and recruiting all these friends and supporters was to keep you out of the courts' greedy hands until your powers were honed and you were ready to defend yourself when they come knocking."

"The question," Dorian said calmly, "was never whether you would be discovered–but when."

"Which means it's time to go to bed," Miss Lillian said, returning from the kitchen. "Jamie, you're going to help me clean the table. Soo Min, I need your help with washing dishes. Aithan, you and the others check the perimeter. And you two," she whirled on me and Julia, "will go to bed. You've both had a big day, and you need to be well-rested in the morning."

Jamie began protesting, saying he wanted to go on patrol, but all he received for his troubles was a smack with Miss Lillian's wooden spoon. Everyone else got up and began talking quietly amongst themselves. Unbelievably, there was a potent feeling of excitement suddenly palpable in the air. But I didn't share that same enthusiasm as Julia and I turned slowly and started walking up the stairs.

Before we got halfway up, however, there was a knock at the door, which was answered by Aithan.

"Yes?" he asked coldly as Julia and I peered down over the banister. I couldn't see who was standing outside the door, but as soon as the person on the other side spoke, Julia and I turned to one another in horror.

"Oh. It's you," said Georgie, not at all sounding pleased. "Do you... live here now?"

"I'm a friend of the family," Aithan said, crossing his arms over his chest. "The Clarksons have kindly made mine an open door invitation."

"Um... okay. Uh, look. Julia left her notebook in economics today, and since she wasn't at her house–"

"You assumed she'd be here," Aithan finished. "That's quite a drive, seeing as we're all the way across town from the university."

There was a pause. When Georgie spoke again, his polite tone was gone. "Okay, fine. I wanted to see if she was okay. Both Everleigh and Julia have been ignoring their phones today. And now that you're here... This whole thing is just off. And I want to make sure they're okay!"

I dragged Julia back down with me before Georgie began to get louder. The last thing we needed was more attention from the neighbors than we'd probably already attracted.

"Hey, Georgie," I said, a forced smile on my face as I ducked around Aithan. "Thanks for checking on us."

"Yeah." Julia's smile looked faker than plastic surgery, but at least she was trying. "And thanks for my notebook!"

"What's going on here?" Georgie asked, trying to see past Aithan into the house. "You guys have been really distant these last two days." He sent Aithan an annoyed look and lowered his voice. "Does this have anything to do with the stalker?"

"Oh, just a family-friend get-together." I waved my hand casually over my shoulder. "And my parents asked Aithan to hang around more until we get the whole stalker thing resolved. With them being detectives and all, they wanted to handle it themselves."

Which was true. I was sure of it. And they would have... if the supernatural courts hadn't chosen to get involved.

"So. A get-together, huh? Like a party?"

I wanted to groan at the hopeful look on Georgie's thin face.

"More for my parents than me," I said with a shrug. Then I yawned, which wasn't hard to do. "But Julia and I were just getting ready to go to bed."

"Yeah," Julia said, yawning much less believably as well. "Thanks for the notebook. I really appreciate it."

Instead of leaving, however, Georgie kept trying to see inside. "Hey, is that Soo Min?" he asked. But I was already shutting the door.

"Night, Georgie. We'll text you later."

Once the door was locked, and Aithan used the driveway camera to make sure he was really gone, I shook my head and started back upstairs.

"You sure you want to send him away?" Soo Min snickered as we walked by. "Two pets would be even more exciting than one."

Julia turned and looked at her with an expression of contempt, but I just waved her off.

"I can think of lots of exciting things, Soo Min. Like how the courts might be really excited to hear that you put magic in your bubble tea purchased by humans–"

"I do not!" she hissed. But she still glanced around to see who might have heard.

I turned and grinned at her. "Then good night."

When we got to my room, we changed into our pajamas in silence, speaking only to thank Miss Lillian when she brought up two steaming cups of tea.

"To help you sleep," she said softly before kissing the tops of our heads and then turning out my light. She was treating us like we were five, but after the day we'd had, I was more than ready to accept it.

After she left, we were quiet for a long time. In my head, the day continued to play back over and over, despite me wishing I could just forget it all.

I didn't realize I was shaking until Julia, who had been lying still on the cot beside my bed, reached out and took my hand. And though I had no reason–or right–to expect comfort from her, I squeezed back and drew strength from it.

"I know I shouldn't," I finally whispered. "And... I'm more sorry than I can say. But Julia?"

"Yeah?" she whispered back.

"I'm glad you're here with me."

She waited so long to reply that I thought maybe she'd gone to sleep. Until, just before the tea sent me into unconsciousness, I heard a nearly inaudible, "Me, too."

Then, breathing easier, I fell asleep.

Chapter Fourteen

Aithan

I CHECKED my phone again as I leaned against one of the giant support columns in the airport baggage claim. This guy's plane had arrived on time, but for some reason, he was somehow twenty-five minutes late coming to pick up his stuff. Annoyed, I took a sip of my coffee, only to realize it was empty.

The bitterness of what had been my drink now matched my mood. Because no matter whether I wanted to or not, I saw Everleigh's defeated, despondent expression over and over again in my head.

Oh, she'd done a good enough job that morning of waking up with a bounce in her step and a smile on her face. And she'd probably fooled most of the others, chatting up a storm as she helped Miss Lillian navigate her way around the kitchen, and doing her best to make everyone feel comfortable. She'd even managed to get off a few snarky comments that were ornery enough to shake Jamie's perfect self-confidence.

Not that I expected anything less. As a kid, Everleigh's spunk and vivacity had drawn people to her. They were a part of who she was—the indomitable spirit that refused to be quenched, even when the supernatural world turned its back on her. In fact, their betrayals had made her more determined than ever to thrive.

And thrive she had.

But this morning when she'd thought no one was looking, her shoulders had slumped, and she'd closed her eyes, breathing in and out slowly as though the world lay on her shoulders.

In a way, it did. The girl who was supposed to be the hero had spent her entire childhood thinking she was worthless and unwanted. And I wasn't sure how this perception would play out.

A steaming cup of coffee was shoved into my hands, and I looked up to see a face I hadn't glimpsed in two years carefully studying me.

It took everything in me not to throw myself at my big brother as he casually leaned against the column beside me and sipped his own cup of airport tea. I knew better, though. Just because he'd surfaced to help me address this massive shift didn't mean I could blow his cover.

"You look worried," he said in a low voice, his now thick beard concealing much of his naturally expressive face. He angled his head so that his sunglasses and the brim of his baseball cap completely covered his eyes.

"This guy better be good," I murmured, "considering how much he charged."

"That's not what's worrying you." Alexander stared down at his cup.

How did he know these things? For a moment, I considered lying to him. But then again, he was my big brother. I knew better than that.

"I'm worried about Everleigh," I admitted finally. "She has a lot to take in. And her confidence in her own abilities is in the toilet."

"Everleigh's a sharp girl. She'll be fine." My brother glanced at me. "Just... don't get too close. It'll hurt you both."

"You think I don't know that?" I snapped back but regretted the words as soon as they left my mouth. With a sigh, I tried again.

"I suppose you don't have any change of plans in the near future?" Asking pointed questions was not an option. I might not know much about Alexander's work for my grandfather, but I *was* aware that it was too secretive to risk sharing any specifics.

Alexander swirled his tea around his cup for a moment. "There's... some sort of power shift going on," he finally said. "The larger courts and families are eating up the smaller ones, forcing them to join their numbers. Calling in loyalties and favors that haven't been mentioned in centuries. People are panicking." He met my gaze, his green eyes blazing even through his sunglasses. "Be careful."

I nodded. "Noted."

Alexander looked as though he wanted to say something else, but his phone buzzed. He pulled it out and looked at the notification. "The wizard will be here soon. There was a delay in disembarking."

Then he was gone.

I wanted to run after him, to beg him to stay and not make me do this all on my own. But crying and protesting like a preschooler wouldn't help anyone. So instead, I returned to the bottom of the escalators yet again to wait for the wizard.

My brother was right. A moment later, I could feel the wizard before I saw him. When he finally appeared at the top of the escalator, he was wearing khaki cargo shorts and a garish red Hawaiian shirt over a bright blue t-shirt. The outfit was completed by the big, red, plastic shoes—the kind with holes in them—which were covered by a variety of dirty rubber shoe charms. He sported a graying brown beard and mustache, but it was carelessly trimmed. And just in case his outfit wasn't loud enough, he exuded magic like a frightened octopus leaking ink.

An airport employee followed him, somehow carrying more bags than should have been physically possible. No doubt, the wizard had tapped his magic for that. And it was drawing attention. People stared, gaping, at the young man who was bearing the weight of seven suitcases stacked on top of one another. Even worse, however, was that as soon as the wizard saw me, he began to scowl.

"I assume you're Bradley Langford?" I asked as he came near.

"*Neglected* would be a more fitting name!" the wizard spat in a heavy Carolina accent. "No one to even meet me at the gate! I had to find my own help just getting here!"

I frowned and glanced back at the baggage claim's sixteen carousels. "You mean... you checked *all* of your luggage as carry-ons?"

The wizard growled at me before coming so close I could smell the peanuts on his breath. "Just shout it to the whole world, why don't you?" he hissed. "*Obviously,* I couldn't check my luggage! What if someone went through it?" He turned to the poor airport employee, who was sweating profusely under the weight of the suitcases but had obviously been charmed so he would follow the wizard around blindly. "You. Find me one of those cart thingies. Then take it out to..." He looked back at me. "Where's my limo?"

I sighed and pulled my wallet out. "I'm your ride. And we can find our own luggage cart. Now let him go."

The wizard gaped at me. "You mean you want me to—"

"To stop making a scene," I hissed, glancing around at the growing number of people who were now watching with open curiosity. "We're trying *not* to attract attention here, in case you forgot."

After saying this, I went to retrieve an empty luggage cart, the wizard growing so red in the face I wondered if he might burst a blood vessel. But once I returned and loaded the suitcases onto the cart—having to subtly use a bit of my own magic to shrink them to size—he snapped his fingers, and the young man blinked rapidly before looking around in obvious confusion.

"Thank you," I said to the employee, handing him the folded ten-dollar bill I'd pulled from my wallet, as I could tell the wizard wouldn't be tipping him. "I'll help my friend from here."

The young man still looked confused, but his face lit up when he saw the tip. "Thank you! Happy to help!"

Once we set off for the parking garage, I endured a barrage of questions about where and when my guest would be fed, and how anyone could expect someone to travel on such paltry sustenance as peanuts and pretzels.

"Humans do it," I said wryly as we came to the truck I'd borrowed from Christian. I began loading his suitcases into the back.

"Humans are also unlucky enough to need deodorant," he sniffed. "That doesn't mean I want to use it."

"It wouldn't kill you to try," I murmured as I climbed into the cab.

"*Excuse* me?"

"Nothing." But I grinned to myself as I turned on the truck.

The wizard insisted on being taken to one of the big resort five-star restaurants to be wined and dined the way he'd seen in a commercial—on my dime, of course. But I told him he had to be content with In-N-Out Burger instead. He protested and threatened to leave again until I handed him the bag from the drive-through. Two bites in, and he finally shut up.

He began to get nervous again, however, as we drove farther and farther toward the northeast corner of the city, passing the Air Force base and the Speedway, and finally leaving Las Vegas behind.

"You said I'd be staying in a house with running water and electricity," he said, glancing back at the city behind us. "This looks an awful lot like the desert!"

"It is." I allowed myself a grin as I turned off the main highway onto a side dirt road.

"Okay, then. If I have to spell it out for you, *why* are we in the desert? Ouch! Slow down!"

This road was why I'd borrowed Christian's truck. I grinned again as I took another bump even faster, taking no small amount of pleasure when he hit his funny bone against the door.

"You know that Las Vegas is now the supernatural capital of the world," I said as we neared an opening in the barren desert mountains north of the city. Finally, I had to slow as the road got worse. "There are countless elven strongholds throughout the valley, and even more belonging to the fae, the shifters, and all other supernaturals. Did you think we'd start her training in a hotel?"

"This kid must be on the broad side of stupid if she's so bad we have to hide her in the– Ow!"

I'd stopped so suddenly he'd hit his head on the dashboard. When he sat up, glowering at me as he rubbed his forehead, I glared right back.

"Before we get there, I'm going to make something very clear. In the last twenty-four hours, this girl has lost her parents, learned that she's a wizard, and accidentally had to make her human best friend into her pet. She's been through a lot, and she's doing the best she can. So keep that in mind." I began driving again.

"Everyone loses people eventually," the wizard sulked. "Might as well get used to it now."

Chapter Fifteen

Everleigh

"Isn't this awesome?" Jamie beamed as he punched my arm just a little too hard. We were all in my garage, finally squeezed into the backseat of Miss Lillian's tiny sedan.

I'm pretty sure the man forgot he was a chupacabra shifter on an hourly basis, and that the people around him were not. But then again, he had the body of a mastiff with the personality of a Labrador retriever. I suppose he didn't know anything else. "Maybe you'll get good enough to beat Aithan in a face-off!" he continued, his dark eyes dancing. "I'd pay to see that."

"Something I'm assuming you've been failing to do?" Soo Min called from the front seat.

Jamie shrugged. "Every man's gotta have his goals."

"I have words for his goals," Julia muttered under her breath as she pressed herself against the door on my other side, huddling over her to-go tumbler of coffee like a wolf guarding her bone.

I gave my friend an apologetic grimace. Miss Lillian—with good intentions—had added a good dose of sleeping magic to our tea last night. And while it had done its job, putting us to sleep quickly so we could wake up rested for the day, waking Julia up that morning had not been a fun task. Not only had I spent half an hour convincing her that yesterday had actually happened, but Julia wasn't a morning person to begin with. Convincing her to get out of bed had required the promise of an extra large latte when the wizard's experiments were through.

"I'll get you extra whipped cream," I whispered as she continued to grumble at the window.

"I still don't get it, Everleigh," Jamie said as Miss Lillian finally buckled herself into the driver's seat. "You have, like... the coolest magic ever. And you don't seem excited about today. What gives?"

Soo Min turned around to face him again. "Miss Everleigh Clarkson doesn't *use* magic. Remember?"

At that moment, Christian walked out of the house and motioned for Miss Lillian to roll down her window.

"Everleigh," he said when it was down, "do you have your concealed carry permit?"

"My dad made me get it as soon as I turned twenty-one," I told him.

His face broke into a grin. "Awesome. And are you carrying now?"

I held up my backpack, and his grin somehow widened. It was the most I'd seen him smile in the two years I'd known him. Then he turned to Miss Lillian.

"The plan is to meet Aithan and the wizard at the designated place. He has my truck, so Aaron is taking me and Dorian in his. If you follow us, we should all arrive in about thirty minutes. Sound good?"

"Lead the way," Miss Lillian said with a smile. Then she turned to all of us and held up a lunchbox. "I brought snacks!"

The drive wasn't particularly enjoyable, as I was cramped between Jamie and Julia. Julia did her best to curl up against the door, but consistent with his Labrador personality, Jamie seemed to forget for most of the ride that he was over six-foot-three, and he had a bad habit of trying to straighten his legs whenever he got excited.

As we drove, I closed my eyes and did my best to prepare for whatever was about to happen. According to Aithan, the wizard would want to test my abilities. And as I wasn't used to accessing my magic on purpose, nor did I seem capable of any sort of precision, it was best to test my abilities away from the general public. So to the desert mountains north of the city we went.

Miss Lillian promised that once I had proper instruction, I would be just fine. In fact, she was more than sure I would excel. Likewise, Christian and Aaron had given me kind words that morning, and Jamie had declared at least twice that he couldn't wait to see me fight Aithan as soon as my magic was "up and revving." Even Julia had mumbled some sort of awkward encouragement. But with each bit of encouragement and every kind word I received, the stone of anxiety sitting in the pit of my stomach just felt heavier.

I didn't realize I'd begun to doze off until the car stopped, and Jamie's jubilant exclamations made me startle in my seat.

"We're here, wizard!" he cried, giving me a friendly shake that felt like it jostled my brain around in my skull. "Time to make things go BOOM!"

I crawled out after him to see that Aithan and the others had already arrived. A disgruntled-looking man in really... *really* bright clothes stood beside Christian's truck, glowering at everyone and everything. When his gaze met mine, his eyes narrowed, and my heart sank.

"The boundaries are all up," Christian was telling Aithan. "Aaron's double-checking them now. We should be able to stay hidden from all aircraft and radar for at least two or three hours, as well as any hikers who choose to get nosy."

"Good." Aithan nodded. "If you could triple-check them, though, that would be great."

Christian nodded once before his eyes took on the same orange glow they'd held the night before. Julia–who was standing behind me–gasped as wings of fire unfurled behind him, and he took off into the sky.

"Everyone," Aithan said, raising his voice. "I'd like to introduce you to Bradley Langford." He gestured at the brightly arrayed man beside him. "Bradley will be our resident wizard for the time being. Bradley, these are the friends responsible for protecting Everleigh. And this," he leaned over and put his hand on the small of my back so he could push me forward, "is Everleigh."

"Hi." I stuck my hand out, not sure what else to do. As I did, I wondered if I would feel a rush of various magics when he shook my hand.

But Bradly only stared at my hand as though it were a dead fish. Then he glanced at Aithan, and when he spoke, he used the strongest southern drawl I'd ever heard. "You said she's never actually used magic?"

Aithan frowned slightly. "She's... always struggled with accessing it. Something her parents think stemmed from–"

"No need to explain." He glanced at me, and I could feel the judgment clouding beneath his thick, surprisingly dark brows. "I'm going to have to start from the top, then. Fantastic." He turned to face me and huffed. "What do you know about wizards? I'm assuming not much."

What was that supposed to mean? I was bad at magic, not stupid.

"I know that wizards have access to all kinds of–" I began, but he interrupted me.

"Well, bless your heart." His voice was acerbic. "The correct answer is that wizards have a *greater capacity* for magic than any other race."

"Wow," Julia muttered into her coffee. "Rude."

"Ignorance is rude." Bradley sniffed. "As I was saying, wizards are different from all other supernaturals in that, yes, they have access to other kinds of magic, but their capacity for magic is far greater than all the others combined. Without this, they wouldn't be able to use more than one kind."

"I have a question." Jamie raised his hand, suddenly looking very much like an overgrown fourth-grader bouncing in his seat.

Bradley scowled at him before glancing at Aithan. "Does my pay cover answering him?"

But Jamie plunged on. "Since you're a wizard, and Aithan is a Nomos, which of you would be more powerful in a fight?"

Bradley shook his head and frowned. "No. No, you're understanding it all wrong. A wizard isn't necessarily stronger than other supernaturals. It simply means he has access to a much larger arsenal of magic." He looked back at me, his gaze suddenly sharp. "But... if a trained elf like the prince here were to fight, Everdee–"

"Everleigh," Julia interrupted.

"The wizard," he huffed, "would most likely have weaker elf magic. You're royal?" He fixed his beady eyes on me.

I nodded. "Minor courts, though. On both sides." My grandparents were all technically kings and queens, but their lines weren't nearly as powerful as others.

"Fine. You're of royal blood, but not Nomos blood. That means that if you were fighting your pretty boyfriend here," he waved dismissively at Aithan, "using only elven magic, you would definitely lose."

I felt my face go bright red. But not having the courage to even glance at Aithan, I kept my eyes glued to Bradley.

"However," he held up an index finger, "if you were to use a combination of elven, fae, vampire, and dragon magic all at the same time, for example, you'd have a much better shot at winning."

"You have *dragon* magic?" Julia squeaked in my ear. "You didn't tell me that!"

"I can hear you, you know." Bradley glared at Julia, who just shrugged and went back to sipping her coffee. "And yes, she could technically use dragon magic. But shifter magic is much harder to access, and it usually takes countless hours of practice to master using all different aspects of it." He turned back to me. "It will take you years, if not decades, to hone your skills, so if you're expecting me to teach them all to you in the next few weeks, you're going to be mighty disappointed. What *you* need to remember is that all magic is about change."

He lifted his hands toward the mountaintops that surrounded us. Above him was projected a transparent image of an atom. "*All* magic," he said again, his voice a little less sour this time, "is about change. Elves change the world around them. Shifters change themselves. Oracles can cut through time just enough to glimpse various versions of it. And vampires... Well, they're interesting in that they *stop* change."

I knew all of this, of course. Every supernatural child did. But I was curious about the fact that he'd left one major magic system out. "What about fae magic?" I asked.

This time, his eyes lit up. "Fae are the most unlike all the others. They change what others *perceive*, rather than the thing itself. So yes, elves can make themselves camouflage into the world around them, but fae can make you *believe* they're invisible." He moved his hands, and the atom image disappeared. Instead, dancing above his palms were the subatomic strings I had told Julia about the day before. They were all pulsing with a particular rhythm, almost as though they were part of a group dance.

"To switch out your magic, you have to use the right rhythm. The strings' rhythm within the quarks of your atoms will determine the type of magic you have access to. The quicker you're able to trade out your strings' rhythm, the faster you can switch between magics. There was one wizard I knew," his eyes went distant, and his voice softened slightly, "who was able to use several magics all at once." Then he blinked a few times and shook his head. "There. Go to your fae friend." He pointed at Soo Min. "Fae girl, stick out your hand and let her touch it."

Soo Min looked for a moment like she was contemplating

murder. But then she rolled her eyes and held her hand out toward me.

"Close your eyes," Bradley ordered. "Focus on finding the rhythm."

I did as he said, and for a moment, I felt nothing. Only panic welling up in my stomach. But then, as my heart began to slow...

Something *was* there after all. It was difficult, and so subtle I nearly missed it. But the longer I focused on the magic humming beneath her skin, the more I could sense the beginnings of what felt like... like a song after all. And the longer I sensed it, the more I began to realize that it had been there all along. I just hadn't known its name.

As I continued to sense Soo Min's magic, I began to feel a spark of something dangerous.

Was it hope?

My whole life, I'd been unable to use *any* magic the way I should have. My parents had tried teaching me, of course, and they'd sent me to tutors and teachers. Nothing, however, had worked.

But now that I knew they weren't allowed to talk directly about my magic, it only made sense that they would have failed. Likewise, I'd never had a magic teacher or tutor who didn't get frustrated with me by the end of the lesson. Then again, I suppose the king's edict would have applied to them, too, even if they hadn't known it at the time. They wouldn't have been able to talk about *my* magic.

Besides, if they hadn't known I was a wizard, it probably hadn't occurred to any of them to talk about different kinds of magics. For all they knew, I was a useless mixed-race supernatural kid who had little potential and wasn't worth the time.

But... What if I had just needed a better teacher? My heart began to beat faster in my chest.

"Now." Bradley's voice broke through my thoughts, and I opened my eyes to see him pointing at Aithan. "Try him."

Aithan looked surprised, but to his credit, he held out his hand toward me, palm up. I closed my eyes and tried not to blush, Bradley's ridiculous reference to Aithan as my "pretty boyfriend" still ringing in my head as I placed my hand on his.

I'd touched Aithan countless times before that day. Half of my childhood had been spent lying in wait to see how well I could tackle him to the ground when he was least expecting it.

The answer was never. I'd never been able to catch him by surprise.

But this was different. There was an immediate sense of warmth that flooded me as my hand touched his. And it had nothing to do with magic.

"Can you feel it?" Bradley asked, his tone impatient.

"Just... just a minute," I said, scrambling to focus my thoughts. And after a moment, I did feel it. I was surprised again, however, once I found his elven rhythm and realized that I knew it already. In fact, I had known it most of my life in the same way I knew my father's and mother's magic. Its pulse was similar to my father's magic, of course, as they were both elves. But Aithan's rhythm was even stronger.

How had I felt this all my life and not made these connections?

"Okay, that's enough canoodling," Bradley snapped. "Not that you'll reach his level anytime soon. But here. Show me now. What's the best you can do?"

"Um, we're not dating," I stammered, red-faced. "And... you mean you want me to do magic? Right here and now?"

"No, I want you to learn the violin," he snorted. "Yes. Obviously, I want you to do magic." He crossed his arms. "You may begin."

I looked stupidly down at my hands. Feeling magic was one thing. I'd done that my whole life, even if I hadn't known all that about strings and rhythm. But *practicing* it was a whole different story. Still, as everyone's eyes were on me, I closed my eyes and reached down inside of myself. Surely there was some sort of rhythm in there. I *did* have magic. I'd used it by accident too many times to count. For so long, though, I'd kept it stuffed down inside, refusing to let it see the light of day. Now I had no idea how to get it back out.

Bradley huffed. "I'm waiting."

Still, no matter how much I tried...

"I can feel it!" I finally cried.

"It's about time!" Bradley muttered. "Now let it out!"

"I... I'm trying." I frowned but kept my eyes squeezed shut. "It's like... It feels like there's something like... like plastic wrap all around it."

"Well, that's dumber than buying all the eggs and milk before a hurricane," Bradley said. "This time, you're going to take *my* hand. Then try again."

But just as I heard him come near, I also heard the distinct sound of wings on the breeze. I opened my eyes in time to see Christian landing, his wings of fire folding neatly back into his shoulder blades. "We have company," he said.

As he spoke, I could feel many different kinds of magic closing in on us, though I couldn't tell what kinds. And as it often did when I was surprised, a heavy dose of power leaked out from behind whatever invisible barrier was inside of me. A miniature bolt of lightning leaped from my hands and aimed at the closest person to me, which happened to be Bradley. He let out a startled cry as supernaturals–winged and those they carried–filled the sky.

Chapter Sixteen

Everleigh

I TRIED to count the intruders as they descended upon us, but there were too many. And not only were they everywhere, but those without wings were being carried by those who had them. I spotted at least three fae, an elf, three shifters, an ogre, a troll, and a pegasus and another fae struggling to carry a giant before I lost track.

"How did they find us?" Soo Min hissed. "I thought our glamour was secure!"

"No clue!" Aithan snapped. "Everyone, positions around Everleigh!"

Two seconds later, Julia and I were surrounded by my friends. Eyes wide, Julia clutched her stun gun as I racked my pistol.

A fae with vivid violet wings, hair, and eyes landed directly in front of Aithan. These visitors were apparently under the assumption that they didn't need to even try looking like humans way back in the canyon. Not a single one that I could see appeared to be wearing a glamour stone.

As I realized this, however, I also realized that the violet fairy was the same one we'd encountered at my school. But I'd been wrong about her. Back then, I'd believed she wasn't even trying to blend in. But now I could see that she had, apparently, been trying to hold a glamour of some kind back on campus, because her colors were now twice as bright as the first time I'd seen her.

Which meant she either had a cheap glamour stone, or she must be really, really bad at holding a glamour of her own.

"We don't have to fight," she continued, holding up her hands in a gesture of innocence. "We're on the same side."

"That depends on what you want," Aithan said warily. As he spoke, I could feel his magic building in his hands. He was so dang *strong*. "So tell me," he continued in an even voice, "what do you want?"

"Funny question, considering you wouldn't be way out in this canyon, all wrapped up in heavy glamours unless you wanted to escape the courts' notice." The fae smirked. "But just so you know, we're not interested in catching the courts' attention either." She paused. "Yet."

"That still doesn't tell us what you want," Aithan said.

"We want to see her." The fae pointed at me. "Just to talk. Nothing more."

Fear had warred with frustration inside me since our visitors had appeared in the sky. But as she said these words, my anger outstripped them both.

"I suppose you just wanted to *talk* yesterday too?" I snapped, tightening my grip on my pistol. "Sending a squad of unskilled kidnappers is a really interesting way to ask."

The fae's smile faltered slightly before appearing again. "No offense, Miss Clarkson, but you're a bit on the skittish side. I've been trying to talk with you for a week now, and all you've done is run away."

Was she flipping serious?

"Stalking," I hissed, "is *not* trying to talk to someone! Nor is attacking me in broad daylight at my school!"

"A bit of forthrightness does amazing things for trust," Aithan said cooly. "And I think Miss Clarkson has made herself clear.

Now," he waved vaguely at the desert canyon floor. "If you wish to stay here and *talk*, we would all love to hear you." As he moved his hand in the lazy circle, I felt a wave of magic roll over me. Oh, he was good. Layering a magical shield without even seeming to try. "Especially," he said carefully, "if we're all on the same team."

The fae woman, who looked to be in her mid-to-late twenties, stared at him for a long moment, and then at me.

"You won't speak with us alone, then? This is your choice?"

I narrowed my eyes at her. "You heard him."

The fae scratched her head and then smiled. "Well, we tried."

A massive ball of elf magic exploded behind us. The hit would have been devastating, and probably would have killed several of my friends, if Aithan hadn't been projecting his invisible barrier around us, the one he'd been silently building as he distracted the fae with talk.

The man might drive me crazy, but he was insanely good at magic.

"I can't maintain this barrier for long," he called in a low voice, just loud enough for us to hear, "which means Soo Min and Aaron are going to take the fae. Jamie, you've got the elf. Lillian and Dorian, you have the vampires. Christian takes the giant from above." Then he looked at Bradley. "Wizard, your job is to protect Everleigh and Julia at all costs."

"What?" Bradley sputtered. "I came here to teach! Not to fight!"

"And if you want to get paid, you'll need *live* employers to do it," Aithan snapped.

"What about the others?" Soo Min asked, glancing back at me uneasily. More supernaturals had continued to land in the canyon while Aithan and the fae had talked.

Aithan gave her a predatory smile. "They're mine."

I felt it the moment Aithan brought down his magical barrier. My would-be-kidnappers must have too, because they began pouring in like a wave from every side, outnumbering us now at least two to one.

But it was quickly obvious that while there were more of them, these fighters—like the ones from yesterday—were neither well-trained nor disciplined. They rushed in without a second thought, seeming secure in their numbers rather than their skill.

Unfortunately for them, Aithan not only had more skilled team members, he'd chosen to divide them up well. Soo Min and Aaron immediately set to work on the three fae, who appeared to be identical triplets. They all had matching blue wings, hair, and eyes, which made telling them apart difficult. Or was it just one fae projecting two images of herself? I couldn't tell.

Either way, Soo Min took their attack head-on. She didn't strive to win, but neither did she lose. Instead, she made just enough trouble to keep them occupied as Aaron, already in his werewolf form, faded back so he could make a wide circle around the trio.

The fae didn't seem to think she might do anything else but give them her all. So they stayed focused directly on her, tossing alternating charms embedded in clay marbles at Soo Min, no doubt trying to hit her with a blinding or paralyzing curse.

But Soo Min was as graceful as she was sarcastic. Not only did she evade the first several attacks by her fae opponents, she managed to deliver her own freezing charm directly to one via a hard slap across the face.

The second sister screamed as the first went down, and she crouched to spring at Soo Min, her face twisted with rage. Before she could attack, however, a large wolf leaped in from behind, knocking her down with a snarl, opening his jaws just enough to place them lightly over the back of the fae's neck.

The third fae began to raise her hands, obviously holding more marble charms. But Soo Min, her own arms outstretched to sustain an arc of magic, loudly clucked her tongue.

"I wouldn't do that if you want your sister to live. Or remember her name in the morning."

"I thought fae could only persuade," Julia whispered loudly in my ear. Her eyes were locked on the screaming fae, who was still on the ground, cowering beneath Aaron's jaws. "I didn't think they could paralyze them!"

"They do persuade them," I replied, stretching my fingers as I spoke, trying to find the magic within them. "They forcefully persuade their victims that they're incapable of moving. It takes a really, really strong supernatural not to be convinced."

Meanwhile, Jamie and the elf were moving around one another so fast they were nearly a single blur. The elf continued to loose what was probably paralyzing or pain-inducing magic at Jamie. But Jamie, in his chupacabra form, evaded every dart the elf threw at him, even managing to get in a bite here and there that made the elf cry out in rage.

Lillian and Dorian were facing off against two vampires, both of whom had their eyes locked on Lillian and were licking their fangs hungrily, eager to deliver their poisonous bites directly into her elven blood, no doubt.

Julia had grabbed my arm and was now squeezing so it hurt. Whether it was from worrying for Lillian and Dorian, or for herself, I wasn't sure. But she needn't have worried.

Lillian sent out six of her own paralyzing darts, forcing the vampires into a slight retreat. Which was exactly the distraction Dorian needed. Less than a second later, he seemed to materialize behind them, his hands on both of their necks, squeezing until their eyes looked like they were about to pop.

Christian was tormenting the giant, meanwhile, making him roar in frustration as he flew low enough to land on the giant's shoulders and set his shirt on fire before flying up out of reach again, obviously trying to lure him away from the larger group where he could do the most damage.

Unfortunately, Christian was so busy with the giant that he didn't see the Pegasus who had risen into the air behind him.

The Pegasus would have kicked him solidly in the back of the skull if I hadn't raised my pistol and let off three rounds in the Pegasus's direction. I knew I wouldn't hit him, of course. He was moving too erratically for me to do much damage with just a pistol. But the sound of the bullets whizzing past his head were enough to pull Christian's attention up so he could see his new attacker as well.

Then there was Aithan. And though I'd seen him spar before, I'd never seen him fight like this.

Somehow, he'd already managed to wrangle two shifters, a troll, and a small ogre into submission, wrapping a magically conjured magic suppressant around their wrists like handcuffs on a rope. And each enemy he subdued was simply added to the line of prisoners.

Unfortunately, each new bit of magic he had to sustain drained his magic that much more. His muscles were already straining and I could see the stress on his face as he faced each new opponent who tried to get through him to me.

"Bradley!" I shouted over the sound of battle, but Bradley was now facing off with a werewolf, whom he had temporarily blinded as it kept trying to bite him.

"What is wrong with them?" he shouted over his shoulder at Aithan. "They should have given up by now!"

"I told you!" Aithan called back, though his words were more grunts than speech. "They're stronger than they should be!"

And it was true, just as it had been yesterday. My friends had done a good job of keeping our enemies away from me, but they weren't subdued. Not yet. There were just too many.

"Young lady!" Bradley shouted as the werewolf took another blind swipe at his face. "It would be a great help if you could find just a *little* magic to share with us!"

"I'm trying!" I cried. And I was. From the start of the battle, I'd been flexing my muscles until they hurt, trying to dredge up any magic that would appear, pausing only to aim my gun at this or that kidnapper to distract them from my friends. Heck, I'd suffer one of my own poorly placed lightning bolts right now if it meant helping Aithan as he struggled to reign in a particularly vicious pixie that seemed determined to bite him.

But I might as well have been trying to set fire to rain-soaked logs. Every time I felt a sliver of something deep inside of me trying to escape, whatever hole or leak I'd discovered would snap shut again.

The door to my magic, it seemed, had been locked.

Aithan let out a cry of pain as one of his magical bindings snapped, three of his prisoners fighting even harder to get free from the remaining strands.

Come on! I screamed silently in my head. *Find the rhythm. Use it. Let it free!*

But no matter how hard I tried, I could get nothing more dangerous than a sparkler on the Fourth of July, and for no longer than a few seconds.

How do I fix this? I silently prayed.

But then Soo Min let out a scream, and Aithan cursed, and I couldn't stand it anymore. Magical I may be, but my learned humanity was more loyal to me by far. With a sour taste in my mouth, I abandoned my magic and lifted my gun. Then I opened fire at each and every enemy in sight, pausing only to switch magazines each time I ran out of rounds.

Very few of my victims went down. Most of them seemed to have gained some sort of strength to withstand bullets, or were fast enough to escape them, yet another testament to their strange strength. Still, I could feel the fight change tides as I switched to my last full magazine. Enemy after enemy began to flee, and those who had fallen to my human wrath were immediately taken up by their companions and carried back into the sky the way they'd come.

Less than a minute later, we were somehow all alone again. And five minutes later, we were back in the cars, heading for my home.

I should have felt relief as we drove back over the rocky, bumpy dirt road we'd taken to get there. None of my friends had died. I'd met the wizard. We were all safe.

But all I could feel was disappointment. Not in my friends, but in me.

Chapter Seventeen

Everleigh

THE CAR REMAINED silent for the duration of the ride home, with the exception of Lillian muttering protection spells as she drove. The words themselves didn't conjure magic, but many supernaturals used rhymes and rhythms to help keep their minds focused when they had to use magic during times of stress.

Julia reached out and took my hand as we turned back onto the main highway, and I gave her the best smile I could muster. But even her comforting presence did little to quell my angst.

An entire battle had raged around me. And not a single bit of the magic used had been mine. Heck, I couldn't even conjure the self-injurious lightning bolts I seemed to spawn when I was stressed. My magic was getting worse, not better. There was no way on earth I could be a wizard born to save the helpless from some great upheaval to come.

Because if I was, the world was doomed.

The silence lasted until approximately thirty seconds after we got home. Just enough time for Bradley, who had been riding in the car behind Lillian's, to follow us inside.

"You!" he snapped as he stalked in, pointing his finger at me as he fumed. "You are nothing like the girl I was told I would train." He turned to glare at Lillian, who was staring at him, keys still in hand. "There's no way I can train her. I don't care what that oracle or whatever crackpot said to convince you all she's a wizard, I'm done!" He turned to glare at me again. "She didn't even try!"

"I *was* trying!" I retorted, doing my best to keep my voice strong and my tears of frustration at bay.

"Oh, *were* you?" He made a face at me. "Did you really try *really* hard, sweet pea? Did you do your very bestest?"

"Hey!" Julia cried. "Rude much?"

"And just why do you think we hired you?" Lillian asked, her Irish accent more pronounced than usual in her anger. "We told you she needed help!"

"And there's no need to talk to her that way," Jamie growled, a bit of his shifter voice leaking through.

As he spoke, I realized I had the outright desire to hug Jamie. That was a first.

"You might think coddling her will help." Bradley shook his head. "But tell me this, wizard. Is this how you always react when your magic doesn't do as you please? Pretend you're a human instead of a supernatural?"

I wanted to tell him to get lost. I really did. But I couldn't. Because no matter how much I wanted to deny the accusation, he was right.

I did run.

Every.

Single.

Time.

"See?" Bradley waved a hand at me. "This is why I can't teach her. She won't be taught. Someone take me to the airport. I'm leaving."

"You're not going anywhere," Aithan said firmly as he walked in, Dorian on his heels.

"And why not?" Bradley glowered up at him.

"Because we already paid you," Aithan said in that same low voice.

At that moment, Christian and Aaron walked in, too, so deep in conversation that they didn't seem to even notice the tension in the foyer.

"We still don't even know who we're dealing with," Aaron was saying. "But they're sure determined."

"I can answer that," Dorian said grimly. We all turned to him in surprise.

"You can?" Lillian asked, blinking.

Dorian nodded but didn't smile. "I'd had my suspicions before, but after I subdued one of the younger vampires today, I forced him to admit it outright."

"You can *do* that?" Julia squeaked.

"Oh yes, dear," Dorian said with a wry smile. "It's one of our greatest strengths. We can temporarily project our lack of change at a victim if he's weaker than we are. In doing so, we can briefly freeze his inhibitions and get him to admit what he wouldn't before."

Julia's face turned an odd shade of green, but Dorian didn't seem to notice.

"I didn't have nearly as much time as I would have liked to probe his mind. He was ridiculously young to be out on a mission of this magnitude, and whoever sent him is either desperate, foolish, or both. Either way, however, I was able to ascertain that Everleigh's admirers are from a group called Pandora's Key."

The room was silent. Even Bradley looked confused.

"I believe," Dorian continued, "that this is the group the courts have been whispering about, though I'm not sure how many actually know their name. My young friend couldn't tell me how many there are in total, but I gather the group is much larger than we first thought." He paused again. "I did get one more question in before they fled, though."

"What was that?" Jamie asked.

"I asked him what they wanted."

"And his answer?" Aithan asked, his jaw slightly flexed.

Dorian took a deep breath before fixing his eyes on me. "They want the princess. Badly. So badly, it seems, they will start a war just to get her."

"Well, we knew *that*," Soo Min muttered as she tapped away on her phone.

Bradley snorted. "And I can't imagine why."

"And *that* reminds me of one of my own questions," Aithan said, his voice turning cold. "I couldn't help noticing that while we were fighting, you only used fae magic." He took a step closer to the wizard and stared down at him. "Fae magic... and fae magic alone."

"I noticed that, too," Christian said, his own eyes taking on a slightly orange glow. "I also noticed that several other magics would have been far, *far* more useful."

"Why is that?" Aithan continued, coming to stand just in front of Bradley. "Why, in the midst of battle, would you—of all people—only use one kind of magic?"

"I think I can answer that."

We all turned to look at Soo Min, who was still staring at her phone.

"I did a reverse image search," she said. "It took me a bit of time to dig it out, but it turns out that this guy," she lifted bright eyes from her phone to Bradley, "isn't a wizard after all."

"What?" I breathed, not sure if I was relieved or crushed.

"Here." Soo Min held her phone out, and we all gathered around it. She had zoomed in on a photograph of two men, one obviously Bradley when he was much... *much* younger. The man beside him appeared to be about the same age. The picture had to be decades old at the very least.

"Where did you find that?" Bradley asked, his voice oddly choked, his eyes transfixed on the image.

"It says in this news article that this *other* guy was the wizard." She squinted at the small text beneath the picture. "Bradley Langford was his name." Then she began to smile like a cat. "And it says here that his friend pictured on the right–*Maverick Thompson*–was his right-hand *fae*." She looked up from the phone and grinned. "Well, what do you make of that?"

Bradley–or rather, Maverick–glared at her as though he was contemplating violence. But then he looked at the rest of us and seemed to deflate from within.

"Fine," he finally pouted. "My name isn't Bradley. It's Maverick."

"And you took the wizard's identity... why?" Aaron frowned.

Maverick huffed and ran a hand through his uneven beard. "Bradley was my best friend. We grew up together. We were as good as brothers."

"I'm going to put on some tea," Lillian said in a low voice before disappearing into the kitchen.

"When we got older, Bradley and I were drafted into the army together," Maverick continued, staring at the ground. "While we were in Vietnam, away from polite society, he had the freedom to teach me more than I'd even known was possible with magic. Saved a bunch of lives, too."

He paused and glared at Aithan, as though that was enough of a reason to excuse the rest of his bad behavior.

"And when we were done, we traveled the world. He was a do-gooder, and I just followed along, doing what I could to help." He ran a hand through his hair. "When he died a few years back, though... the calls for help just kept coming. And I wanted to do what would have made him happy. To honor his memory, so... I pretended I was him and just kept on going."

He looked up, and his gaze flitted from each face to the next. "I didn't plan to do it at first. But people were just so desperate. And no one wanted a *fae* to help. A wizard, though..." His eyes went distant. "And a lot of what they struggled with, I *could* fix. They just... didn't want me to help as me."

"All for a price, I'm sure," Aithan guessed.

"A man has to make a living!" Maverick scoffed.

"Great." Soo Min rubbed her temples. "So we've got a dud wizard and a pretend one now. Honestly, why even bother?"

"All right, that's it!" Julia shook her head. "For so long, I thought you were nice!" She shook her finger at Soo Min. "But I'm done listening to you–"

I didn't hear the rest of what she said, though. Because inside of me, the panic that had been simmering throughout the day moved to a roiling boil. And I couldn't contain it anymore.

I grabbed my dad's keys off the hook by the door and threw the garage door open. Then I ran into the garage, and with shaking hands, tried to unlock his car. But try as I might, my suddenly blurry vision kept me from hitting the button the right way.

"Hey."

A large, calloused hand covered mine. I looked up to see Aithan standing beside me.

"Give me that," he said gently.

"Aithan," I snapped, trying to keep the stupid tears from running down my face. But it was too late. They were already there. "I'm going for a drive, and you can't stop me–"

"I'm not saying no," Aithan said with that same infuriating calm. "I'm saying, let's take mine."

Chapter Eighteen

Aithan

The engine purred beneath us as Everleigh came to a stop at the light before the on-ramp.

She turned to me, a challenge in her blue eyes. If I hadn't known better, I would have said her fae magic was trying to peek through in their rebellious shine.

"This is your last chance to bail and get me my dad's car instead," she said. "Just so you know, I'm going to be violating a few traffic laws."

A voice in my head murmured that this was a bad idea. It was wrong. It was dangerous. But something inside of Everleigh had snapped. The magic that was bound up so tightly seemed to be demanding she *do* something.

As I thought these things, I could fairly feel the magic inside her pulsing from within. How awful it must be to have no way to express the emotions that so often took their form through magic in most supernaturals. But here they were, all tied up inside her, trying desperately to escape. No wonder she wanted to get away.

So I just shrugged. "Why do you think I have this car spelled to the hilt?"

She blinked at me, clearly surprised by my reaction. "What's that supposed to mean?"

The light turned green, and I gave her a small smile. "It means *go*."

Everleigh hit the gas and sped through the intersection at a velocity that pushed me back in my seat. But that was nothing compared to the way she gunned the engine once we were on the freeway.

I had done my fair share of speeding through the years, particularly after I'd gotten my driver's license. Evading the police and escaping most human notice wasn't a difficult thing if you had the right kind of magic, I had learned as a teen. And I'd taken full advantage of my natural abilities until my parents found out and spelled my car so it couldn't go over a certain limit. (It's just what happens when your elven parents also happen to be police.)

But even I wasn't ready for the way Everleigh took control of the road.

Fortunately, there weren't many cars out and about at the moment, but after a moment of measured breathing, I realized I didn't need to worry. Even if my car hadn't been spelled so that it was currently invisible to human drivers and repelled anything it might come into contact with, she would have been just fine. Everleigh, it turned out, was a skilled driver.

Part of this was probably due to the fact that her parents had sent her to several professional driving schools when she was seventeen, and her magic still hadn't come in.

But the aggression with which she met the road tonight made it abundantly clear what a precarious place Everleigh was in. The Everleigh I knew was cool and controlled at all times. She kept her head, just as she had when the stalker had used a *Seira* spell on her, and when she had thought to adopt her best friend so the strange fae couldn't. Even when she was doing "adrenaline junkie things," as Julia phrased it, she acted within the parameters of safety. All the safety harnesses were buckled, and all the rules were followed.

This, however, was a side of Everleigh I'd never seen before. For her to drive this recklessly meant she was likely at her breaking point.

But maybe...

Maybe breaking was exactly what she needed.

As if hearing my thoughts, she looked over at me, her eyes daring me to warn her to slow down or stop.

"What do you want to know?" I asked instead.

She turned back to the road and cut in front of a semi in a move that would have made a NASCAR driver cringe. Was she too angry to talk? Would she just need to wear herself out first?

"I want to know everything," she finally said. "Everything else that's been hidden from me all these years."

I drew in a deep breath through my nose. "How about I tell you what I can?" I asked. "Pull off at the speedway exit."

For a moment, I thought she would be mad with me for telling her what to do. But after a brief second of indecision, she gave me a sharp nod and made her way toward the exit.

It was one of the last main exits on the northeast side of town, so there wasn't a ton of traffic when we got there. The massive parking lots that surrounded the main race track and the smaller tracks that surrounded it were mostly empty, so I directed her toward a particular side road until we came to a chain link gate, which I used my magic to unlock before telling her to slowly drive through.

Wordlessly, we parked in a shadowed corner used for deliveries and found our way up to the empty red, white, and blue stadium bleachers, where we had a good view of the empty oval track and the military jets as they took off and landed on the long runway at the Air Force base beyond.

Neither of us spoke for a long time. We simply listened to the roar of jet engines and watched the sky go from sky blue to orange to purple to the blue of twilight. I snuck a glance at her several times, but she never seemed to notice, lost in thought as she stared up at the sky.

It was strange, really. For so long, I'd thought of her as a kid. But now that we were sitting here, I sensed a new kind of camaraderie that I'd never shared with her before. We'd both gotten the short end of the stick in the saga that was our families. And now it felt like we were balancing on a precipice, neither willing to jump, but knowing we couldn't stay.

"So," she finally said, turning to me with a grim smile, "what's your part in all this?"

"Don't you remember? I'm your unwelcome babysitter." I reached out to muss her hair, but she ducked and slapped my wrist.

"I mean it." She scowled up at me. "I *know* you don't want to be here. You wouldn't have been gone so much if you did. So what brought you back?"

The teasing died on my tongue as my smile fell. Why indeed? But when I looked at her again, I knew I couldn't keep this truth hidden. I might be unable to tell all of it. But I could tell her some. She deserved that.

"I was thirteen," I said slowly. "My parents told me the truth about who and what we were. I mean, I knew what we were, but until then, I didn't know most of the details. They also told me who *you* were... and *what* you really were. How your parents had left their own families to join my parents and a number of other allies out in the common world. How they wanted to keep you hidden and safe from the courts and anyone else who might want to use you before you were able to defend yourself."

I looked down at my hands. "My brother knew already, of course. He'd been older when we left the courts, and remembered more. But once I knew it all, they asked me to be a part of it, too. For the sake of the world."

For the sake of you, I wanted to say. But I didn't.

Everleigh, who had been watching me with wide eyes, now looked crestfallen. "So they *made* you protect me."

Oh, crap. I hadn't meant it that way. "No," I hurried to assure her. "The decision was my own. I took the Binding Oath completely of my own will–"

"You... you took the *Binding Oath?*" Everleigh whispered, her jaw falling open. Then she put her hand over her mouth and shook her head. "Aithan... Aithan, that oath is forever! *Why* would your parents ask you to make that? Why *did* you make it?"

The utter horror in her expression reminded me once again of why I had taken the oath in the first place. Why I would take it again.

"Aithan?" she asked, making me realize I'd gotten lost in my own thoughts.

"Right. Sorry." I shook my head and drew a deep breath. "I took the oath because my brother–as my dad has abdicated–is technically first in line to my grandfather's throne, so he was obviously not the choice candidate. And because you," I said, tweaking her nose, "deserve to be protected."

I tried to smile as I spoke, but I failed. Instead, my voice dropped to a whisper. "There are so few good things in this world, little wizard. And you're one of them. I knew that even then."

Everleigh slowly turned to look back at the flightline, clearly shaken. But I didn't look away. Even as we sat there, I could feel the magic bond the vow had created between us stirring. Similar to the tie between a fae and the fae's pet, this bond would link us for life. But unlike the fae-pet bond, there were absolutely no ways out of such an oath. And rather than her being tied to me, I was tied to her.

For life.

As long as there was breath in both of our lungs, my purpose was to protect her. Sure, I'd had a brief reprieve in my teen years and early twenties, as my parents and hers were watching her as well. But when the call had come, I'd known my life would never be the same again. I could feel it deep within my soul, where the magic of the oath had begun to stir.

As long as Everleigh lived, I would live for her.

If Everleigh died, I would die as well.

If I neglected my duties, my descent into madness would be long and full of pain.

It was one of the heaviest burdens a supernatural could bear. But suddenly, for the first time in a long time, I realized I didn't mind the weight.

"I was telling the truth, by the way," I added.

She turned to me. "What?"

"Back in high school, at that Christmas party. When I told you that I wasn't trying to avoid you."

Everleigh shook her head, a lock of brown hair falling in her face. I resisted the urge to push it out of the way.

"I didn't have any idea what you meant." She sighed. "I just wanted you back as my friend."

"I know. And you guessed right back then. I was running, but it wasn't you I was trying to free myself from. I ran just—"

"Just to be free," she whispered.

"To be free," I echoed. And that was the truth. Sure, there was a brief time when I'd blamed Everleigh for the weight of the oath that I'd only understood *after* I took it. But even in my angstiest of teen moments, I'd known deep down I wasn't angry at her. It wasn't her fault she needed protection. It had been the expectations that frightened me, a life I began to grasp the magnitude of only with time.

But even that might not have been so bad if it hadn't been for my grandfather's curse. Not that I could share that with Everleigh.

Crickets began to chirp somewhere nearby. It was early in the year for them, but I was thankful for another noise to fill the silence that had fallen since the fighter jets had taken a break.

"I know you can't tell me specifics about your curse," Everleigh said, her mind seeming to be on the same track as mine. "But... can you hint to me about it? Just so I don't do something... something stupid that might make it worse?"

I gave her a wry smile, and she sighed.

"Figures."

That little sigh made me want to groan. Even in this, my grandfather had cursed me to loneliness forever.

Which meant, that little warning voice inside whispered, that this–what we were doing here and now–was dangerous. My brother had been right to be concerned. Everleigh might have been like an annoying little sister to me once, but she was neither little nor annoying now. And she *definitely* didn't feel like my sister.

Sure, it was still strange to see her... shaped like a woman. But I wasn't surprised at all by the way she'd turned out. She'd been gorgeous since her fourteenth birthday. She didn't know it, but I'd threatened more than one idiot in high school when I'd overheard inappropriate conversations involving her name.

Why was I here, I mused, torturing myself with what I could never have?

And yet, in spite of all this, I couldn't get myself to suggest we leave.

Time to focus on something else. "Do you see now why it's so important you learn how to use your magic?" I asked. "Everyone around us gave up everything because they believed in you."

"They shouldn't have," she answered softly.

"If you can't believe in your own abilities," I said after a moment, "believe our families and friends. Trust that they were wise enough to make the right decision, even if it seems crazy right now."

She turned her blue eyes on me. "I don't know how."

Dang, she was beautiful.

I stood and held my hand out so it faced her. Carefully, I projected just enough magic from my palm for it to form a swirling sphere of green about the size of a softball.

"Stand up," I said. When she obliged, I nodded at the swirling ball of magic. "Put your hand out to feel this. The way you did with Bradley–Maverick–whatever his name is. But take your time."

She closed her eyes and put her hand out so it was in contact with the magic. For several minutes, she was silent, sometimes turning her hand this way or that, until a slight smile turned the corners of her lips.

"I can feel it," she said, her eyes still shut. "Not just the magic itself. I can always feel that. But... the rhythm. Just like he said."

"Good." I took a step closer, knowing I would regret it later, and pressed the palm of my hand against hers so they were touching. Her skin was cool, and I briefly wondered what it would feel like if she were to run her fingers lightly across my face.

No, Aithan.

That was *not* going to help.

"What about now?" I asked.

Her breath hitched slightly, though whether it was from my touch or the magic, I didn't know.

I kind of hoped it was both.

"It's stronger now," she said, sounding somewhat breathless. Then she gave a slight laugh. "How many dates have you brought up here, Mr. Nomos, asking them the exact same thing?"

She'd obviously said it to lighten the tension, but I couldn't get myself to smile. Then she opened her eyes, and I knew it the moment she recognized the pain in mine. For the briefest of eternities, our eyes stayed locked, neither of us seeming able to break away.

"No dates," I said softly. "Just a friend."

She edged forward, until she was nearly touching me "The way you date girls," she said softly. "Always a new one, never longer than a cycle of the moon. Does that have something to do with your curse?"

I could only swallow.

Everleigh held my gaze for a moment longer before closing her eyes. And what she said next was not what I was expecting.

"That demented donkey!" she snapped, removing her hand from mine and running it through her hair.

I blinked at her in surprise. "I'm sorry... What?"

"Your grandfather." She turned to me, blue eyes burning brightly again. This time, however, there was no denying it. Her fae magic was shining through, obvious in the glowing ring of pink that had appeared around her irises. "I don't know what he did to you and your brother. But once my magic comes in, I'm going to schedule a meeting with that moron and let him know *just* how difficult he's made everything for–"

"Everleigh! Look!" I grabbed her hands and lifted them up. A very thin, but very *real* layer of pink light was now covering the entirety of both of her hands. She gaped, as did I. And though the magic flickered out nearly as fast as it had begun, I let out a laugh.

She stared at me as though I'd lost my mind. "What's so funny?"

"Clarkson," I said, continuing to chuckle, "I've been trying to get that reaction out of you for years. I'd always wondered if it would work. Especially after the Christmas party incident!"

"Is... is that why you tormented me so much in high school?" Her jaw dropped. "Aithan, you dyed my hair pink for a *week!*"

I grinned at her. "And I was apparently on the right track! Everleigh, you have *magic* in there!" I pointed at her heart. "The trick is just getting it out!"

"Your grandfather may be a jerk!" she said, still scowling at me as she smacked my finger away. "But so are you!"

I grabbed her and gave her a nuggie, drawing another shrill protest about her hair. "You're a weird kid, Clarkson. But there's hope for you yet."

"And if you want any sort of hope in *your* future, you're going to get me some Mexican rice and bubble tea on the way home." She pulled her scrunchie out to fix her ponytail as she made her way back toward the car, her movements agitated and jerky in her rage. "And an apology wouldn't hurt, either!"

"Anything for you, Clarkson." I grinned at the back of her head as I followed. "Just as long as you don't give up on your magic."

Chapter Nineteen

Everleigh

I WOULDN'T HAVE BELIEVED it possible so soon, but I realized that I felt much better as we made our way home. I even let Aithan drive. Of course, his promise to feed me might have had something to do with that as well. The prospect of an In-N-Out protein wrap and a cup of bubble tea improved my mood and optimism immediately.

Humans don't know it, but hanger functions a lot like a curse. (If only curses could be broken with a drink and a side of fries.)

In a miscalculation, Aithan made the mistake of trying to steal one of my french fries at a stop light, but I slapped his hand away.

"No stealing! You could have gotten your own."

He made a face at me. "You going to eat that like a normal person, or hoard it like a dragon?"

"Aithan, I am *starving*, I'm cranky, and I just learned that I'm part vampire. Don't think I won't bite you."

Aithan shook his head. "Okay, first of all, you know that's not how your magic works. Second, very, *very* few wizards have ever been recorded to have accessed their vampire magic."

I gave him a look, my mouth stuffed with a bite of juicy burger. "Try me."

He glanced at my fries, then muttered something about the difference between being brave and being stupid and then kept his hands to himself.

Wise man.

By the time we got home, however, I had finished my food and my bubble tea, and was already starting to feel more than a little embarrassed about my earlier outburst. Yeah, the whole situation sucked, but it wasn't my friends' faults. I couldn't blame them. So it was with a red face and a tied tongue that I stepped back into the house.

"Everleigh? Aithan? Is that you?" Miss Lillian's voice called from the kitchen.

"It's us," Aithan called back. "Where is everyone?"

"In here," Miss Lillian replied. "Come and join us. We have a proposition for you."

A proposition? That felt official. My heart started to beat even faster as I removed my shoes and went to the kitchen, and my breath caught in my throat again when I realized that all of my friends–and Maverick-the-liar–were there.

After my terrible display of non-magic and then my temper tantrum... What did they think of me now?

"Sit down," Miss Lillian said, with a smile. "We were just talking, and I think we've come to a possible arrangement." She gestured to an empty barstool beside hers, but I shook my head.

"I have to say something first. I'm... I'm sorry." I reached up with my left hand and rubbed my right arm uncomfortably. "I wasn't trying to ignore my magic during the fight today." Shame and embarrassment flooded me more with each word, so I shoved them out as fast as I could. "I really... really just didn't know what to do. And then I panicked, and..." I swallowed hard. "I'm just sorry."

"We know this isn't easy," Miss Lillian said gently. "You always give your very best. I've known you long enough to be confident of that. And it's not *your* fault that Mr. Thompson is not a wizard."

She paused long enough to shoot him a scathing look, but he just scoffed.

She rolled her eyes, then went on. "As I said, we all had a long talk—"

"And we're *all* going to train you!" Jamie interrupted with a grin.

I had been staring at the kitchen tile beneath my feet, but at this, I looked up. "You... *want* to train me?"

Soo Min made a face at her phone, and Maverick just continued to sulk, but the others—even Julia—nodded happily.

"It's quite practical," Dorian said in his smooth British accent. "Betwixt our company, we have two elves, two fae—

"I am *not* here of my own volition," Maverick snapped. "I just want to point that out."

"You've already been paid," Aithan said with a frown. "You're going to do what you promised. Which is to stay here and train her."

"Two elves," Dorian repeated, sending an uncharacteristic look of annoyance at our visitor, "two fae, myself, a phoenix, and two shifters."

"That's more than enough to get you started," Christian said kindly, the gun he was cleaning spread out all over the kitchen island. "You can hire more tutors in the future as you wish."

"You've had a lot of change in a short amount of time," Miss Lillian said apologetically. "And it's only right that we help you navigate it, as we're relying on you to one day help us."

"We owe you that," Aaron said with a nod.

"I... thank you." I gave them a hesitant smile. "I wish I could promise that I'll learn it all right away. I can't promise that, but... I'll do my best."

"And that's all anyone can ask," Dorian said sternly. "Well, that and for another cup of tea. Miss Lillian, is there any more of that chamomile you brought the other day?"

The others began to talk amongst themselves again, but as I

watched them all this time, I didn't feel nearly so bad. I had meant what I had said.

I was ready to try.

Chapter Twenty

Everleigh

I KNEW TRYING WOULD BE EASIER SAID than done. But I really did mean I would do my best.

The next morning–because Miss Lillian insisted I have another good night's sleep before my lessons began–I started with the magic that would *probably* be more powerful than all the others.

So elven magic it was.

When I headed into the backyard, I was pleased to see that Miss Lillian would be my teacher. I had wondered the night before whether it would be Miss Lillian or Aithan, and though I felt like we'd crossed some barrier during our chat, for some reason, having Aithan as my teacher made me feel...

I decided not to give it too much thought.

"We'll start with what the humans call telekinesis," Miss Lillian said pleasantly. She'd positioned us on the deck beside the swimming pool, an odd assortment of household items in a pile at her feet. Soo Min had cast a glamour over the entire backyard in case any nosy neighbors tried to peek, which meant that short of me blowing up the house, no one could see my experimentation but us.

Miss Lillian was wearing her usual outfit of a thin yellow sweater and a knee-length skirt that flared out just below her knees. She was the very picture of spring. I, on the other hand, was wearing jeans and a hoodie because March still hadn't given up on winter, icy blasts of air continually whooshing over us. I couldn't manipulate the air around me to stay toasty and warm the way I was sure Miss Lillian was.

"Generally, elves enact change upon the world around them using direct energy," she began. "But it's also possible to directly summon objects–given they're not too big, of course. Students usually start this by summoning objects sitting on a surface the student can touch. For example, if I put this golf ball on the ground." She paused and placed the golf ball on the pool deck at her feet. "If I touch the same surface the ball is touching, I can use the surface as a conduit..."

She pressed her hand against the ground several inches from the ball. No normal human would have been able to see it, but a thin line of green energy shot from her hand to the ball via the pool deck. The ball began to roll toward her hand, following the green line, but before it could touch her fingers, it shot into the air and landed directly in mine.

Miss Lillian gaped at me, as did Julia, who was sitting on a pool chair nearby. Jamie, standing beside Aithan, let out a loud *Whoop!* and began to laugh. Only Aithan looked unsurprised.

"Everleigh, that was... wonderful!" Miss Lillian stuttered. "But... how did you do it?"

I gave her a guilty smile. "I'm afraid it's the only thing I'm wonderful at."

"But how did you do that?" Jamie repeated, shaking his head. "For a girl who hits herself with lightning bolts on a regular basis, that's not bad."

Aithan just met my gaze with a cool expression as he continued to sip his coffee. Oh, he was going to play innocent then, was he?

"I don't know, Aithan," I said, crossing my arms. "How *did* I get so good at telekinesis?"

But Aithan just shrugged. "Just goes to show that you should be thanking me and Alexander." He turned to Miss Lillian and raised his coffee mug. "Our wizard is an excellent pickpocket. We're all saved."

I turned to Miss Lillian, too, and rolled my eyes. "When I was little, Alexander and Aithan liked to steal my dolls and hide them. Like, a lot. Eventually, I realized if I didn't want my favorite babies to disappear for days or weeks, I had to get really good at saving them." I looked at Aithan again. "I had to learn to snatch them right out of their kidnappers' hands."

"Like I said." Aithan stretched his shoulders and neck. "Gratitude is owed. And yet, I don't feel as much gratitude as you'd think I would."

Miss Lillian had taken her glasses off to stare at him, her accent growing thicker with her disapproval. "You, young man, had better watch your back. That was no way to treat a lady, and if I'd known what trouble you were up to, taking this poor girl's babes, I would have tanned your hide. And your parents wouldn't have minced a bit either. Probably would've saved them a load of trouble if I had."

"But... can you do it all on your own?" Julia sat up and put her book down. "Or does someone else have to start the magic for you?"

"This one thing," I said, "I can do all on my own."

I turned and smirked at Aithan, but he just shamelessly grinned.

"Now that we have that established," she said, giving Aithan one more meaningful look before turning back to me, "and it seems you've mastered that little trick, I guess we'll move on. Let's work on changing water into ice, then back into water, then steam, then back again. After that, I'll have you start fermenting grape juice into wine. These are nice simple ways to introduce elven students to their magic."

Unlike her telekinesis lesson, Miss Lillian's ice lesson went about as well as I had expected all of my lessons to go. In other words, it was like pulling teeth.

Enacting change upon a substance was much harder than simply summoning it. It took me six cups of spilled water before I managed to create a thin layer of ice on the surface of water in a cup. And I rejoiced too soon at even this. I then lost count of how many drinking glasses exploded as I expanded the ice too quickly inside of them.

Miss Lillian, much to my relief, turned out to be excellent not only at protecting all of us from flying shards of glass, but at repairing the drinking glasses themselves.

It took me three days to learn that very simple skill. At first, many of my protectors came out to watch me when they weren't on guard duty. But my progress was so painstakingly slow that after the first two days, they generally spent their free time elsewhere, sparring and training downstairs in the basement, or chatting while scrolling on their phones. Dorian continued going to work half of the time and spent his other half playing strategy board games with Christian. Maverick only left the guest room, which Aithan had traded him for the couch, when Aithan told him he had to. Julia, however, continued to be amazed, cheering me on the same way she had when we were twelve, and I'd chosen to try out for the local ballet theater. Aithan, too, was often present when he wasn't working out downstairs.

Five days and countless broken objects later, Miss Lillian declared that I was ready to move on to my next teacher. In no way had I mastered my elven skills, and if I was honest, I had to admit that my skills were still severely stunted. If I tried really hard, I might rival the average elf child as old as seven or eight. And yet, the more I practiced, the more it felt like I was poking holes in whatever magical plastic wrap seemed to be holding my magic in. I was undeniably better than I had been before.

Maybe there was hope for me–and the world–yet.

***

Shifting with Jamie and Aaron was next. The afternoon of my fifth day, we met out in the backyard again, and they both took their shifter forms, which–if I was telling the truth–were more than a little unnerving. Aaron looked like any werewolf might, but his status as an alpha's firstborn put him head and shoulders above those of a normal wolf. And Jamie, who I'd decided had the temperament of a Husky rather than a Labrador, looked like a creature straight out of a nightmare.

He wasn't at all ugly the way the internet made chupacabras out to be. But he was just as terrifying. His large, gleaming red eyes, knife-like teeth, and sharp spikes that ran along his spine made me shiver nearly every time I looked at him. And unlike the pictures on the internet, he wasn't skinny or emaciated. Instead, muscles rippled out of his shoulders, sides, and hindquarters, and his claws were longer than Aaron's. Side by side, the two shifters were about the same size, and the low growls they often emitted while in their shifter forms made me shudder, though they probably had no idea they were doing it.

"Okay," Jamie said, a blur as he shifted back into his human form. "Now it's your turn to try."

I stared at him. "Um, how? And... what am I supposed to shift into?"

Aaron changed back into his human form as well. "Miss Lillian taught you to enact change upon the world. This time, you're changing yourself."

"That makes sense in theory," I said, holding up my index finger. "But it still doesn't tell me *how* to do it or *what* I'm supposed to try changing into. Do I picture it in my head and just hope I turn out the same?"

Even as I spoke, I wanted to groan. Knowing me, I would shift into something that was half chicken, half water buffalo.

Maverick, who had been forcibly stationed on a lawn chair nearby, put his book down and rolled his eyes. "You're a wizard, not a shifter. They're limited to the shape they were given. You turn into whatever *you* feel like."

I looked at Julia, who was clapping her hands. "Oh! Everleigh! Turn into a tuxedo cat!"

"Seriously?" Soo Min scoffed as she came outside. She was carrying a tray of the new milk tea flavors she'd been mixing up in the kitchen. "Why in the world would you want her to turn into a tuxedo cat?"

Julia sniffed daintily. "Because I've always wanted one."

"And here I was thinking *you* were the pet." Soo Min smirked.

Julia's eyes went wide, then shrank down to angry slits as she glared at Soo Min.

"Most wizards," Dorian called lazily from his shady corner, "have one shape they're most comfortable in. I knew of one about a hundred years ago who preferred to shift into a sparrow, although he could also become a bear when the occasion called for it. Technically, you can turn into any kind of animal you can imagine. But usually, unless I'm mistaken, there's one form that's easier than all the others."

"Bradley," Maverick grunted, "liked to turn into a Golden Retriever."

Jamie snickered. "That's about the least threatening animal he could have picked."

Maverick's scowl turned into a smirk. "Maybe," he said, his southern drawl a little sharper than usual. "But have you ever thought to keep a secret from a pet?"

I shook my head, trying mentally to separate the good information from the useless. "Okay. So I need to..." I looked at Jamie and Aaron, then Maverick. "How do I do this?"

Maverick huffed dramatically before getting to his feet and

coming to stand by my side. "Last time, you *pushed* the magic out. This time, you're going to suck it in, like you're drinking it through a straw."

I closed my eyes and imagined pulling my magic in through a straw.

And to no one's surprise, nothing happened.

Maverick growled. "Well, if you're not going to even try–"

As he spoke, though, the world around me began to spin. And yet, it wasn't the world spinning. It was me. I felt as though the world and I were switching places. I closed my eyes and tried not to topple over.

I had no idea how long I stood there, trying to keep my balance while the magic wreaked havoc within me. But when I finally felt steady enough to open my eyes, I let out a squeak.

Everyone else had risen up around me, taller than the tallest giant I had ever seen. Their eyes were wide, and their mouths hung open, an expression I felt mirrored on my own face. We stared stupidly at one another for a long moment before Jamie began snickering. Then laughing. And the harder he laughed, the harder it was for him to speak.

"You... of all things!" he gasped, hugging his sides. "Of all things, you choose... You turn into..."

"A chipmunk," Soo Min said, disbelief written all over her face. "You shift into a *chipmunk?*"

Maverick only shook his head. "Go figure," he muttered to himself as he returned to his lawn chair and his book.

"Hey!" I snapped after I'd shifted back into my human form. "A chipmunk can be very useful!" Okay, so I might have been aiming for a cat, but they didn't have to know that. And I was simply relieved I'd been able to change back at all.

Jamie continued to roar with laughter. Soo Min rolled her eyes and went back inside, and Aithan wore an amused smirk. Miss Lillian took a very long sip of her tea, making her face impossible to read, and even Julia was very obviously trying not to laugh. But

Aaron, who was now my *new* favorite person, only gave me a kind smile.

"You transformed into your shifter form and back on your first day. That's a win. Let's acknowledge that win and keep on going."

We only spent that afternoon on shifter magic, as Aaron decided I knew enough to keep practicing on my own. And while I couldn't turn my entire body into one giant flame the way Christian could in his phoenix form, I was able to conjure a single tiny flame on the tip of my finger by the end of the day. I went to sleep that night feeling somewhat encouraged. I was actually getting this! Maybe fae magic, which we were tackling tomorrow, wouldn't be so hard after all.

But fae magic, as it turned out the next morning, was the hardest magic I'd encountered yet.

"No, no, you're still doing it all wrong." Maverick, who had been forced to participate, rubbed his temples. "You're making the lawn chair invisible the way an elf would. The fae wouldn't actually make the chair disappear. He would cover it with a glamour to *convince* others it was invisible." He shook his head and huffed. "Try again."

I gave a huff of my own and turned back to the lawn chair. I knew I was supposed to glamour it. I just couldn't figure out *how*. So with a sigh, I lifted my hands again.

Slowly, slowly, the corner of the chair became invisible. Just when I began to think I'd nailed it, however, Maverick pinched the bridge of his nose.

"Everleigh, bless your dadgum little–"

I whirled around to face him. "If you bless my heart again, I'm going to slap you."

"What else am I supposed to do?" he exploded. "You're no

good at this! How am I supposed to teach someone who refuses to do better?"

"Maybe if you were a *real* wizard instead of a *fake* one," I snapped, "you'd be smart enough to figure this out! I've told you a million times that it feels like there's something inside me that's holding me back! I don't know what else you want me to say!"

Maverick's face grew so red I began to wonder if he was working on a heart attack. But before I could ask, the back door slid open, and Aithan strode out.

"Time for a mental break," he announced, coming to my side and quickly whisking me back toward the house with him, away from the annoying fae. "Let's go, wizard."

"Where are we going?" I asked, my mood immediately improving with each step away from the jerk in the backyard.

He gave me a smug smile. "I'm not sure you'll like it much better."

"Oh..."

"I talked it over with Aaron and Miss Lillian last night, and we all agree that you need to practice using your magic during a fight."

I took a moment to process that. "Oh," was all I could think to say again.

"Which means," he said as we entered the basement, "that you need to stretch. First style is Jiu Jitsu."

***

I wasn't as bad at the magical sparring as I'd been at the other magical skills. I was far, far worse.

To my relief, the martial arts part was second nature. I'd trained in multiple styles for more than ten years. Unfortunately, coupling my fighting skills with magic introduced me to a whole new slew of stuff I was bad at.

Not that my opponents said so out loud. The only one who trash-talked me was Soo Min. And as she'd never taken martial arts, I could *sometimes* beat her if I attacked fast and hard enough. The problem was that most of the time, I found myself relying on my human skills instead of my magical ones. Which meant the moment I dropped my guard, I was fae toast.

And that got me into loads of trouble with everyone else as well. Less than five seconds on the training mat with any opponent who wasn't Julia had me tapping out.

After the first two opponents, my magical sparring matches made me long for my regular magic lessons once more. Which we started again the next day. Only now I was lucky enough to be practicing *both*.

Dorian, much to my relief, was the easiest magical teacher to understand. Although I was pretty sure that had a lot to do with the fact that he was hundreds of years old and knew how to verbalize his powers inside and out.

"Will I have to drink blood?" I grimaced at the thought.

He laughed softly. "No, Princess. Just know that vampires drink blood because our bodies stop producing it. We're permanently in stasis, for lack of a better description. Now, if you decided to remain unchanging the way we do for days or weeks, you might, but as that's highly unlikely, and you take in regular food on a daily basis, I doubt it shall ever be necessary."

"I wonder," Julia said slowly, "if you could do the opposite, Everleigh. Like, speed yourself up instead of slowing yourself down."

"It's... possible, I suppose," Dorian said, his pale forehead developing a slight crease.

"It would take a crazy amount of calories and energy," Maverick called from his favorite lawn chair. Instead of reading today, he was sucking down one of Soo Min's new drink creations and watching us with lazy interest.

"And," Dorian said firmly, "*not* something you would do as a habit. That would be more dangerous than I can spell out." Then he paused. "I'm curious, though. What situation might you need that for, should you listen to your friend here and try?"

I shrugged. "I don't know. But it's a good question. And now *I'm* curious."

"Curiosity killed the cat," Maverick muttered from his chair.

"Well then," I snapped back. "It's a good thing I'm a chipmunk!"

Chapter Twenty-One

Aithan

I FROWNED as I watched Everleigh practice adding elven magic to a basic punch. Jamie had been kind enough to volunteer his own body as the punching bag for this lesson, something Soo Min seemed to enjoy watching just a little too much.

"She's improving," said a smooth voice. I didn't have to look over my shoulder to know that Dorian had joined me. Vampire magic was cool, almost minty, and being hundreds of years old, Dorian fairly oozed it.

"You're off early," I murmured as he studied Everleigh as well.

He shrugged. "Don't tell the police, but I can do my day's work in about an hour's time. I simply remain at the lab to make the government feel better about how much it pays me." His lips curved into a near smile.

I smiled, too. Knowing what little I did of vampire noses, I had no doubt a vampire Dorian's age could do the work of ten human experts in about three sniffs. And he was right. Telling the humans that he could smell poison in a victim's blood would do more than freak them out.

"What's wrong?" he asked, giving me a furtive glance.

I shook my head. "I just can't figure out why she's progressing so slowly. Everleigh is bright. And in the ten days we've been at this, she's *learned* nearly everything we've taught her... in theory, at least. But for some weird reason, she's good at telekinesis and nothing else." I reached back and rubbed my neck, which had started aching from the unusual amount of tension I'd been feeling since last week. "All I can think is that it must be some sort of... mental block."

"Almost as if she's afraid of success?" Dorian asked.

"Yeah."

Dorian scanned the basement before his eyes lanced on Maverick and narrowed. "What about him? Have you asked whether his friend ever had this sort of trouble?"

"Well," I let out a gusty breath, "I have an idea of what he'll say, but I guess there's no better time." I walked around the perimeter of the room until I was standing beside the fae, who was sitting on a weight bench looking like a thundercloud as he watched Everleigh.

"Hey," I said, coming to sit beside him.

He made a face at me before scooting to the far corner of the bench. "What do you want?"

Oh, we were going to be *that* way then?

"I wanted to ask you something about your wizard friend, Bradley. Do you remember him ever having... these kinds of struggles?" I nodded at Everleigh, who had finally managed to pack a literal handful of magic into one of her punches.

"That was awesome!" Jamie was saying. "I almost got nauseous!"

Maverick rolled his eyes. "Bradley had *talent*, boy. This girl's got..." He waved his hand at her, as though searching for a word. Then he opened his mouth, but a quick look at me seemed to warn him away from whatever he was going to say. "Sass," he finally finished lamely. "She's got sass."

Wise choice of words, fake-wizard.

"I just wish I knew what she needed," I murmured, inwardly

bemoaning–again–Everleigh's parents' absence. "She *knows* it all, technically speaking."

"She can't get the magic to meet the mind," he said with a snort. Then he turned and fixed me with a shrewd look. "What'll it take for you to let me go, now that we've seen she–"

"You can leave," I said evenly, "once Everleigh's parents are restored to her."

He gaped. "But we agreed–"

"That you were a wizard who could teach her all that you knew," I interrupted.

He stared at me for a moment before giving a huff. "Fine. I don't know. Maybe... maybe she just needs a win of some sort. Something beyond figuring out she can turn into a squirrel."

"Chipmunk," I murmured, but my mind was already spinning. "Actually, that's not a bad idea." As I spoke, I remembered a text I'd received from my brother earlier that day. And I couldn't help it as a smile spread across my face. "And I think I know just the way to find it."

"All right, everyone, listen up. I've got news," I said as Miss Lillian doled out dessert, which happened to be matcha ice cream topped with something crunchy–Soo Min's newest experiment. Jamie had already eaten most of his and was eyeing his neighbor's as he finished. I would need to talk fast, or there would be nothing left of mine by the time I was done.

"I got a message from Alexander this morning. It was about Pandora's Key."

That got their attention. Even Jamie quit eating.

Satisfied, I continued. "There's going to be some sort of hand-off at a club called Amethyst that's located downtown. He couldn't tell me everything, of course, but I get the idea that if we can intercept that hand-off, we'll probably learn something really important about who they are and what we're dealing with."

"When is this hand-off happening?" Aaron asked.

"In four days. Which means we have some time to prepare." I looked around. "Has anyone heard of or been inside this club?" In my time as a personal security guard, I'd scoped out a few clubs ahead of celebrities, but I'd never had any interest in hanging out in one.

"I have," came a small voice.

We all turned to Julia, whose hand was half-raised as though in class, her face paler than usual.

"You have?" Everleigh echoed, sounding shocked.

"Um, yeah." Julia gave her a smile tinged with guilt, her shoulders hunching slightly. "I went there with my old roommate a few times before she moved out."

"Oh." Everleigh blinked at her. And though she said nothing else, I could see the wheels spinning in her head, most likely in shock at learning that her friend had done something without her.

"I have, too," said Soo Min. "It's fae-owned, and the security's pretty tight. We'll need to use our glamour stones, as a lot of humans attend, but the fae guards are no joke. So we'll need more than just that, especially if we want to go unnoticed."

"That will complicate things," Miss Lillian said, shooting Dorian a worried look.

"Do we know what we're even looking for?" Christian asked.

"No," I said, "but I have a picture of one of the men involved." I held up a blurry image on my phone, and everyone leaned in to look. His facial features were hard to make out, but his hair, which was so red it was nearly orange, was a dead giveaway. He wouldn't be easy to miss.

"That'll definitely make things easier," Jamie said. "But the question is, how do we get close enough to distract him? He probably won't be too susceptible to a fae mind charm."

"Isn't it obvious?" Soo Min scowled at him. "You use *us*."

"Just you?" Jamie asked blankly. "Or all of us?"

Soo Min rolled her eyes. "The ladies, dumb-dumb. Unless *you* want to flirt with the stranger?"

"Oh. *Oooh,*" Jamie said, his face turning slightly pink.

I suppressed a smile. "If that's the direction you ladies are comfortable with, that's fine. But the boys and I will wait nearby in case things go south." I turned and looked at Everleigh. I wouldn't push her into this if she didn't want to do it. But...

I hoped she would.

Because the more I thought about it, the more I was sure Maverick had been right. Everleigh *really* needed a win.

"What exactly would we need to do?" she asked uncertainly.

"Ideally, you and Soo Min would find a way to steal whatever it is that they're trading," I said. "But if not, we could use any information you can get about *what* they're trading instead."

"If Everleigh's going, I'm going too!" Julia blurted.

"Julia, dear," Miss Lillian said, "that's so kind of you... and courageous, but–"

"Actually," Soo Min interrupted, tilting her head thoughtfully like a cat. "Having a real human along might be useful. It'll make us look less threatening. Besides," she shrugged, "if she's been there before, she'll be able to help guide the wizard, should we get separated."

A wicked glint appeared in Jamie's eyes. "You know, we could make our *senior* wizard put on a mini skirt and flirt with our targets. That would distract them for *sure.*"

Aaron snorted, and Everleigh bit her lip and looked down as several of the others openly snickered. Only Maverick seemed unamused.

"If y'all are just going to mock me–"

"You," I said, taking charge again, "are going to remain with Dorian and Miss Lillian to help advise us. We'll be wearing cameras and two-way earpieces, and I have little doubt Jamie can hack into the fae's security system." I looked at Jamie. "Yes?"

Jamie held up his hands. "Not a problem."

"Which means our next lesson," Soo Min said, her dark eyes sparkling in a way I hadn't seen before, "is going to be focused on glamours!"

Everleigh blinked at her, obviously as taken aback by her sudden enthusiasm as I was. "But... didn't you say we'd be wearing our glamour stones?"

"Yes," Soo Min flipped her ponytail, "but you need to learn to hold a glamour in case someone takes your stone. In a fae club, that is *more* than a possibility."

The others began to chime in, plotting excitedly as several started pulling up the club's social media accounts on their phones.

"Everleigh," I said softly, "come talk to me."

Everleigh hesitated briefly before pushing her chair out and following me into the kitchen.

"Tell me what you're thinking," I said once we were alone.

She drew in a deep breath and let it out slowly. "I'm... I'm not sure I'm ready." Her blue eyes finally met mine. "I don't want to get everyone into trouble. And... I've never been to one of those clubs, but my parents have told me enough about what they've seen to know how easy it is to find trouble, even if you don't want it."

I nodded. "Understandable. But if you'll let me, I also want to point out that you—none of us—will ever be one hundred percent ready. Not without actually putting some skin in the game." I shrugged. "Think about it as if... How do I say this? Oh, okay. So imagine that using your magic in the field is kind of like having kids. You just... jump in, and you learn along the way."

She gave me a skeptical look. "That's the *only* analogy you could come up with? One that compares raising kids to dealing with magical terrorists?"

"Look, my point is this." I shook my head. "If you want to get our parents back, the elven and fae courts will have to be convinced that their assets–AKA, our parents–aren't at risk.

Which means you're going to have to stretch yourself–a whole lot. But remember, you're not going in alone." I put my hand on her shoulder and immediately regretted it. She was so small and warm. I reminded myself that now was not the time or place to pull her in for a hug like I wanted.

A long, lingering hug.

Even if she looked unsure and adorable, and I suddenly had the nearly overwhelming desire to chase the anxiety from her face.

"I... know that," she said slowly. "And it's funny. The last few nights, I've started having this recurring dream about my magic. Almost–almost like a memory. But..." She closed her eyes and shook her head. "Not that it matters–" She paused and pulled her phone out of her pocket. After glancing at it, she huffed, shot off a quick text, and put it back.

"Who was that?" I asked.

She made a face. "Oh, Georgie's still freaking out. I think he's half-convinced you've kidnapped me."

"You know, I'm sure Soo Min would be more than happy to do a memory charm on him. Make him forget you ever existed." I, for one, would be more than fine with that.

"*That* would cause more problems than it would solve." She shook her head. "A more important question is whether there will be any way to sneak my gun inside with me."

"Only if you can find a way to glamour it so well you trick the fae security guards." I gave her a smirk and reached out to ruffle her hair, but she ducked out of the way before turning and making her way back to the dining room.

And though I knew better, I had to work *really* hard not to admire her as she walked away.

Chapter Twenty-Two

Everleigh

THE NIGHT before the club infiltration–or what everyone had come to call our "heist"–Aithan decided we should all brush up on our defense skills.

Or, in my case, continue learning them as quickly as possible. Most of the team had been taking turns facing off on the sparring mat in the basement throughout the week, but this, Aithan announced, would be an *official* practice.

"You'll do fine," Christian said kindly as I glanced nervously at the mat. "You've been improving all week. Just... try to clear your mind. Let your instinct run."

"My instinct wants my sidearm," I muttered as Soo Min and Jamie walked in, bickering about whether pineapples belonged on pizza.

This made Christian laugh. "I know the feeling. Unfortunately, phoenixes and sidearms aren't always compatible. I learned long ago that I had to keep a vanishing charm on my guns for that very reason."

"Let me guess," I said as Aithan and Aaron entered "Fire shifting made guns go boom?"

Christian grimaced. "I've lost more of my favorite guns that way than you can count."

"Okay," Aithan announced as the rest of the crew walked in. "This is how we're going to do it. Since Everleigh is new at this, everyone else is going to take turns first so she can watch our technique. Then she'll jump in." He looked at me, his green eyes piercing. "Sound good, Clarkson?"

I swallowed hard but nodded anyway and forced a smile. "Yeah. Show me what you've all got."

I'd seen most of them face off throughout the week, so I had an idea of who could do what. But to my surprise, even Dorian and Miss Lillian were participating tonight. Dorian, being a vampire, could handle himself—I had no doubt about that. But when sweet, petite Miss Lillian, still in her pleated skirt, baby blue sweater, and heels, stood up to face Jamie, my blood ran cold.

"What is Aithan thinking?" Julia hissed in my ear. "She can't face off against him!"

We shouldn't have worried, though. Because two seconds later, while Jamie was still shifting into his chupacabra form, Miss Lillian interrupted the shift by projecting what looked like a green electrical sphere around him. Jamie let out a half-growl, half-human screech as his metamorphosis came to an abrupt halt. Keeping her hands raised, Miss Lillian sent more and more power into the sphere until Jamie was fairly glowing, floating frozen in midair.

Her green prison lasted so long that I was beginning to worry about Jamie when he finally managed to twitch one shoulder just enough to slash at the sphere with his half-formed claws. The sphere disappeared, and Jamie finished shifting while he pounced in Miss Lillian's direction.

Miss Lillian immediately conjured a magical bow and arrows in her hands. These, like Aithan's magically conjured sword and whip, glowed brightly in her hands. I was sure she would loose the arrow, but just as it was fully formed and pointed right at his neck, Jamie's claws were at hers.

"That's a draw," Aithan said. "And a good way to start our evening. Soo Min and Dorian. You're next."

Soo Min's weapon of choice, I'd learned that week, was disorienting her opponents by making them believe the world around them was pitch black. It usually worked well but turned out to be a mistake with Dorian. Because Dorian relied far more on his nose and ears than his eyes. And Soo Min, thanks to all of her time in the kitchen, smelled strongly of sugar and tea.

She used this to her advantage, however, by projecting the imagined scent of matcha tea and sugar throughout the room, which forced Dorian to stop so he could get his bearings. Leaving his back wide open.

Soo Min sprang, and she might even have won if Dorian's hearing wasn't so sensitive. Just before her feet hit his back, however, he whirled around and caught her in his arms, and placed his sharp, shining canines just millimeters from her throat.

"And that win is Dorian's," Aithan said. Aaron marked it on the whiteboard hanging on the wall, which I realized had all of our names written on it.

"What's that for?" I asked.

"Bets," Jamie grinned. "We've all put our money on who we think is going to win."

"Not all of us," Soo Min scoffed as she walked off the mat. "Only those who are stupidly immature."

"As if a Nomos would give anyone else a chance," Maverick grumbled.

"Keep it up, and I'll stick *you* in a round as well," Aithan threatened.

As the sparring continued, I was more and more thankful that Aithan had given me time to watch. Despite the feeling that I was still fighting my magic from within, I was starting to see how creative one could get with magic. And as I had nearly every kind at my disposal—in theory—the possibilities were unlimited.

If only my body could get on board with my brain.

Unfortunately, Aithan did eventually call my name. So with a sigh, I stood and stretched as I slowly walked toward the mat, waiting with trepidation to hear my partner's name.

It was Christian that Aithan called first. I let out a sigh of relief, as Christian had somewhat taken on the role of an older brother to Julia and me throughout the week. Julia had found this most disappointing, but I was grateful for any help I could get.

Still, despite Christian's many attempts to help, my first match was over faster than any of the others had been. I made the mistake of trying to make it rain over the sparring mat, forgetting that to do so, I needed actual water already nearby. And the pathetic remnants I stole from Aaron's water bottle didn't do the trick.

No sooner was there a slight hiss from the quarter cup of water I dumped on Christian's fiery wings, than Christian used those same wings to briefly create a wall of flame, completely encircling me.

If this had been a real fight, I would have been literally cooked.

"Your instinct wasn't bad," Christian said as he shifted back into his human form. He casually raised one hand and recalled his fire into his hand before it could set the basement ablaze. "But you need to make sure you have the resources available if you're going to try something like that."

"How much water would it take to completely douse a phoenix?" Julia wondered aloud.

Christian thought for a moment. "About five hundred gallons."

"You'd have to drown him in one of those country fair dunk tanks," Maverick added with sly satisfaction from his corner.

I looked stupidly back at the open water bottle. "Oh."

Aaron was next, and despite my attempt to blind him the way Soo Min had, he had his giant wolf jaws wrapped around my neck in about ten seconds flat. Likewise, when I went up against Dorian, my attempt to fill the air with all the dust from every surface in the room wasn't a bad idea, I was informed. But I would have to make sure not to choke myself with the dust as well.

"I tried," I mumbled to Julia after Aithan had cleared the air. "I just don't have the right amount of control."

Still, despite losing every round I fought, I began to learn new methods of fighting that I'd never thought of before. My biggest eureka moment happened when I was standing across from Jamie in his chupacabra form. And though I knew it wouldn't do much good, I ran through my readily available resources in my head.

Elven power was the quickest to conjure. But it would be a lot more useful if I could use that *and* another power at the same time–

Jamie lunged. Throwing my hands up, I brought a rain of raw green energy sparks down over his head. Jamie let out a yelp and jumped back, only to shake his head like a dog and come at me again.

But as I'd released the energy above him, the thought had occurred to me to try separating the magic that resided in my mind from that in the rest of my body. The mental block I still fought seemed to fit like a rubber band around my mind. *That* wouldn't be disappearing any time soon. But Christian had said to trust my instincts. And my hand was suddenly itching to use more of its elven power.

So I tried something new.

I raised one hand again the way I had to create elven energy. Seeing this, Jamie dodged it easily before launching himself forward, both claws raised.

With all my might, I pushed back against the mental rubber band for just long enough to send a burst of fae magic into the space between Jamie and me. And I could see by the expression on his face that it had worked. In his mind, a cinderblock wall was raised in front of him. He tried to stop, but he had too much momentum. So instead of stopping, he tripped and fell at my feet, where I conjured the most pathetic elven knife imaginable and held it above his throat.

The whole room stood still.

"You... you won."

This statement came from a very bewildered-sounding Jamie, who was still lying at my feet, gaping up at me. His words, however, seemed to wake everyone from their stunned silence. And then the room exploded with shrieks and shouts of joy and congratulations.

I laughed as it felt like everyone was suddenly on top of me, hugging me or patting me on the back. Jamie, to his credit, didn't even seem to be annoyed that I'd beat him. On the contrary, he seemed more enthusiastic than anyone else.

The cheering only quieted when Aithan's voice broke through the joyous cacophony.

"That was good, Clarkson. Which means it's my turn now."

I blinked at him. "Excuse me?"

"You heard me. You've got half a minute to prepare."

I studied him, trying to decide if he really meant it or not. He didn't appear to be joking. On the contrary, his eyes glittered like those of a predator that had just sighted its prey, and I could feel the magic fairly rolling off of him in waves.

"I've won *one* match," I reminded him, holding up my index finger. "One. Need I remind you that you're a *Nomos?*"

He only gave me a feral smile and began to stalk forward toward the training mat. "And you're a wizard. I would say the odds are very even."

"That's a lie, and you know it." But while I spoke, I went back to the same place I'd stood a few minutes before.

Most of the others watched like they were about to see the sequel to their favorite movie. Miss Lillian and Dorian, however, exchanged concerned glances before Miss Lillian cleared her throat pointedly as she glared in Aithan's direction.

But Aithan ignored her. Instead, he took his place across from me and nodded. "All right, Clarkson. You've got ten seconds left to think up a game plan. What'll it be?"

My mind felt blank as I tried to brainstorm strategies. He was an elf. Elves changed the world around them. So that obviously meant I should...

What should I do? I screamed in my head. But my mind remained blank.

I barely had the time to react when he conjured his energy whip in his right hand. Thankfully, due to all the training I'd endured that week, my first reaction was to conjure for myself an energy shield.

"Good," Miss Lillian called out. "And a helm!"

Just in time, I was able to visualize the helmet on my head as Aithan's long whip came cracking down over me.

My heart raced in my chest as I held my energy shield with my left hand, and used my right to sweep a wide arc in front of me. Unlike Soo Min's illusion, which had been directed only at Dorian, mine was big enough that we *both* saw my rainforest creation around us. This made him—and as a result, me—more difficult to see.

Unfortunately, I couldn't wield two kinds of magic at the same time. My energy shield sputtered and disappeared as I held the rainforest illusion to separate us. But that didn't last long either, as Aithan sliced his way through the false trees with what was now an energy ax. The speed at which he did this took me by surprise, and I accidentally dropped the illusion as I backpedaled quickly.

In its place, I tried to conjure fire the way Christian had taught me, but it quickly sputtered out in my hand, completely useless as Aithan snapped his energy sword back into a whip, then snapped it over and around my left wrist.

I knew I should use magic, but instinct and annoyance were too strong as he yanked me toward him with the whip. I let him pull me close enough that I could throw a roundhouse kick at his head. He blocked this easily, but before he could reset, I moved to a sidekick combination and was able to nail him hard enough in the side to push him back a step.

"Would you look at that?" Despite just getting kicked, his voice was smooth and taunting, and not at all out of breath the way I felt. "Clarkson's riled."

Riled was right. Frustration and anger were quickly boiling up inside me as he easily countered everything I did. Even my kick, while it had pushed him back, hadn't seemed to hurt at all.

It was a mistake to let my anger show. Anger made fighters sloppy. And just as I'd known he would, he took advantage of my frustration by yanking me closer with his whip again, which was still wrapped around my wrist. I could tell from his stance that he was about to throw a kick of his own.

He was toying with me. But that was about to end.

Quickly, I shrank into my chipmunk form, loosening the whip enough for it to fall uselessly to the ground. Then, still in my chipmunk form, I projected the illusion that there were twelve of me scurrying in every direction. Aithan's head whipped from side to side, confusion wrinkling his brow as he tried to look at all the chipmunks at once.

But as I still couldn't hold two magics at the same time, my chipmunk form disappeared, and I reappeared in my human form—all twelve of me. Without pause, I took two bounding leaps toward him, my eleven doppelgangers doing the same. Just as we began to converge, I went for an elbow to his throat.

As fast as I was, however, the last thing I expected was for him to whirl around and grab me—the real me—firmly with his left arm. At the same time, he snapped his whip around my waist, drawing me in and then yanking my back against his chest. It was the favored position of any vampire, leaving the victim completely helpless, her back to her enemy. In fact, he did it so well that I nearly expected him to put his teeth inches from my neck the way Dorian had done with Soo Min.

But to my surprise, he only put his nose close to my neck and sniffed. And I was suddenly very aware of just how close he was holding me. A shiver ran down my back

But oddly, it wasn't from fear.

"That was good," he murmured smoothly. "But you made a mistake."

"Oh?" My brain tried to grasp the concept of words. What was wrong with me? Why couldn't I think? "What was that?" I managed to croak.

He sniffed again. "I've always liked that perfume," he murmured in my ear. "Maybe wear less when going into a fight."

I turned to look back at him over my shoulder. And for some reason I couldn't name, we seemed frozen that way for what felt like an eternity before he finally let me go.

As soon as I was free, our friends converged, congratulating me yet again.

"He's the best of the best," Christian said. "All things considered, you did really well."

"You're starting to get the hang of this!" Julia crowed.

"Shouldn't be too long before someone *actually* stands a chance at kicking his royal butt." Soo Min smirked.

But when I tried to find him again, Aithan had already turned away and was frowning as he made his way up the steps to the door.

Chapter Twenty-Three

Aithan

I stalked out to the pool, but couldn't bring myself to sit in any of the chairs on the deck. I was too tense for that.

Not all supernaturals were aware of it, but not only did elves contain more powerful magic than the other races, we also felt more... passionately than most other races. Kingdoms had risen and fallen throughout history based on mere elven sentiments. And tonight...

The sliding glass door behind me opened, and I heard the soft murmurs of Dorian and Miss Lillian. They were thick as thieves these days, though I supposed that made sense, as they had both taken on the roles of stand-in parents since joining the group. Dorian was older by far than Miss Lillian, but what she lacked in vampire years, she made up for in wit and wisdom. Fond as I was of both of them, however, this time I didn't turn around to greet them.

I just couldn't.

There was a pause in their conversation.

"I'm going inside for a drink," Dorian finally said in a soft voice. "The case of that new blood substitute that I ordered arrived today, and I want to test whether it's actually as good as true O neg."

Miss Lillian murmured something in reply before coming out to stand beside me. But to my relief, she said nothing.

Unfortunately, however, it seemed I was unable to do the same.

"I did a dangerous thing," I said, glaring down into the water.

Miss Lillian only sighed.

"I don't know why I let myself hold her like that." My throat grew tight as I spoke. "I don't know why I let myself wish."

As I said the words, however, I knew they were lies. I knew *exactly* why I'd held Everleigh like that. Sure, it was part of the sparring match. I'd put over a dozen male opponents into submission that way in my line of work, though that usually involved some sort of blade to their ribs or neck. No one could deny my technique had been good.

But I could have let her go immediately. Heck, if I was honest with myself, I would admit that I could have finished the match a dozen other ways, none of which involved bringing her that close to me.

I *had* pulled her close, however. And having her there had felt *good*. The same way it felt good when I heard her laugh, or saw the fire of determination in her eyes.

Miss Lillian waited another moment before she finally spoke. "Have you tried telling Everleigh about your curse? The way her uncle told her about hers, perhaps?"

I shook my head and ran a hand through my hair. "My grandfather was sloppy when he cursed her. It was given out of spite, considering he didn't expect much out of her anyway. But mine..."

My curse had obviously been carefully planned. The wording was specific enough that there was no way he could have thought it up on the spot. No, my grandfather had crafted my curse like a potter shaping his favorite kind of clay.

"The others, to my knowledge, don't know about it either. They're too young. Except Dorian, of course. He knows.' Miss Lillian pursed her lips. "I guess that comes from recruiting a younger generation of fighters, rather than the older ones. If we had more volunteers your parents' age..." She let out another sigh and shook her head. "Just... be careful, Aithan." Her smile was sad. "But I suppose I don't need to tell you that." She turned and headed back toward the house before pausing at the door. "I just don't want either of you to get hurt."

Chapter Twenty-Four

Everleigh

I TUGGED at the hem of my dress again as I stared into my bedroom mirror. It just seemed so *short*.

"Stop doing that," Soo Min ordered. When I rolled my eyes at her, she just rolled hers back. "Good grief, Everleigh. If I didn't know any better, I'd think you'd been raised by nuns." She squinted as she focused on perfecting my eyeliner.

"Besides," Julia added as she applied her own makeup. "You're wearing leggings underneath it. I've seen you in less at the gym."

"At the gym, I wasn't dressed like a walking disco ball," I grumbled. It was the night of the heist, and Julia and Soo Min had miraculously moved from mutual resentment to annoying besties as they conspired to make me "club-worthy."

Soo Min's words. Not mine.

"Look, can't we just glamour the club look on?" I whined as Soo Min moved to the other eye. "This is taking a ridiculous amount of time. We're going to be late."

"I can see why you never took her with you," Soo Min said as she leaned back to study her work.

"Right?" Julia answered. "I never would have gotten her out of the house. Everleigh, look at these and tell me which color you like best." She held up one silver heel and one black.

"I'm right here, you know. I can hear you," I mumbled. "Okay, fine. If I have to wear heels, give me the black."

"Silver it is," Julia sang.

"Everleigh, what you don't understand because you apparently weren't *listening* the first time," Soo Min continued, "is that the less glamour we use, the more realistic our little game of pretend will be. There. Finished." She glared at me as she capped the eyeliner. "And don't you even *think* of touching your face. If you smudge my masterpiece, we won't need to infiltrate Pandora's Key because I will kill you myself."

Julia's phone chimed. She looked at the screen, then sighed.

"What is it?" I asked.

"It's Georgie," she said, giving me a grim smile. "He keeps demanding to know what's going on and if we're all right."

I winced. He was still texting me daily as well, despite my insistence that we were fine, and just had to sort out some family stuff. "I'm sorry," I said, "but we can't tell him. If we do—"

"I know, I know." Julia huffed. "He'll end up a pet like me. I told him the other day that I was helping you through some family stuff. I'll tell him the same thing again."

Soon after that, Soo Min and Julia began to chat about makeup and Soo Min's signature streak of pink hair, so I put on the shoes Julia had handed me. Then I stood and studied myself in the mirror.

Despite all my protests, I had to admit that the look was cute. Really cute. Even if it did draw attention to my legs. The dress had spaghetti straps that widened until they met in a V below the little hollow at the bottom of my throat. The cut was simple, and whatever fabric it was made out of shimmered like glitter.

It was also Soo Min's. Because there was no way in the world I would have ever dropped cash on something so glitzy. Unfortunately, it was also shorter than any dress I'd ever worn in my life, and I was pretty sure Julia and Soo Min had bonded only because they'd had to talk me into wearing it. After a very... *very* long argument, they'd grudgingly realized that the only way I would ever walk out of my bedroom in that thing was if I was allowed to wear leggings beneath it. So we'd eventually settled on a pair of black leggings that reached just below my knees.

The silver bangles I wore on my left hand were also cute, but they were actually useful too, having been charmed by Miss Lillian against drink tampering and to monitor my consciousness. I still wore the tracking necklace Aithan's family had given me, and I'd added my own crystal earrings to match. And, apparently, I now topped the whole look off with low, strappy, glittery heels.

At this rate, I'd be lucky if the astronauts on the International Space Station didn't spot me before the night was over.

Still...

As I studied myself in the mirror again, it hit me that–sans leggings–I was dressed in what Aithan's girlfriends tended to wear.

Huh.

What did one make of that?

What would *Aithan* make of that?

"And now that we're ready, it's showtime," Soo Min announced with a grin.

My jaw dropped. "You guys had like...five minutes! How did you get ready so fast?"

"We don't squawk at every item of clothing we put on." Julia grabbed my hand and pulled me out the door. "Let's go!"

I had to focus on not tripping as we started down the stairs. Hopefully, no running would be involved tonight. In addition to martial arts, I'd taken twelve years of professional ballet classes and was a competent dancer. But walking in heels was another skill entirely.

The men were waiting for us at the bottom of the stairs. As we started down, their eyes widened, and beside me, I could almost feel Soo Min's growing smirk.

Standing a little way from the others, however, Aithan watched us with an expression I couldn't read. But judging by the tense set of his shoulders, he was in a bad mood.

I didn't want to admit it, of course, but I couldn't help feeling a little disappointed. I had wondered... Okay, so I'd *hoped* he would notice. Especially after the way he'd looked at me last night at the end of our match, while I was still in his arms. But then he'd let go and walked away, and had avoided me ever since.

Not that I needed his attention. I sniffed and smiled at Miss Lillian as we reached the bottom of the stairs. I hadn't needed his attention when I was fourteen, and I didn't need it now.

"Soo Min." Miss Lillian was frowning at my friend. "That is a very... *very* short dress you're wearing."

Julia and Soo Min exchanged an amused look.

"Soo Min," Aithan said, his words clipped. "May I have a word?"

Soo Min glided over to him, and they stepped into the kitchen. I couldn't hear what was said, but a moment later, Soo Min emerged, looking quite pleased with herself.

"Are you sure about this?" Aithan followed her, looking even more like a thundercloud than before. "Or are you just having your way for the sake of winning?"

"Excuse me." Soo Min whirled on him. She didn't lose her smile, but her eyes narrowed. "This is a *fae* establishment, yes?"

His frown deepened. "Yes."

"And fae tend to prefer a certain... aesthetic, yes?"

Aithan pinched the bridge of his nose and closed his eyes. "Fine. Just... fine."

Soo Min turned happily and began to glide toward the garage once more. But no matter how many times I asked her on the way to the car, she refused to tell me what their argument had been about.

"Get in the car," was all she said. "It's time to go. We'll finish our glamours on the way."

Once all three girls were in Dorian's car, with Dorian at the wheel and Miss Lillian beside him, Soo Min flipped open her clutch and pulled out a little package. Inside was a single green mochi snack.

"Eat this," she told Julia. "It's charmed so we can keep track of you in case your earrings fall off. It should last four to five hours."

Only then did I realize that someone must have charmed Julia's earrings, just as they'd charmed my bangles.

"Julia, this is your last chance. Are you sure you want to–" I began, but Julia rolled her eyes.

"If you ask me one more time whether I want to do this, I'm going to scream. Yes, Everleigh, yes! I'm coming on this mission! And there's nothing you can say to talk me out of it!"

I sighed but nodded. The more I thought about Julia in a fae establishment, the more worried I felt. But then again, she'd been to this club before. And that time, she hadn't had anyone with her for protection. Now that she was my pet, weird and horrifying as it was, she would actually be safer than any other human there. Stealing another fae's pet was forbidden.

"Now," Soo Min turned to me after Julia had taken the charmed treat, "it's time for us to glamour ourselves. We'll need to hold the glamour for at least two hours. Do you think you can do that?"

I took a deep breath and nodded. I'd done it several times in practice over the last few days, and I was decently confident in my ability to do the same in the club.

Mostly confident.

Closing my eyes, I tightened my core and imagined myself pushing back against the strange barrier that walled off my magic. As I held this image in my head, I also imagined the vivid colors in my eyes dulling, and the slight point in my ears tapering off. The glamour stone I held in my purse should already be doing this for me, but in the case it was taken, I had to be doubly sure the glamour would hold. Allowing my human facade to drop in a fae establishment would *not* go over well.

"Everyone take one of these earpieces." Miss Lillian turned around to face the backseat. "I've charmed them to amplify sound directly into your head so you can place them anywhere on your person without having to physically place them in your ears. Jamie tapped into the security system, so we'll be able to see the goings-on around you. Just be listening for our instructions. Do you remember the plan?"

Soo Min grinned. She'd been the one to devise the plan, and was quite delighted to have done so. "We'll be looking around for the guy in the photo. Once we find him, we'll pretend we're out for a fun night and do some flirting. Once we know who has the package, we'll do our best to take it. Removing his coat so he can dance, or using our elven pickpocket skills." She fixed a sharp eye on me.

Miss Lillian nodded. "Yes. And the men will be stationed at the bar to run interference if something goes wrong. Everleigh." Her voice softened. "Lean into your fae magic tonight. It's going to be everywhere. Just... keep it subtle, and you should be fine."

"Speaking of the club, we're here," Soo Min announced. Her glittery nails flashed in the setting sunlight as Dorian pulled up at the large casino's roundabout entrance, and she flashed me a brilliant smile. "Everleigh, it's time to see you shine."

Once Dorian dropped us off, we made our way through one of the many flashy glass doors and into the hotel lobby. To our right, slot machines stretched all the way down the wall, and beyond those, card tables. The air smelled of cigarettes and something synthetically sweet. But we turned left and followed the pulsing sound of music instead.

I'd never been inside a club before, but after doing a quick search, I'd learned that this particular club was one of the more popular ones for locals. It was fairly new, and a few years ago, they'd done a huge ad push all over social media and on the local television stations. And once I knew what it was, I couldn't believe I hadn't recognized it as fae-owned the few times I'd seen it advertised before. Now, as I looked at the sign outside the club doors, I realized that the fake diamonds edging the vivid pink and purple sign should have given it away. It practically screamed *fae*.

Just like in the movies, there were two guys in suits stationed outside the doors from which the pulsating music was coming. One checked each person's ID as he or she came to the front of the line. The other kept an eye on the line itself, which was sectioned off by pink velvet ropes on each side.

When it was our turn to walk through the doors, I nearly panicked, sure they would see right through us. But I did my best to look cool and nonchalant as I handed them my driver's license, along with Soo Min and Julia. And I must not have done too bad a job because the one looking at IDs barely glanced at the cards before nodding at us to go in.

The music, which had seemed low and rhythmic outside, was nearly deafening in the open space, and I had to take a deep breath as we walked in. It felt like my heart was changing its rate to match that of the nearly hypnotic beat. The pulsing colorful lights flashing on the pearlescent ceiling tiles only made it worse. People lounged or danced all around, and I could immediately see why my friends had insisted I wear something shiny. If I'd worn purely solid colors the way I'd wanted to, I would have stuck out like a sore thumb. But by wearing Soo Min's disco ball dress, I simply blended in.

They're already here, Soo Min mouthed.

I glanced casually at the bar to see Aithan and Christian leaning against the far end, each holding a beer. Aaron and Jamie sat at the other end, closer to us. To say their presence was enormously comforting was the understatement of the century. I hadn't realized I was holding my breath until the sight of them had me breathing easier.

"Let's get our drinks," Julia called, just loud enough for us to hear over the music.

Soo Min and I nodded. The plan was to have drinks from the start so we could pretend we were already having fun when we found our target. So we went over to the bar to stand beside Aithan and Christian as we waited for our drinks–ignoring them, of course, as we did. I got a ginger ale, and the girls both ordered virgin mojitos. As soon as we had our drinks, we turned around and began to search.

As we wandered, keeping watch on the doors, Julia and Soo Min giggled and laughed as though they went to clubs every night. All the while, however, I noticed Soo Min's sharp eyes taking note of everything she could see. And Julia's chatter was just a bit too bubbly for her usual level of cool calm.

"There," we heard Aaron's deep voice in our earpieces. "eight o'clock. By the pegasus sculpture."

Casually, I turned toward the towering glass sculpture of the ancient fae creature. Sure enough, there was the man from the picture standing beneath it. He was of average height, and probably in his mid to late-twenties. He had orange-red hair and dark eyes, and based on his physique, I guessed him to either be a fae or some kind of smaller shifter.

And he was looking around just as carefully as we were.

"Here we go," Soo Min murmured, taking another swig of her drink before flouncing over to him.

Our timing couldn't have been better. As we headed over, a second man joined him. This guy was slightly bigger, but not big enough to be a werewolf or anything horrendously large. He had magic of some sort, though I couldn't tell exactly what, as he was obviously using some sort of a glamour stone. My bet, however, judging by the strange shade of brown in his eyes, was that he was a vampire. They shook hands just before we reached them.

"Hello, gentlemen," Soo Min purred. "Looking for friends?"

I had to hand it to her. The girl was a born actor. Gone was the cynical, snarky, bossy bubble tea master. And in her place stood a sparkling young fae with a single pink stripe running down her silky black hair and a daring gleam in her dark eyes.

Julia, though she didn't have magic, was just as good. She sidled up to the unknown man's arm and gave a giggle as she flipped her blond hair.

Which meant I had to step up my game.

And for a moment, I panicked.

I didn't flirt with guys. I sparred with them. I baited and debated them. But flirting? Where in the world was I supposed to learn that on the fly?

Before I could completely blank out, however, inspiration struck. I didn't flirt with guys... but Aithan's girlfriends did. Each one seemed to do nothing but flirt when they were with him. All I would have to do was imitate everything I resented about them. So ignoring the suddenly strong desire to send a wicked grin back at the elf watching us from the bar, I leaned in slightly and gave the men my sweetest smile.

Okay, so I felt as dumb as a doorknob, but to my amazement, it seemed to work. The two men blinked at us a few times before grinning. And sure as clear skies in the Mojave desert, the second guy's canines were just slightly more pronounced than his other teeth.

We had ourselves a vampire.

"Can we buy you ladies another round of drinks?" Pandora Guy asked. I didn't miss the way he puffed his chest out as he spoke.

"We want to dance!" Julia pouted, finishing her drink and putting it down on a table nearby.

"You up for it?" Soo Min indicated the dance floor, which was already full of men and women moving in time with the music's heavy beat. "Or should we find someone else?"

Vampire Dude looked like he had reservations, but Pandora Guy was already letting Soo Min lead him out to the floor. And even Vampire Dude's reservations seemed to evaporate when Julia put her hand on his arm and gave it a slight tug. I giggled for good measure before running and squeezing myself between them, taking his arm as I pushed Julia out. Vampire Dude looked amused, and Julia seemed surprised, but I only giggled stupidly and held his arm tighter. He seemed—and smelled young, which meant he'd probably been changed only recently.

Which also meant he and Julia were *not* going to dance.

Once we were on the dance floor, I had a chance to really study the two men as our little group began to fall into rhythm. My first conclusion was that they were both creeps, and I would be happy to be rid of them. But as we had a job to do first, I did a quick scan of their outfits.

Whatever they were handing off was probably small, as both wore jeans, and the Pandora Guy wore a simple sports coat. Vampire Dude didn't even have that, wearing only a button-up shirt with one front pocket. Pandora Guy's sports coat probably had several inner pockets, but they wouldn't hide much even if he had them.

Soo Min seemed to be thinking along the same lines. She play-fully slapped Pandora Guy on the arm before telling him to take his coat off. Vampire Dude snickered, but Pandora Guy refused.

"You're a killjoy!" she laughed.

He laughed along, but this time, it sounded forced. "I'm afraid I'll forget it," he said, shaking his head. "I did the last time I was here and lost my wallet with it!"

Soo Min gave him an absurd pout, but I felt like jumping up and down. We'd found it. Whatever he was hiding was in his coat.

But now that we knew where it was, how did we get it out?

Even as I thought the question, however, the answer struck.

"I need to use the restroom!" I called over the music. "Julia, want to come with me?"

"Sure!" Julia said, flashing one more smile at the men. "We'll be right back!"

Julia and I went to the bathroom. After making sure it was empty, I dragged Julia with me into the big stall at the end.

"What are you doing?" she whispered. "Why are we in here?"

"That guy is not going to give his coat up. Which means we need a plan." I took a deep breath. "So this is what I need you to do."

Chapter Twenty-Five

Aithan

Soo Min came up to the bar and stood beside me to order another drink.

"Are they making the trade?" she asked in a low voice as she kept her eyes on the bartender. "I left them alone for a moment to see if they would try."

As she was speaking, the Pandora's Key operative said something to his friend while watching Soo Min's back. He touched the opposite breast of his sports coat as he spoke, seeming nearly unaware he was doing it. No pockets were visible in the place he touched, so I could only guess that whatever he was checking was on the inside of the coat. A hidden pocket or something like it.

"Everleigh, where are you?" I growled, knowing she would hear me over the earpiece. Everleigh was definitely up to something. I could hear her and Julia speaking, but they were talking low enough that I was having a hard time hearing them over the music.

"Keep your shirt on, Nomos," she replied a little louder. "We've got a plan."

I glanced at Christian, who just shrugged.

At that moment, Julia walked back out. But Everleigh wasn't with her.

"Clarkson, what are you doing?" I asked. "Where are you?"

But this time, there was no reply. Instead, Julia walked straight up to the two men, who were back at the table near the Pegasus and deep in animated conversation. No trade had been made yet, but whatever they'd been discussing looked intense. Soo Min took her drink from the bartender and walked back quickly to join her.

Still no Everleigh.

The itch to slug the second guy had been growing inside me as he'd danced and laughed with Everleigh on the dance floor, and I'd nearly lost it when she'd grabbed his arm and hung on it like she was drunk. Only the knowledge that I could be at her side in less than two seconds had kept me in place.

Which was stupid. This was what we were here for, after all.

Nonsensical as it might be, however, it was all I could do to keep myself from marching over and demanding that Julia tell me where Everleigh had gone. The sweet, innocent girl I'd watched over for years had disappeared in a club full of supernaturals and tipsy humans, and the need to have her safe at my side was eating away at my gut.

"Lillian," I said in a low voice, "can you tell wher–"

Julia let out a shriek as she reached out and grabbed the Pandora's Key operative's sleeve to catch herself as she tripped.

He and the other guy hurried to right her, and she let them, laughing as though she were embarrassed. The drama of the fall, however, had me convinced that the whole thing had been a ruse.

A ruse for what, though?

Soo Min pointed back at the dance floor and asked if they wanted to dance again. The Pandora's Key operative began to nod, but then he frowned as his right shoulder twitched. Then it twitched again. Looking more confused, he grabbed his right shoulder with his left hand and began itching viciously.

The other man stepped back and stared at him like he had lost his mind. Meanwhile, more and more people not involved in the scene were beginning to stare as well. Some on the dance floor were even taking notice.

"You girls are drawing too much attention," Christian said in a low voice. "The club owners are going to notice if they haven't already."

I stood and began to make my way toward them, trying not to look too hurried but walking with as much speed as I could manage.

Had they given the guy an itching spell? And *where* was Everleigh? If I didn't see her soon, I was going to start looking.

Soo Min reached out to the guy as though to help. And though the snarky fae drove me nuts nearly every time we talked, I had to admit her brilliance. The Pandora's Key operative was full-out writhing like he was possessed, which allowed her to drop her drink as though he'd accidentally hit it out of her hand. The sound of breaking glass immediately directed everyone's attention to her and away from the Pandora's Key guy.

"I'm sorry!" she cried, her eyes glistening with glamoured tears. "I was just trying to help! Ugh! What's wrong with you?"

The Pandora's Key guy immediately stopped. He looked down at himself and then at Soo Min in dismay and confusion.

"I... I don't know!" he stuttered. "It felt like there was something moving in my coat!"

"What's going on?"

Christian and I turned to see Everleigh walk out from behind a pillar. Her hair was a bit windblown, and her dress slightly rumpled, but otherwise, she simply looked like she was returning from the bathroom.

I was staring at her, trying to discern what she'd been up to, when Miss Lillian's voice came through the earpieces. "Be ready! Another one is headed your way!"

Before I could ask what she meant, a new voice called out from my left.

"Everleigh Clarkson?"

All my senses went on high alert as I turned to find a fae woman approaching the group. When I recognized her, I accidentally let out a low growl. She was one of the fae we'd fought in the canyon. And the same one, in fact, who had led the attack at the university campus.

"Can I help you?" Everleigh crossed her arms and looked up at the woman defiantly. Out of the corner of my eye, I saw Aaron and Jamie headed our way. Knowing this woman wouldn't be fooled by our little act, I made my way to Everleigh's side, where I could stare down at the fae.

"What a fantastic coincidence to find you here!" The woman beamed. "We meant what we said about just talking. We have a room reserved." She stepped back to gesture at the hallway down which the bathroom was located. "Surely you wouldn't mind chatting now, seeing as you've already made friends with another of our members." She nodded at the guy we'd been watching.

"I'm not interested in the way you 'just talk,'" Everleigh snapped.

"Perhaps," the fae woman said slowly, "but I think you'll agree we ought to talk now." She glanced around. "You'll want to ensure the safety of everyone here, of course."

She was threatening us—using the humans and supernaturals in the club to force Everleigh's cooperation. Our little party stiffened and drew closer together, while the second guy took one look at her and bailed.

These people did not know how to take no for an answer. For a moment, however, I wondered if Everleigh was considering it. Compared to most supernaturals, she was a bleeding heart when it came to humans. Would she agree to their demands because they were threatening people?

But to my surprise, Everleigh only lifted her chin in defiance and put her hands on her hips. "I'm not sure whether you're an idiot or whether you just like playing with fire. But this club is fae-owned. And considering the... competency of your previous attempts to get my attention, I have serious doubts about your willingness to start that firestorm here and now."

The sound of my earpiece going dead created a crackling noise in my ears as yet another woman's voice called out above the music,

"My niece is quite right."

We all turned to see a tall fae woman in an expensive pink suit and gold name tag enter our circle. "That would be more foolish than I can express," she said with a smile.

I stifled the curse I wanted so much to utter out loud. *This* was a face I knew far too well. And it was not one I had hoped to see tonight.

<hr>

Princess Fiadh looked around at my group like a cat who had stumbled upon a mouse nest. Her blond hair was pulled back gracefully into a feminine but business-like knot at the back of her head, allowing just a few tendrils to hang down, framing her face. Shiny pink heels made her legs look a mile long, and her suit had obviously been custom-made.

If I'd been asked to come up with a code name for this woman, it would have been "Name Brand."

Name Brand, youngest daughter of the fae King Daniil of House Gallagher, oversaw most of the Gallagher business enterprises. Shrewd, close-fisted, and cutthroat, the entire supernatural community as a whole was loath to cross swords with her. And though she closely resembled her oldest sister, Everleigh's mother, they were as different as sisters could possibly be. Only her father seemed to have any sway over her dealings. And, of course, the Nomoses. But even they usually ignored her.

She was also *supposed* to be out of town. I'd known this club was in the Gallagher territory, so I'd asked Miss Lillian to do some research ahead of time. And according to Miss Lillian, Princess

Fiadh was scheduled to speak at a business conference in Portland. The last thing I had wanted was for Everleigh to accidentally run into her aunt.

"Everleigh," Fiadh said, her tone warm and inviting. "The last I'd heard was that you'd sworn off magic."

Everleigh swallowed, but to her credit, she didn't stutter. "I knew early on that I wasn't gifted in magic," she said slowly. "So there didn't seem to be a reason to try."

Fiadh's sharp eyes slid over Soo Min and then moved to Julia. Her mouth curved up into a smirk. "You tell your human friends about us, dear one?" Her tone was politely curious, but it had a cruel undertone.

Typical fae.

Everleigh stiffened but answered, "She's my pet." Only then did I realize that Soo Min must have also done a charm to cover Julia's tattoo-like pet mark on her arm.

Fiadh stared for a moment, then let out a bubbly laugh. "Maybe you *are* part of the family, after all."

Everleigh bristled.

"I am curious, though," Fiadh continued. "Everleigh Clarkson is a name I've heard mentioned often as of late. And it makes me wonder why." As she spoke, she waved a hand lazily toward our little group. Fae men in suits appeared from the shadows and forcibly removed the Pandora's Key operatives. One moment, they were there. The next, they were gone.

I held my breath as Everleigh paused. She had to be careful. Her parents had wisely never introduced Everleigh to her aunts or uncles, aside from Finn from the bookshop. Now her aunt was fishing for information.

"Word has it that my parents were recently taken by King Kostas due to some sort of threat," she said bitterly. "But *apparently*, I wasn't important enough to be considered worthy of royal protection." She straightened. "So I'm staying with friends."

I let out a small breath. That was a *good* answer.

But her aunt continued to study her. Finally, she asked, "Are you holding a glamour now?"

Everleigh sent a pointed look at the many people walking around. "You want me to drop it *here?*"

Fiadh raised her left hand. Immediately, I could feel a thin glamour shield us from view.

Everleigh huffed, then closed her eyes. A few seconds later, she opened her eyes again, their blue much more vivid than before, and her ears regaining their slightly pointed tips.

Her aunt blinked at her, then laughed. "You aren't very good, are you? If you were trying to stay under the radar, no wonder that woman recognized you."

The words had to sting. But to Everleigh's credit, she didn't argue. Smart girl. As much as the insults might hurt, it was better to let her aunt think her an incapable *Anikos* than to hint at the truth.

"I think," Fiadh continued, her eyes finally coming to rest on me, "that we ought to continue this conversation somewhere more private." As she spoke, we were suddenly surrounded by guards. Aaron and Jamie hadn't made it all the way to us, so they faded back in the background, out of sight.

Fiadh turned and strode back toward the darkened hall from which she'd come, her shiny pink heels clicking against the tiled floor. "Follow me, please."

***

We followed her silently down two halls and into a large sleek office, where her propensity toward name brand clothing apparently extended to furniture and decor as well. There was a cylindrical fish tank in the center of the vast office, the kind that professional companies custom-make for TV shows. Everything else, including the desks, tables, chairs, carpet, and curtains, was pale pink, white, or gold, and expensive artifacts and jeweled ornaments dotted the room.

Fiadh seated herself behind a long glass desk with the largest computer monitor I'd ever seen and what looked like a customized keyboard. There were several chairs and couches spread about the room, but she didn't ask us to sit.

"My niece coming here with friends I can understand," she said, steepling her fingers. "We have records of both of them visiting us before." She nodded at Soo Min and Julia. "But you and your friend, Nomos, are a surprise."

I chuckled. "And not a pleasant one, it would seem." I paused. "I'll admit that I also didn't realize you owned this establishment. It seems we're both learning things today."

Her smile froze. "Recently purchased. But what I want to know is what you're doing with my niece."

This was a trap. There was no way she was oblivious to our family ties, as her sister had eloped with my father's best friend. The two elven princes, abandoning the courts with their wives, had been the scandal of the century.

"Watching out for her," I answered. "Since her *family* decided not to."

My jab hit its mark. Probably too well. Fiadh snarled, and for the shortest of moments, I saw the unbridled fury of the ancient fae cross her face. There's a reason legends describe fae as cruel and sadistic. Not all are, of course. But there are... enough to merit human lore.

"If my sister had kept contact with her family, she might have *told* us what Everleigh needed," Fiadh snapped. The words were said quickly enough, but I noted the care with which she chose them. She said Everleigh's mother *might* have told them about what Everleigh needed. Which, I could only guess, meant her family had *known* the elven courts had left Everleigh alone.

They'd just chosen to do nothing about it.

Fiadh's eyes, which had streaks of vivid purple in them, narrowed. Then she smiled and stood. "And... I suppose this is all done out of the kindness of your heart? Giving up money, time, and..." She glanced at Everleigh, and her cruel smile widened. "Entertainment? Or are you entertaining yourself at her expense?" She took a few steps closer, and her voice dropped to a near whisper. "What will King Kostas think if he gets wind that his grandson is playing games with an *Anikos?*"

If we had been in danger before, there were now tornado sirens going off in my head, complete with flashing red lights. In just a few simple words, Everleigh's aunt had laid multiple traps.

More than anything, she was trying to bait me into giving up information about Pandora's Key. She and her guards had obviously seen that something was going on. And when they'd intervened in the meeting, only the two Pandora's Key members had been taken. She knew who was with who. She simply wanted us to plead our case, to give up every bit of information we had so they would set us free.

At the same time, she was also doing her best to create cracks in our glue. She'd just accused me of playing with Everleigh's heart because I was bored. She was also baiting Everleigh, insulting her split-blood heritage just as she had Everleigh's weak glamour. Groups like ours were unusual in the supernatural world. People tended to stick around their own kind.

Third, she was testing me. I could deny it all I wanted, but the simple truth was that being a Nomos meant I was one of the most powerful supernaturals on the planet. And one of the unfortunate parts of having royal blood—even if one didn't live as a royal—was that royal children made fantastic stepping stones for anyone who was trying to scale the heights of power. If Fiadh knew how much Everleigh meant to me, I had no doubt in my mind that she would abuse Everleigh to death and back to leverage me for her own good.

Everleigh was in more danger now than she'd ever been in her life. And I hated myself for the words that I knew had to come out of my mouth. Because they would cut Everleigh to the heart. But they just might save her life.

"If you're insinuating what I think you are," I scoffed, "then you should know that half-breeds aren't my type. I promised her parents I would guard her for a price." I folded my arms and stared down at her with all the elvish disdain I could muster. It was a lie, of course. They weren't paying me. But Fiadh didn't need to know that.

She sneered back, but after a moment, she just rolled her eyes and made a sound of disgust. "You're not so unlike your grandfather after all."

As she said this, I glanced at Everleigh. She only looked bored and annoyed, much to my relief, studying her nails as she leaned against the doorway between Christian and Julia.

"Fine." Fiadh waved a hand at us. "You're all dismissed, but I don't want to see you at my club again. Understand?" She gave me a sharp smile, like a piranha. "And I do thank you, Your Highness, for clarifying Everleigh's situation. I'll admit that I've been remiss. Something I'd like to remedy in the near future."

I gave her the smallest bow allowable by supernatural standards, and the others followed suit. Then I turned and strode back down the hallway, more than ready to be back outside in the night air, where I could finally breathe. But it really didn't matter how fast we found Jamie and Aaron and then escaped. From now on, Princess Fiadh of the House Gallagher was going to be watching.

Chapter Twenty-Six

Aithan

Our group was subdued as we left the club, nothing like the way we'd come in. Aaron and Jamie met us by the food court just outside the club doors.

"Dorian rented a private limo to pick us up," Aaron said quietly. "We restored the audio connection after you left, and he figured it would be best not to use our personal vehicles to head home now that we're on their radar. We can pick them up early tomorrow morning when we're not being followed out."

I gave him a tired smile. "A good idea."

He smiled back, but we both knew that trying to hide our personal information would do little good. Everleigh's aunt likely knew the names of all the kids in Everleigh's third grade class by now. Fiadh would have had her minions doing research the moment she recognized her elusive niece on the security cameras.

No one else talked until Dorian pulled up in a limo, and we all climbed inside.

"Are you all well?" Miss Lillian called from the front seat.

"We are, thank you," I told her. As well as could be.

"I've never been inside a limo before," Julia whispered to Everleigh. "Are we allowed to eat the little snacks?"

"Well," Jamie said, looking more morose than I'd ever seen him, "not only did we fail to get the package or learn what it was, we also gained ourselves some notoriety with the wrong fae."

Julia shivered. "It was so weird to see Mrs. Clarkson's face on such a horrible person."

Soo Min didn't say anything. She just glowered out the window.

"Who said we failed?"

We all turned to Everleigh.

"Everleigh," Soo Min snapped, "have you *been* on planet Earth for the last hour?"

Everleigh opened her purse and pulled out a tiny ziplock bag the size of a postage stamp. "Unless this wasn't what we were looking for?"

Our jaws dropped as we all leaned in to see what the bag held. A chalky white stone no larger than the head of a sewing pin sat inside.

The car erupted into cheers and shouts as everyone demanded to know how she'd gotten the bag.

"Never," she said with a sly smile as she slipped the bag back into her purse, "underestimate a determined chipmunk."

Laughter broke out as she started to recount the way she'd ridden in Julia's clutch, and then slipped up the Pandora operative's jacket sleeve when Julia "fell" and grabbed his arm. It was then that I remembered her hair looking so windblown when she'd finally reappeared.

"He nearly squished me twice," she said ruefully. "And it was all I could do to get away without someone seeing or stepping on me.

Immediately, the questions began to fly again. Despite everyone else's excitement, however, I couldn't join in. Everleigh spoke with animation, but she was very clearly avoiding my gaze.

I hated myself for what I'd told her aunt back in the casino. It couldn't have been further from the truth. But I'd spent too much time dealing with sticky fae to risk Everleigh's life more than I had to. Pretending to be cut from the same cloth as my grandfather and many of my other family members was my best bet at protecting Everleigh from her aunt. Fae were sneaky and cruel, but the Nomos family was strong and proud. I'd had no choice but to fight fire with fire. If Fiadh had sensed even an inkling of affection for her niece in me, she would have whisked Everleigh away, claiming that it was their duty to protect her. By hiding the depth of my... *connection* to Everleigh, I'd created at least a temporary barrier between the two women.

Still, the whole situation shook me more than it should have. For so long, I'd succeeded in keeping my distance–emotionally and physically–from anything that could be used against me. But these last few weeks had forced me into proximity with situations and people I wasn't used to interacting with. I was getting too close to the edge. And that was without even considering what my grandfather's curse would do to me if I leaned even an inch the wrong way.

No security job I'd ever taken had been as dangerous as the game I was playing now.

"Don't get too excited," I called as Dorian pulled onto the freeway. "We still have some major problems to figure out. And we've complicated a few more."

Soo Min let out a snort. "Do we have to talk about this *now?*"

"Yeah!" Julia added indignantly. "Everleigh just did what no one else could back there!"

"Has anyone stopped to wonder how Pandora's Key seemed to *expect* that Everleigh would be there?" I asked. "Because there is no way they rented that club room just for kicks. They came *ready* to talk to Everleigh."

That sobered everyone quickly.

"It means," Christian said slowly, "that we either have a traitor–"

"Or they have an oracle," Jamie interrupted in a hushed voice. "Which might be worse."

"What's the other problem?" Aaron asked.

"The other problem is that Everleigh's aunt wasn't fooled. And economically speaking, she's even more powerful than she was a few months ago." I pointed out at the Las Vegas Strip as it sped by. "Somehow, we missed that she recently purchased that club. I'd like to know what other acquisitions she's been making and why." I leaned back. "There's also the problem of her promise to 'remedy' Everleigh's situation." I fixed my eyes on Everleigh, but she only stared down at her purse, her shoulders slumped and her smile gone.

"Maybe she feels guilty, now that she knows Mrs. Clarkson is gone?" Julia asked hopefully.

"If you're going to survive this world, Julia," I said, not bothering to soften my tone, "you need to learn one thing. Fae aren't *nice*. They're not nice people. In general, they don't do things out of the goodness of their hearts."

"Soo Min's a fae!" Julia objected.

But Soo Min held up her hands. "Notice I'm not arguing with him."

"Not the royal families, at least," Christian said softly. "The common ones are often more like everyone else."

"And the nice ones," I added harshly, "die."

Julia looked at Soo Min in horror.

But Soo Min just shrugged. "He's not wrong." Her voice hardened. "I guess you never heard about how my mom died."

"I think," Miss Lillian called back over her shoulder, "that after this exciting evening, we could use some food and rest. Let's be done with this conversation until we're all feeling a little more nourished."

Her words were gentle, but no one dared argue with *that* tone. As I watched Everleigh stare out the window, though, I knew that no amount of food or rest would fix what I had just done to her heart.

The drive back to Everleigh's house seemed to last a lifetime. When we finally arrived, Everleigh was barely out of the limo when I touched her arm and waved her over to the corner of the front yard, to the rocks behind a squat palm tree. But I waited until the others went inside before speaking. Christian, to his credit, stood quietly in the shadows where he could keep watch on both us and the property barrier I'd erected. Only when I was sure we were alone, though, did I raise a sound shield to block our conversation from anyone who might try to listen.

"Everleigh," I said, suddenly unable to look her in the eye. "I just want you to know that what I said back in your aunt's office–"

"I know. You were just covering so she would leave us alone." But even as she spoke, she stared down at her hands.

"If she'd figured out..." My voice cracked, and I had to lick my suddenly parched lips. "I've dealt with her people before. They're ruthless and won't hesitate to use any possible weakness against you."

"If she had figured out what?" Everleigh asked, finally looking me in the eye. Glamour completely gone, her eyes burned with the tell-tale fae glow inside them. "What were you so afraid she would find out?"

My voice caught in my throat, and in spite of the countless hours I spent in the gym training my muscles and my magic, I felt more helpless than I ever had.

If she had figured out how I feel about you... hovered on the tip of my tongue. But I couldn't say the words. Because if I did, I would be practically diving headfirst into the shallow end.

"You haven't been immersed in the magical community the way I have," I said, shaking my head. "I know you think you understand, but you've never witnessed firsthand the cruelty we inflict on one another on a daily basis." I spoke the words carefully, but I wondered if she heard the silent plea behind them.

She studied me for what felt like forever, but I saw the moment the hope in her eyes finally flickered out. She had been hoping I would tell her how I felt—*what* I felt. And she wouldn't have been mistaken. I'd slipped up too many times in the last few weeks for her not to at least have some guess.

But I couldn't give her what she hoped for.

And thanks to my grandfather, I would never have a way to try.

Finally, she swallowed hard and blinked several times. "I get what you mean." She let out a harsh laugh. "I mean, she's *my* aunt, after all." Then she turned and went inside, leaving me alone behind her.

Chapter Twenty-Seven

Everleigh

I DID my best to glamour my face as I went into the house, so any tears that had escaped my eyes wouldn't show. As my aunt had so kindly pointed out, my glamours were far from amazing. But no one gave me a second glance as I made my way into the kitchen where everyone else was still celebrating, so my glamour must not have been too bad.

Aithan and Christian followed me inside, but I didn't wait for them as I practically ran to stand beside Julia.

"What are we doing?" I asked, forcing a smile.

She beamed at me. "We're having root beer floats!" Then she frowned and leaned closer. "What's wrong?" she whispered.

Maybe my glamour wasn't so great after all. But then again, Julia was my best friend, and she could read me like a book. At least that hadn't changed.

"I'll tell you later," I promised.

"I used something called a grocery delivery app!" Miss Lillian was exclaiming to anyone who would listen. "It was like magic, only better! They just take your money and deliver the food, and no one tries to kill you or extract a favor!"

"No offense, Miss Lillian," Jamie said, bending over to kiss Miss Lillian's cheek. "But you need to get out more."

Aithan silently stationed himself in the far corner of the kitchen, where he could see everyone and talk to no one. Instead of watching him, however, I decided to mind my own business and enjoy the moment.

Even if his words back in my aunt's office seemed to have been burned into my brain.

He claimed that he didn't mean what he'd said about dating half-breeds. And I believed him. The dangers presented by my fae family were very real. Blood relatives or not, many of them would happily sacrifice their weakest link without a thought if it meant gaining power for the whole.

But that didn't mean his words didn't hurt.

Two hours later, when everyone else but the assigned night watch was asleep, I let the tears silently fall.

Not because Aithan believed what he said—but because I did. I'd figured out young that no one in his right mind would date—let alone marry—a half-breed. And though I knew now that I wasn't a half-breed, it was still how I felt. A wizard I might be, but I wasn't powerful or fast or competent in my magic. I was barely better than I'd been three weeks before, and that was only because I had *really* patient friends.

As a fourteen-year-old, though—all starry-eyed and brimming with blissful ignorance-I had hoped that maybe one day the charismatic Aithan Nomos would see me for me. Not as the annoying little kid who used to follow him around, but as a *girl*.

But Aithan hadn't spared me so much as a glance in high school. Instead, he'd always gone for the obvious ones, the girls who looked like they spent an hour on their makeup before they left the house each morning. Popular human girls. Full-blooded supernatural girls.

The kind of girl I would never be.

My phone buzzed twice on the corner of my desk closest to the bed, and I held my breath, wondering if it would wake Julia. But it didn't, so I grabbed it and glanced at my screen. It was from Georgie.

> Everleigh, I know I'm texting a lot, but I'm really worried. Are you okay? Is Julia fine? I just need some answers, and I'll leave you alone.

I smiled before the tears began to fall even harder, and I had to press a pillow against my face so as not to make a sound.

Just a few weeks ago, I would have answered him immediately to allay his fears. I would have talked to my mom until I felt better, and then I would have snuggled against my dad's side on the couch while we watched *Office* reruns. The next day, Julia and I would have gone to Soo Min's tea shop, where I would have protected Julia from Soo Min's experiments.

It all sounded so wonderfully mundane.

But now things were different. Heck, my fae blood wouldn't even let me lie to Georgie through a text to tell him we were all fine. Because we weren't fine. And though I lay in a house full of people, I realized I had never felt so alone. I finally texted him back when the tears had died down.

> Crazy family get-together due to an extended relative emergency. Thanks for checking on us. I'll catch you up when this is all done.

If only I had an idea of when.

Chapter Twenty-Eight

Everleigh

THE NEXT MORNING held blue skies and less wind, and while I still wasn't ready to talk to Aithan, I perked up when I learned that we were all making a trip to the local farmer's market.

"What are we doing there?" I asked as I made my bed. Soo Min had already been downstairs, chasing everyone away from the coffee machine like she did every day so she could then brew her creations. She'd returned with mugs of her experimental coffee and the news.

"Aithan says there's a jeweler there that he trusts to look at the stone you stole." She sipped her coffee and wrinkled her nose. "Too much cinnamon. Julia, what do you think of yours?"

"You didn't put any weird magic in here, did you?" Julia stared doubtfully into her mug. "I won't grow green freckles or anything?"

Soo Min rolled her eyes. "If you must know, I added some calm." She took another sip, her eyes narrowing at me over the rim of her mug. "Everyone knows you could use it."

I sniffed my mug then Julia's. "She's telling the truth. You're fine." I turned back to Soo Min. "If we're going to the farmer's market, we'll need to leave soon to get parking."

"Aithan wanted to go alone." Soo Min smirked. "But I put an end to that fantasy."

"Why would he want to go alone?" Julia asked.

"I have *no* idea," Soo Min replied, but the way she stared at me while she spoke made me squirm. And she was able to get away with it because she wasn't lying. She was being sarcastic. "Anyway, I have a bunch of stuff I need to get while we're there, so I told them we should all go so Everleigh can practice her glamouring. So guess what *you* get to do when we arrive."

The West Canyon Outdoor Shopping Center was one of my favorite hangouts in the city. The sprawling outdoor grid of glass-fronted stores was close to Red Rock Canyon, one of our local nature spots just west of the city. The canyon was infamous for its towering red sandstone cliffs surrounded by high desert. The proximity to the edge of the city made the outdoor mall a logical place for the farmer's market. They would shut down several of the mall's streets to make space for vendors every Saturday. And though there were few foods that grew in Vegas, and even fewer farmers who knew how to coax anything living up from the ground, there were plenty of artists, food vendors, and other small businesses to make up for any lack.

And unbeknownst to humans, a large portion of the stalls there were owned by supernaturals.

Not that any of us could advertise our true natures or magical goods. But for one who knew how to look, there were signs. The bakeries that advertised comfort food? Probably fae. The singer on the corner with an open guitar case? Mermaid. The wood and metalwork that seemed impossible to comprehend? Elves. You get the picture.

It made sense that Aithan would want to talk to a supernatural jeweler at the market. A locally owned small business would be far less likely to have connections to the supernatural courts than the well-known high-end ones in the downtown resorts and casinos.

As had become the norm, Soo Min, Julia, and I rode with

Dorian and Miss Lillian. Dorian was old enough and strong enough not to be bothered by the sun, as long as he didn't linger directly in it for too long. Aithan and his fancy car drove Christian, Aaron, and Jamie, and when they forced him to accompany them, Maverick. (When I asked how they all fit, Miss Lillian said there was a kind of physical space-altering elf charm she would try to teach me at a later time.) We all parked on the north side of the outdoor mall and then met up just outside the market's edge.

"Before we head in," Aithan said in a low voice, "is there anyone that needs to go to the bathroom?"

"No, and I wouldn't tell you if I did." Soo Min folded her arms. "I would just go. But I do need to visit a particular brownie's stall. There's one here that has some herbs I need for potion-making. I also need to pick up some ingredients for mixing flavors."

"And as Soo Min said, this is the perfect place for Everleigh to practice her glamour," Miss Lillian added. "Try turning your eyes brown today, and see how long you can hold that. Then, if you have to drop it, you can just rely on your glamour stone instead."

I nodded and took a deep breath before closing my eyes. A moment later, I opened them again. "Did I get it right?"

"Yeah, but now your hair has blond highlights," Soo Min said.

"It looks fine," Aithan snapped. "Let's go."

I tried not to feel hurt as he turned and strode toward the market, but it was hard not to feel the same rejection that I had last night. He hadn't so much as looked at me that morning.

I bet he didn't even know what color my hair was. He was just in a hurry to get away.

Still, I had to admit that it was a lot more fun to go shopping with Julia, now that she was my pet than it had been in the past. We'd been to this market a thousand times before, but now I could point and whisper about all the supernatural stalls as we passed them. And the sidewalks were so packed that our going was slow, and we had time to linger.

"What's he selling?" Julia nodded at a stall owned by a man

with very long, very sleek hair. He wore a sleeveless shirt so everyone could see his toned arms, and his golden skin nearly glowed.

"He's a fae," I whispered back. "And he's selling skin and hair oils. He's spelled them just enough to enhance their shine and strength. Nothing that would be noticeable to humans."

She frowned slightly. "I don't see anything supernatural about that."

"There's not..." I paused. "Unless you see that he has a separate box behind him with slightly different bottles of oil. Look! See him handing one to that woman?"

Judging by the sharp features on the woman's face, I could only guess she was a troll wearing a glamour stone.

"But what are the special oils for?" Julia asked as softly as she could in the bustling crowd. "Why do the supernaturals need their own?"

"We don't need them," Jamie said, edging his way into our conversation. "But the rich and powerful often wear oils that coat their hair and their skin with a residue that magnifies their power. Anyone who touches them picks up the residue on their hands, and then they're left feeling that supernatural's magic for hours."

"That's... odd," Julia said with a frown.

"It's a power move," Christian said in a low voice. "Meant to remind them of who they've dealt with and just how powerful they are."

Dorian, who had slipped on ahead as only vampires can, found us in time to tell us that the stall was indeed there, but the owner had stepped away for a few minutes.

"Great," Soo Min announced, seeming to appear out of nowhere. She had somehow already purchased three bags of goods. "I'm going to the food court. Anyone who wants to come is welcome to join me."

"I don't think we should split up." Aaron frowned. "There are a lot of people here."

Soo Min scoffed. "I don't know about you, but three weeks ago, I was a *big* girl, and I went anywhere I wanted."

"How about," Miss Lillian intervened, "I go with Soo Min and her group, and Dorian, you stay with Aithan and his." She held up her cell phone. "We can stay in contact with one another that way."

So it was agreed that Soo Min, Julia, Jamie, and I would go with Miss Lillian. The rest would stay with sulky Aithan and his babysitter, Dorian.

And no, I wasn't bitter about the night before at all.

No sooner had we reached the food court than Soo Min spotted a bubble tea food truck and insisted we get some for "research" purposes. She ordered the traditional brown sugar bubble tea, and Jamie ordered coconut. Upon receiving her drink, however, she declared the human bubble tea to be disgusting. Then she immediately demanded a taste of Jamie's. When she decided it wasn't bad, she handed him hers and walked away with his, muttering to herself about ingredient proportions.

"Um, what just happened?" Jamie asked, watching her walk away, still muttering to herself, before looking down at her drink in his hand.

"Not *what*, but *who*." I grinned. "And the answer is always Soo Min happened."

We followed Soo Min into a large department store. But before I could join her and Julia where they already were exclaiming over some new style of jacket, Miss Lillian touched my hand.

"Wait a moment, dear. There's something I want to ask you."

I nearly sighed aloud. That tone of voice was far too conciliatory to be good. Still, I stopped.

Miss Lillian folded her hands and pursed her lips. "I know... I'm aware that something happened last night between you and Aithan," she said carefully.

I looked down at my purse. "Nothing really happened, but–"

"What I mean is that I'm aware something has been happening

for the last few weeks." She gave me a sad smile. "And I just wanted to say... to encourage you to give Aithan grace." Her smile faded. "He's suffering a terrible fate in silence. One he has no control over and probably never will."

I swallowed hard. "Is... Does it have something to do with his grandfather's curse?"

"It's something none of us can speak of," she said, avoiding my question in a way that told me I was right. "But no matter how he acts–how he pretends it's nothing–he's hurting deep inside."

As she spoke, her phone buzzed, and she glanced at the message on the screen. "And that's our cue. Let's go back to the stall. The proprietor must have returned."

"We're here," Aithan called as our group approached. We came to a stop in a corner stall, one so close to the back of the line that I might have missed the entire table if Aithan hadn't been standing beside it. The table was covered with pretty beaded bracelets and colorful stones set into simple rings and necklaces, and a few dozen earrings were scattered about. I could feel a bit of magic coming from some of the jewelry, but barely.

The girl behind the stall was tall and painfully thin. She wore cute round purple glasses and a set of overalls over a white flowered shirt. And she constantly fidgeted and blinked, as though we all made her very nervous. So instead of looking directly at her, I fingered one of the bracelets–a pretty little silver chain with pink gems dangling from it, the same color as fae magic.

"Everyone," Aithan said, "this is Cara. Cara, these are my friends." He leaned slightly closer. "Do you have a place we can talk that's more private?" He glanced back pointedly at the crowd.

"Oh, um, yes." She swallowed and nodded quickly. "If you'll follow me."

She put a sign up on her stall. The sign must have been spelled because as soon as she did, the contents of the table vanished under a glamour. Then she waved us back to what looked like a maintenance door on the side of the nearest building, and we followed her through. Once we were all in and she had shut the door, however, I realized we weren't in a storage closet or maintenance space at all, but in a pretty little cottage made of stone and mortar. Something straight out of a fairy tale.

Julia clutched my arm. "Where are we?" she squeaked.

"We took a private portal," I told her. "Like the one we took to get to my uncle's store."

"Oh," she said softly. "Okay."

I sighed. The poor girl had been forced to learn so many new things in such a short amount of time. I tried to think of the simplest way to explain it. "Elves create magical paths to shorten distances between different places on Earth. Which means now we're..." I looked around. The cottage windows were open and I could see the green of what looked like a forest outside. "I'm assuming we're at her home... wherever that is."

"My grandfather bought it for me," Cara said, beaming. "Well, the portal came with the house, so I guess he bought that, too." She looked at Julia. "Kind of like a private road. It's not open to the public for travel. Only my guests." Then she turned to Aithan. "What was it you wanted me to look at?"

I barely knew the girl, but her kindness to Julia had me liking her already. Most fae would have made fun of or ignored the human pet tagging along.

Aithan removed the little ziplock bag I'd given him the night before. The tiny chalky rock inside was still there, to my relief, though some of it had rubbed off as powder inside the bag. The stone must not be very hard, I realized.

Cara took the bag and squinted at it as she stretched her hand out like she was enlarging a screen.

"She's making the stone appear larger," I whispered to Julia, who looked very confused. "So she can see–"

Cara let out a shriek and dropped the bag as she jumped backward. "Where did you get that?" she demanded, still staring at the stone where it had landed on her table.

Aithan and Dorian shared a significant look. "We took it," Aithan said as he reclaimed the bag. "From a group that's repeatedly attacked one of our members." He paused. "I take it this means you've seen this kind of stone before?"

Cara nodded emphatically, but she didn't smile. "Some... people came to see me a while ago. They wanted me to make a special metal charm that could hold one of those stones in it, about that size."

"Do you know what the stone does?" I asked, holding my hand out to Aithan. He dropped the bag in it, but was careful not to touch me as he did.

Choosing to ignore that, I studied the stone more closely.

"I... I don't know exactly what it is." Cara bit the inside of her cheek. "But that rock—whatever it is—is powerful. Like, so powerful that I only touched it once. And I never want to touch it again." She shivered.

"Did you take the commission?" Aithan asked.

She shook her head, her long ponytail swinging behind her. "No. I mean, to begin with..." She held up her hands and gave us a self-conscious smile. "I'm not actually very good at metalwork. Or adding magic to metal. I mean, I'm not terrible, but I'm self-taught, and..." She waved a hand. "Not that that matters. Anyway, when I said no, they tried to wipe my memory."

My friends and I inhaled sharply. Memory wiping humans was a pretty regular occurrence for the sake of both the human and the supernatural. Julia was a testament as to why such a thing was necessary. But only minimal wiping at most. Anything extreme that exposed us to humans would be dealt with swiftly by the courts. Wiping the memory of another supernatural without legal allowance, though? It was punishable by life in the elven dungeons.

Or worse.

"Wait, you said they *tried* to wipe your memory," Soo Min said. "Did they fail?"

That was even more unheard of.

Cara blushed slightly. "I mean, they hid some details. But I don't think the guy that tried to do it was very good." She scrunched her nose. "Also, I have a photographic memory. All I can guess is that maybe that made it harder for them to remove everything?" She shrugged. "Anyway, I can't remember the guy's name or the date, but I remember what everything looked like."

"Can you show us what you remember?" Miss Lillian asked gently.

Cara nodded, then frowned. "But... before I do, I have to ask. What are you all trying to do with this information? I don't want to get in anyone's way, but like I told them," she stood taller, "I won't be part of hurting people."

"That's very noble of you, dear." Miss Lillian smiled. "And we would never ask you to hurt anyone. As my friend said, though, this same group has targeted one of our friends several times." She nodded at me. "They've tried to abduct her three times now."

"And we want to know why." Aithan's voice was hard.

Cara's gray eyes grew wide. "In that case, I'll tell you all that I can. Or rather... I'll show you." She pushed her bangs out of her eyes and lifted her hands, frowning in concentration as light began to emanate from them. Julia gasped as Cara projected a silver image before her.

"An infinity symbol?" I asked, thinking back to the phone with the engraved key. "They wanted you to mount a stone on that?"

"Yes." Cara moved her hands, continuing to add details as she strengthened the projection. "One that could be worn as a pin or on jewelry. And they wanted a lot. Hundreds of them."

I sucked in a sharp breath. And despite my determination to ignore Aithan the same way he was ignoring me, our eyes locked.

Hundreds.

Just how many members did Pandora's Key have?

"And here," Cara said, the image changing before her, "is the face of the guy who tried to take my memories.

My mouth went dry as everyone else went silent. Except for Julia, who began, "But that's–"

Her voice cut off so she couldn't say his name. Probably silenced by Miss Lillian.

I felt like someone had just kicked me in the chest. Everyone else–even Dorian–looked as though they felt the same way.

"What's wrong?" Cara asked, looking from one face to another. "You know this guy?"

"Thank you," Aithan said tersely. "We'll not take any more of your time."

"But if you know who he is, can't you tell me?" Cara followed us as Aithan opened the portal once more and led us back through the door. We all stepped out into the space behind Cara's table, Cara still pleading with us to tell her the attacker's name.

"We'll contact you if we learn anything of significance," Aithan said, ignoring her pleas. He looked down at her table and spotted the bracelet I'd been admiring earlier. "I'll take that one." Then he pulled his wallet out and handed her a hundred-dollar bill without looking at the price.

Cara gaped at the money in her hand. "But the bracelet only costs–"

"Keep the change," Aithan said gruffly, before handing the bracelet to Miss Lillian. Then he turned and led us away.

Chapter Twenty-Nine

Everleigh

As we made our way back toward the parking lot, I stared at the bracelet as Miss Lillian cooed over it, thanking Aithan for such a sweet gift. There was no way he'd coincidentally chosen the bracelet *I'd* admired. Not that I would begrudge any gift given to Miss Lillian. But that one? Seriously?

"What's going on with you and Aithan?" Soo Min whispered as we walked.

"*Nothing*," I snapped. And nothing was going on with us. Because there was obviously nothing there.

Soo Min just rolled her eyes. "Clearly." Before she could prod further, however, Aithan was at my side and had grabbed my hand. Then, without a word, he was dragging me in the opposite direction.

"What are you doing?" I protested as he yanked open the door of one of the hallways that led from the marketplace to the bathrooms. But he still didn't answer as he pulled me halfway down the hall, which was air-conditioned and darker than it had been outside. But then I realized that he didn't have to answer. Because through the glass door, I could see three very large men in security uniforms standing just outside the hall.

Except I knew they weren't security guards. Their matching silver earrings marked them as elven soldiers. They were simply wearing glamour stones so they could go where they wanted without being questioned by humans. And they were looking all around. In only a few seconds, they would be sure to spot us.

And while I had no idea what the elven soldiers wanted, I knew I had no desire for them to spot me.

The soldiers didn't surprise me nearly as much, however, as Aithan twining his fingers with mine and pressing me against the wall. His lips brushed my left cheek the moment one of the soldiers tried to look through the door.

"Um." I did my best to breathe, my heart beating frantically in my chest. "Are we trying to hide in plain sight?" As I spoke, I was *very* aware of the way his rough fingers tightly held mine, and the way his breath was warm against my neck. And...

Was he *kissing* my face?

"Yes," he whispered, his lips still brushing my cheek as he spoke. "Don't look directly at them. Just keep them in your peripheral vision." He paused. "And try not to look so horrified." There was a breathy laugh behind the words. "Most women aren't disgusted when their boyfriend kisses them."

I knew what he meant. He was trying to hide our faces from the soldiers. Still, that was easy for him to say. It wasn't like I had guys waltzing up to kiss me all the time.

Least of all, Aithan Nomos.

But then one of the guards put his hand on the door.

"They're coming–" I began, but I didn't get to finish. Because Aithan Nomos, prince of the ancient Nomos line, serial dater and commitment-phobe, was kissing me. His lips, surprisingly warm and gentle, were on mine, bold yet inviting. And like charmed chocolates, one taste made me want *more*.

Before I knew what I was doing, I was kissing him back. And it was so much better than anything my thirteen-year-old imagination had ever conjured. Somehow, with his hands gently holding me close as he positioned himself between me and the door, I felt safe and cherished. And I never wanted it to end.

But just as I began to lean into him, the door at the end of the hall banged shut.

And like that, Aithan was gone.

I opened my eyes and blinked rapidly as he strode down the hall to peer out the glass door as though nothing had just happened.

"They've moved on," he called back to me. "Let's go before they circle back."

I tried to respond, but my voice had fled me. Or rather, it was attached to the tears that suddenly wanted so desperately to fall. But I wasn't about to emerge from the hall back into the farmer's market, sobbing my eyes out. *That* would cause questions galore. So instead, I only nodded and followed him.

Chapter Thirty

Everleigh

When we got home, Aithan announced that he was changing clothes and going running, and that he expected to be left alone. This meant that I had no choice but to change into my running gear as well. Georgie, I found as I changed, had left me about three more panicked messages while I was out that morning, the last one saying we *had* to talk. But I chose to ignore those and set out after Aithan instead.

I let him keep pace ahead of me until we left the neighborhood, and he turned toward the local park. It was a large, sprawling piece of land with three playgrounds, several tennis courts, and a padded jogging trail.

Once we were both on the padded trail, however, I increased my speed.

"What was *that?*" I demanded as soon as I pulled up on his right.

He huffed. "Hello, Clarkson."

"No." I shook my head, my words coming out in puffs louder than I meant them to. Even jogging, Aithan was fast. "What *was* that?"

"That," Aithan said without looking at me, "was a fire hydrant.

Firefighters use them. They're full of water. And before you ask again, that one," he pointed to a grassy area, "is a tree."

"Aithan, this is not funny," I snapped, suddenly aware that I sounded way closer to tears than I meant to. "You *know* what I'm talking about."

Aithan came to a stop and put his hands behind his head, stretching his chest as he turned slowly from side to side. "Look, I saw my grandfather's goons coming, and I made sure they didn't see you. It's as simple as that."

"No." I put my hands on my hips and glared at him. "You and I both know that that kiss wasn't just a cover." As I spoke, the memory of the way he'd held me on the sparring mat flashed through my mind, followed by the way he'd reached out to touch my hand at the racetrack. And, of course, the way his mouth had felt on mine today.

That memory would be burned into me until the day I died.

Aithan scowled. "Everleigh, my grandfather has been trying to recruit me away from my parents since I was twelve. Do you think this was the first time I used a girl to avoid his men?"

I flinched as the face of every one of his girlfriends came to mind.

That hurt.

But it didn't mean I was ready to give in.

"No." I stubbornly folded my arms. "There was something more in that kiss. I know there was more." I shook my head. "Aithan, *talk* to me."

He finally turned his green eyes on mine. They were cold and hard, the way I always imagined the high king's eyes to be. "Yeah, well, there wasn't." He ran a hand through his hair and looked out toward the edge of the park. "There can't be."

I was contemplating grabbing his face and dragging him down for round two to test that hypothesis, when a familiar car pulled up to the edge of the sidewalk near the running path, and the right front window rolled down to reveal Jamie at the wheel. I nearly let out a frustrated scream. *Could we not have five minutes to ourselves? Was that too much to ask?*

"What is it, Jamie?" Aithan asked in a tired voice.

Jamie had been looking back and forth between us with wide eyes, but Aithan's question seemed to snap him out of his trance.

"Dorian figured out what the stone does," he said, still looking back and forth between us. "He says you need to come see."

Aithan sighed but nodded and made his way off the path toward the car. I considered mutiny for a moment. But as Jamie was present, and it wasn't just Aithan who would suffer my wrath, I stomped down after him and got in.

The drive home, short as it was, was suffocating, the silence so heavy I wondered if anyone else was struggling to breathe. But when I glanced over at Aithan's face, it was so passive that I realized it must just be me.

Chapter Thirty-One

Aithan

I SILENTLY BLESSED Jamie's timing as we neared Everleigh's driveway. A few more minutes with her pleading, beautiful eyes, and I might have done something I couldn't take back.

As it was, emotions were swirling inside of me, my elven nature bringing them to a temperature no human could have conceived.

Worry and frustration at my brother for touching poor Cara's memories. That he'd failed to fully remove them had been no accident. My brother was far too powerful and too controlled to make a mistake like that. But he'd put himself at risk by taking some memories and leaving the rest. Not just that, but if he was removing memories now, how much of his soul was he willing to trade to stay in my grandfather's good graces? Or was it Pandora's Key's good graces? Who was he ultimately working for? And why did he have to make this more complicated than it already was?

And now that the flames of my fury at the world had been properly stoked, I felt like someone was pouring gasoline on the fire, intent on destroying me from the inside out. Hatred in spades for myself, and for all the ways I'd slipped up in the last few weeks.

A deep, abiding hatred for my grandfather and his curse.

There was even anger at Everleigh and her mosquito-like

persistence that kept her hoping when anyone else would have just given up. Why couldn't she just leave me be? Why couldn't she just be happy with our friendship the way it had always been?

She might have, an annoying voice whispered inside me, *if you hadn't shown her what could be.* Except it couldn't *be.* Not now. Not ever.

No matter how much I might want it to.

After we parked, I took a deep breath and waited for Jamie and Everleigh to enter the house ahead of me, using the need to check the safety spells as an excuse to clear my head before following them inside. Once I had checked every single spell three times over, I finally made my way inside to find everyone gathered in the kitchen.

"Thank you for joining us, Your Highness," Dorian said in his languid way. He was sitting at a barstool in front of a makeshift science lab that had nearly driven Miss Lillian out of her mind, as it took up nearly the whole kitchen island and got in her way every time she tried to cook. Everyone else was gathered around him.

"I thought about what young Cara said today," Dorian began, turning his attention back to the small stone that was sitting on a tiny plastic specimen square, the kind scientists used with microscopes. "And her mention of power made me consider what Prince Aithan noted about the Pandora's Key operatives every time they attacked."

"That they're stronger than they should be?" Everleigh asked.

"Precisely." He frowned thoughtfully down at the little stone. "After doing a few tests, I've discovered what I think the nature of this stone is. And if I'm right..." He paused, his face unusually grave, even for a vampire. "It will change the entire supernatural world."

No one dared to breathe.

"It seems," he continued, "that this stone is a natural power enhancer. Only, it's much... much stronger than anything we know today. Oils, gems, even spells, this stone—if I'm not mistaken—takes the power of the one wearing or touching it and makes him exponentially more powerful than he would have been."

"So it's like a magical steroid?" Aaron asked.

"That's *exactly* what it is," Dorian said. He leaned forward and moved the stone beneath his microscope. "Of course, due to the presence of other elements and impurities, I would say that this piece has been mined out of the ground and not in any way purified."

"There's lots of mining in Nevada," Julia said. "I wonder if it's local or from somewhere else."

"The better question," Christian said, frowning, "is how much more of this is there? And what's more, who has control over it?"

Before anyone could answer, the doorbell rang.

"I'll look to see who it is," Julia said quietly.

I studied the stone again. "Something tells me that Pandora's Key isn't the only group that knows about this. Considering the courts took my parents and Everleigh's to keep them safe, I would say they're at least aware of the stone's existence. And there's an even better chance that they're somehow involved."

"Las Vegas wasn't the royal supernatural capital until the mid-twentieth century," Miss Lillian said slowly. She looked at Dorian. "You were here at that time. Do you think the courts making their move here could have had anything to do with this?"

"The question you should be asking," Maverick called from his chair in the corner, "is why now? Why would these two groups make their move after waiting all this time?"

All eyes went to Everleigh.

Julia came back to the kitchen, her face ashen. "There are five black SUVs parked in the street," she said in a whispered voice.

I let out a curse.

Chapter Thirty-Two

Everleigh

AITHAN MOTIONED for me and Julia to stay in the kitchen while
he went to answer the door. Miss Lillian and Dorian remained
with us while Aaron, Christian, Soo Min, and Jamie followed
Aithan closely, staying just out of sight of the open door.

"Aithan," came a man's voice. "It's good to see you!"

"Angelo," Aithan responded coolly. "To what do I owe this
pleasure?"

"Good afternoon, nephew," came a softer, deeper voice. "I'm
sure it's no surprise to you, but we've come to collect you, Everleigh, Miss Lillian, and your friends. Your grandfather is calling in
every member of the family in order to ensure their protection."

Fantastic. He said family, but they were taking our friends as
well. I closed my eyes and drew a slow breath in. If the Nomoses
themselves were here, and not their goons, we had no hope of
escape.

"Oh?" Aithan retorted. "The way you protected Everleigh
when you took her parents and left her to fend for herself?"

There was a chuckle. Then the younger voice spoke again.
"Was she ever truly alone? Everyone knows the Nomoses and the
Clarksons are never far apart."

"That," the older man said in a gentler tone, "was an unfortunate oversight. One we've come to correct." His words reminded me sharply of those my aunt had spoken the night before.

Without warning, I felt magic surround me. The summoning spell was so fast I didn't even have time to fight it as I was whisked to the front door and dumped beside Aithan. With as much dignity as I could muster, I straightened my clothes and glared up at the two men in suits standing on my porch.

"And this," the younger man said, his green eyes slowly traveling down my body, "must be Everleigh Clarkson. I apologize, Everleigh, that we haven't met before."

I felt Aithan's magic roiling beside me, and I could only guess what he thought of Angelo–a cousin, I assumed–as he looked at me in a way Aithan *never* had.

The older man, who looked exactly like the younger one might in twenty years, turned a sharp gaze on his companion. "Angelo." His voice was velvety soft, yet absolutely terrifying.

The young man–Angelo–immediately looked down.

"I apologize," the older man said, smiling at me. "My son sometimes forgets himself. I am Atticus Nomos, Aithan's uncle. And I've been sent to bring you to your parents." He looked at Aithan. "You, Miss Clarkson, and Miss Lillian will ride with me so I can catch you up on recent events. Your friends will have comfortable rides in the other vehicles."

"Where will you take them?" I asked suspiciously.

"You'll all be reunited at my father's hotel," he said. "We simply don't have room for everyone to ride together."

I turned and looked up at Aithan. He looked furious, but after a moment, swallowed and looked down at me. He held my gaze for a long moment, almost as if weighing options–though what options were possible, I didn't know. A dozen powerful elves in suits littered my front yard behind the two I'd just met. What options were there?

"Everyone," Aithan finally called, still holding my gaze. "go grab a few toiletries and a change of clothes. Then meet us down here."

My friends stared at him in shock. Even Soo Min looked speechless. But when a few more men in suits appeared in the backyard, everyone seemed to finally realize that we had no choice.

We were surrounded.

Julia was nearly in hysterics when Soo Min and Jamie guided her into the back of another SUV. I gave her the best smile that I could, but inside, I wanted to be sick. *I* had done this to her. I had done this to them all. All of my friends were here for me, and now they were going to pay for it.

Angelo tried to strike up a conversation with me on my walk out to the nearest SUV, but Aithan quickly maneuvered his way between us. And for that, I was grateful. Miss Lillian, pulling her flowered suitcase, stayed close behind me as well. Even now, facing down an enemy we had no hope of defeating, they were still protecting me.

Still, as I sat stiffly on the leather seat between Aithan and Miss Lillian, I realized I had no idea what to expect.

Did I want to see my parents again? Absolutely.

But they had been adamant that I never set foot in the high elven king's resort and casino. And if being reunited in the royal resort was a good thing, my friends wouldn't have looked so upset. Miss Lillian's lips were pinched in a thin line, and Aithan, solid and unwavering as ever, stared, unseeing, ahead. And I didn't like that look, I decided. It only took me a moment, though, to realize that I didn't like it because it made me fully aware that Aithan Nomos, for the first time in my life, was *not* in control. Not even in the bowels of the club with my vindictive aunt had he looked so...

Resigned?

The car pulled out onto the road and headed east. And as we got closer to the epicenter of the royal courts–the famed Las Vegas resorts and casinos–it dawned on me that I was about to step into a world I could never step out of again.

Chapter Thirty-Three

Everleigh

I KNEW where we were going, but for some reason, that didn't stop my heart from kicking into high gear when we turned from the famed (and crowded) Las Vegas Boulevard into the entry of the tallest building on the Strip. Taking the shape of a double helix, the building elegantly twisted toward the sky, its green glass windows dotted with random red, yellow, blue, and purple, like glass flowers in a lush forest. In large rose gold flourishes, the words, *The Realm* were hung near the top.

This was the building my parents had forbidden me from ever setting foot in. And now my friends and I were going to walk through the front door. But would we ever walk out again?

Without meaning to, I grabbed Aithan's hand where it rested beside me. As soon as I realized what I'd done, I wondered if he'd shake me off. But to my surprise and relief, he only squeezed my hand back.

The black SUVs didn't park, but pulled into the valet lane in front of a long row of glass doors with rose gold frames and elegantly swirling handles. Angelo Nomos got out and opened the door for Aithan, who helped me out, and then Miss Lillian. Once we were all out of the car, however, Aithan didn't take my hand again.

"Your things will be taken upstairs to your rooms," Atticus said politely. "If you'll follow me."

What other choice did we have?

Julia darted over to me as soon as she was out of her car and grabbed the hand Aithan had dropped. I held it tightly, sending up a prayer of thanks that I had my best friend to walk with me.

I also prayed that she would make it out alive.

A doorman ushered us into the most opulent lobby I'd ever seen or even imagined.

The green and brown floor tiles were solid like stone, but their colors swirled slowly beneath our feet so smoothly I couldn't tell if they were spelled or just high-tech screens. Real trees and flora stuck out from the walls and hung down from the ceiling, and little colorful lights appearing here and there, and more zooming around behind them like fireflies. And though I could see the casino further in, I realized that it truly smelled like a forest, not the usual casino scents of carpet and cigarettes. Water bubbled up in a colorfully lighted brook that had been built into the floor, and the music that played over the speakers sounded eerily similar to siren songs, too quiet to bespell anyone who heard them, but loud enough to make the magic palpable even to the humans. Not that they would recognize it as such.

Tourists, oblivious to the true nature of the building they were walking into, pointed as they walked through the doors, exclaiming excitedly about the elaborate details of the intricately crafted enchanted forest.

But Atticus didn't stop for us to admire the craftsmanship of the building. Instead, he led us toward a roped-off set of elevators with a sign hung in front of them that said *V.I.P. Guests*. He unhooked the velvet rope and indicated the rose gold elevators. Obediently, we all squeezed into one. And though I wondered if anyone would break the silence to ease the tension, not even Soo Min had something sarcastic to say.

Then we began to ascend. And ascend. And ascend. And because the back of the elevator was made of glass, once we passed the first twist in the double helix, we found ourselves looking out over the entire city.

How, I wanted to wail in despair, *did we ever believe we could hide?*

What felt like ten minutes later, the elevator dinged, and I let go of Julia's hand as we all quietly stepped out. Once out, we found ourselves in an expansive room with outer walls made of nothing but glass, providing a full three-hundred-and-sixty-degree view. This might have given the space a very modern feel, except it was offset by the dais and rose gold throne in the center of the room. Thick, round columns and pillars held up the distant ceiling, which was painted with mosaics of a classical style. The crowd of elegantly dressed people milling about the dais and the tall elf wearing traditional elven garb elegantly draped across the throne made it look very much like something out of a storybook—a castle in the sky.

Which meant we could only be standing in one place.

This was the royal court of the elven high king, Kostas Nomos.

I didn't recognize most of the dozens of people who stood near the throne, but after a moment of searching, I spotted Mr. and Mrs. Nomos, and behind them, my parents. Uncle Finn stood beside my mother. They were also wearing the more traditional court fashion, which bore echoes of Greek and Roman fashion. (All supernatural races had preferences, but they tended to absorb pieces of any culture that pleased them.)

Their eyes were all trained on us, and their postures were tense. My parents had put off this moment for as long as they could. And now they watched me, their eyes wide and full of fear. But still, they didn't make a move. I met their gazes as we walked, but resisted the urge to call out to them. If they weren't running to me, it would be a mistake to try running to them.

Then again, they were no longer in control. Aithan was no longer in control. Everyone in this court was subservient to the king. A king who, I knew without a doubt, would try to use his power and position to control me. But I wasn't a toy. Which meant that I, Princess Everleigh Clarkson, wizard-of-sorts, would have to act like I had some inkling of control myself.

Even if I had no idea what I was doing.

The man reclining on the throne straightened as we walked in. He wore a rose gold circlet on his head, as well as a long gold robe draped over a fine green tunic, belt, and trousers. His leather boots made no sound as he climbed down the dais steps and smiled at us as we approached.

Aithan had the good sense to kneel, so the rest of us followed.

"You may rise," the king said in a rich voice, somehow even deeper than his son's. Only then, as I stood, did I allow myself to study the face of the supernatural high king.

It was strange to see Aithan, Alexander, and Mr. Nomos's kind features in such a cold, calculating face. His emerald green eyes were sharp and didn't look like they missed a thing, and his long hair, though graying slightly, was still thick and shone like gold. And despite his layers of clothes, the contours of his powerful muscles were obvious even through the fabric. Of course, even without seeing those, his walk alone was the tread of a predator. Which was exactly what he was.

"Good afternoon, everyone," he said pleasantly, looking each of us in the eye before moving on to the next person. "I hope you will all make yourselves comfortable here for the time being.' He looked at Aithan. "I also hope, Grandson, that you've been giving my last offer some thought."

"I have," Aithan said. His voice was polite but distant, and he kept his eyes ahead.

"And?" his grandfather pressed.

Aithan finally met his grandfather's eyes. "That depends on a number of factors."

I turned to stare up at him. Working for his grandfather? He couldn't mean it. Aithan would rather die than serve his corrupt grandfather.

Wouldn't he?

Or did he no longer have a choice?

"And you, Everleigh dear," the king said, coming to stand before me. "I've been looking forward to meeting you. You've practically set the city ablaze." Short as I was, I felt much like a dwarf or brownie as I stared up at him. Still, I decided I wasn't going to cower before him. What good would that do after all? He was known for being brutally honest.

I could be brutally honest, too.

"In what way, Your Majesty?" I asked, doing my best to sound as cool and detached as Aithan.

His green eyes lit up, and he grinned. "I was hoping *you* could tell me."

"What I *know* is that I've become the target of a group of supernatural zealots. Though why they picked me out, I haven't the first idea."

There. That was honest enough. Okay, *obviously* they'd chosen to try recruiting me because I was a wizard. But how the zealots had found that out before I had was beyond me. So in truth, I didn't know just why they'd chosen to seek me out. Or rather, how they'd known to do so.

"Be that as it may," the king said, "you seem to have amassed quite an army to protect yourself."

"I have *friends,*" I retorted, "who were kind enough to come and watch out for me when my family wasn't able to do so."

The people watching us—mostly elves—had been whispering quietly to one another. But this little jab at my relatives' courts silenced them.

The king stared at me for a long moment. Just as I was starting to wonder when the beheading would begin, however, he let out a laugh. "You're quite direct, aren't you? I like that, especially in one who's half-fae."

I gave him a respectful nod, not trusting my mouth to say anything more. I could almost hear my mother silently lecturing me to keep it shut.

"But it is a good question, isn't it?" he continued. "Why would a gang of misfits be so obsessed with adding you to their ranks?" His sharp eyes went up and down my person—not in the disrespectful way Angelo's had an hour before—but like a wolf might size up a deer.

"Announcing King Daniil of the royal House Gallagher!" called a man standing by a large set of doors. Everyone turned to see the doors open to reveal an unusually portly fae hurrying into the room, followed by an entourage of his own. He stopped at the edge of the dais and gave a surprisingly elegant bow, considering his shape and size, his blue wings somehow bowing with him. He had iron-gray curls and wore a circlet of silver studded with pink and purple gems. Even if he hadn't been announced by his name, however, I would have known him immediately by the striking resemblance he bore to my Uncle Finn and my mother. He had their eyes.

My eyes.

"Your Majesty," he said, puffing slightly. "I came as soon as I heard the news."

King Kostas stared at him. "My dear fellow, whatever for?"

The fae king blinked rapidly. "Well... to meet my granddaughter, of course!"

For the first time, my mother spoke. "Father—"

"No, Princess Erin, he's quite within his rights," King Kostas said, though from his amused smirk, I could only guess he was allowing this intrusion for his own entertainment. "By all means, King Daniil, meet your granddaughter."

I began to curtsy as the fae king approached, but before I could lower myself all the way to the ground, he pulled me up into a surprisingly warm embrace.

"I heard what happened at the club with Fiadh," he whispered as he hugged me. Then he pulled away and studied my face. "Child, what have you gotten yourself into?"

Seeing what looked like genuine concern in the fae king's round face was not what I had expected upon meeting my maternal grandfather. I didn't have time to puzzle it out, however, because King Kostas was suddenly standing over us again. And though my grandfather was not a short man, King Kostas was even taller.

"Such a sweet reunion," he crooned. "Of course, it makes me wonder even more why the Clarkson family would hide such a pretty little face from their own relatives and friends." His sharp gaze went to his eldest son, Mr. Nomos. "And why their friends would hide her as well."

"I think," my grandfather said, placing his arm around my shoulders, "that we ought to postpone this conversation until she's had time to rest and–"

His mouth continued to move, but his words were silenced. I looked back at King Kostas to see a malevolent grin spread across his face, a single finger of his right hand raised. "I think that in the future, Daniil, you would do well to remember that this is *my* court, and that I give the orders," he said softly.

My grandfather's face turned red, but he stopped trying to speak. Instead, his arm tightened around my shoulder, and I found that I had the oddest sensation of wanting to lean into him. Anything to put distance between myself and the high king of the elves.

"Grandson," King Kostas said, turning back to Aithan. "You said there were stipulations surrounding your willingness to work for me. Might I ask what those stipulations would be? You make me curious. Up until now, you've merely turned me down."

Aithan hesitated, meeting my eyes for the briefest of seconds.

But even that single look was too long. For as soon as King Kostas had seen it, he clapped his hands together once, a new look of delight crossing his face.

"Perhaps," he said slowly, "I should ask Princess Everleigh if she knows. After all, you two have been spending an extraordinary amount of time–"

"I took a *Binding Oath* years ago!" Aithan snapped. "Because our families knew the courts wouldn't *stoop* to protect an *Anikos!* How else was she supposed to remain alive after our parents disappeared?"

"An honorable thing to do," the king said cordially, patiently. "Still, I can't help thinking there's more to this story that you're not telling me." He tilted his head thoughtfully as he studied me. "Perhaps if I just apply the right amount of pressure..."

Pain like I'd never known could exist hit my body, hurling me out of my grandfather's arm and slamming me against the stone floor. When I opened my eyes, I could only see green light. Several people screamed, and others shouted, but the ringing in my ears made it impossible to know who.

Wizard. I was a wizard. Searching deep inside myself, calling to memory every lesson I'd received, I tried to find the magic to fight back. To shift. To at least dull the awareness of the indescribable pain that racked my body. But King Kostas's magic made mine look like a little girl playing pretend. I couldn't even try. My magic was trapped within me more tightly than ever before.

And I knew instinctively that if it lasted much longer, I was going to die.

Chapter Thirty-Four

Aithan

I DIDN'T THINK before releasing my magic. There wasn't time. All I knew was that my grandfather would lose no sleep over killing someone he considered a useless half-breed.

I had to stop Everleigh from dying.

My magic, though not as strong as my grandfather's, still bore the ancient strength of the ages. I was a prince of the direct Nomos line, after all. And while I couldn't stop him entirely, my burst of power hit my grandfather hard enough to send him stumbling to the side. As he fell, his flow of magic ceased, leaving Everleigh whimpering on the floor as her parents ran to her side.

No one spoke. They didn't have to, though. Because a second later, a nearly mind-numbing pain ripped through my chest as the sound of cracking stone echoed through the large hall. I fell to my knees with a loud cry, clutching at my chest as though it might relieve the pain.

"So," my grandfather said, walking toward me with a strange smile, "after all these years. You fell in love after all."

My friends stood nearby, looking back and forth between us like they weren't sure what to do. And as the pain continued to ripple through my chest, I prayed with all my might that Miss Lillian would keep them from following my example.

Even as I thought this, however, the inevitable feeling of numbness began to creep over me. Unable to keep from groaning, I looked at Everleigh one more time. She was conscious and propped up on her elbow now, and her mouth was open as she stared at me in horror.

Silently, I pleaded with her to understand. To know why I hadn't been able to love her. To understand why I'd had to push her away.

To recognize that—because I loved her—saving her life, and in doing so, activating my grandfather's curse upon myself, was my choice and my choice alone. And I didn't regret a thing.

Chapter Thirty-Five

Everleigh

I staRED at Aithan in horror as he slumped against the stone floor. But I wasn't allowed to linger.

"Come," my grandfather whispered, gently lifting me up off the ground. His strength was surprising, considering how out of shape he looked. "You can't help him now. It will be better if you're out of sight when he comes to."

I wanted to argue with him, to fight my way back to Aithan's side. But my strength had been drained by King Kostas's attack, so I had no way to resist him when he lifted me up in his arms and carried me out of the hall.

"My parents," I breathed, realizing as we turned a corner that they were no longer with us. "My friends!"

"King Kostas is keeping a watchful eye on both his son's family and yours," my grandfather whispered. "Best to talk about it when we're in my quarters. And not to worry. I'll bring your friends to you as soon as I can."

Unable to fight him, I closed my eyes and let my head roll onto his shoulder.

If you had asked me three hours before if I would have ever

trusted a strange fae as though my life depended on it—particularly one from my estranged family—I would have laughed.

But now I had no choice.

We soon entered a large suite. It looked like something out of a travel magazine with a large open-concept room that included a sleeping area, living space, dining table, and kitchen. Altogether, the room was at least as large as the entire first floor of my house. Instead of stopping in the first room, however, my grandfather waved off his entourage and carried me into a smaller bedroom beyond the first. Carefully, he pulled the covers back and laid me in the softest bed I'd ever felt.

"This is your suite?" I rubbed my eyes as I tried to think straight. "But... isn't your hotel the Midsummer's Dream?"

My grandfather, who had begun tucking me in like I was five, paused before resuming his work. "King Kostas prefers to have places for his more... important guests to stay when he needs us on hand."

I finally managed to pry my eyes open to see his grim smile. "You mean you're a prisoner."

"Much in the way your parents are. Though King Kostas is more hesitant to put such open restrictions upon myself as he has on them. I'm allowed to come and go as I choose, just as long as I mind myself and keep my people on their best behavior. He knows that if I weren't given *some* leeway, my people would begin wreaking havoc in the city as only fae can."

I looked down at the surprisingly excellent job he had done in making me feel comfortable in the bed. I wondered if he'd done this for my mother when she was a little girl. Many of the royal supernaturals kept nannies to do such for them, but judging by his tucking-in expertise, I could only guess that he'd had practice with his own children. I'd have to ask my mother when I saw her next.

If I was allowed to see her in private ever again.

I opened my mouth to ask, but then flinched, my muscles still screaming with the echoes of King Kostas's magic. As if reading my mind, my grandfather rang a bell and called for tea.

"Was he telling the truth, though?" I asked once the muscle spasm had passed. "I mean, about taking my parents out of an abundance of caution?"

My grandfather drew in a deep breath and sighed, and I had to remind myself not to put full stock in anything he said. Not yet, anyway. A few moments of kindness from any fae didn't merit immediate trust. Especially when that kindness came from royalty.

"You aren't mistaken," he finally said. "Your father has been like a brother to the eldest Kostas prince since they were very small. And King Kostas treated him as such. All the royal families knew about the friendship, so it was no great surprise when Prince Nikos followed your father and my daughter into the human world. I eventually figured out the real reason for their escape, of course." He gave me a pointed look. "But word quickly spread that they were embarrassed about... Well." He shook his head. "It doesn't matter."

"About their half-breed," I said with a dry smile.

"I suppose you could put it that way." He wrinkled his nose. "Of course, King Kostas always kept a good eye on both your families even after they left. Neither was allowed to leave the city or take any portals that would lead you far away."

Which meant, a corner of my mind reasoned, that Cara's cabin was most likely on Mount Charleston, which overlooked the city.

"What happened to Aithan?" I whispered, knowing it wasn't Cara I was really thinking of.

"You know about your punishment by now," my grandfather said, staring out the window as he did. "But far worse was how he chose to punish his own son." He scowled and shook his head. "Cursing both of Nikos's sons. Any parent or grandparent who can do that... Well, put nothing past a Nomos, I suppose. Anyway, none who were present were allowed to speak of the curses until they fell." He looked down at his hands, lines of sorrow creasing his face. "I was there, of course."

"Grandfather," I said, the word feeling strange on my tongue, "What specifically was Aithan's curse?"

My grandfather gave me a sad smile and reached out to gently tuck my hair away from my face. It was such a natural gesture, and so sweet that it reminded me of my own father. "Young Aithan was cursed so that if he ever fell in love, his heart would be locked away so he could never love again."

I stared at my grandfather in horror. "Never love..." I was unable to finish the sentence.

I had been putting two and two together as my mind slowly cleared, but the full weight of this revelation was nearly too much. All the times Aithan had pushed me away... Dating without depth so he could have companionship without getting attached. Keeping himself separate and alone. He was trying to stop his grandfather's curse from falling. And I had blindly pushed him harder and harder toward that line until he literally threw himself over it. And now...

The tears I'd been suppressing all day began to fall. Before I knew it, I was sobbing into my grandfather's arms. And to my surprise, I decided not to fight him.

"King Kostas delights in forcing others to tell half-truths and sow discord and miscommunication," he said, his voice bitter. "Even among his own blood!"

"But I don't understand!" I croaked, leaning back to study his face. "What does any of this have to do with that strange white rock? And Pandora's Key?" So many lives had been—and would be—upended soon. And it always seemed to come back to me and that stupid rock.

My grandfather gently pushed me back into my pillows like I was a tired rag doll and rose to get the tea from the servant who had appeared at the door.

"So you've discovered the Pandora Stone, have you?" he asked after the servant was gone. As he spoke, he set about serving the tea.

"So you know about it?" I sniffed.

"All heads of clans and courts know about it," he said, frowning. "But it's a secret that's been kept for a long time. And must be kept still, difficult as that's turning out to be." He studied me. "What do you know of the stone?"

"Dorian—one of my friends—discovered that it enhances the strength of the person holding or wearing it. But that's all we know so far. Well, that and that Pandora's Key..." My words trailed off. "Wait! That's what they're named after! Pandora's Key, I mean!"

My grandfather nodded. "Why do you think so many hotels just popped up in the middle of the desert back in the middle of the twentieth century? The stone was discovered by a dwarf, which comes as no surprise, but as soon as the courts found out about it, they moved their main operations here. King Kostas's grandfather was king then, and he decided quickly that the stone must be kept hidden from the supernatural public. He and the other supernatural heads bought up all the land around the mining site, and as a payment for their continued cooperation and silence, the high elven king to this day allows the other heads to use small pieces of the stone in order to strengthen their warriors through proximity. And the warriors themselves swear an oath of binding silence before taking a post that would allow them such proximity. But no individual is allowed to take a piece of the stone for him or herself. Not even the king does that."

"Why?" I asked, thinking of the Pandora's Key operatives' request of Cara.

His thick eyebrows rose. "Aside from it most likely killing them on the spot if handled incorrectly? Can you imagine the chaos if the supernatural community found out that there was a stone that could exponentially increase their strength?" He shook his head. "As much as I disagree with King Kostas in many ways, this is not one of them. Which is what makes Pandora's Key such a threat."

"Are... are they new? And what do they want?" I asked, taking a sip of the tea he'd handed me. It was lemon and licorice. My favorite. How had he known that? I could also feel a bit of sleeping magic in there as well. Not that I minded. I suddenly realized I desperately wanted a nap, if for no other reason than to escape

"They've been on the fringe for about two decades now, but only recently have they gained in both traction and numbers.' He frowned at me. "The timing is... curious."

"What do they want?" I asked again, though I had a feeling from our prior encounters that I knew.

"They want the Pandora's Stone to be made available to all." He scoffed and glared down at his own tea. "They claim that supernaturals have become soft, and that a purge would be beneficial for us. Those who remain and are strong enough to use the stone should rule the earth as God intended." His frown deepened.

I shivered. A purge? "As in... they want the weakest to die?"

He gave me another sad smile. "So it seems."

And they had been delusional enough to think I would join them?

"Which brings us back to the timing—something I find oddly suspicious, as their sudden flurry of activity lines up with your reaching adulthood. It has many supernaturals worried." He nodded at the window. "Hence King Kostas recalling the entire royal family so they're under his protection here. Other race heads are doing the same. Even the vampires are on edge." Then his voice dropped, as though someone might be listening. "And word has it that the dragon marshals are listening in."

I stared back. Dragon shifters were few in number. But, as they were the only race who could rival the elves for power—and they had their own sense of justice—the appearance of one of them was never good. It usually meant heads were about to roll.

"So," I asked slowly, "what do we do now?"

He sighed. "To be honest? I have no idea. My children—your mother and Finn excluded—all turned out just as conniving and cold as most fae. Everleigh, you can't under-stand—I wanted so much to know you." His eyes suddenly glistened with unshed tears. "But I left your parents alone in the hopes that Kostas would, too. I played the part of a tyrannical fae king and affronted parent so they wouldn't suspect what I already knew." He shook his head. "But I think that things are about to get very ugly. Whether he knows what you are or not, you've proven yourself to be resourceful, and therefore useful. And from what I understand, the high king has plans for you to get your hands dirty on his behalf. Very dirty."

I blinked up at him and swallowed. "Do you think he knows what I am?" That my grandfather knew was bad enough. Kind as he seemed, the fewer people knew of my fledgling powers, the better. At least until I got those powers under control.

"I honestly don't know," he said. "But I'm afraid we'll soon find out."

My grandfather told me to sleep soon after that and left me alone in my bedroom. I knew I ought to push to find out where my friends were being held, but before I could ask, Julia came bounding in, sobbing like a baby but, from what I could tell, unharmed.

"I thought you were dead!" she cried into my shoulder. I still felt weak, but I did my best to hug her back. "When he hit you with that magic—"

"I'll be fine," I promised her, doing my best to dredge up a smile. "But what about you? And the others? Where are they?"

She sat back, still sniffling. "From what I can tell, they're all getting rooms of their own. We're not allowed to leave, and they took all our cell phones, but I think everyone seems fine otherwise. They were going to do that memory spell thing to me until I told them I was your pet." She gave me a fierce look. "They weren't going to get rid of me that easily."

"Julia, you should have let them!" I chided. "You would have been safe by now! And then they would let you leave!"

"No, I'd still be your pet. Only I'd feel lost and confused. You said yourself that it's nearly impossible to sever the fae-pet tie."

"Yes. But I've also never met a human so determined to remain a pet!" I glared at her in frustration. "You *have* to know that he's keeping you here to remind me that he can kill you all in an instant. If we ever get out of here—"

"Oh, but you will!" Julia's face transformed into a feverish determination. She leaned forward to whisper in my ear. "Before they took my phone, I was able to text Georgie! And he's already planning to break you out of here!"

Nausea suddenly swirled in my stomach. "You texted Georgie to come here? Julia, I can't have two pets! I can't even protect the one I have!" I shook my head. "Besides, if they read your texts—"

Julia just folded her arms and lifted her chin. "I sent him a few short messages to tell him where we were and what was going on. And I figured they'd check my phone, so I deleted it all. But I was able to fire off a few texts about magic and the king and The Realm Resort first. And from what he responded, I don't think he's as ignorant of this world as you think he is."

I stared at her, shaking my head in disbelief. "Julia, I don't know whether to call you the bravest girl I ever met, or the most bullishly, foolishly determined."

"Everleigh," she said, taking my hands in hers. "If there's anything I've learned over these last few weeks, it's that you *have* to be kept safe. For all our sakes."

I held her gaze, unable to give words to the sudden fear and affection that now battled inside. But I wished more than ever that I could figure out why my magic was still so limited.

And what I could do to loosen it so that I could protect this precious—albeit naïve—friend of mine.

So I could protect *everyone* I loved.

270

Chapter Thirty-Six

Everleigh

I slept harder that night than I had meant to. With Julia sharing my room, my plan had been to stay awake during the night and think as I stood guard. I had so many things to figure out.

But either my grandfather's sleeping magic or the physical shock from King Kostas's attack made that impossible. I only woke up the next morning when someone pounded on my door.

"What?" I mumbled, bolting upright as I tried to remember where I was.

"His Majesty, High King Kostas, is expecting you to join him for breakfast," a familiar voice called through the door.

The sound of Aithan's voice had me suddenly wide awake. And as I came to, the day before came rushing back. I grabbed my head with both hands and groaned as I squeezed my eyes shut.

King Kostas had taken us.

Aithan was cursed.

We were all prisoners in The Realm Hotel.

I groaned and lay back in bed, rubbing my eyes as though it might change what I saw when I opened them again. My dreams had been so vivid the night before that I'd been convinced just before waking that they were just that—dreams. Unfortunately, when I did open my eyes again, everything looked the same. Which meant I had no choice but to go.

"I'll be there in a minute," I called back to Aithan, my heart thundering in my chest as I tried not to think about the fact that he, supposedly, could no longer love.

Or that he *had* loved me.

Julia, to my relief, was already up and watching the news on the TV across from the bed.

"I don't want you eating or drinking anything without me," I told her as I rifled through my suitcase, which had been brought up the day before. Court-appropriate clothing–the kind from story-books–had also appeared in my wardrobe overnight, but I ignored those and pulled on a pair of jeans, a graphic t-shirt, and a hoodie. "Wait, what are you eating?"

I paused brushing my hair to look at the plate of what looked like... "Julia, are those *tarts?*" This girl wasn't going to last an hour in the supernatural world without me, let alone live out the rest of her life.

But Julia only waved me off. "Girl, your grandpa is awesome. He brought these up this morning. Said he'd made sure they were safe. But you wouldn't wake up, so he told me to have as many as I wanted, and he would bring up more later. Also, they have the *best* coffee machine in the kitchen! Soo Min would be so jealous!"

"Julia." I ran a hand down my face. "You can't just go *eating* anything offered to you by a fae!"

But Julia only scoffed. "They were for you. It's not like your grandfather would poison *you.*"

"Okay, that's it." I pulled my hoodie over my head indignantly. "When we get out of here, the first thing I'm doing is buying you a fairy book! And not some happily-ever-after one! Like... the real lore! And you can learn about all the *kind* things fae have done to humans throughout the history of the world!"

"Princess." Aithan, sounding bored, knocked again. "King Kostas is waiting."

I huffed but pulled on my sneakers. Then I took a deep breath and opened the door.

Aithan stood before me dressed, to my relief, in street clothes like I was. I'd been half afraid the curse would turn him into some medieval European prude. But when he saw me, there was no spark of relief or joy—not even the hint of a smile. He only gave me a passing glance, as though making sure I wasn't still in my pajamas, before turning and waving for me to follow him.

I did so, my heart squeezing in my chest as I did. *Aithan loves me,* it seemed to beat over and over again in amazement.

Or at least, he *had.*

And knowing exactly what his grandfather's curse would do, he had loved me anyway, enough to save my life at the cost of his own heart.

I might have cried again if the whole situation didn't make me so flipping angry. But I would cry later. Right now, anger was good.

Anger would help me win this war.

Armoring myself with my anger, I allowed him to lead me to a pair of doors—the same ones, I was sure—that my grandfather had carried me through the day before.

Only then did Aithan turn and address me. His tone was flat. "His Highness, King Daniil, was called away this morning on royal business. But he says he should return by the time you're finished taking brunch with the high king." Then he turned and stationed himself outside the doors.

Doing my best to forget that the man now standing beside me no longer cared, I squared my shoulders and faced the doors. Brunch with the high king, was it? Such a sophisticated meal for such a scummy jerk. But I knew better than to voice that thought out loud. King Kostas could kill me much in the same way he could swat a mosquito. He'd proven that yesterday.

When the doors were opened, I walked in, doing my best to appear confident and unaffected by Aithan's presence. The appearance of strength in the supernatural world was everything.

But to my surprise, the magnificent room was empty of all its courtiers and soldiers. Only the high king and his personal guards were present. And the decor had been transformed to make the large room look much like a large flower garden. Flowers seemed to sprout right out of the walls, and the ground beneath my feet was no longer stone but soft, green moss. The king was also nowhere near his throne. Instead, he was sitting beside a sunny window at a small, round table piled high with food. The kind you might find on an apartment balcony. A single empty chair sat across from him.

"Sit, please," King Kostas said after I curtsied. "I hope you like eggs."

"I do," I said cautiously as I sat.

The king spoke as he salted his own plate. "I'm aware enough of your personality to know that you don't appreciate fluffy nonsense, so I'll get to the point." He put the salt shaker down and met my gaze. "You might be an *Anikos,* but you've proven yourself to be unusually skilled at survival, and as such, will be quite useful."

In my mind, I let out a scream of triumph. He didn't know I was a wizard. At least... Not yet.

"With that in mind," he continued, "I will press further and also say that it's your duty, as a member of not one but *two* royal households, to work in some capacity for your people."

"You mean," I said carefully, "to work for you."

He nodded. "I'm glad you see my point."

"I never said I agreed," I argued back. Elves were nearly as tricky about word choice as fae. And unlike fae, they could lie. "I was only clarifying the point."

He gave me a dry smile. "Your parents have taught you well. Yes, I would like for you to work for me. But not only for me, mind you. In addition to your mother's side, which is also loyal to me, you are, in fact, an heir of a lower elven house that has pledged fealty to the high elven crown. Both have sworn to support the high king in my endeavors to protect all supernaturals from human knowledge and harm." He paused. "For example, Pandora's Key."

"What would you want from me?" I asked slowly.

"I'm glad you asked." He took a bite of a strawberry crepe and chewed slowly. "As I said before, I'm not unaware of the stir you're making in the city."

The same stir, I wondered silently, as the one that led him to attack me the day before? But to my relief, he didn't press the subject.

"You and your friends, unsupported as you were, were able to gather quite a bit of useful information on your own. And I would like for you to continue that kind of work for me."

"Not to be rude," I said, knowing perfectly well that I was risking rudeness, "but to be equally candid, won't your court mind having a magical mutt working under you?"

"I don't think you'll need to worry about what my court does or doesn't think." He leaned forward and fixed his emerald-green gaze on me. "They do and think as I say without question."

Which, I was perfectly aware, would be expected of me if I were to join their ranks.

"You'd be paid handsomely for your work," he continued, turning back to his food. "From what I understand, you work for your Uncle Finn whenever your schedule allows. But I would pay you far more. And I would also ensure you're given time to finish your degree. I prefer my employees to be well-educated. In addition, you would be provided comfortable living quarters, of course. And..." His smile grew. "We would find you an adequate teacher. Much better than that dried old prune your friends hired. *Anikos* or not, you deserve something better than *him*."

I nearly choked on the bite of cantaloupe I'd just taken. Did he know *why* we had hired such an ill-tempered prune? Had Maverick told him my secret, and he was simply playing dumb? Or did he simply think we had really bad taste?

"I suppose," I said, "that you would wish for me to live that comfortable life here at The Realm."

He nodded once. "Naturally. This is where you and your family will be safe. At least until we can get this gang of zealots under control."

Meaning he had no plans to ever let us out again.

"Everleigh," he said, seeming to read the suspicion on my face, "I need you to understand something. I am a king, yes. But my work isn't to grow fat and live on the backs of those under my rule. Whether you choose to believe it or not, I'm the arbiter of peace in the supernatural world. I keep the fae from manipulating every human they come into contact with and robbing them blind. I keep the elven kings and soldiers in check when they grow too... enthusiastic about enforcing law and order through permanent and lethal force. I keep the vampires from killing and turning humans at will, and I ensure that there are laws and systems in place to keep that peace. Then I must also oversee those systems, not only here in this city, but all around the world." His green eyes brightened. "You wouldn't know it, of course, but since being crowned, I've stopped civil war from breaking out amongst the supernaturals no less than three times."

"That makes sense," I said slowly. For though I didn't want to, I believed him. I might not be at the center of most supernatural life, but I was aware enough to understand the raw aggression that was so common among supernaturals as a whole.

He twirled his glass of water so its refracted sunlight danced on the flowers around us. "I gave your grandfather permission to tell you more about the Pandora Stone. Now imagine what would happen if the information about the stone were to be leaked to the entire world."

He met my gaze again, his eyes suddenly narrowed. "It would be a feeding frenzy. Every power-hungry supernatural—which is many of them, if not most—would be on his way to Vegas in an instant, intent on doing whatever harm necessary to make sure he got a piece of that stone. The humans and the weaker or non-violent supernaturals would be slaughtered. Our existence would be broadcast, and all the remaining supernaturals would be hunted down by human governments as enemies of the public."

He leaned back. "It's happened on a small scale in the past, but now human technology has gotten so good that no true war could remain hidden. Essentially," he held his hands out in a helpless gesture, "a huge population of all life on Earth would be wiped out.

I hated it. I really did. But every word he said was true. If Pandora's Key got what they wanted and found a way to distribute the Pandora Stone to supernaturals on a grand scale, or even chose to simply release the information about it, the result would be a bloodbath.

We were, I realized, on borrowed time already.

Of course, I also wasn't unaware that the king was threatening everyone I loved if I didn't obey.

"I've explained my piece. And yet, you still hesitate," he said, his voice dipping dangerously low. "Whatever for?"

"I... want to prevent war," I said slowly. "And as I've been personally attacked by Pandora's Key, I have no desire to join or help them."

He leaned back. "So I see no problem."

I paused, fully aware that my hesitation may set off yet another round of deadly torture. And this time, there would be no Aithan to save me. "My... struggle," I finally said, "is that I'm not convinced I can agree to obey you without question. Not without abandoning my conscience–" As I spoke, the memory of Alexander's face in Cara's memory came to mind. I shivered.

The king abruptly stood and went to look out a window, gesturing for me to join him. Knowing I had no other choice, I did.

"Child, the Nomos name has denoted the most powerful fae bloodline for the last millennium. We've perfected our methods of persuasion over centuries of practice and experimentation. And while I can feel that you're... *curiously* strong for an *Anikos*–

because I *can* feel it." He turned to study me with burning eyes. "I doubt you're strong enough to withstand watching everyone you love suffer the way my grandson just did."

I stared back at him, my stomach curdling inside me. Strong? What did he mean, I was strong? And what exactly did this tyrant have in mind bringing up–

"I happen to know that your father's right knee is particularly susceptible to injury because he broke it playing football with a troll on his fourteenth birthday. I also happen to know that your mother gets migraines when the sun is too bright, although…" He smiled slightly. "I might have had a hand in that when they got married against my particularly useful advice."

As I listened, I dug my fingernails into the palms of my hands to keep them at my sides. Never had I wanted to punch anyone this much.

"Julia, of course, would be the easiest of them all, seeing as she's perfectly human. And your friend, Soo Min, was only allowed to return to her father because he's been quite useful to me." He sneered slightly. "Unlike her mother. But either way," he met my gaze again, "I know exactly where she is at all times. Just as I do the rest of your little posse. And as for my grandson–"

The door burst open, and a servant ran in, a look of horror on his face.

"What is it?" the king snapped.

"There's been a staff mixup, Sire! Someone downstairs–"

Before he could finish, the elevator dinged, and not one but both of the elevator doors opened. Dozens of tourists immediately poured out of each. They began to *ooh* and *ahh* over the beautiful statues, the columns, and the throne, taking pictures and streaming video on their phones as they did.

"Please!" a doorman was calling frantically as he ran after the quickly dispersing guests. "There was a mistake! These are private quarters!"

I stared stupidly at the confusion as King Kostas immediately began to address the people in a calm, languid tone. His guards stood by, but I could only guess they were staying back because a number of the humans were obviously streaming from their phones. Before I could see what he would do about it all, however, a large hand covered my mouth, while another was wrapped around my waist.

I was about to scream when I looked back and recognized Georgie's warm brown eyes.

He jerked his head toward a door that led to what looked like emergency stairs, but I glanced back at King Kostas. Surely he'd notice if we disappeared. We were far too many stories high to try escaping on foot without being noticed or caught. Especially as I would be running with a human.

And even if I got away... What would he do to my family?

But then Georgie pulled something out of his pocket and raised a finger to his lips, his eyes dancing, and I nearly fell over.

Georgie had somehow gotten hold of the most powerful–and presumably, the most expensive–glamour stone I had ever seen. It literally pulsed with power.

The sight of that stone made up my mind for me. The elven king didn't hold all the cards. And if I escaped now, I knew there was no way he would murder my family and friends to get me. It would cause too many waves in the world of politics that he was so desperate to control. No, I would be far more receptive to coercion if I were under his control. He had me where he wanted me, right here and right now.

Which meant it was time to get out.

How Georgie had gotten the stone, I decided I would ask later. Instead, I let him lead me to the stairs. We slipped through the exit door and began making our way down the dizzying, countless rounds of steps.

Unfortunately, my usual stamina was still drained, my body sore from the king's attack the day before. It wasn't long before I started to fall behind. Again, however, Georgie seemed to be one step ahead of me. Just before my knees gave out, he took my hand and dragged me out of the stairwell and back into the hotel. This one, however, was a public area, a long hall with general hotel rooms lining both sides. From there, he dragged me three doors down to the regular guest elevator. We dove in, and he hit the button to close the doors several times.

"Come on! Close!" he muttered.

Unfortunately, the doors didn't close in time, and a large woman in a very shiny pink dress walked in carrying her dog. The dog was of the tiny variety—the kind my dad called "pretend." And in pretend dog fashion, it took one look at me and Georgie and began to bark.

"What's wrong, Tiko?" the woman crooned. "We're the only ones in here!"

How the dog knew we were there, I didn't know. The glamour stone was obviously working well enough that the woman had no idea there were two other people present. But the dog continued to bark until we made it down to the ground floor.

My heart leaped as the elevator opened, and the hotel's main doors came into sight. But my relief came too soon. We hadn't taken more than three steps out of the elevator when a deafening buzzing filled the whole building, followed by lights flashing overhead. A smooth female voice sounded over the speaker system.

"For the safety of our guests, a hard lockdown has been engaged. Please remain where you are. Caution. For the safety of our guests, a hard lockdown..."

The voice continued to repeat itself as Georgie veered away from the main doors and back toward a smaller red emergency exit sign. When we were twenty feet from the door, however, two large elven soldiers in suits appeared and stationed themselves between us and our escape.

We stopped in front of them. They didn't seem to see us, but even the best fae magic could only camouflage. There was no way we'd be able to slip behind them without them noticing, and I wasn't skilled enough yet at elven invisibility to get either of us through.

Georgie frowned hard in concentration, but I just wanted to kick myself. If my magic wasn't so bad—

The moment I thought the words, however, I realized I did have one elven skill that was unfettered by the odd rubber band-like sensation that kept my magic trapped inside.

"Get ready," I breathed.

"For what?" he whispered back.

Unfortunately, the soldiers' sensitive elven ears picked up our whispers, and their heads snapped in our direction. Knowing I now had no time to rethink my decision, I reached out with my magic and grabbed whatever the men had in their pockets. Instead of magically pulling the objects to me, however, I simply sent their glamour stones and wallets flying.

The soldiers were unable to use their elven magic in front of the guests, who were staring at them with wide eyes, so the best they could do was go hurtling after their belongings while Georgie dragged me toward the doors.

But the doors were locked.

Cursing under his breath, Georgie fumbled in his pockets for what I could only guess was some sort of purchased fae lock-breaker charm. But as he did, one of the elven soldiers reached out wildly and managed to grab my arm, hidden as it was, dragging me away from Georgie's protective stone.

People screamed as I stumbled, seeming to appear out of thin air as the guard threw me to the ground. I hit my head hard on the stone floor, and the soldier twisted my arm hard. Blood ran from my nose into my mouth, and I was just conscious enough to realize that they were preparing to handcuff me on the spot.

This was not good.

An explosion rocked the building, however, knocking the guards to the ground. Sunlight streamed into the casino from where the door had been. I gave up trying to stand as my ears rang so loudly that I couldn't tell which way was up. But a second later, Georgie had lifted me in both arms and began running again. I could tell from the sudden flood of light that we were finally outside, but my head hurt too much to open my eyes.

Georgie slowed as I heard the sound of a car screeching to a halt in front of us.

"The door! Get the door!" he shouted.

I heard a car door open, and Georgie half-climbed, half-fell into some sort of vehicle. He dropped me into the seat, slammed the door shut, and shouted for the driver to go.

The next thing I knew, we were speeding down the road.

Chapter Thirty-Seven

Everleigh

WE DROVE for about ten minutes before coming to a stop. I wanted to sit up to see where we were, but Georgie told me to stay down.

"We don't know if they're following us," he said, glancing around. "Just lie low and rest."

So I did, staying huddled on the floor of the backseat until the car stopped about ten minutes later, and the guy who was driving announced that we'd arrived.

"Here." Georgie handed him a wad of cash. "Thanks again."

The driver had a hoodie and sunglasses on, so I couldn't see much of his face. But based on the slightly musky smell of the vehicle, I guessed him to be a shifter of sorts. He took the cash and thanked Georgie, then he waited politely until Georgie had helped me out of the car and deposited me into his own. Once I was laid out in his backseat, Georgie insisted I drink several elven healing elixirs before getting into the driver's seat and setting out again.

"Where are we going?" I mumbled. The elixirs were making me nauseous, and my head still spun from hitting the ground.

"We're going to my house, actually," he said. Then he glanced back at me and grimaced. "I'd take you to yours, but it's being watched. So is Julia's apartment."

"How…" I had to stop to lick my dry lips. I hadn't drunk much during my brunch with the high king. And healing elixirs were no Gatorade.

"Here." He handed me a bottle of water. I pushed myself up on my elbow and drank greedily, thankful I didn't have to wonder what kind of malicious magic someone might have spiked it with.

"So," I said more clearly once the bottle was half-gone. "I'm guessing you're not just a human." As I said it, I wondered how in the world I could have missed his magic.

"I'm not," he said with a sheepish smile. "But… I'm also not anything you've probably spent much time around."

I smiled ruefully. "I have absolutely no idea how I never sensed that. Color me impressed. Or totally oblivious. Whichever you prefer."

"Oh, you're not oblivious!" he hurried to assure me. "I mean, I doubt you would have been easily able to feel me because my magic is, as I said, less common than most."

I lay back down and closed my eyes. "Georgie, I would love to guess what you are, but my head hurts so much right now—"

"I'm an oracle."

His words were so quiet that I nearly missed them. But as soon as what he'd said dawned on me, I nearly sat upright, only for my head to burst into flames again. "You're… what?"

"Not an extremely talented one," he continued, keeping his eyes on the road. "My dad is way better than I am, as is my uncle. My dad actually worked for several of the local kings before he moved away." He glanced back at me. "Including your fae grandfather. And King Kostas."

I put my hands on my head and did my best to breathe slowly. This changed… so much. "Did you know I was a supernatural when we met?" I asked. Although, the better question was whether he knew *what* I was.

He let out a strange laugh. "Of course I did. My dad told me about you ages ago." He paused again. "He was the one who went behind King Kostas's back and told your parents who and what you would be." Now his smile was undeniably proud. "He was the reason you escaped! Not that I could have talked with you before about all of this. Dad made it clear that you were under some sort of curse by King Kostas, and when he described you to me, he had to use a lot of vague inferences. But I... I'll admit that I sought you out as soon as I could." He chuckled. "It was kind of like meeting a celebrity I'd heard about my whole life."

"*Why?*" The word was out of my mouth before I could consider that it might sound rude.

But he just shrugged. "From what my dad told me, you were... a one of a kind. I figured you would be lonely... like I was." He paused, and when he spoke again, his words were slow and deliberate. "Also... your birth heralded the advent of something big. All wizard births do. And I wanted to be on the right side of history whenever it happened." His smile broadened. "Then, when I finally met you, you were everything I'd hoped you would be. Everything my father hoped you would be—and more. That was why I wanted to be your friend."

A hard lump rose up in my throat, and I had to clear it several times so my voice wouldn't crack. "Oh. That was... really thoughtful." And I meant it. For so much of my life, I *had* been lonely. Julia was there, of course. But she'd been blissfully ignorant up until a few weeks ago. An unsuspecting human who knew nothing of the secret world in which I lived. Having Georgie there to discuss supernatural stuff with would have made all the difference.

We didn't talk for a while after that. I just lay in the backseat, wondering how I was supposed to pick up and start again after all of this. Before King Kostas had intervened, I'd had my friends to turn to when things fell apart. But now...

My heart twisted painfully in my chest as I remembered the evening Aithan and I had spent out on the racetrack. He'd been so open then. So close to saying what he often seemed to shove back down. If only I'd known–

"We're crossing into North Las Vegas now," Georgie announced. "You can probably sit up if you like."

The city line between North Las Vegas and Las Vegas was pretty much nonexistent. But North Las Vegas was a lot less crowded than downtown, and it was less likely that we'd be followed out here without noticing. Grateful for the clearance, and finally feeling the effects of the healing elixirs, I sat up and looked around. Then I gave a little start.

"Hey, I used to live near here!" I exclaimed.

"Where?" he asked.

"Over there." I pointed just south of the beltway. "Near the golf course."

He put on his blinker and took the next exit. "How about we take a trip down Memory Lane? I'm still not certain we're free of any followers. I used several strong tracker decoys in the parking lot, but that doesn't mean we're in the clear. While we're driving, tell me what you remember."

I knew he was trying to distract me. This usually would have been annoying, as I preferred to face problems head-on, but at the moment I didn't mind. My brain felt like it was in tangles.

"There." I smiled as I looked out the window as we moved into a more residential area. "That was my first park. My parents took me nearly every day. I broke my arm falling out of that tire swing when I was five. And there's the field where my dad took me to fly my first kite!" I craned my neck to see better. "Down this road, there's a gas station that used to sell the best soft serve banana and walnut chocolate chip ice cream!"

Georgie let out a laugh. "You got ice cream at a gas station?"

"Hey, no hating! It was the only thing out here, back when most of this was desert. Oh! And that's the school where I took my first..."

I had pointed excitedly to the elementary school that bordered the park. But even as I spoke, something stirred inside me—like an estranged memory trying to find a foothold in my mind. One that felt oddly close to the surface, but I had no idea why.

"What is it?" He parked against the curb and turned around to look at me.

I stared at the school, the unsettled feeling growing stronger by the second. Then the dreams—or nightmares, rather—that I'd been having lately hit me.

As did inspiration.

"Georgie, oracles can retrieve hidden memories, can't they?"

"Well, usually. I mean, it takes some work, but generally, they can."

My heart began to beat faster with each second I stared at the school. "Even ones that were erased?"

Fae memory charms didn't *actually* erase memories, though that was how it was often described. Instead, the fae built a wall, so to speak, in a specific part of the mind to make the memories on the other side invisible. When it wasn't done illegally or as part of a court operation, it was sometimes done to those who'd survived serious trauma in order to protect their minds, though the technique was highly controversial. Humans, however, might as well have had their memories put in a wood chipper, as they had no medical means by which to retrieve them. For supernaturals like Cara, who were the victims of other supernatural crime, retrieval was still difficult. But now that I knew Georgie was an oracle. . .

He scratched his chin, which was starting to show the beginnings of a shadow. "I mean, I studied it a little at the oracle school I attended before starting at the university." He paused and met my pleading gaze, then sighed and gave me a wry smile. "I can't guarantee anything, but I'd be happy to try." He looked back at the school. "What makes you think you might have a stolen memory?"

"I can't say exactly." I frowned. "But seeing this building .. We moved to our current house when I was in first grade. I know this was where I took my first magic class. But there's something about this place that makes me feel like something important happened here."

"Well," he said, "seeing as I haven't spotted any cars trailing us, let's go back to my house and try."

Chapter Thirty-Eight

Everleigh

I WAS FEELING NEARLY normal again by the time he pulled into the garage of a cute one-story starter house. Elven healing elixirs are nasty, but they work *really* well.

"Georgie, it's adorable!" I exclaimed, walking back out of the garage to see the front. And it was. The front yard was small but neat, with two kinds of white filler rock, bushes, and artfully arranged cacti. The stucco and roof had been painted three variations of blue-gray, and the door was red. "Julia and I drove through this neighborhood once by accident, and I told her I'd love to live somewhere like this one day."

He gave an odd chuckle as he unlocked the door. "That conversation was actually what led me here. I decided I wanted to see what you were so excited about. And... I guess I loved it too."

He went inside, so I followed.

"Please make yourself at home on the couch. I know you're feeling better, but you probably need a few more elixirs and a couple days of rest before you're ready to get back to those workouts you and Julia like so much." He went into the kitchen. "I'll get you some fae potions as well, and some juice to get your blood sugar up."

I sank into his couch and let my head rest on the back. "That sounds amazing."

And it really did. After a weekend of my fae aunt's interrogation, learning about the Pandora Stone, nearly dying, watching Aithan crumple under his grandfather's curse, and then escaping the elven high king's demands, simply sitting in a normal house on a normal couch with one of my normal friends was deliciously bland.

Not that the house was bland. The inside was just as cute as the front yard.

"No offense," I called as I studied the way the gray floor tiles complemented the blue walls and white trim. "But this house doesn't look anything like a bachelor lives here."

He laughed. "I guess it doesn't. My mom's an interior designer, so I asked her to come and work her magic when I moved in."

I continued to study the room. Most of the wall decor was made up of tastefully selected art, but there were a few pictures in frames on the mantle. And one of them caught my eye. Was that...? I stood up to get a better look.

It sure was. And I couldn't help smiling. Georgie had not only framed pictures of people I assumed to be his mom and dad, but there was also one of him, Julia, and me. It was a selfie we'd taken at Soo Min's shop.

"This is so sweet," I said as he walked back in with a cup of red juice. I pointed at the picture.

"Oh," he said, his face turning slightly pink. He put the juice down and nervously adjusted his glasses. "Yeah, I guess I liked how that one turned out." He looked down. "Um, here's the juice. And I just put in a grocery order for some food. I'm sorry I don't have more. After getting Julia's text, I didn't want to fool around with waiting for a delivery." He handed me two chewable tablets.

"I have some of my own," I said, taking my little tin out and shaking it. "You don't have to give me yours. I know they cost a fortune."

He waved me off. "One of the really useful things about being an oracle–even a mediocre one–is that it's easy to make money on the side." He laughed a little. "A lot of supernaturals are willing to pay heaps of cash for future possibilities–even if they're warned the visions may not be that accurate."

I wanted to argue with him. But after watching him adjust his glasses again, his eyes looking anywhere but at me, I decided to simply thank him and take the tablets with the juice.

Elven elixirs and tablets are different from fae tablets and potions in that elven magic truly heals. So they're really, *really* expensive. Fae potions and tablets are also expensive, but as they only mask the sensation of pain, they aren't quite as pricey as those of the elves.

"Look," I said once I'd finished the juice. "This day has been insane, and though I know it's not enough, I just want to say thank you." I gave him a sad smile. "And... I'm sorry for not answering your calls and texts recently. I thought–"

"You thought I was human. I get it. Telling me would have been dangerous." He paused and looked down at the rug. "I'll also say that I probably should have told you what I was sooner. But you wanted so much to leave the supernatural world behind that I thought I'd wait till... Well, I'd planned to tell you by taking you out. But then Aithan Nomos appeared, and..." He shrugged, his smile suddenly gone.

Well, this had just gotten awkward fast.

"Have you heard anything new from Julia?" I asked. "I don't have my phone, and hers was confiscated."

He frowned, seeming glad for the change of subject as well. "Unfortunately, no. I was shocked she was able to text me from The Realm at all. My father often lost contact with my mother whenever he was there with King Daniil or King Kostas. They could be there for hours or even days, and she wouldn't hear a word from him."

"Do you think she's really safe?" I pressed. "I mean, she was in my fae grandfather's care this morning, so—"

"She'll be fine." He took my hand and squeezed it once before letting go. "The law automatically protects her as long as she's in your grandfather's retinue. His title will give her way more political protection than she had while she was with you. And before you start blaming yourself," he gave me a reproving look, "she was right in sending you away. A lot of people are depending on you, Everleigh. You have to be kept safe. For all their sakes." Then he laughed. "Is it true that Julia's now your pet?"

I let my head fall back and groaned. "It was the only way I could think to protect her!"

He only shrugged. "Unfortunately, something like that was highly likely. I even glimpsed it as a possibility a few times."

"And you didn't say anything?" I asked.

He gave me a half-hearted grin. "She was running around with two somewhat rare supernaturals. It was only a matter of time." As he spoke, the sound of a tea kettle went off in the kitchen, and he stood. "Excuse me." When he returned, he carried a mug of tea. "Drink this."

"What is it?" I took the mug and sniffed it.

"It's not magical if that's what you're asking. Our main work is seeing visions of the future, of course. But oracles also learned a long time ago that memories are easier to retrieve if the person is unconscious or relaxed. It helps us break down that wall created by the memory charm." He nodded at it. "This blend is a bedtime tea and should help you unwind." He glanced at the couch. "Drink it, then lay down. I don't want you falling over."

"I'm not sure unwinding is possible right now," I said. But I sipped it anyway, doing my best not to gag as its bitterness scratched my throat. Still, to my surprise, I was tired enough that within two minutes, I was putting my head on the pillow and stretching out on the couch, hovering on the brink of unconsciousness. I probably had King Kostas's attack to thank for that.

"All right," Georgie said, though he sounded somewhat far off. "I'm going to be searching your mind for a wall of some sort. A kind of charm. But let me know if I get into anything you don't want me to see."

I nodded but didn't speak, hoping I was relaxed enough for him to try. A part of me wondered if this was a wise idea. I had a lot of people's secrets in my head. I was also, however, out of options. I needed something... anything to fight back with.

For example, my magic.

If this strange secret—whatever it was—gave me even an inkling as to how I might access that magic, I might have a better chance of going up against both Pandora's Key *and* Aithan's grandfather. And for some reason, seeing that elementary school again had given me hope. Something had happened there. Something important. I *felt* it.

"Think back to the time you went to that school," Georgie said. "Or at least, as close as you can." As he spoke, I could sense him creating a thin layer of magic around me.

"I... I know my parents sent me there," I said, trying to remember the details of the day my mom had dropped me off.

"Was it for school?" he asked. "Like kindergarten or first grade?"

"I don't... No. It wasn't. It was in the summer, and I was signed up for some sort of class. Or camp—Yes, it was a camp."

"Okay, good." He worked in silence for a moment, continuing to weave the sheet of magic around me. "I think I've found it. Keep going."

I took a deep breath. "I remember her dropping me off with a lunchbox. It was going to take most of the day, she said, but she would be back to get me after—" I paused. Details of that day were becoming more and more clear. It was like putting on a pair of glasses. "There's white and blue-flecked linoleum. And the walls are made of those big cinderblocks painted blue. The windows are the thick glass tiles you can't see out of, but they let in light."

"Good. The more you tell me, the more I can feel the holes in the charm."

I couldn't help pausing. "There are holes?"

"*All* spells and charms have holes in them," he said firmly. "No charm is perfect because no supernatural's magic is perfect. I just need to find them. Keep going."

"Um..." I did my best to focus. "I'm seated with other kids. And they're... they're all fae. Oh!" I was so excited I nearly opened my eyes. "I remember now! My first magic lessons! My mother signed me up to see if I could start honing my fae magic!"

"Do you remember what happened once the class started?" he asked.

"I..." I felt my smile fade as an oddly familiar sense of shame overcame me. My stomach turned, and my face and neck grew hot. "I'm not very good," I said, inexplicably on the verge of tears. "I'm sorry," I laughed as my voice warbled. "I don't know why I'm crying." As I spoke, large tears started rolling down my face.

"Don't be sorry," he said gently. "It means you're accessing the part of your mind that's been closed off for a long time. You never got to finish experiencing or processing those emotions, so they stayed frozen right where they were." His voice hardened. "It's a cruel thing to do to a child."

I swallowed and did my best to focus, though that was hard, as my memories were now stained with tears. It was like trying to see through a rainy windshield.

"I'm not very good at the lessons," I said again. "The teacher is frustrated with me. And there's someone else there who's not very good either. A boy about my age. After we fail several times, she takes us into the hallway away from the other children." I paused, watching it all happen through the eyes of my past self. "She's asking us questions about our parents. He says his father is a fae, and his mother is a shifter. I tell her about my parents, too. That... Oh, she doesn't like that."

"What does she do?" Georgie asked in a tight voice.

"She's... She's telling us that we're called *Anikoses*. And that it's best for the world if people like us don't use our magic at all. That we can hurt people and expose supernaturals." The tears were coming faster. "Now she's telling us that she's going to teach us to bind our magic so we can't use it anymore. Then we won't have to worry about hurting anyone. And... and she says not to tell anyone. It will be our little secret."

Unable to watch any longer, I sat up and put my face in my hands, heaving sobs shaking my body. I could feel Georgie's magic dissipate, but it didn't matter. I knew what had been stolen from me.

Georgie put his hand on my back. And I let him.

"I'm... I'm so sorry, Everleigh," he whispered. When I glanced at him, he had tears running down his face as well.

"I just..." I sniffed. "I don't know why remembering feels so *lonely*."

"She must have put the charm on you when she was finished," he said, his voice terse. "The kind of memory charm she used on you to block your memory was one that's easy to slide into food. That would have been easy to give to small children." He paused, then shrugged. "But... for what it's worth, at least you know why you have such a hard time using your magic."

"It was me," I whispered, hugging my knees to my chest. "I sealed off my own magic. With her help, I imprisoned myself."

"Hey. Here's the good news." Georgie lowered his face so it was level with mine. And he was smiling. "This was never your fault. It was due to age-old resentment and prejudice. The kind a lot of supernaturals are tired of. Believe me. You were just the victim. Not the villain."

I gave him a tired smile. "Yeah, but–"

"And better yet," he continued, wiping my face with the corner of a blanket. "You know now that you can undo it!"

I stared at him. "But how? Can you teach me?"

"No. My magic only works in extending my own *sight* to you in a way. But I think I know someone who can." His grin was wide now. "In fact, I was hoping you would want to meet her. I think she can help you—" Before he could finish, his phone buzzed, and he glanced at it. "Oh, that's my mom. I'd better not ignore this. Give me a minute?"

I waved him off. "Don't want her to ground you." And as I spoke, I realized I was smiling, too.

Georgie went into the kitchen to talk to his mom. Suddenly feeling restless, I stood and began to look at all the pictures on his walls. But a minute later, I realized that all those elven healing elixirs had gone through me, so I stuck my head into the kitchen. *Bathroom?* I mouthed.

Georgie nodded and pointed to the hallway. I waved and left.

The bathroom was like the rest of the house—small but tidy. After I was done, I noticed a line of pictures that had been hung in the hall, similar to the ones on his mantle. I stopped to study them.

There were several people in the photographs that I expected were probably cousins or grandparents, and then the people from the living room pictures that I assumed were his parents. Then, to my surprise, I found a picture of me and Julia again.

I studied this one and tried to remember when it was taken. We weren't looking at the camera in this picture. We were laughing, each of us holding an ice cream cone, but I couldn't tell where we were.

Huh. Then I moved to the next picture and froze.

Chapter Thirty-Nine

Everleigh

THE WHITE AND black photograph that had been printed, framed, and hung in Georgie's hallway was a picture of me in the mountains. I remembered the day clearly because it had been a last-minute day trip, one we'd taken only a few months before when my parents and I had thrown caution to the wind and driven up to the mountain lodge on a whim. I was even wearing the baseball cap my mom had purchased for me from the lodge gift shop.

By all photographic standards, the image was well-positioned and exceptionally clear—perfect for that kind of frame. It looked professional.

But it was also a photo neither of my parents had taken.

From a trip to which Georgie had not been invited.

Heart suddenly pounding in my chest, I glanced back toward the kitchen. I couldn't see him, but I could hear Georgie still arguing with his mother, and he didn't seem as though he would be done any time soon. She sounded worried about something, and he was doing a terrible job of assuaging her fears. So I took a deep breath and darted down the hall toward the open office.

As soon as I burst in, my worst fears were realized. There were pictures of Julia, Georgie, and me everywhere. But mostly me. My stomach twisted even more as I recognized one of them as the framed photograph that had gone missing from Julia's apartment. And the friendship bracelet hanging on its corner was also far too familiar.

I ran to his desk, where his laptop sat open, and quickly looked around the desk. To what extent had this obsession gone? Was I in danger?

Besides the pictures, there wasn't much to go off of based on the desk itself, which was as neat and tidy as the rest of the house. So the computer it was.

I had to guess the password twice, but to my horror, I succeeded. It was my name with no caps. And there, on the screen's wallpaper, was a picture that Julia had taken of Georgie and me.

I bit the inside of my cheek to keep my nerves at bay as I quickly expanded the browser window that was already open and then opened a new tab so I could pull up the university's portal. I logged into the portal and then went back to the original page. Georgie's voice was louder now, and I knew I probably didn't have much time. Fortunately, the site that had been open was his email. A quick search of my name revealed exactly what I had been looking for.

And what I'd feared.

There were far too many emails involving my name. The other recipients of these messages had names I didn't recognize, but many of the messages were, at a glance, about me. The most common, however, were exchanges with a person named "Sam."

The most recent email exchange was long, and as I could hear Georgie bidding his mother an exhausted goodbye, I knew I didn't have much time. I did have enough, however, to learn for certain that not only were "Sam" and Georgie involved in Pandora's Key–I discovered that Georgie was behind nearly all of it.

Every attack Pandora's Key had made against me had been planned using information only Georgie could give. Many of his predictions about where I would be had, apparently, come from his visions of the future. Other details were given simply because he knew me so well.

I was nearly ready to click off the page when one final email caught my eye. I opened it and nearly gasped aloud as "Sam" ordered Georgie to infiltrate the high king's meeting that would take place, apparently, in three days. It read,

Even if you fail to reach the wizard, skipping the king's meeting is not an option. There is no second chance for this. The wizard will be useful if you can get her to help you, but you're an oracle. Extort the king, wizard or not. If you don't, you will be answerable to the entire Key.

"Everleigh?" Georgie called, his voice slightly muffled by the partially shut door. I quickly clicked back onto the university portal tab and opened one of my class links just as he walked in.

The look on his face was one of terror, but it quickly changed to relief when I looked up from the class roster and gave him my sweetest smile. If he asked me directly whether I'd been snooping, I wouldn't be able to lie. But as long as he didn't ask anything directly, I could play pretend.

"I hope you don't mind," I said, hunching my shoulders slightly. "I haven't been able to log into my classes since last week."

"Oh, um, of course not." He rubbed the back of his neck and gave me a strained smile. "Everything okay?"

"Well, Professor Gable thinks I have a chronic condition involving neuropathy. His unofficial, unrequested diagnosis, not mine." I forced a laugh. "But I think I might still pass my classes if the high king doesn't decide to murder me first." I paused, choosing my next course of action as carefully as I could on the fly. "Do you think you could take me to the store tonight to get some clothes?

And some hygiene stuff? I'm going to need to pick up a few things if I'm lying low for a while."

Which I had *zero* plans to do.

"Actually," he shifted from one foot to the other, "it would be best if you stayed out of sight for a while. Oh, and Julia beat you to it!" He beamed. "She sent me a list of your favorite stores and brands so I could have stuff ready. And your sizes. They're in the spare room."

"Oh." I struggled to keep a smile on my face, the sensation of a noose quickly tightening around my soul. "Awesome. Thanks. I guess I'll go look at those."

I stood and followed him to a bedroom down the hall. But when I saw the pile of clothes on the bed, I nearly threw up. Not only had he gotten my favorite styles and brands, he'd even gotten my sizing right. And while Julia had been quick enough to message him about coming to my rescue, I very much doubted she'd had the time to detail my favorite brand of sneakers.

The man was *clearly* obsessed. And as I reluctantly pawed through the clothes, I made a mental note to burn them all once this was over.

He was still standing outside the door when I emerged, and the sensation of a noose tightened even further.

"I know I shouldn't be in public too much," I said, trying yet again. "But we should be fine if you take me through the bank drive-through to pick up some cash, right? My parents have an emergency fund for–"

"Everleigh, relax," he laughed softly. "I have everything you could possibly need." As he spoke, he reached out and put his hands on my shoulders. The gesture would have been sweet–if I hadn't just seen the two dozen pictures of myself hanging around his home.

"In fact," he continued, his gaze narrowing, and his shoulders squaring up, "I... I probably shouldn't tell you this, but..."

"But what?" I echoed.

He broke into a bashful smile. "Everleigh, I bought this house for *you*."

I stared at him. Surely I hadn't heard that right. "You... bought this house... for *me*." I meant it as a question, but it didn't come out that way. Instead, I simply sounded incredulous. But his eyes grew brighter, as though I hadn't said anything. And when he spoke again, he slid his hands down my arms, his voice breathy and excited.

"The day you told Julia you wanted a house just like this, I knew what I had to do. I went out and bought this house for you... and for me." His fingers tightened slightly. "For our children."

The guy was insane. Absolutely stark-raving mad. And somehow, I'd missed it entirely. Forget overlooking the fact that he was an oracle, I'd somehow completely failed to realize that Georgie was certifiably insane.

"You have no idea just how perfect this can be!" he whispered, his eyes bright. "I've seen it all! Every year, every birthday..."

He continued to ramble, but at his mention of his visions, I was hit with the sudden recollection of the bone-dry supernatural textbooks my father had made me practically memorize as a kid.

Oracles could see glimpses of the future. That much was true. But their visions weren't always as sure as other supernaturals assumed they were. Georgie had admitted as much when he'd said he warned his clients that what he saw might not actually happen. Instead, oracles often saw what might happen... should the people or circumstances continue on their current trajectory. Statistically, their visions were generally better than the average person's guess. But really, whatever outcome they saw was likely to take place, as opposed to a surefire guarantee.

The oracle who had seen my future as a wizard had been one hundred percent certain about his vision because I was *already* a wizard—albeit in utero. The future he'd seen was actively in play.

But in the few short seconds all this took to pass through my mind, I realized that Georgie had fallen prey to the temptation that oracles had faced since the beginning of the world. There was actually a term for it: *Elpasthéneia.*

This mind sickness, as it was often referred to, had driven many oracles mad. Because oracles, in seeing what might be, were often prone to losing themselves in what they *wanted* to be. Not what actually was. And Georgie seemed to have glimpsed a possible future with me that he'd set his heart–and mind–on without giving a whole lot of consideration to what was actually likely to happen.

What was less likely to happen with each passing second.

I tried gently to pull my arms out of his grasp. "Georgie, I–"

But he only gripped me more tightly, his eyes taking on a feverish shine. "That's why you're perfect for Pandora's Key! We're fighting the very people holding your family–and your future–captive! They want to lock you up and control you! But the Key wants to release you! And to give you as much power as you were meant to hold!"

I pulled back harder this time. "Georgie, let go."

"You have to see it, Everleigh!" He tightened his grip so violently that it jarred my body. "We're trying to free people! I want to free *you!* Not just from your grandfather, but once and for all! No more rules or societal restrictions. No more fear or hiding! And once the Pandora Stone is ready for distribution to the public–"

I had to escape. That was not a question. In fleeing the elven high king, I'd unwittingly rushed into the arms of my attempted kidnappers. But Georgie's assurances that the future was certain and everything would be fine now were growing in fervor and intensity, neither of which was good for me.

But I also knew from my parents' police training that people in a frenzied state could turn violent when they were denied what they wanted. If I wanted to make a clean break, I would need to placate him until a chance to escape presented itself. Even if I fought him hand to hand, who knew what kind of charms he had rigged around his house and yard? Fighting both him and his expensive purchased magic did not hold good odds for me.

The simple fact that he was an oracle made him a formidable opponent. Not only was he much bigger than me, but his magic would give him insights into what I might do, which would make a planned escape much harder. I was trained in mixed martial arts, yes. But my magic was still bound, and fighting in such a small, enclosed space meant his height would give me a sizeable disadvantage. This left me no choice.

I'd have to wing it.

"I know you weren't expecting the Key to follow you to campus," he was saying, a frown now on his face. "And I should have foreseen that it would frighten you. My friend, Sam, had wanted to talk to you first. She was afraid I'd explain it all wrong, so she kept sending her protege to talk to you."

Protege? I tried to remember all the times we'd been attacked. Did he mean the purple fae girl? Girls? Was there one or three? I couldn't remember. Georgie, however, unaware of my questions, was still talking.

"But... I was wrong to let her make that decision. I should have just talked to you myself." His grip tightened. "But if you would just listen to my friends now, they can tell you all about how we're going to free *and* empower supernaturals so we no longer have to be in hiding!"

We? Oh no, sir. If he thought there was a *we* here, he had another thing coming.

"Georgie," I said, trying to sound sweet and not totally panicked or annoyed. "Have you ever stopped to think about the carnage this kind of revolution would cause? How many people are going to die?" I gave him the most winsome smile I could muster. "I never saw you as someone to discount the lives of human children or the elderly or–"

"I'm not," he said solemnly. "But Everleigh, think about how many great causes were soaked in blood."

My temper got the best of me. "Blood of the *innocents?*" I asked, a hint of my rapidly growing frustration seeping into my words. "Georgie, the humans aren't at war with us! They can't even try to defend themselves or their vulnerable if they have no idea what's coming!"

"We must protect the innocents of the future," he said patiently, as though I were a small, stupid child. "Innocents like *our* children." He leaned closer. "You have no idea how long I've wanted to tell you all of this. I just wish they would have let me share it with you sooner." His eyes fluttered shut as he lowered his face toward mine.

Seeing my chance, I looked desperately around me. The closest thing that might even pass as a weapon was a small scented candle jar from the decorative shelf beside us. So with all the strength I could quickly conjure, I twisted out of his grasp and snatched the jar off the shelf. Then I smashed it against his jaw with a hard right hook.

To my relief, his head snapped sideways. Then he crumpled like a rag doll, unconscious before he even hit the floor.

I paused only to make sure he was really unconscious. Then I sprinted back toward the front door and snatched his keys off the front bureau. Thirty seconds later, I was in his car, cruising down the road.

Chapter Forty

Everleigh

I DROVE until I was in a part of town I was unfamiliar with. When I was sure no one was following me, I pulled into a shopping center and parked there so I could think.

A month ago, life had been simple. It was me and my parents against the world. Julia was free, and Georgie was just that sweet, awkward friend who seemed perfectly content with his lot in life.

Then my parents had been taken. But even after that, I'd still had Aithan and our friends.

And just when it seemed as though all of *them* had been yanked away, Georgie had literally charged in and saved the day. Only... he wasn't the white knight on a war steed, it turned out. He was part of the problem.

Which meant now it was just me and only me, with King Kostas on my tail and Pandora's Key waiting in the wings. Sure, I knew *why* my magic was bound now, but I still didn't have an idea how to free it. To make matters worse, nearly everyone I loved was being held captive in order to force my hand one way or another.

That I needed to do something was obvious. But Georgie was an oracle, and King Kostas was the high elven king. How in the world was I supposed to outmaneuver them both in order to free the people I loved?

And where did we go after that?

Even as I wondered these things, however, anger began to pulse hot inside of me.

How *dare* King Kostas curse his own grandson? And who did Georgie think he was, revealing my secrets to the stupid Key in order to gain power?

Supposedly, curses couldn't be broken. But the longer I sat stewing in the car, the sharper my wrath became, until I could feel the binding that encased my magic threatening to tear at the seams.

I was done ducking my responsibilities. I was taking this fight to *both* of the parties who had done their best to ruin my life and the lives of everyone I loved. Pandora's Key seemed to think–encouraged by Georgie, most likely–that they had a weird claim on my loyalty just because I didn't subscribe to King Kostas's way of life. And King Kostas was far too comfortable in thinking I couldn't shake his world.

The hotter my wrath burned, the stronger the magic within me pushed against the binding I had spun as a child. My first instinct, as it had always been, was to quench it so I wouldn't risk damaging anything or anyone with my unpredictable magic. But then I stopped.

What would happen if I just let it burn?

In a way, Aithan and I were in somewhat similar situations. We were both bound–Aithan by his grandfather's curse, and me by a binding of my own making. Unlike Aithan, however, I should theoretically be able to destroy my own binding as well.

Right now, I felt like I was in a spider's web, wrapped and ready to be eaten. The binding had grown so tight it was nearly physically painful. But that was good. It meant my magic was fighting to be free.

Georgie, on behalf of Pandora's Key, was going to crash the king's big meeting in three days. And I was done playing defense.

Which meant I was going to join them and set them *all* straight. But first, I would need to practice. And to do that, I would need both privacy and safety.

My first instinct was to go to Professor Petras. But as I was putting the car into *Drive*, I stopped. Professor Petras was too well-known in the magical community for me to risk it. King Kostas most likely knew that he had helped my parents, and was probably keeping an eye on him as well.

No, I would have to do this on my own—human style.

Unfortunately for my enemies, however, I excelled at being human.

Chapter Forty-One

Aithan

As I MADE my way down my grandfather's resort corridors, I did my best to look as though everything was fine. But my body might as well have been someone else's–a costume, for lack of a better word. And if I could just find the zipper, I felt as though I should be able to simply take it off. But it wasn't coming off. Not now, and not ever.

Because everyone knew that elven curses were for life.

Much in the way a fae memory curse erected a barrier around a memory, this curse had created one around my heart. Only this barrier was physical, and not just a spell. It was so real, in fact, that if I held my breath and pressed my fingers against my chest in just the right place, I could feel it. And though something had been added and not removed, it had left me with the sensation of being hollowed out, like something was missing inside.

Love was missing.

I knew that, though. Everyone knew that, as the supernatural gossips had been having a field day online and in person now that the news of the curse was out.

But that wasn't all. The curse hadn't just deadened many of the emotions I was used to feeling–it had also cut off some of my magic. I'd quickly learned that while being thoroughly thrashed during combat training with my grandfather's guards that morning. But this, unfortunately, made sense, too. Natural magic was highly reliant on the link between a supernatural's heart and mind. If I wanted to regain my edge, I'd have to learn to fight without my heart.

A more lethal style by far.

"Ah, there you are," my grandfather announced as I opened the door. "Come. I've made plans that involve you, and I want you to know what they are so we can be ready as soon as the time comes."

I glanced around the room I'd been summoned to. It was my grandfather's personal theater. A large projection screen hung against the wall at the front, and facing it were four rows of twelve seats each, anchored into a gentle carpeted slope with an aisle going down the middle. Green velvet carpeted the walls to absorb the sound, and there was even a wine and snack bar set up in the back. Despite the recreational setting, my grandfather was all business today. His long blond hair was pulled back at the nape of his neck, and he wore a tailored business suit with a touch of elven flair in his emerald cufflinks. He was studying a bottle of white wine when I reached his side.

"How can I be of service?" I asked. My voice was respectful, but I made sure to keep it uninterested. I might not feel love anymore, but anger and resentment took turns nearly drowning me in waves. I would have to make sure they stayed at bay if I wanted to live long enough to see the next day.

"I've decided that I'm going to pair you with Miss Clarkson to investigate Pandora's Key once she returns." My grandfather kept his eyes on the wine. "With your magic and her sharp mind, I think you'll make an excellent team."

My plan had been to remain as emotionally sensitive as a toaster, but at this, I found myself blinking in surprise. "Has Everleigh been recovered then?" I hadn't expected that so soon.

"No." My grandfather put the wine down and finally looked at me. "But she will be."

His placid self-confidence made my eye long to twitch.

"You doubt me," my grandfather said. His words were still pleasant, but there was a dangerous glint in his eyes. "Might I ask why?"

I considered my answer carefully. I didn't love Everleigh anymore. And it wasn't for lack of trying. I'd tried desperately to find my former affections the night before until I'd nearly passed out on the floor of my new room. Still, my vow to protect her tugged at me from within. And even if I hadn't been held by my vow, my personal apathy toward her didn't increase any feelings of affection toward my grandfather either. The enactment of my curse by the one person who might have been able to call it off, or at least alter it, only confirmed my long-held conviction that trusting him would be a deadly mistake.

"Everleigh," I said carefully, "has shunned magic for so long that she's learned successfully how to blend in with humans and utilize their tools. I've been under the... conviction that she'll be harder to find than most supernaturals if she truly desires to remain hidden."

My grandfather stared at me for a long time.

"Tell me," he finally said, "who are you loyal to?"

That was a question for the ages. My affection for my friends was gone. For obvious reasons, I wanted nothing to do with my father's side of the family, and my loyalty to my mother's side had always bordered on nonexistent, as they'd moved to Milan after my parents abandoned the courts. But even my immediate family held little draw now, other than offering the comfort of the familiar.

And I liked my grandfather less than any of the others.

Still, disloyalty to him wasn't even an option. Elves *had to* retain power if supernatural society was to survive. My father's line had prevented magic and race wars more times than I could count on both hands in the last hundred years. Just as fae loved beauty and luxury and word games, and shifters were passionate about strength and family, elves were the race of law and order. It was the only reason the dragon marshals—the only group who rivaled us in power and passion—didn't snatch control of the supernatural world. But my grandfather didn't have an ounce of altruism in his heart. And I had no desire to help him take advantage of others the way he had done to me.

"The law," I finally answered.

My grandfather stared at me another moment before surprising me with a chuckle. "A very elven answer to give. Perhaps I should curse more people if the result is this." He shook his head, his long blond hair moving gracefully with him. For some reason, even this bit of perfection angered me more.

"As I said, when we get Miss Clarkson back—and we *will* get her back—you'll investigate the Key as partners. This will satisfy your vow and serve my purposes." He picked up another bottle of wine. "Any questions?"

None that *he* would want to hear. "No," I simply said.

"Very well then. You're excused."

I nodded respectfully before turning to go. But as my fingers touched the door, he called from behind me, "I know you feel lost now, Aithan. But I promise. It won't be as bad as you think."

As I stormed away from the theater, I passed my brother and father in the hall. The sight of Alexander slowed my steps.

What was *he* doing here?

My father waved at me to join them.

"Come with us, Aithan. We're going to get something to drink."

Alexander nodded as our father spoke, but I could read the hesitancy in both their eyes.

They were right to be hesitant. The love that had kept me loyal was gone, and my vow to protect Everleigh and my own curiosity were the only ropes tying me to the stern of this insane ship. Still, I had no desire to hurt my family. Well, not *this* part of my family. So I nodded and joined them.

We silently left the resort and made our way down to the sidewalk of the busy boulevard that ran in front of it. I half-expected my grandfather's security to tackle us as we left, but to my surprise, they merely respectfully nodded as we went.

Everyone in my family, I decided with disgust, had been thoroughly broken in. The security guards seemed one hundred percent confident that my father and brother wouldn't try to escape, and they must have trusted that I wouldn't do anything while I was with them either.

I'd have to remember that for later.

We stopped at an outdoor coffee shop a block down and ordered our drinks. Then, while my father waited, my brother and I found a table outside. Alexander created a muffling charm around us so we could talk freely without the humans hearing more than an indistinct rumble of words.

"How long are you here?" I asked Alexander as my father remained at the window to wait for our orders. "I thought you were undercover."

"I'll be returning." Alexander frowned at the passing cars. I expected him to go on, but that was all he said.

"To that fae named Cara?" As I spoke, I carefully measured his reaction.

His eyes snapped to me. "Why do you think I left holes in the memory charm?" He snarled under his breath. "Getting the work done is one thing. Ruining people's lives because they were in the wrong place at the wrong time..." He shook his head as he scowled. "There's been more than enough of that, what with what happened to Julia and all."

I'd suspected as much. As soon as I'd seen my brother's face in Cara's memory, I'd guessed that he was working undercover for my grandfather within Pandora's Key. And her description of the memory charm as *shoddy* had been telling as well. My brother was in line for the Nomos throne. No one as powerful as him would accidentally perform or enact a memory sealing charm as badly as the one performed on Cara. Still... whether I was cursed or not, what had been done to her bothered me, and I no longer had the affection for my brother to cushion the truth of that.

"Aithan," my dad said as he returned with our drinks. "I want to tell you a story."

I took my drink and said nothing.

"When I was young—probably about fifteen," my dad said, settling in his chair, "my father tasked me with removing the traitorous sire of a particular vampire coven. He had sworn allegiance to my father, but then had gone behind his back and expanded his coven to be far larger than my father had wanted it to be."

"Why did Grandfather want it to remain small?" I asked.

My father stirred his coffee slowly. "Vampires are jealous creatures. There are a few, of course, who aren't. People like Dorian or Caspian West, who have integrated themselves into human society. But those who choose to remain within the coven family structure are far more likely to harbor and act upon the more... traditional sentiments of vampires."

I drank my coffee and let him talk. I knew all of this, of course. But as I was currently free of my grandfather's resort at the moment, I had no desire to return so soon.

"All that to say," my father continued, "that my father had decided this particular vampire coven had gotten out of hand. And the day of my fifteenth birthday, he decided it was time for me to handle the situation myself."

I put my coffee down. "How so?"

My dad fixed me with a hard stare. "I was sent with several of his soldiers to remove the sire and destroy the coven completely."

I stared at my dad. "You're telling me that Grandfather sent you—at the age of fifteen—to lead a takedown of the city's largest vampire coven?"

"Yes." My dad didn't blink. "But it got worse. Because when I finally managed to subdue their sire, I realized that I couldn't kill the man in cold blood. I'd known him since I was small, if only as an acquaintance. So I brought him back to my father in chains, sure my father would let him barter for his life."

I read my dad's face like a book. "He didn't, did he?"

My dad looked down at the ground.

Alexander was like a statue the whole time, still glaring out at the traffic as though it had done him wrong.

"I tell you all of this to warn you," my dad said, "to be wary of working for my father. I know he's been planning to use you in—"

I scoffed. "Just because I no longer feel love for Everleigh doesn't mean I *love* the king, if that's what you're implying. I've still got the vow. With that in mind, as Everleigh is still missing, following him right now is the... logical thing to do. Besides, as much as I despise the man, he's keeping the supernatural community from consuming itself."

"You're not wrong," my dad said slowly, his eyes still on mine. "That's the only reason Alexander, your mother, and I are going along with his plans for now as well. But just... try not to become him."

I let out a harsh bark of laughter. "I have no ambitions to—"

"It's what he wants, Aithan." My dad's voice was hard now. Harder than I'd ever heard it. Almost like my grandfather's. "I abdicated when I left the court to follow the Clarksons. And now he's working as hard as he can to mold both of my sons into his own image."

Alexander still said nothing but looked nearly as though he were in pain. He'd agreed to work for Grandfather years ago, after deciding we could keep a better eye on the high elven king if one of us was in his court. Then he could warn us if he saw anything particularly dangerous to us or Everleigh. But now he was in so deep, I wasn't sure if he'd ever find a way out.

"Well," I said, standing and grabbing my coffee cup, "I hope it was worth it. Following the Clarksons' brat at the cost of your own."

My dad looked as though I'd slapped him, but my brother turned his burning green eyes to mine.

My dad's reply was so soft I nearly missed it. "You'll never know, son, what it cost me."

My brother didn't speak. He only stood and followed me as I opened the courtyard gate and stepped back out onto the sidewalk.

"You look worried," I said without looking back at him.

"I have every right to be."

I shrugged. "Aren't you supposed to be looking for Everleigh?"

My brother gave me a sharp look. "That was supposed to be a *secret*." As he spoke, he glanced nervously around. But he didn't need to. We were alone. It was too early in the morning for most tourists to be out and about. "What are you up to, Aithan?" he asked, leaning toward me and pitching his voice low. "You're planning something. I can tell."

I smiled sardonically. "Just because I'm cursed doesn't mean I appreciate what our grandfather has done."

My brother studied me. "You don't want him to find her," he finally guessed.

I stopped walking and turned to face him. "Despite Grandfather's curse, I'm still bound by my vow. Grandfather has looked down on Everleigh her entire life for what he perceives to be her lack of magic and her refusal to use what little he thinks she has. But what he missed in all that was seeing how Everleigh's lack of magic changed her."

"I don't get your meaning."

"In case you haven't noticed, Everleigh is an adrenaline junkie," I said, our drive in my car flashing through my mind. "You've seen it. Going on every fast ride she could buy tickets for at the fair. Attempting every kind of martial arts she could afford. Zip-lining. Going up in hot air balloons. The list goes on."

My brother gave me a funny look. "So she likes going fast. What of it?"

I snorted. "Obviously, you've never let her drive. My point is that if you put all of that together and glaze it with wizard magic, you've created one of the cleverest, most resourceful creatures to ever walk the planet—one who can exist in the supernatural world *and* in the human world, all the while, camouflaging perfectly as she moves seamlessly back and forth between them. So do I believe Grandfather deserves to get everything she's about to serve him? Absolutely, I do. And as I'm perfectly aware that Grandfather will send you after me if I try to find her, she's safest on her own right now. In fact, whatever she's planning, I can't wait to watch her serve it to him hot and ready in Everleigh style."

My brother folded his arms and studied me with a furrowed brow. "Whose side are you on, Aithan? And don't try to lie to me."

That was the second time someone had asked me that question this morning. "Like I told Grandfather, I'm stuck with this vow. That aside, I'm on the side of law and order. I like it when my city isn't in ashes." I lifted my coffee cup. "Doesn't suit my way of life." With that, I turned and started walking toward The Realm again.

"Even the cruelest of dictators often have the best intentions," my brother called after me. "Try to love in actions, even if you can't in feeling. She deserves that."

I didn't look back as I neared the resort doors. But in spite of the nonchalance I wanted so much to project inside and out, my brother's words bothered me more than I could say. And I didn't know why.

Chapter Forty-Two

Aithan

THE NEXT DAY, I was summoned to attend a meeting with my grandfather, his top advisors, and some of the most powerful race representatives in the world—though most of them were local. My brother was absent, though that was no surprise, as he was probably out looking for Everleigh again. My father, I learned upon arriving, hadn't been invited.

What was interesting, however, was that my former companions had been invited as well. Although the more I thought about it, the more I realized that *invited* was probably a strong word for what my grandfather had said to get them there. My friends were not the kind to attempt to climb the social ladder.

They were seated at the far end of the ridiculously long rectangular table by the time I arrived, each looking more uncomfortable than the last. Aaron, Christian, and Jamie all tried to catch my eye, but I ignored them. As usual, Dorian and Miss Lillian sat together at the back. The guys had seated Julia at the center of their group, doing their best to shield the frail human as she stared at everyone and everything as though it might eat her. Maverick was staring blankly at the wall. Mentally, that man had checked out.

Still, even if my affection for my friends had remained, they should have known that I couldn't show favoritism in front of my grandfather. In fact, that was likely why he'd brought them. To test to see if his curse had taken full effect. There was a high chance one of them would die before the meeting was over to prove it.

But I was glad it wasn't prudent for me to give them my attention. If my heart hadn't been locked away, having them present would have been incredibly awkward and probably painful. For just as with Everleigh, it was strange to look at them... and feel nothing.

In addition to my former companions, there were about three dozen supernaturals squeezed around my grandfather's long conference table, which sat in the middle of his famous greenhouse built onto the roof of The Realm Resort. Elves, vampires, werewolves, trolls, a variety of fae, merfolk, trolls, and several other shifters filed slowly into the room as the time for the meeting neared. They all knew better than to be late to any meeting my grandfather called, but most were also smart enough to know not to arrive early enough to attract his particular attention. As each entered, he or she knelt and kissed my grandfather's emerald ring before finding the correct name placard on the table.

It was always easy to tell the new representatives from the more experienced. Their looks of confusion when they were led up to the greenhouse were obvious. And to an outsider, their curiosity would make sense. A glass structure built on top of a skyscraper might seem a strange place to hold some of the most private meetings in the world. Especially considering that the majority of my grandfather's guests were far stronger than humans, and it would take very little provocation for many of them to do something that might destroy the glass itself.

Besides the glass panes being magically reinforced, however, so that it would take more than a charging elephant to break through them, the setting provided two crucial elements to what my grandfather considered an appropriate royal environment. First, the greenhouse was regularly pumped full of raw elven magic and decorated with magical flora of every kind. At night, the flowers glowed, and during the day, they moved out of your way if you asked politely. A few were spelled to swallow a full-grown man alive if my grandfather so desired it. And there were, of course, the wide variety of healing herbs that grew right next to the poison ivy and poison oak. Not a single piece of surveillance technology was allowed inside. It was the stuff of storybooks and fairy tales.

The old German kind.

It's to mimic the supernatural world before human technology became too vast, my mother had once explained. It also served to provide an excellent view of my grandfather's chosen domain.

Most of the guests were smart enough not to question the location, even if they didn't understand it. And if they were foolish enough to ask aloud, one of the more experienced attendees usually silenced them quickly. Many had been around long enough to witness my grandfather make a lesson of the situation every couple of years.

A female werewolf–in her human form, as shifter forms weren't allowed at the meetings–leaned toward me. "Your Highness, do you know why we've been called?"

"I haven't been informed," I said before turning my attention back to my grandfather. And while this was true, I knew why I'd been summoned. With my father removed from the line to the throne, Alexander was supposed to be the next king. But he was doing his best, from what I could tell, to stay as far from our grandfather as possible without raising his ire. He had never told me why, of course, but I had a feeling it had to do with his own curse. Which meant it was highly likely that my grandfather would try to crown me in my brother's stead.

I had no desire to be king. I never had. Growing up in the Las Vegas suburbs with parents who actually cared for my brother and me had cured me of ever wanting a part in the stupid politics that supernaturals liked to play. But as I had little choice at the moment, I decided to simply watch for the entertainment factor to see how things played out.

"It appears everyone is–" My grandfather sat at the head of the conference table and scanned the room. He smiled benevolently until his gaze settled on the single empty chair ten seats down on his right.

"Oh dear. It seems we're missing Madame Olgath. Does anyone know where she is?" His words were pleasant, but everyone in the room shifted uncomfortably.

"Um, yes, Your Majesty," said a thin, high-pitched voice from the other side of the room.

"Ginisea." My grandfather gave the young vampire a sweet smile. "Please, do tell me."

"Uh, yes." Ginisea's eyes darted around before she stood and offered my grandfather yet another bow. "My grandmother sends her deepest apologies, but she's very ill, and has sent me in her stead." The young vampire swallowed loudly. "She's summoned the fairy godmothers this morning."

My grandfather put his hand over his heart. "I'm so very sorry to hear that. In fact, I shall be sure to visit her later to wish her better myself. Maybe there's even something I can do. One of my personal elixirs, perhaps?"

"Oh, yes. I mean, that would be most gracious of you, Your Majesty," Ginisea said, her voice quivering. "She would be most honored."

My grandfather gave her another warm smile, but I could see a few of her neighbors offering up silent prayers that the popular vampire mother was truly ill. If she was, my grandfather would most likely do everything he had said. He could be most generous when it suited him. But if she wasn't...

That elixir would most likely be the last thing she ever swallowed.

"My friends," my grandfather said, raising his hands for quiet, as though the room wasn't already silent. "I've spoken with many of you individually on this matter several times in recent months, but the situation has changed enough that I believe it's time to address the issue of Pandora's Key directly."

The room stiffened at the utterance of the zealot group's name, but I held back a scoff. Most of them obviously hadn't actually encountered a member of the group. If they had, they wouldn't be nearly so scared.

"We've known this group was planning something for a long time, but recently, they've been extraordinarily active and have been pursuing new recruits with a vigor unlike before. But one of my undercover contacts has worked their way deep enough into the group to have discovered that the group believes..." He paused, as though wondering if he ought to tell them. And to my surprise, I found myself leaning forward with everyone else. Finally, he seemed to make his decision. "This group seems to believe they've found a wizard. And they wish to add this wizard to their ranks."

This time, audible gasps went up around the table, and my companions shared anxious glances, but my grandfather continued.

"I don't know whether this wizard exists, but I do know that the group has become large and unruly. They've been making blatant attacks in broad daylight where humans are beginning to take notice, and it's getting more and more difficult to clean up the messes they've made."

As my grandfather spoke, his voice began to harden into something like granite, and his gaze was sharp enough to cut glass. "Even more brazen, they've begun attempting to abduct supernaturals they think will benefit their cause but refuse to join. We've recovered all of their most recent victims, of course, but this makes me think they're in their final stage of planning."

Gerald, one of the less stupid trolls I'd ever met, stood and bowed to my grandfather. "My Liege, we are ready to follow your orders. All you must do is issue your command."

"A sentiment I am most appreciative of," my grandfather said, gesturing for the man to be seated. "Which is why I'm telling you this tonight. You are the representatives of our people. Millions depend on you and your leadership. And in this case, they need you to prepare them for war."

The doors burst open as he spoke. I froze as a person I disliked immensely walked in, my grandfather's personal elven guards crumpling to the floor behind him. About a dozen supernaturals in combat gear embroidered with the now familiar key symbol followed the intruder and encircled the room.

How in the world...

The annoying sop Everleigh and Julia were so fond of stared back at me, pride obvious in his slowly spreading grin. But I didn't get it. "Georgie," as Everleigh called him, was a human. What was he doing here? And how had he taken out my grandfather's best elven guards?

My grandfather lazily held up a single hand, palm out, at the intruder and his entourage.

Green magic should have crackled as it branched from my grandfather's fingers like lightning. But his magic only fizzled.

My grandfather's eyes looked like they might fall out of his head as Everleigh's dopey college friend gave him yet another smarmy smile. And though I wasn't in any way sorry for my grandfather, I just couldn't get the situation to work in my head. Everleigh's annoying human friend was here with members of the Key? And my grandfather's magic had just... failed?

"Good morning, everyone," Georgie chirped as he looked around, as though he was used to being in a room full of the most powerful and influential supernaturals in the world. "I hope–" He stopped and glanced over his shoulder. "Soo Min, are you coming?"

Soo Min walked in behind him. She carried a to-go tray holding two sealed bubble tea drinks. I smelled Everleigh's favorite flavor, rose milk tea, coming from the pink drink. But unlike the soldiers who had followed him in, whose body language was clearly submissive, Soo Min looked like she'd much rather turn into a cat and scratch his eyes out than do as he said.

"There you go," he said with condescending politeness as she put the tray on the corner of the table. "See, that wasn't so hard."

"I hope you choke on a tapioca ball," she spat as she marched toward our companions, positioning herself as far from him as she could get.

He only chuckled. "I've looked ahead, and that's highly unlikely. But thank you for your concern."

My grandfather took advantage of Georgie's distraction and tried again to fling magic from his hands at Georgie and his entourage. But again, it just fizzled.

What was going on?

For the first time in my life, I saw fear in my grandfather's eyes. And though I hated Georgie, the sight of it was delicious.

"You're a powerful man," Georgie told my grandfather as he picked up his straw and broke through the drink's plastic seal. He took a sip of the drink and then held it back to study it appreciatively. "Wow, that's good. Anyhow, as I was saying, you're not easy to reach, King Kostas. We had to try several times to get one of our people into your house."

"And who would that be?" my grandfather growled through his teeth.

But Georgie only smiled. "You should always check who's delivering your personal oils. It would be a terrible mistake if one of them was replaced with... I don't know, a magic suppressant elixir."

In spite of the situation, I wanted to laugh. My grandfather's vanity—his need to leave those he touched with the lingering sensation of fear—was seemingly responsible for his downfall. Magic suppressants were extremely rare and exorbitantly expensive. No one even knew where or how they were made, and there was only one known living supplier. It seemed, however, that someone had figured out not only what kinds of oils my grandfather used, but they had also managed to sneak the magic suppressant into his personal oil. Which meant he had literally drenched himself in the very oils that would ultimately declaw him.

"You!" my grandfather snapped, his eyes going wide. "You're... You must be related to Dustin Flavel. I would recognize your face anywhere." He scoffed. "Your father gave me a bad prophecy regarding my son's goddaughter. So I suppose we needn't expect too much out of you."

At this, Georgie straightened, and his eyes flashed. "Oh, did he?"

"Yes." My grandfather's smile was mocking. "He said her life as an *Anikos* would be of no consequence. So imagine my surprise when the Key decided to set a bounty on her head for her to be brought in alive."

As my grandfather spoke, I began to put the pieces together. Georgie wasn't just Everleigh's dorky human friend. He was an oracle. And if my grandfather was telling the truth, Georgie's father was the reason our families had escaped the high courts to begin with.

But what, I wondered silently, *were the odds of Everleigh* accidentally *befriending the son of that same oracle?*

The answer was slim to none. Georgie must have been planning this–whatever it was–for a long, long time.

"Your Majesty," Georgie said, turning back to my grandfather. "I know it's not in your nature to listen to commoners, but I recommend you try this time. Because if you don't, these people are going to die. And if they try to stop me, *their* people will die as well." He gestured to the people crowded around the table. As he spoke, the soldiers closed in on the table, each bearing several pairs of handcuffs. The handcuffs looked greasy, and whatever was smeared on them let off a pungent smell.

Growls and hisses rumbled through the air as several shifters pushed their chairs back. But Georgie held up his hand.

"I'm telling the truth. I have sleeper groups hidden within

every supernatural region in the world. And though I have no desire to do so, if I give the word, your people will pay. So if you want your citizens to live, allow my people to place the handcuffs on you for the time being. It's all temporary, of course, but I need everyone to listen to my proposition before you make up your mind."

I could only guess that my grandfather was regretting banning all electronics from this particular part of the palace. And so was everyone else. The ability to shoot off a quick text would be super convenient right about now.

There were more sounds of furious protest, but no one seemed ready to test Georgie's claim. Every single one of the guests, with the exception of my companions, oversaw thousands or even millions of supernaturals. And now this oracle was threatening them all.

I let the soldier nearest me click the handcuffs onto me as well. I didn't plan to give them the upper hand in the end, but now wasn't the time to try to escape.

As soon as the oily metal touched my wrists, I was absolutely certain that these cuffs had been rubbed with the same magic-suppressing oil that had been slipped into my grandfather's toiletries. But as I subtly tested the cuffs' strength, a body whizzed by me in a blur.

Georgie must have seen it coming, however, for by the time the vampire had reached him, fangs bared, a small silver knife had been slipped between the vampire's ribs.

Baron Kwame–the oldest vampire in Africa–stared down at the knife's silver handle in shock and horror. His expression was shared by my grandfather and his guests.

"I'm very sorry to do that," Georgie said as he looked down at Kwame, who was now gasping for air. "But I did warn you." He sighed. "And now I must punish your people. It really is a pity. Zambia is such a lovely place." He nodded at one of his soldiers, who pulled out a phone and began to text. Which probably meant my grandfather's anti-electronics charm had been removed from the greenhouse as well. So *they* could use their phones, it seemed, while we still had no way to communicate with the outside world.

I was no longer amused. Though I held no personal affection for the vampire, Kwame was a sensible and effective leader. He'd single-handedly stopped a large group of rogue vampire gangs from terrorizing South Africa several years ago, and he had led the supernaturals living on the continent in peace since—not just the vampires but all main groups of supernaturals.

"I wouldn't do that," Georgie said, his gaze flicking from the impaled vampire toward one of the werewolf shifters two seats down. I could only guess that he must have foreseen that the werewolf had been planning a similar attack. "I had every intention of letting you all live—if you do as I say. But if the lives of your people aren't enough..."

He pulled a small vial of white pearlescent powder out of his pocket and held it up.

"This is a piece of the Pandora Stone, ground down into dust. All it takes is a little bit..." Georgie let go of the silver knife, which sent Kwame crashing to the ground. Then he held out his hand. One of his soldiers handed him a long, thin dart. He uncorked the vial and dipped the tip of the dart in it. Then he closed the vial and handed the dart to the soldier nearest him. The guard took the dart carefully and slid the dart into a small tube about twice the length of his hand.

"You've made your point!" my grandfather hissed. "Now what do you want?"

Not wanting to lose any more useful heads of state, I decided it was time for me to step in. Unlike the other people here, I had no community or jurisdiction. And I'd told my brother the truth when I said I didn't enjoy chaos. This stupid boy thought he was being brave, prancing around with a vial of poisonous magical steroids, and in doing so, was about to bring the whole supernatural world crashing down. But as soon as I'd made the decision to intervene, Georgie turned and looked right at me.

"I'm afraid," he said, a mocking smile stretching across his face, "that you're no longer the knight in shining armor." He tossed a fae charm at me with his right hand at the same time that he motioned to his soldier with his left.

In what felt like one eternal second, I disintegrated the charm easily, despite the handcuffs. But as I did, cries went up from all over the room.

The soldier, it seemed, had tried to use the blowgun dart on an older wood nymph from Germany. My grandfather and several other fae in the room had successfully broken the dart before it had reached her. But as the pieces of the dart hit the table, a merman let out a cry. Too late, everyone looked over to realize that one of the other Key soldiers had let loose a second dart. This dart had hit the merman, who slumped to the ground, his open eyes glazing over.

"You asked me why I'm here, Your Majesty," Georgie said, his voice less pleasant this time. "My name is Georgios Flavel, and yes, I'm an oracle. And I'm here to represent my organization, Pandora's Key. You don't need to look so surprised. We've known about the Pandora Stone for a long time now. And in short, we believe you've controlled its supply long enough. This is our formal claim upon both the stone and the mine in which the Pandora Stone was found."

"Oh," my grandfather drawled sarcastically. "And what do you plan to do with it once it's yours?"

"From there, we aim to redistribute the stone you've hoarded for yourselves to the supernatural community at large, so all have access to this power." Georgios glanced at my grandfather in disgust. "You boast in your pomp and its splendor. But look at you now." He gestured to the room. "It took just a handful of zealots and a single oracle to imprison the top supernaturals of the world. Our ancestors would be ashamed." He spat on the ground.

What had Everleigh ever seen in this guy to let him come within forty feet of her?

"And if we refuse to give you what you want?" my grandfather growled, his fists clenched within the cuffs.

"You saw what just happened to Lord Axos there," Georgios said, gesturing to the fallen merman. He put the vial in his shirt pocket. "We've managed to get our hands on a small bit of the stone. And though you *should* know this already, the magic contained in this powder is so incredibly potent that it will kill any supernatural who not only gets it in his bloodstream, but so much as inhales it."

"If you know all of that," my grandfather spat back, "then you should also know that it's dangerous to handle *any* of the stone in person! Tell me, how many friends did you lose because of your pompous stupidity? Why do you think we've kept it locked away for so many years? Not even *I* keep it on my person! It remains hidden, and the local supernaturals benefit from a distance."

But Georgios only shrugged. "They died for a noble cause. And because of their sacrifices, we've learned enough to know precisely how to handle it."

I snorted. "I sincerely doubt that."

Georgios scowled at me. "Then you should also know that I–"

He paused as a knock sounded at the doors behind him. He nodded to the two soldiers closest to the entrance. They went to the doors and swung them open.

Everleigh walked in.

My grandfather's eyes went wide, and many of the guests began to murmur. Most of them, I could only guess, had no idea who Everleigh was. And those who did had no idea of what she was or what she could do.

Our companions looked stricken.

If I had been myself, and my grandfather's curse had never fallen, I would have leaped out of my chair to throw myself between her and Georgios's men. But now, despite knowing what I *would* have done, I remained cool and calm. My vow compelled me to wish to protect her, but that desire was unclouded by emotion or feeling.

Of course, the jaded part of me also harbored a morbid hope that she would bring everyone in the room to their knees.

That would be fun to watch.

"Everleigh!" Georgios exclaimed, as though he was welcoming her to a dinner party. "You're right on time!" He went to the table where he'd left the two bubble teas. He grabbed the pink one and handed it to her. "After I'm done here, you and your family and friends will be free to leave with us." Then he made a face and looked at me. "Except for him. I hate him even more now than I did before."

"Believe me." I grinned sardonically. "The feeling's mutual."

Everleigh watched him impassively. But knowing her as well as I did, I could see her anxiety begin to rise. She had made a misstep already.

Georgios had seen that she was coming.

Chapter Forty-Three

Everleigh

"Georgie, don't," I said. But even as I spoke the words, I wanted to kick myself. Apparently, I'd already blown the element of surprise. My goal had been to walk in and catch him off guard, but it seemed I'd been so calculated that he'd not only expected me to come, but he'd brought me bubble tea as well.

As though the offer of a treat would make up for all that he'd done. It was he and his group, after all, that had put my family and friends in this mess.

"And I'm so sorry to say this," Georgie said, cringing slightly as he did, "but I need you to wear these magic-suppressing handcuffs. Just for now. They're oily from the potion, and I apologize for that. I just have to be on the safe side this time. Because... you know... you're really good at getting away." He grinned and shrugged before turning his chin so I could see the bruise from where I'd hit him with the candle.

Was he seriously trying to be cute? He sounded almost proud of me.

I wanted to hit him again.

But he wasn't the only one who had made plans. I'd figured he would have *some* inkling that I was going to show up, with him being an oracle and all. I just hoped now that he hadn't foreseen the majority of my fallback schemes as easily as he'd seen my plan to show up.

Two of the Key members, recognizable by the giant key embroidered into their uniforms, placed a pair of handcuffs around my wrists. I didn't fight back, but I did test the cuffs silently as the guards looked back at Georgie for directions. The cuffs were strong, but not perfect.

I gritted my teeth. Just like me.

But even though I knew how to slip out of the cuffs, I'd have to wait until Georgie was focused somewhere else. Right now, there were too many people looking at me, and the room was full of raw, explosive, unspent magic. I would have to take care, or a lot of people could be hurt.

"I'm curious," King Kostas said dryly. "Would you like to explain why you're cuffing my son's goddaughter as well? Her magic is terrible, just like all half-breeds'."

If the king kept this up, I was going to rescue his sorry butt last.

"See, and that's why you've already lost." Georgie rolled his eyes. "If you could look for five seconds beyond your shiny hotel doors, you'd know that Everleigh Clarkson isn't some half-breed." He looked at me, and his eyes softened. "She's our wizard."

Sounds of shock went up from the table, and King Kostas turned to stare at me so hard that his eyes bugged out. Aithan sat in the seat to his right. He was looking at me, too, but I couldn't read his expression. My friends, who were sitting at the far end of the table, had gone stone still.

"With this wizard's help," Georgie continued, the excitement returning to his voice, "we can make this resource available worldwide. Supernaturals everywhere will once again meet their full potential, and we won't have to live in fear of the humans discovering us anymore!"

As Georgie continued to describe all the wonderful ways I was supposed to aid their cause, I did my best to focus on my magic.

Unfortunately, despite my continual attempts over the last few days in the scummy motel I'd rented with the single stash of my parents' cash I'd been able to recover, my magic hadn't come completely free. I'd loosened it enough, however, to know I should at least be able to *help* the king. Of course, the cuffs made summoning that magic even harder. But as long as he–

I jumped. I had felt a source of raw, potent magic since entering the room, but in that moment, as Georgie took a step toward me, I finally sensed exactly where it was coming from. Georgie had a piece of the Pandora Stone with him. In fact, he was *wearing* it.

Change of plans. My new goal was to get rid of the stone before he could use it to hurt anyone. Anyone *else*, rather, as two bodies already lay on the floor. Which meant I would need a distraction. But even if I managed to steal the stone, what would I do with it? I couldn't hide it. Someone within Georgie's ranks was bound to sense it if it was kept in the room. And I couldn't very well dump it over the side of the building onto who knew what below. If only...

My gaze fell to Dorian, who was leaning close to Miss Lillian. And like a dream remembered, his lessons came back to me in a flash.

That was it.

I knew how I had to stop Georgie.

The thought of it made my stomach turn. I would not only have to lose these cuffs, but I'd also have to free my magic entirely to pull this off–something I hadn't yet figured out how to do despite having the last two and a half days to practice by myself.

But really, there was no other way.

With grim determination, I closed my eyes and summoned my elf magic. It was still slow in coming, made even slower by the cuffs, but after a moment, I found it. Taking a deep breath, I subtly nodded my head at the farthest Key guard.

And nothing happened.

I bit back a growl of frustration and tried instead for the Key member who stood a few feet closer.

Still nothing. The dratted handcuffs were working better than I'd thought they would. I'd have to do this the human way. It would be slower, but at this point, it was the only chance I had.

I plopped down on the ground and sat criss-cross, where I could lean against the wall, making sure to look as annoyed as I possibly could, like I was throwing a temper tantrum. Looking annoyed wasn't hard, though. Dealing with the problem like a toddler was sounding more and more appealing by the minute.

The guards standing on either side of me jerked around at my sudden movement, but when I made it clear that I was just sitting down with my cuffed hands in my lap in front of me, they relaxed and looked back at Georgie.

Slowly, slowly, I moved my fingers down to my sock, where I always kept a bobby pin whenever I wore sneakers. One of the perks of having parents in law enforcement is living with their paranoia. I'd known how to bust out of handcuffs since I was ten.

Moving at a snail's pace, I stretched the bobby pin out as Georgie moved from praising Pandora's Key to interrogating guests on how they might be of service to the organization. Several times, one of the guards looked at me, and I had to stop to scowl up at him. And when he looked away, I would start again.

As I worked, however, I felt a new pair of eyes on me. Sure enough, when I looked up, it was Aithan.

My heart skipped a beat as we locked eyes. Even though he'd loved me before, he didn't now. He couldn't. So where did that leave us? Did he have any loyalties left at all? Or was he only here to please his grandfather?

To my relief, he didn't rat me out. Instead, he just returned his focus to Georgie, who was still lecturing a belligerent troll about why he was wrong to object to the Key's schemes.

For a few minutes, I began to sweat how long the escape was

taking me. But just as Georgie's lecture seemed to be drawing to a close, I felt the satisfying click of my right handcuff sliding open.

Unfortunately, everyone else heard it, too, and all eyes turned to me. But now I could summon my elf magic faster, and with my free right hand, I knocked one of the Key soldiers into his neighbor, sending both of them to the ground.

Chaos broke loose.

Sensing their chance, half of those at the table jumped up and attacked the soldiers, fighting in spite of their handcuffs. The others remained at the table, trying to get their magic-suppressant handcuffs off. Strangely, King Kostas stood as well, but he did no more than clench his hands as he glowered at the scene surrounding him.

I quickly set to freeing myself from the other handcuff, but before I could finish, Georgie was at my side, clasping my left arm.

"Everleigh, what are you doing?" he pleaded in a whisper. "I'm trying to save your family! If you'd only wait—"

I jumped to my feet and tried to yank my arm out of his grasp. Unfortunately, despite all my martial arts training, he was bigger and stronger than I was, and he grabbed my loose handcuff with a firm grip, effectively chaining me to his side.

Which meant I had to fight dirty. So acting on instinct, I kicked him in the knee and watched in satisfaction as he went down. I tried to kick him again, but he must have sensed it coming because he swept my other leg out from under me so I hit the ground hard.

Just then, the room went pitch black. I did my best to search on the ground for my missing hairpin, but failed until small female hands grabbed mine. My first instinct was to yank away from these, too, until I heard Soo Min's voice.

"Girl, would you *stop*?"

I realized then that Soo Min must have freed herself enough to make the room dark. Unfortunately, her darkness didn't last long enough for her to help me escape. The room flooded with light once more, and she had to let go of me to leap out of the way as a large supernatural standing near her came crashing down.

To my relief, however, a very angry troll also chose that moment to attempt running head-first into Georgie's stomach. Georgie dodged the blow, but it gave me the chance to scurry away, searching the battle as I ran until I found my fae grandfather at the edge of the fray.

As soon as our eyes met, he let out a sigh of relief and fought his way to my side.

"Why did you come back?" he demanded, but I shook my head.

"Where's the stone?" I had to shout to be heard. "I know Georgie brought one!"

"It's not a stone anymore! He ground it up into powder! The vial is in his pocket! But Everleigh, that powder is so potent it's toxic to humans and supernaturals alike! One whiff can–"

We were thrown apart by a random bolt of lightning that exploded between us. I had no idea who'd loosed it, but I knew if we didn't stop this madness soon, the green glass around us, reinforced as it probably was, would shatter.

That would be quite a way to introduce supernaturals to the human world.

Georgie was still at the front of the room. Which meant I had to get back to where I had just been.

I dove under the table, hoping it would be easier to cross the room on my hands and knees, rather than trying to dodge the fights that seemed to be everywhere. The Key soldiers were holding their own, but only because everyone else wore the handcuffs.

I hadn't shuffled more than three feet, however, before getting tangled in a selkie's net. I looked to my right to find a Key member holding the other edge of the net, trying to drag me out.

I struggled for a moment, tangled as I was, before remembering my tiny phoenix fire. It was even smaller than usual, thanks to the cuff still on my left hand, but it set the net ablaze just fine. The selkie let out an ear-piercing shriek as I rolled out of the burning net and began scrambling again toward Georgie, where he stood beside the door.

I hadn't gotten two feet more, however, before a clawed hand grabbed my foot and yanked me out from beneath the table, and I found myself staring up at a large werewolf wearing a Key uniform.

I kicked at his leg with what should have been a painful shot to the shin, but werewolf strength is no joke. He didn't even blink. Just as he began to pull me to my feet, however, I looked up to see Jamie and Christian in their human forms yank *him* backward.

"Everleigh, go!" Christian shouted as they struggled to pin the werewolf to the ground.

I didn't need to be told twice. I got on my hands and knees yet again and darted back under the table, hoping no one else would find me.

A brownie did see me, thanks to her diminutive stature, but a flick of my hand sent a thin burst of temporary blindness directly at her. She screamed and threw her hands over her eyes, which freed me to finally reach the end of the table, where my boba tea was still sitting.

But getting to the front of the room was only the first part of my plan. Now I had to find the vial. My grandfather had said it was in Georgie's pocket, but upon looking at Georgie again, I was dismayed to realize that he was wearing cargo pants.

Georgie had been fighting an enraged fae and didn't see me as I emerged from beneath the table, but my focus on him meant I missed the Key soldier who was aiming what looked like a tranquilizer gun my way. Too late, I watched him shoot a tranquilizer dart right at my heart.

But it never reached its mark.

I watched in horror as Aithan, for a second time that week, leaped between me and my attacker, taking the shot that had been meant for me.

But this time, he didn't do it out of love. He couldn't have. His heart was incapable of love.

The soldier stared stupidly down at Aithan, seeming as confused as I was, until Soo Min hit her over the head with a chair.

I ran to Aithan's side. "Aithan, what—"

His eyes were already rolling back in his head, but he lifted his cuffed hands and patted the left part of his chest, then pointed weakly at Georgie before slipping into unconsciousness.

The vial. It was in Georgie's left breast pocket.

Bless you, you annoying, devastatingly handsome, aggravating elf.

I looked back down at Aithan, who lay unconscious and vulnerable now with enemies all around him. Once again, he'd made himself vulnerable... for me.

He might not feel the love, a small voice inside my head whispered. *But his actions are drenched in it.*

The same anger I'd felt in the shopping mall parking lot a few days before began to burn within me. Too many times, the people I loved had been hurt for me. My parents had been ostracized, mocked, and dethroned. My friends had been captured and weakened. And now the leaders of the free supernatural world were being attacked with the hopes that I would join in. And Aithan....

After Aithan had given nearly everything he had to protect me, he had risked his life yet again for my sake. Even under his grandfather's curse, he was upholding his vow to protect me.

The flame within me burned yet hotter as I decided I was finished watching others take the fall for me. But this time, it wasn't just an uncomfortable flame. No, this was my phoenix's fire burning within me, along with my fae determination. My elven desire for order. My shifter's bullish intensity. My dragon's sense of justice. My vampire's jealous, possessive nature. Every bit of magic within me seemed to burn along with that flame.

And this time, I let it all consume me.

A little at a time, like a rope being cut to pieces by a pocket knife, I could feel the layers of my magic binding fall off. And at some point, though I don't know exactly when, the handcuffs fell off with them.

The fighting around me stopped as nearly everyone–Pandora's Key members and the supernatural leaders alike–began to edge toward the other end of the room. And that was probably wise. The colors of my many magics began to whirl around me, faster and faster, encasing me in a sphere of power as Georgie and I stared one another down.

I could sense the magic flowing through him as he received a vision, and immediately, he moved his left hand protectively over his shirt pocket.

He already knew what I wanted to do.

At the same time, he also raised his right hand, a powerful charm clasped in it.

"Don't try it, Everleigh," he pleaded, taking two steps back. "I don't want to do this! Please don't make me–"

I didn't wait for him to finish his pleading. Instead, I closed my eyes and focused my mind on every inch of my being, calling to arms every drop of vampire magic within me.

I had never tried this before, and wizard or not, I had no idea how long I could make it last. So, choosing not to think about the danger of what I was about to attempt, I yanked my body from its briefly frozen vampire state that I had just activated, and mentally flipped that magic in the other direction. As I did, Dorian's words echoed in my head.

That would be more dangerous than I can spell out.

Dangerous or not, I did it. And when I opened my eyes, the world around me had stopped as though encased in ice. I had successfully reversed my vampire magic, just as Julia had once suggested. Which meant I had to act *now*.

I sprinted to Georgie's side and removed his hand from his breast pocket. Yanking the vial out, I ran back to my side of the room. The edges of my vision were already beginning to waver and blur as I snatched up my bubble tea cup and dumped the powder inside. Then, after stirring the milk tea in several frantic circles, I popped the straw in my mouth and began to drink.

As I drank, I could immediately feel the powder begin to react inside of me. Colors flashed before my eyes, and I wondered if I might melt to the ground or explode. Or possibly both. But I forced myself to drink the entire thing anyway, slurping up the final drops as the world around me burst back to life.

Georgie immediately looked down at his empty pocket, then at my cup, then at me, his eyes growing wide with horror. "Everleigh, you didn't!"

"What did Everleigh do?" Julia shouted, running toward me as the entire room stared at me in silence. "What did you *do?*"

My grandfather, though silent, was right on her heels.

I stared at them, smiling as I put the cup down, even though I was beginning to sway.

"I finished my drink," was all I could say. Then my knees buckled.

Chapter Forty-Four

Aithan

I woke up to find myself on the floor and to hear the fighting around me cease. Still somewhat dizzy, I pushed myself up onto my elbow to see that everyone was staring at.

Everleigh was facing Georgios, her stance wide like she was getting ready to run. That alone wasn't strange. Everyone had been running or fighting when I'd lost consciousness. What was extraordinary about the scene was the cloud of magic encircling her. Countless magics of all colors and varieties mixed together, lighting the cloud surrounding her like she was her own personal sun.

This was the Everleigh everyone had been waiting for.

This was our wizard.

My grandfather's mouth was hanging open, and I could see the greed in his eyes as he watched. Everleigh had gone from a supernatural point of shame, to a curiosity, to the thing which he now coveted and would likely continue to covet until he had her. Of all the soldiers in his army, hand-selected and extensively trained at great expense, she could be his shining gem.

But Everleigh wasn't paying attention to my grandfather or anyone else other than Georgios, who had already fallen back several steps as he placed his hand protectively above his shirt pocket where the vial of powder sat.

"Don't try it, Everleigh," he begged. Only then did I realize what was in his other hand, and it made me stiffen.

A Malayan Tiger Charm.

One of the most expensive and destructive charms known to the supernatural world, it combined tiger shifter magic and elven magic upon impact to inflict the same scars and injuries a human might suffer upon encountering a Malayan Tiger. It could place a hardened elven soldier at the door of death.

"I don't want to do this! Please don't make me—" he began to beg. As he did, I coiled my muscles, ready to leap up and take him out. Almost immediately, however, I realized that while my elven blood had burned through the tranquilizer quickly, I was still stiff and slow from its effects. And I was still wearing the cuffs. But I would have to push through it. This loser had gone too far, and if he was willing to hurt and disfigure the girl he so obviously admired for the sake of his cause—

But then something strange happened. Without seeming to take so much as one step, Everleigh moved from one side of the table to the other. Also confusing was that her magic cloud was there one moment, then gone the next. And though I didn't see her actually lift the cup of bubble tea or put the straw in her mouth, she was suddenly draining the remnants of a drink that had been full a second before.

Georgios patted his breast pocket again, then whipped his gaze down to look at it, his expression moving to one of horror. I couldn't tell for sure, but... The pocket looked empty. Then he looked back at Everleigh. When his eyes moved to the cup, however, they bulged.

"Everleigh, you didn't!" he cried.

My mind was still frustratingly groggy as I tried to figure out what she had just done.

Julia shoved a very large vampire out of the way as she charged across the room toward her friend. "What did Everleigh do?" she screamed as she ran. "What did you *do?*"

Everleigh's fae grandfather, whom I hadn't noticed before, followed on Julia's heels.

"I finished my drink," Everleigh said, sounding more than a little drunk. As she spoke, she swayed slightly right as Julia reached her. And in my mind, the pieces suddenly came together.

"You drank the powder," I said, sitting up. "Didn't you?"

The look she gave me was scared and slightly sick as she pressed her hand to her stomach and grimaced.

I pushed myself to my feet but wasn't sure what to do after that. Was I supposed to try to help in some way? Was there anything I *could* do? I hadn't the first clue.

This was why supernaturals needed their hearts to properly use their magic.

My heart *should* have been beating a million miles a minute. But the stone prison that my grandfather's curse had formed in my chest kept my heartbeat steady and strong, as though the girl I was sworn to protect hadn't just drunk a vial full of poison. And even though I didn't have a single drop of personal affection for her now...

I wasn't ready to watch her die.

But... she didn't. Instead, after another long moment of loaded silence, Everleigh only gave a very small, very girlie burp before standing up straight and smiling as Julia wrapped her in a hug.

"Everleigh!" Georgios said, putting his Malayan Tiger charm back in his pocket. "I didn't think... I was afraid–" His voice shook, and he walked toward her slowly, as though in a dream, his right arm outstretched.

Julia, despite being the vulnerable human that she was, tightened her hold on Everleigh and pulled her away from Georgios, as though she could protect the wizard from their former friend.

She needn't have worried, though. My grandfather, who had

been standing in the corner observing, pulled a saber from his fallen guard's belt. He stalked the oracle silently, and with one swift move, ran the saber through Georgios's heart.

Everyone—the Key members in particular—watched anxiously as he then used the saber to break his own handcuffs and shake them off. Next, with one swipe of his arm, he destroyed the magical barrier that had been placed over the door. The rest of his personal soldiers outside had obviously figured out that something was wrong, and immediately came charging in.

"Take the remaining Key members for interrogation," my grandfather ordered as they continued to spill in. "And see if there's anything that can be done for the injured. Well, *our* injured." He kicked Georgios's lifeless body as he passed him.

I took the time to get to my feet as he did.

"As for the rest of you," he said, raising his voice to be heard over the sudden din of chatter and arrests. The room immediately went silent. "What happened here today is a sign of things to come." His voice was sharp and ominous. "The events that have taken place here are a symptom of the reason I summoned you."

"We knew things had changed," called a brave woman's voice. "But you didn't tell us a *wizard* had been born!" The woman, the wife of a werewolf alpha, looked at Everleigh, who was still standing arm in arm with Julia. "Wizard, how old are you?"

Everleigh stood taller. "I'm twenty-one."

The werewolf looked back at my grandfather. "She was born more than two decades ago, and you didn't *tell* us?"

My grandfather hesitated. His reputation had already suffered a damaging blow today. Being attacked in his own sanctum didn't do much to stir up confidence. Admitting that he hadn't even known about the wizard's existence would further erode the trust the supernatural world at large had held for him just hours before. But lying to them could prove even more disastrous in the end.

"I didn't realize she was a wizard," he finally said, his words slow and deliberate. "I had her watched as she grew, and she proved to be rather poor with magic." His eyes narrowed at Everleigh. "Until today, it seems."

Everleigh gave him a wry smile. "It's a long story, Your Majesty."

"One I can't wait to hear," he said. Then he turned back to his guests. "I release you all to go clean up now. I'll speak with you individually later concerning what is to be done about the Key. As you've witnessed today, this is not a threat we can ignore any longer. I trust, of course," he paused, searching their faces, "that you will all keep this to yourselves. You were invited here because I knew I could rely on your discretion." Then he nodded once. "You are dismissed."

Everyone in the crowd bowed or curtsied, but many did so stiffly. They knew his demands were not a request. And while their trust in him and his abilities had been shaken, they weren't stupid enough to object beyond what the werewolf had dared to do.

"Miss Clarkson." My grandfather turned to Everleigh as the room began to clear. "You handled yourself quite... creatively with the oracle."

Everleigh gave him an uneven curtsy. "I am honored, Your Majesty." Her curtsy was proper, but I didn't miss the fire in her eyes as she met his gaze yet again. She hadn't forgotten about what he'd done to her family and friends. And when her gaze moved to me, I could sense her wrath burning deeper still.

He, however, simply nodded and looked around. I could only guess that he was counting how many people were in the room, most likely calculating how many ears might be listening, and how many people might know if he later double-crossed the wizard who had saved them.

No one said it out loud, of course, but I knew what was on his mind and everyone else's. As a wizard, Everleigh would be his crowning jewel, should she choose to declare her allegiance. But given time and training, she was also one of the only creatures in the world who had the potential to eventually stand against him.

"Perhaps," he finally said, "we got off on the wrong foot. I would like to negotiate terms with you. Your skills would be highly valued by the supernatural world at large, and... I think we could work together nicely to protect our people from Pandora's Key."

"I do want to stop the Key," Everleigh said with slow deliberation. "But I won't give you unquestioned obedience. I can't."

My grandfather's jaw tightened, but she went on.

"My friends and family also need to be freed and allowed to go back to their normal lives. And... I'll also need some sort of... of paycheck. Chasing down Pandora's Key is starting to eat up a lot of my time."

"That's fair enough," my grandfather said, nodding slowly. But knowing him as well as I did, I could see him already scheming how he might turn this to his advantage.

Everleigh's objections weren't a stop sign to him. They were merely a speed bump. He wasn't even close to giving up his plans to add her to his personal arsenal of power and keep her securely under his thumb.

I turned to survey the damage. Servants had already appeared and were cleaning up the chairs that had been broken during the fight. Kwame and the merman had been taken to the healing rooms, and several of my grandfather's soldiers were taking statements from the remaining visitors. Everleigh's fae grandfather began fretting over her as soon as she was done with my grandfather. But his fuss was nothing compared to the shriek her mother let out as she and Everleigh's father sprinted into the room.

"I don't understand!" Mrs. Clarkson cried, running her hands up and down Everleigh's face. Her father, pale as a ghost, stood behind his wife. "You... you *drank* the Pandora Stone powder? But... how are you alive?"

"That's easy," Maverick grunted. The grizzled old fae had been standing against the wall, his hands in his pockets as though not sure what he was supposed to do. But now, when everyone looked at him in amazement, he just rolled his eyes.

"What did I tell ya'll? Wizards aren't powerful because they're the strongest in this or that kind of magic. What makes them unique is their ability to *contain* magic. Everleigh survived because she's able to hold more magic than anyone else."

Everleigh's father frowned. "But the Pandora Stone powder is so potent—"

"So potent it would kill any of *us*. Obviously. But she's not one of us." He looked at Everleigh again with the closest thing to admiration—or maybe it was tolerance—that I'd ever seen on his sour face.

Someone slapped my back, and I turned to see Christian and Aaron standing beside me. They were smiling, but their smiles were uneasy.

"Hey, we saw what you did back there," Christian said. "Good job."

"Yeah," Aaron said. He lowered his voice and looked at Everleigh. "So what now?"

"My grandfather will let you go, just like Everleigh said." I frowned. "So I suppose you're free to go back to your lives."

Christian and Aaron looked at one another, and then at Jamie and Soo Min, who had walked up beside them. None of them said whatever they were thinking aloud, but at the moment, I didn't care because I was looking at Everleigh.

My arms felt strangely empty as I watched her assure her parents she was all right, going repeatedly from one parent to another, then to Julia, and then starting all over again. If I had been myself...

If I had been myself, I would have been holding her close, too. She'd nearly just died, and that was *after* disappearing for three days. What she'd done with the powder was the kind of recklessness I'd expected but dreaded from her before the curse. But now?

Now I didn't know what I felt except... empty.

We'd won—well, this battle, at least. Their joy made sense.

Slightly jealous, I rubbed my chest as I watched them celebrate. All our years of planning and recruiting and sacrifice had paid off in the end.

But at what cost?

Epilogue

Everleigh

I SHELVED the rest of the books in my box, then paused to stretch.

"Done with that set?" Uncle Finn called from the other side of the room. He was carrying a box of what looked like children's picture books.

"I am," I said. As I spoke, I lovingly ran my fingers over the colorful spines before pulling one out and taking a big whiff of the pages. In the week since I'd started working there–two weeks since Georgie's attack–I'd taken exceptional joy in returning to the mundane.

There was something so satisfying about the evenly spaced rows of hardbacks I'd just shelved. And even more so about putting the missing book back in place so the row was complete.

"Thanks again for letting me work here with my crazy schedule. It should get easier once the semester ends, but I can't make any guarantees once the king decides where he wants me." I rolled my shoulders. "I decided last night that I'm not taking any summer courses this year. I need some time to reset and figure things out."

Sure, the king's paycheck was enough to get a really secure apartment. And Julia and Soo Min had agreed to room with me, which made the money go even farther. But I *needed* a way to

348

escape back into moments of what had once been my life. Even if it was only for a couple hours at a time.

"You know I'm happy to have you whenever you're free." My uncle put his box down and adjusted his robes. Today, they were a bright blue with a hint of green that shimmered when he turned at just the right angle. Oddball of his family that he was–being obsessed with books and other human pleasures such as pumpkin spice lattes and scented candles–the fae flare for fashion hadn't passed my mom's older brother by in any sense.

He went over to his mini fridge and pulled out a bottled fruit smoothie. My personal favorite–one that he'd only started stocking after I'd begun working for him in my spare time. I took the bottle gratefully, popped the seal, and downed a big swig.

My uncle picked up his own cup of tea from his desk and swirled it thoughtfully with his pinky finger. "So King Kostas hasn't given you any assignments yet?" His tone was casual, but I could tell from the way he was wrinkling his brows that he was worried. Out of their five siblings, my mom and uncle definitely took after my grandfather's side. I'd never had the chance to meet my grandmother, as she'd died when I was small, but rumor had it that she'd been even more calculating than my Aunt Fiadh.

"No. He said he wants to wait until finals end." I capped my drink. "Want me to take those?"

He handed me the box of children's books, and I went over to the children's corner and began to arrange the books cover-out. It was the newest part of the store, complete with miniature chairs and a couch that would grow or shrink depending on the sizes of the people who wanted to sit on them, and the cutest little rug in front of a magical, non-burning fireplace. There were plates of miniature cakes and chocolates that refilled themselves on the little table beside the couch, and a non-staining magical elixir that was sprayed over the area twice each morning to protect the furniture and the books from sticky little fingers.

I would have loved that corner if it had been there when I was a kid. Once, when my uncle hadn't been looking, I'd decided to test it out myself, and it was so comfortable, I'd fallen asleep with a book open on my chest and chocolate stains on my mouth.

Creating a children's section was part of my uncle's initiative to get supernaturals to actually *read* their children books instead of charming the books to read themselves aloud. "A lazy habit," he liked to say, shaking his head in disgust. But then again, my uncle wasn't exactly a paragon of tradition in the supernatural community. He'd bucked his parents' advice and had gotten a human master's degree in library science, and had then returned to Las Vegas to open this bookstore for supernaturals. His willingness to mix with the human world was the only reason my parents had allowed him to get to know me.

And though everyone had predicted his bookstore would fold in a year, he was now thriving—though I was somewhat convinced that the novelty of the store kept it afloat, rather than its practicality.

As I stacked the books, however, my mind slid from the spines' presentation to all that had happened in the two weeks since King Kostas's disastrous meeting.

By some miracle—a miracle that I suspected had to do with Professor Petras's influence—Julia and I had managed not only to *not* fail our classes, but we'd even maintained decent grades. King Kostas had also declared that in the fall semester of my senior year, I would do online classes only. He'd quickly decided that it wouldn't be safe for me to attend in person until we learned more about Pandora's Key and its plans.

To my surprise, Professor Petras had agreed with him. "Just for the fall semester," he'd told me with a kind smile.

That conversation had taken place at the *second* supernatural meeting, which my grandfather had called three days after the Georgie disaster. Professor Petras had been invited to participate that time, as had even more influential supernaturals from around the city, which meant the second meeting had been even bigger than the first. I had told Julia afterward that seeing my teacher at the meeting had been more than a little weird. Professor Petras was so much younger than nearly everyone else present, and appeared so much more... human.

I had hoped after that meeting that King Kostas would leave me alone. He had, after all, sent all of my friends (except Julia, with her being my pet) their respective ways. Not only were they unnecessary for my purposes now that he was my boss, but they were also unwelcome.

This impossible dream of also being left alone was quickly dispelled, however. After joining forces with the king, I'd soon learned that just because I wasn't attending classes in person didn't mean King Kostas was about to leave me be. I'd been assigned several personal magical trainers and lesson times that I was expected to attend religiously. After Georgie's attack, Maverick had apparently demanded that we let him go home.

"Not that it matters," King Kostas had said, rolling his eyes. "I've never met a worse-tempered man. No, I quite prefer to have my own trainers work with you instead."

For some reason, though I couldn't say why, this made me sad. The new trainers were all experts in their fields, and their lessons were the best money could buy. But none, I'd quickly realized, had the big picture understanding that Maverick had. He might not have been the wizard he'd claimed to be, but he'd spent enough time with one to know loads more about my magic than any of the individual trainers knew or cared to.

On a happier note, I was just two weeks away from moving into a new apartment with Soo Min and Julia. King Kostas had secured it, of course, which meant it was located close to The Realm Resort. The reason we couldn't move in immediately, he said, was because he was having it spelled to the hilt. And though I'd been sure my parents would argue, wanting me to stay home with them, they surprised me as well.

"As much as I hate to admit it," my mom had said, looking at my dad, "I think you'll be safer there. Our house has been compromised, at least for the time being."

"King Kostas might be selfish," my father had added, "but he's deadly serious about protecting the people he considers his assets. And now you, my daughter," he'd touched my face with a sad smile, "are one of his most important assets. Which means he'll be able to keep you safer than we can."

I had my doubts about this. But it was exciting to talk with Soo Min and Julia about our new apartment, so I didn't fight it.

One of the most jarring aspects of my new life, however, was my status. King Kostas had sworn his guests to secrecy the day my race had been revealed. But it was obvious that someone had shared with a spouse or child, and that spouse or child had talked to friends who had talked to other friends, because word in the gossip blogs and podcasts and supernatural social media apps soon had it that there was a wizard in Las Vegas. And though I never advertised who or what I was, I'd lately begun to notice people stopping to stare and whisper whenever I went into public.

Alexander had also popped up a few days after the second meeting. Julia and I had been making a salad in my parents' kitchen when he'd appeared out of nowhere. Julia screamed, and I nearly had a heart attack. But he must have been used to people's shock because he didn't even blink.

"I can't be away from my work often," he'd said quickly as he handed me a small blue card. "This is only for the utmost of emergencies."

I'd gaped at the obviously spelled phone number written in pen on the otherwise blank card. "Oh. Wow," I said after getting my voice back. "Thanks, Alexander. That... means a lot."

He nodded once at me, then studied Julia for a long moment before seeming to disappear again.

And as if my life wasn't complicated enough, I was still stuck with Julia as my pet. The whole situation, as I'd griped countless times to anyone who would listen, was absolutely ridiculous. Who kept their best friend as a pet? Even weirder was that Julia seemed to be taking it much better than I was. But even *if* I had the most amazing, most understanding best friend in the entire world–which I totally did–I had no plans to *own* her for the rest of our lives.

I just wished I knew how to sever the connection between us. My parents swore it was possible, but when I asked them how, they'd exchanged a look that didn't inspire confidence.

"We'll research it more," was all my dad said. "But... it might take a while."

And then, of course, there was the problem of Aithan.

My hands slowed their work as I thought about him. And as no one was around to see, I closed my eyes and let my head hang as I took a deep, grounding breath.

Processing his curse was like... Well, I felt like I was mourning his death, if I was being honest. In a way, he *had* died. The Aithan who had always teased and poked and prodded me just to raise my ire, all while watching over me with the attention of a wolf, was gone. And in his place was a cold, distant protector. He didn't stay with me all the time anymore, now that my parents were free once again, and the king had added enough protective charms to my life to bring a pet rock to life. But now that he was working full-time for his grandfather,I had seen him enough to recognize that the Aithan who remained was different, so unlike the man I had known before.

Yes, he had saved me again during the fight, and I would be forever grateful. But the more I thought about it, the more I got the feeling that his actions had more to do with the binding of his vow than any remnants of affection that might linger for me.

He even looked different now. It was his eyes, I'd quickly decided. They were cold and hard, not warm and full of light and life the way they had been.

The sound of the bell over the portal door jingled, and I sniffed and wiped my eyes, not realizing until that moment that I'd begun to cry. Hopefully, the quick glamour I cast across my face would be enough to make me look normal.

"I'll be there in a min..." My voice died as I turned to find Aithan standing at the door.

Could he tell I'd been crying? I was tempted to look at the mirror on the far wall, but I forced myself to keep my eyes ahead.

"Can we talk?" he asked, frowning slightly.

"Your Highness, we didn't expect to see you today," Uncle Finn said, appearing around a corner of a bookshelf. His tone was polite. His expression, however, was anything but.

"Uncle Finn," I said slowly, "can I take my break?"

My uncle looked Aithan over several times before sighing and giving me a nod.

I thanked him and grabbed my juice before gesturing for him to follow me out to the garden behind the store.

Once we were there, and the door was closed behind him, I waited as he created a muffling charm around us, twirling my juice bottle in my hands and feeling thankful for something to hold.

And I tried *really,* really hard not to notice just how good he looked in his jeans and fitted black tee.

Instead of talking, however, once the charm was set, he only stared down at me. I stared back, suddenly hyper-aware that I'd forgotten to put on makeup that day.

"My grandfather isn't happy," he finally said.

I nodded slowly. "I figured. He's not a man easily pleased."

Aithan's frown deepened as he stared at me. "Everleigh, being enemies with the most powerful sovereign in the world is no small thing."

I scoffed. "I saved his sorry butt. I'm not sure what right he thinks he has to be mad at–"

"You showed him up in front of the leaders of the supernatural world."

"He got the kill shot. All I did was swig down an iced drink fast enough to get a brain freeze." I rolled my eyes and knelt to pull a weed from my uncle's patch of chrysanthemums.

But Aithan didn't smile or laugh. Instead, he looked...

Was he *worried?*

Was he even capable of being worried?

For the briefest of moments, he looked almost like the Aithan I knew.

"The king made an enemy of me first," I added, standing and brushing the soil off my hands. For some reason, though, my voice was slow and soft, and the words didn't sound the way they had in my head.

Aithan didn't answer. He only stepped closer and slowly, slowly stretched out his hand to brush it lightly across my hair.

And just like that, the fire inside me was burning again.

"I'm going to free you," I heard myself blurt.

Where had *that* come from?

But I didn't stop. Words just kept coming. "I'm going to break this curse." As I spoke the words, however, I realized that I meant every one of them. I *would* free him. And I would track down every last book on magic and magical history if it meant discovering how.

I raised my right hand slowly, as though he was a rabbit that might dart. But he didn't dart, so I sucked in a deep breath as I placed my fingers against his chest. Then I traced the shape of the hard stone beneath.

***

Aithan

I stood perfectly still under Everleigh's touch. It wasn't flirtatious in any way, but the light pressure of her fingers was the gentlest, most soothing sensation I'd ever felt.

And I didn't want it to end.

I didn't understand this... desire to be near her. I didn't love Everleigh, after all. I didn't love anyone. And if asked why I had come to warn her, I would have answered that my life was less chaotic if war wasn't breaking out within the ranks. At least, that's what I told myself. But whether I believed that answer or not...

I *had* loved her. Just as before the curse had fallen, I'd experienced the most potent flash of emotion and desire I'd ever felt. And strangely, even now, I realized that I didn't dislike her either, the way I disliked most people these days. She amused me. She always had. And she was really a useful little creature to have around.

She was also trouble, however. And it seemed she had absolutely no idea how small and helpless she'd looked next to those warmonger soldiers my grandfather recruited and trained from boyhood up. And anyone who attracted trouble and attention the way she did was someone who was sure to rouse chaos wherever she went. And my goal was to avoid chaos—or quell it at the very least.

Yet somehow, these diametrically opposed desires both bloomed within me, and it didn't make sense.

"Curses can't be broken," I stupidly pointed out, my chest still tight as she pressed her palm against it. "Not this kind." Unlike in some of the fairy tales and legends of old, my grandfather had left no way out. No mysterious path to escape or clever riddle hidden.

But, as she so often did, Everleigh surprised me by simply giving me an ornery grin. I could feel her magic now running from her fingertips into me, exploring and pulsing within. The sensation was warm and cool at the same time. Mesmerizing. Then she sucked in a sharp breath, and her eyes began to sparkle.

"That's it," she whispered. "Just like he said!"

"Like who said?" I asked.

But she ignored me. "The imperfections..." she whispered.

I could see the wheels turning in her head. "What?" I asked. "Everleigh, I'm lost."

"I don't have to bring the walls tumbling down," she said,

almost as if she was talking to herself. "All I need is..." She stepped closer, and with a surprising amount of force, placed her left hand behind my neck. And pulling my face down to hers, her right hand still over my heart, she pressed her lips to mine.

It wasn't the first time I'd kissed Everleigh Clarkson. And while the first time had been far more enjoyable than I'd let on—so good, in fact, that I'd nearly broken my carefully crafted act to tell her—this kiss was different. It was sure. Determined.

Fierce.

As she deepened the kiss, something stabbed like a knife inside my chest.

With a sharp cry, I stumbled back and clutched at my chest. But as I tried to catch my breath, pain still radiating through me, she only nodded once and grinned.

"I'll take that as a start," she said. Then she picked up her bottle of juice from the ground and waved at me, blue eyes sparkling. "My break is over. I'll see you around, Aithan."

A Wizard's Worth

So much to destroy, so little time.

Everleigh Clarkson thought embracing her identity as Las Vegas's only wizard would cool supernatural tensions. But her problems have only begun. Sure, she and her friends might have stopped one arm of the mysterious vigilante group, Pandora's Key, but their former troubles can't compare to what the supernatural zealots are sparking next.

To make matters worse, Everleigh's oldest and most trusted friend, Aithan Nomos, accidentally enacted a curse upon him himself when he dared to love her. And everyone knows curses can't be broken.

But Everleigh has never been one to surrender, and she's not about to start now. Not with Pandora's Key, nor with Aithan. And if she has to bring the entire city to its knees to make things right, she's absolutely prepared to try.

Continue Everleigh and Aithan's story with A Wizard's Worth (A Wizard in Las Vegas, Book 2)!

Dear Reader,
Thank you so much for beginning this journey with Everleigh and Aithan. If you want to spend more time with them (and get other free stories), you can get access to their bonus stories when you sign up for my newsletter at BrittanyFichterFiction.com.

You'll also get more secret chapters, sneak peeks at books before they're published, chances at giveaways, and much more!

If you loved this series, it would be a huge help if you could rate and review these books on Amazon or Goodreads. More reviews help new readers find my books, which allows me to keep writing and publishing them.

About the Author

Brittany lives with her Prince Charming, their little fairy, and their little prince in a ~~sparkling~~ (decently clean) castle in whatever kingdom the Air Force has most recently placed them. When she's not writing, Brittany can be found chasing her kids around with a DSLR and belting it in the church choir.

Contact Brittany:

Subscribe: BrittanyFichterFiction.com
Email: BrittanyFichterFiction@gmail.com
Facebook: Facebook.com/BFichterFiction
Instagram: @BrittanyFichterFiction

A WIZARD AWAKENED (A WIZARD IN LAS VEGAS, BOOK #1)

Cover Design by MoorBooks Design

A Wizard Awakened / Brittany Fichter. -- 1st ed.